CIRCLES IN HELL SERIES
Hell's Super
A Cold Day In Hell

A Cold Day In Hell

(Circles in Hell, Book Two)

by

Mark Cain

ISBN-13: 978-1518612633
ISBN-10: 1518612636

All rights reserved. No part of this book may be reproduced or transmitted in any form or by any means, electronic or mechanical, including photocopying, recording, or by any information storage and retrieval system, without permission in writing from the copyright owner.

'A Cold Day In Hell' is published by Perdition Press, which can be contacted at:

hellssuper@hotmail.com

'A Cold Day In Hell' is the copyright of the author, Mark Cain, 2015. All rights are reserved.

This is a work of fiction. All of the characters, organizations or events portrayed in this novel are either products of the imagination or are used fictitiously.

Cover design by Dan Wolfe (www.doodledojo.co.uk)

To Claire, who insisted that I continue Steve's story. Thanks, Red, for everything.

"Don't let go!"

"I'm not letting go!"

"For Go ... for Heav ... oh, shit ... just DON'T let go!"

"I'm NOT letting go!"

I was letting go.

Not by choice, mind you, but the only thing keeping Orson's nearly four hundred ectoplasmic pounds from falling thousands of feet, to be impaled on one of the jagged toe bones of Mount Erebus, was the tenuous grip we each had on the other's wrist. My arm felt as if it was being pulled from its socket, and my fingers were beginning to slip.

My situation was only slightly less precarious than Orson's. A quickly-made lasso of duct tape was fastened to my ankle, a lasso I'd just barely managed to toss over a stony outcropping twenty feet above me; it held me upside down, suspended in midair. Periodically I'd crash into the sheer cliff off of which Orson and I had slipped moments before. Each time I hit, my nose would slam against the rock, and the delicate cartilage in my schnozzle would snap. "Ow! Ow!" I said every few seconds.

"Steve! Do something! You know what will happen if I fall."

Well, actually, I didn't. Falling anywhere else in Hell would just result in a lot of pain, and a passel of broken bones that would knit themselves back together in short order. But this was Mt. Erebus, and the normal laws of the Underworld didn't apply here, according to Satan.

Of course, he is the Prince of Lies. Not the most dependable person to take advice from. Still, he might be telling the truth this time.

My recently-healed nose hit the stones again, breaking once more. It didn't seem to be mending as quickly as it would under normal circumstances, although perhaps being whacked with such regular frequency didn't allow enough time for a proper *nose job.* Since I didn't know for sure what the Erebus Zone did to Hell's normal laws, I could only assume the worst (which was generally a smart attitude toward things down here), i.e., that Orson's immortal soul was in danger, that a fall to the base of the mountain would snuff it out.

With my free hand, I grabbed for a roll of duct tape. If I could just make a few loops around our two wrists, the tape could hold us until we figured out how to get out of this fix.

Our fingers slipped again. Despite the numbing cold, our hands and wrists were beginning to sweat. Bad luck that. It was hard enough to dispense tape one-handed without having to deal with sweaty palms. But I had to save Orson somehow, and we had to get back on the mountain, make it to the top, finish the job. If we didn't, all Hell would freeze over.

And that would be a very bad thing.

Chapter 1

I looked in disgust at the giant boulder, split neatly in two, as if someone had taken a meat cleaver to it. "How the hell did you manage this?"

A heavily-muscled guy, wearing an ancient crown, stood before me and Orson, my assistant. "I tell you, Steve, I haven't a clue. I was just doing what I always do, you know, roll the rock up the hill, watch it roll back down, roll the rock up, watch it go down, up, down, up ... "

"Yeah, yeah, we get it," Orson said, cutting him off. "The old Sisyphean thing."

The brawny royal frowned, as if we'd just offended him. "Hey! It's what I do." He slapped his chest. "It's who I am."

Which was true. We were talking to the original Sisyphus.

"Anyway, I'd just gotten my bolder to the top of the hill and was standing there, watching it roll down as I always do. When the thing reached the bottom, it just," he looked embarrassed, "well it just split in two."

"You didn't hit anything with it, did you?"

"No, no," Sisyphus said impatiently. "Besides, if I had, the boulder would have flattened it." Sisyphus looked crestfallen. "I've had it all these years, and now, look at it. Ruined, just ruined!"

All these years was right. Sisyphus - whom Satan had picked up from Hades, the Greek god, along with a few other colorful individuals that had lent some class to the place, characters like Charon, Cerberus and Prometheus, at the time the big devil-may-care had bought Hell from his Greco-Roman predecessor - had been shoving that damn boulder up the hill for over three millennia. Both hill and boulder looked a little worse for wear.

Sisyphus, though, was in great shape. They say weight training does wonders, and Sisyphus could have put Charles Atlas to shame. Maybe even Atlas himself.

"Do you still have the owner's manual?"

"I have it here somewhere." King Sisyphus patted down the pockets of his tunic - when he had found time to have pockets sewn into the garment I'll never know - and pulled out a dog-eared pamphlet, entitled "Care and Use of Your Boulder (Model BB1000).

"Oh," I commented, "a BackBreaker 1000. Good choice."

"Thanks," Sisyphus replied. "It's served me well. Never had a lick of trouble in all these years, until now," he said, slightly deflated.

I flipped to the index, found the page I wanted, and turned to it. "How many miles do you think you have on your rock?" I asked, as I read the fine print.

Sisyphus scratched his beard in thought. "Dunno. Ten million?"

I exhaled hugely. "Well, *there's* your problem. Says right here on page twenty-three. The thing wasn't designed to go beyond five."

"Is it still under warranty?"

"What do you think?"

"Guess not." Sisyphus sat down on the edge of one piece of the broken rock. "I suppose I could get another one." He patted the surface of the boulder fondly. "Won't be the same, though. Me and Bessie ... "

"Wait a minute," Orson said. "You named your rock?"

Sisyphus hopped off Bessie and made a fist. "So I named my rock. What's it to you, fatso?"

"Nothing, nothing," Orson Welles, one of filmdom's greatest directors, said hurriedly. "Rock guitarists sometimes name their axes, so I guess there's nothing wrong with a Greek king naming his boulder."

Sisyphus relaxed. "Right, and don't you forget it. Anyway, me and Bessie have been together a long time. I've really just gotten her broken in, if you know what I mean."

I looked dubiously at the bisected boulder. Ironically, the millennia of stone hill rubbing against stone boulder had had the same effect as a gargantuan rock polisher. Bessie had become as smooth and polished as a bowling ball - without the finger holes, of course. The hill itself was probably several feet shorter than it used to be. Yep, Bessie looked pretty good … except that she was split in half.

Sisyphus nodded to himself. He had made some sort of decision. "Look, Steve, I don't mean to be a nuisance, but I don't want another boulder. I want Bessie. Can you fix her?"

"Fix a boulder? And how am I gonna do that? SuperGlue?" I turned to Orson, who just shook his head.

"Well, why not?" Sisyphus countered. "You're Hell's Super. You're supposed to be able to fix anything. At least try, please?" The hulking Hellene looked like he was ready to cry.

I don't know where he got the impression I could fix anything. Sure, that was my job: Mr. Fixit for the Netherworld. That didn't mean I was any good at it, though. This was my eternal damnation, chosen specifically because I was lousy at this kind of work. Hated it, too, I mean really hated it, though that's about what you'd expect of an eternal damnation. Still, I had to try. "Fine, fine," I said at last. "But you've got to help."

"Sure," the king said, enthusiastically. "What can I do?"

"Well, first you can help Orson and me get the two pieces back together, okay?"

"Sure, I can do that."

That task was trickier than one might imagine. It wasn't just getting the two halves to touch; it also required a little bit of futzing around to get them to meet at the precise points where they had parted. Orson and I worked one half of the boulder and Sisyhpus the other. Our half alone seemed to weigh a ton. We ended up taking the limb of a nearby dead tree and, using a large rock as a fulcrum, applied all our weight and strength to lever the hemisphere into position. Then we chocked it up with some more rocks that were lying around. Sisyphus had no difficulty with his piece. After all, this was half the weight he was used to handling.

In about fifteen minutes, we had the two halves together. "Now, your highness," I said, reaching to my belt, "I'm going to need you to push the two pieces together as tightly as you can, closing the crack on this side."

"Okay," Sisyphus said, shoving the two bits of rock against each other until a wisp of smoke couldn't have gotten through.

I pulled two strips of duct tape, one from the roll hanging on a spool on the right side of my tool belt, the other from another roll on my left, and taped over the crack. "Orson, take over from Sisyphus."

My assistant's face puckered up as if he had been sucking on a lemon. "Come on, Steve. I can't handle that much weight."

"You and the duct tape can. Besides, you won't have to do it for long." Grumbling, Orson took our places. "Now, your majesty, let's deal with the other end." The king and I went to the far side of the boulder, he held the two pieces tightly together, and I secured things with two more strips of tape. "Now give me a minute to make a few passes around the rock."

I didn't need a minute. The tape flew from my fingers as I did a double-circumnavigation of the boulder, slowed only by my ability to run around the rock, dodging Orson and Sisyphus as I went. Then I had the two of them step back as I began to encase the entire rock in duct tape. In two minutes, everything but the top and bottom was covered. I had Sisyphus roll the rock over so I could finish the job. "There," I said, at last.

When all else fails, use duct tape. It was my fixit failsafe in life, and using it was the only thing I was good at in my afterlife.

Sisyphus scratched his head, dubiously. "I don't know Steve. Doesn't look as pretty as she used to."

"Hey," Orson said, still panting from his time holding his side of the rock together. "She's still gray and a little shiny. Besides, the tape will flatten over time."

"Sisyphus, I'm sorry but it's the best I can do. Why don't you give it a couple of test rolls and see what you think?"

The king shrugged then started shoving the boulder up the hill. He got to the top; the rock rolled down to the other side. He followed. He rolled it up, and the rock rolled down toward us - pretty fast too. We had to jump to one side to get out of the way.

Sisyphus came trotting down, a big smile on his face. "She may not look so good, but the old girl rolls like a dream. This'll do fine."

Whew. Close one.

"Okay," I said, handing Sisyphus a pen and the work order. "Sign here, please."

Sisyphus put a sigma on the form, in the "completed" box. "Thanks again."

"You betcha."

"And Orson, sorry I got a little hot there for a moment. Bessie and me, though, well, like I said, we go way back."

"It's okay," Orson said. "I should have been more sensitive. Thoughtless of me."

He and I made our goodbyes to the burly king and began wending our way back to the office. Steve Minion, Hell's Superintendent for Plant Maintenance, and Orson Welles, his trusty assistant, had triumphed again.

One work order down, an infinity to go, but that's life in Hell for you. Sisyphus had his rock; we had our work orders. He had his version of Hell; we had ours.

My friend and I headed for Hell's Escalator, a one-way affair that stretched from Gates Level, where St. Peter sorted recently deceased souls into lambs (Pearly Gates invitees) and goats (Gates of Hell inductees), all the way down to the Eighth Circle of Hell. As we walked, I noted that the day was an atypically nice one. The sky, or what passed for sky down here, seemed more clear than usual. Sure, it was still gray and smelled of gym socks, but I could see farther than was customary. The view from the Second Circle was spectacular that day, though not scenic, like a view from the Sears Tower or the Matterhorn or anything like that. Hell's spectacles tended to be a bit more grisly.

Off to the right, I could spy a large fiery pit with a gargantuan grill top. Hundreds of souls, bound in chains, were stretched atop it, like so many frankfurters. Beside the grill stood the giant Cyclops Polyphemus, who, like Sisyphus, was a colorful character from Greek mythology and another long-time inhabitant of the Underworld. He was dressed in a white apron and chef's hat, and his single eye monitored his charges as they sizzled on the grill. In his hand was a spatula the size of the digging bucket on a backhoe. Periodically, Polyphemus would flip over one of the souls in order to brown the other side. When one of these unfortunates was well-done - charred to me, but well-done to Polyphemus - the Cyclops would flip him or her off the fire and onto a massive platter. This would give the flesh of the damned soul time to heal, and then the giant would toss the raw meat back on the grill.

All of this, of course, was accompanied by plenty of wailing and gnashing of teeth. That's generally a requirement in Hell. All of us are really good at wailing and gnashing our teeth, seeing as how we've had lots of practice.

At least they aren't stuffed in a bun and eaten. That would be downright undignified. Extra onions. Hold the mayo. Ugh.

In the distance was the cone-shaped silhouette of Mount Erebus, which was sort of an anomaly among all mountains, earthly or otherwise. It hung upside down, suspended from the underside of Hell's First Circle, a gated golf community for virtuous pagans and unbaptized babies.

(Seems a bit unfair about the unbaptized babies, but the early leaders of the Catholic Church, who got to Christianity first and set up most of its basic constructs, are responsible for that. A lot of people don't like that babies are in Hell, but the First Circle is really very nice. Besides, I didn't make the rule, so don't shoot the messenger.)

The mountain is a frigid affair, a gigantic stalactite of ice that dominates the skyline, narrowing as it approaches the surface of Level Two, stopping just a few hundred feet shy of the ground. Erebus provides most of Hell's ice, which is used to punish the damned who in life lived in places like Florida, Hawaii, and Saint Vincent and the Grenadines (which to me always sounds like a Sixties Motown group). Others who get the cold shoulder include former Snowbirds, those northerners in the States who drive south in their RVs and spend the winters in more temperate climes. In other words, Erebus provides torment for people who hate to be cold.

Oh, devils and demons also use ice from the mountain for their martinis.

I remembered from a geography course I took in college that there was a Mount Erebus in Antarctica. At 12,000 feet it was taller than ours, but since it didn't hang upside down, Earth's version wasn't as impressive to me as our own mile-long stalactite.

Orson and I were going to take the Escalator from Two, where Sisyphus had his rock and roll gig, down to Five, where our office was located. We could have taken Hell's Elevator, but while it could traverse the Circles of Hell faster, it was less reliable. You could spend your entire day poking at the down button, trying to get the damn Elevator to stop and pick you up. And the Stairs, well, that was just way too much work. The Escalator was generally very dependable, and while we were on it, we weren't expected to fix anything, giving Orson and me a bit of a break.

"What do you want to do today, Steve?" Orson asked, as we passed some Gluttons on Level Two being force-fed cans of Spam.

I idly wondered why these souls weren't down on Three, in Glutton's Gap, where most of the gluttons tended to be gathered. Hell wasn't as tidy as Dante's *Inferno* suggested, though; I knew you could find sinners of every stripe in almost every Circle of Hell.

We came to the Escalator and hopped on. "I dunno. Fix some stuff, I guess."

"Well, that's pretty obvious," my assistant responded in that supercilious tone he would sometimes use. I had long ago gotten used to it, but I know it pissed off a lot of people down here. I don't even think Orson realized he did it. He was such a big shot in life that he had never quite gotten used to being a flunky down here. "I mean, what are we going to work on?"

We had just passed beneath the surface of Level Two, burrowing into the firmament that supported it. The air, already hot, since things tended more toward toasty than chilly down here, suddenly became superheated. I took a breath to answer my assistant and went into a coughing spell; it's hard to talk when you're sucking in super-heated air. Orson pounded me on the back, which didn't stop the coughing, but it gave him something to do, and he kept it up until the Escalator emerged into the air above Level Three.

"Like I said," I wheezed. "I don't know. Sisyphus caught me right after I clocked in, and I haven't had a chance to look at the work orders yet. Didn't even get to pour myself a cup of coffee."

"Ah." Orson stared off into the distance, daydreaming. "You know," he said, abruptly. "I wish Satan would let me make a film about Hell."

"Yeah, sure, that's gonna happen."

"No, I'm serious, Steve. Hell may be pretty horrible, but it's quite an eyeful. I'd think the devils, at least, would enjoy the movie, and Satan could use it as a recruiting piece to get more demons."

"Keen."

Orson harrumphed. "Stop being so sarcastic. You know he has a worker shortage in that area. He's certainly tried to talk you into being a demon more than once."

That was true. I like to think of myself as a nice guy, but if I don't like someone, well, I guess I have my nasty side. A couple of examples: Thomas Edison and Henry Ford were two of my least favorite people in Hell, and I'd certainly put those two through the wringer more than once. I chuckled nastily then caught myself.

I guess I'm not as nice as I think I am. The thought made me uncomfortable.

"Anyway, I could really do a bang-up promotional video."

"Would you do it in gray?" Orson preferred making black and white films.

"Uh-uh. There's way too much vivid coloring down here. You know, all the blood and bile and stuff. No, it would be Technicolor all the way. And my movie would make 'Satyricon' look like 'Bambi' by comparison."

I brushed some dust I'd picked up from that damn rock off my shirtsleeve. "Well," I opined, "there was that forest fire sequence in 'Bambi.' I thought it was pretty scary when I was a kid."

"Phtt! That was a *cartoon*, Steven." Orson gestured expansively. "Look around. This is the real thing!"

I didn't say anything for a while, and soon we were closing on the surface of Level Four. I noted the fire pits and the Sea of Thorns, where tens of thousands of the damned were impaled. In the air, two harpies sped by, sharp talons extended, as they chased a few understandably terrified souls. Off in the distance, Old Dependable, a perpetually-erupting volcano, spilled its fiery guts onto a town below. The screams could be heard even from the Escalator. "More like the surreal thing, I'd say."

"Absolutely!" Orson beamed. "It would make a great movie, and I wouldn't even need to get Harryhausen to create the effects. Who needs stop-motion dolls, when we have *real* giant apes, three-headed ogres, a volcano that just keeps on giving."

At that moment, Old Dependable's fire simply went out, as if someone had placed an invisible cone over the summit and choked off the oxygen. "Orson," I said, pointing toward the suddenly-inert volcano. "Look at that!"

Orson scratched his goatee. "Well, I'll be damned ... "

"That goes without saying."

"Yeah, but have you ever seen Old Dependable when it wasn't erupting?"

At that moment, the Escalator took us below the surface of Level Four. "Well, now I can't see anything."

Orson grabbed my arm, a little more tightly than he needed to. "But that's never happened before, has it?" he wheezed, the hot air no doubt scorching his lungs.

"No," I gasped. And it could mean only one thing.

Trouble.

Chapter 2

The Escalator reached Level Five, and we jumped off, just before the moving stairs delved beneath the surface on their way to the Sixth Circle of Hell. Five was where we had our office.

Normally, the Escalator platform for Level Five was near Plant Maintenance. Periodically, though, Management would randomly reroute the thing, and this was one of those times. We were at least five miles from the office. For an hour Orson and I tried to hail a cab, but none would stop, despite all of them appearing to be empty. Their "Available" lights were on too. It was pretty aggravating, but about par for the course. Still, our office was a little too far away to walk, so when a bus halted right in front of us, spilling out five sewer workers onto the pavement, we hopped aboard.

"Fuck you," said the demon at the wheel. "Fifty thousand bucks. In the slot. Now."

I rolled my eyes. Money was meaningless in Hell, but it didn't pay to argue with a demon, so I began stuffing all the bills and coins I had in my pocket into the change collector. Yet my mouth, which had gotten me in trouble my whole life, and a fair bit of my afterlife, wouldn't stay shut. "You're full of crap, you know."

Without taking his eyes off the road, the demon, a little puce-colored creep whose name, I think, was Gaap, lifted a whip from his lap and lashed me across the face.

"Ow! Shit, that hurt!"

"Back of the line, you two. It's the rules." He closed the bus doors and slammed down on the accelerator. Orson and I were pitched to the floor. My friend landed on top of me, completely predictable in Hell, since he was much heavier than me. When his considerable personage made its emergency landing on my shoulder, it dislocated.

My assistant pulled himself up by grabbing the leg of a nearby passenger. She cursed and thumped him on the head with her purse. Struggling to keep his balance, Orson helped me to my feet. "Sorr … "

"Skip it," I said hurriedly. You don't dare sincerely apologize for anything in Hell. That results in a rather juvenile, but nonetheless humiliating and painful, form of punishment down here. "I'll be okay in a moment."

There were no seats to be had, and barely any standing room. With some effort, we worked our way to the back of the bus, as Gaap had told us to. I noticed he was watching us through the rearview mirror, and I didn't want any more trouble from him. Between Orson and me, we managed to score six inches of commuter pole, to which we held on for dear life.

Well, okay, not life, since we were already dead, but you catch my drift.

I hated riding in Hell's buses. With cabbies, at least you got a human, even if he or she *was* blind, but with a bus, the driver was always a demon. The cabbies couldn't help scaring the bejeezus out of you. They may have been blind, but they tried their best. Demon bus drivers, though, did everything in their power to make your ride miserable. A demon would seek out traffic jams and contentedly sit for hours without moving the vehicle, pretend the bus had broken down, or just stop to get out and flatten a tire, take a smoke, or throw excrement on one of the bus's windows.

If you were lucky, the window was closed.

Today's ride was no different. We went one block, and the demon stopped the bus and began filing his nails or, rather, claws. The passengers started to grumble.

Gaap reached for the microphone of the bus's PA system. "Shut the fuck up!" he yelled. "Besides, I'm on break."

Back on Earth, some scientist got a grant from the National Science Foundation to study traffic patterns in New York. To me it sounded like one of those story problems we all had to do in high school math. Anyway, it went like this: in Manhattan a man got on a bus that was going from east to west. At the same time, another fellow just started hoofing it. The walker reached the West Side half an hour before the rider. I don't know why the NSF bothered to fund this kind of research. Any New Yorker could have predicted that outcome. But what can you do? Your tax dollars at work.

Our bus ride in Hell promised to be a repeat of the NSF study. I sighed. "Let's just get off and walk."

Orson nodded and prepared to force his way to the back door. Being big as a house, he was just the guy for the job.

Suddenly there was a buzzing sound, like flies. It reminded me of my boss, Beezy, aka, Beelzebub. The noise came from the driver's dispatcher system, his connection with the Authority that managed all of Hell's buses. Gaap put down his nail file. "Shit. Now what?" He picked up his headset and slipped it on. In the mirror's reflection, I saw his eyes go wide. "Right away, sir," he mumbled, and rang off.

Gaap floored the accelerator again, and we took off like a bat out of hell.

Well, not really. I served with BOOH, I knew BOOH, the storied Bat out of Hell. BOOH was a friend of mine, and Gaap was no BOOH, but he moved the bus as fast as he could, running cars and trucks off the road, sideswiping pedestrians on the sidewalks or work crews in the streets that were busily carving fresh potholes into the asphalt, as he pushed his vehicle to its limit. There was the ding ding ding sound of numerous "let me off" pulls on the "let me off" cords, but Gaap didn't stop until he was right in front of my office, then he braked so hard his foot could have gone through the floor.

We were in one of those buses designed to kneel. Back on Earth, they were used to aid the boarding and de-boarding of disabled passengers. In Hell, they served to throw people out of the bus and onto the asphalt. Orson and I had just reached the rear door, when we were tossed through it like bags of garbage. We slammed against the curb.

Orson's face was planted firmly in my butt, and his capacious belly was flattening my face into the concrete. With a groan, he crawled off me again, pulling me up by my sore arm. It hurt like hell, but in the process he popped my shoulder back in place, so things could have been worse.

Orson examined a tear in his coveralls. "What was *that* all about?"

"I'm not sure, but dollars to donuts Beezy was behind it."

My friend nodded. "You know, that's a really stupid expression, but I agree. I thought I recognized Beelzebub's ring on Gaap's walkie-talkie."

Before us was a dilapidated excuse for a trailer, propped up precariously on cinderblocks that were slowly disintegrating. The vinyl siding of the structure was beginning to pull away at the edges; it also needed a new roof. Our office wasn't much to look at. Back on Earth, it would probably have been the first to go in any trailer park when a tornado careened through, cherry picking people's homes, pulverizing them, and then throwing the remains to the four winds. This particular single-wide was our office, not where we spent our evenings, though it felt as much like home to us as any other place in Hell. The peeling wallpaper, damp and moldy from a ceiling leak that we had never been able to find, the rickety furniture, the ancient and rusting time clock: they all were evidence of the drab ennui of our eternal damnation. But at least they were familiar.

Above the roofline of the trailer loomed the twin towers of Hell's Hospital. The hospital was where thousands upon thousands of the damned were unceasingly tormented. I usually called the hospital the "Giant Toaster." There were a couple of reasons for that. One, its twin steel towers, stuck together as if they'd been epoxied, reminded me of the toaster we'd had in my house when I was a kid.

Also, everyone who goes to hospitals ends up dead eventually, and, as everyone knows, when you're dead, you're toast.

Hell's Hospital dished out fear and pain with marvelous efficiency. It was easy, mainly because of that "toast" thing I just mentioned, but the hospital had a major problem preventing it from achieving its full potential as a place of torment. There was a powerful subversive element wandering the halls of the Toaster, an indomitable force for good thwarting the efforts of Management, bringing relief wherever she went.

That would be Florence Nightingale. Unlike the rest of Hell's denizens, Nightingale was not one of the damned, but more of a missionary who was trying to do some good in a backwater place. She was, in fact, the finest, kindest, purest soul I'd ever encountered in my life or afterlife.

Upon her death in 1910, St. Peter was all set to escort her personally to the Pearly Gates, but Florence thought she could do more good in Hell than she could in Heaven, so she came here and began to provide what comfort she could to the denizens of the Toaster. Flo drove Satan crazy, but he was powerless to touch her. She wasn't one of his minions, but a saintly soul who seemed to have the protection and approval of the Top Brass.

Flo. My Flo. My one true love.

Corny, I know, but true, or at least it used to be, and the thought of her brought a familiar knot to my chest as I stood there on the pavement before my office. Flo and I used to be an item. She was helping me find some conspirators down here. In our time working together, we got pretty close and, well, we ended up in the sack. Unfortunately, while we were *in flagrante delicto*, Satan had a couple of devils film the whole bedroom scene; they turned the footage into a porn movie that continued to play in every movie theater in Hell. Flo was humiliated by the whole affair and had been avoiding me ever since.

It was a problem I was still trying to solve.

"Steve? You okay?"

"Huh?" I'd stopped moving once I'd spied the Toaster. "Yeah, sorry. I was just thinking about something." I wiped my eyes on my sleeve before Orson could see any tears.

"Flo, huh?" He smiled in sympathy, putting a friendly hand on my shoulder.

I sighed. "Yeah."

"Come on," he said, gently shoving me toward our office. "Best thing for a broken heart is to stay busy."

"Right," I said and got moving again.

We climbed the rickety stairs, keeping our balance by gripping an even more rickety metal railing. As I grabbed the office door handle and pulled, it came off in my hand. This was not the first time, and by habit, I reached for my hammer, preparing to throw it through the frosted glass.

Orson stopped me. "No, don't. We have enough to do. Let me help." He pulled a credit card out of his pocket. Where he got one, I don't know - maybe he was buried with it; maybe it was one he used in a TV commercial - but the card was an American Express that looked to be nearly a hundred years old. Anyway, Orson used it to jimmy the lock.

I whistled in admiration. "Membership really does have its privileges. That was pretty good. Where'd you learn to do that?"

"A bad spy movie," he said, opening the door. "After you."

We went over to the antediluvian Mr. Coffee and filled our mugs with the burnt dregs from the morning's pot. Funny. All I'd had time to do before leaving to help Sisyphus was turn on the coffee. The pot should have been full, or only slightly cooked down, but the contents of the carafe were more like sludge than java. My cuppa Joe always tasted like hell - that was a given - but I usually didn't have to strain it through my teeth to get some liquid out of the concoction.

Whatever.

Setting our mugs on my desk, a beat-up All-Steel model, we checked the wire in-basket for new work orders. As usual, there were way too many for us to handle, so we looked for any top priority ones.

"What did you think of Old Dependable winking out like that?" Orson asked, as we performed our triage, separating out two work orders from the hundred that had filled the basket while we were gone. Another light bulb had burned out in the sign above Hell's Gate; we'd need to get to that soon. Mussolini's sewing machine - the Great One was spending eternity making panty hose - was broken, and he had nothing to do. The guy was just enough of a baddie to require fairly prompt attention.

"I don't know what happened to Old Dependable. I half-expected to find something in here about it."

A low gurgle of sound emanated from the pneumatic tube above the basket. This was the way we usually received work orders. The noise grew, then with a moist popping sound, the tube spat out a burning piece of paper. It landed in my basket, and I quickly used my needle nose pliers to pick it up, laying it atop the metal desktop.

When the flames died down, I looked to see what was written on the page. "Crap."

Orson glanced up from the work orders he was examining. "What? What is it?"

I handed him the paper. It wasn't a work order but a short note.

Down the rabbit hole. Now. S

"Rabbit hole? What?" Orson's eyes widened. "Does this mean what I think it means?"

"Yeah," I said, unbuckling my tool belt and placing it on my desktop. "I guess I'm off to see the Wizard."

That's two children's literature references in a row. I'll have to watch that. Besides, Satan might not like me calling him the Wizard. You never know what's going to make him mad.

"Do you really, uh, have to take the express train?"

I walked to the front door, swallowing hard. "You know I do. See ya. While I'm gone, go over to the hospital blood bank and pick up a sack-full of blood bags." We always liked to keep bags of blood on hand, in case a certain friend of ours came visiting. I preferred getting them myself, but because of the situation with Flo, Orson had been performing this task for me.

Once outside the trailer, I broke into a run, heading straight for the Throat of Hell, the series of big holes that ran through the center of all circles in the Underworld, from the Mouth of

Hell at Gates Level all the way down to Level Nine, where Satan had his office.

The running was important. Satan didn't tolerate any hesitation or lateness from his minions, and the quickest way to get to him was by

"Aaaaaaaaaaaaaaaaaaaaaaaaaaaaaaaaaaaaaaaaaaaaaaaaa aaaaaaaaaaaaaaa … "

plunging down the Throat of Hell.

This was one of the worst parts about my job, responding to an emergency summons from the Big Guy. My life-long fear of heights, actually one of only a couple of things that really scared me, had persisted beyond the grave. I had made this jump twice before, the last time plummeting all the way from Gates Level, down down down through all the Circles of Hell, before landing in Satan's waiting room. Trying to make the best of a bad situation, I noted that my fall would only be four circles this time - well, five if you counted the splat at the bottom. The last time I'd done a freefall through Hell had involved all nine levels.

I was curled up in a tight little ball, like a pill bug. This was for self-protection. The sides of Hell's Throat were as hot as Hades, well, precisely as hot, and I didn't relish the thought of coming in contact with them. I also didn't want to accidentally catch myself on some stone, throwing off my trajectory and landing on Six, Seven or Eight. Then I'd just have to jump in again.

And Satan would be pissed off because I'd kept him waiting.

I was gritting my teeth, trying to stop the screams, but all I succeeded in accomplishing was muffling the "Aaaaaaaaaaaaaa" down to more of an "Eeeeeeeeeeeeeeee." It didn't seem much of an improvement, and my lips were more exposed to the super-heated air. I hated chapped lips, so I opened up my mouth again and allowed my scream its full throttle.

When you fall through the Throat of Hell, you can't see very much: basically pitch black and then blinding white. That's because, as you descend, you're alternating between the interior of a circle (black) and the mile of air separating it from the next one (white). The trip actually doesn't take very long, because normal physical laws don't apply in Hell. Specifically, you aren't limited by terminal velocity, and you keep accelerating. I guess if this fall were interminable, I might eventually exceed the speed of light. For some reason, this idea intrigued me. Would I go back in time if that happened? Maybe back to before I died?

That would be nice, I thought, as I fell like a BB down the infernal chute. Then perhaps I could have stopped that little prick of a graduate student from blowing my brains out.

Of course, I've been in Hell so long that I surely would have died of natural causes by now anyway.

I was getting a leg cramp from being curled up in my cannonball position for so long.

If I could go back in time, though, maybe I would do it with foreknowledge of damnation. Then I could spend the rest of my life being the best person I could, maybe change the odds and make it to ...

"Aaaaaaaaaaaaaaaaaaaaaaaaaaaaaaaaaaaaaaaaaaaaaaa aaaaaaaaa ... Ouch!"

Chapter 3

My abrupt landing disrupted my chain of thought ... my spine too. As the knee bones, shattered from my impact on the carpet, glued themselves back together and reconnected to the thigh bones, I looked up to see Bruce the Bedeviled, Satan's personal assistant, standing above me. He gave me a hand.

"No applause, please," I said, wincing in pain. "Just help me up."

Bruce was a small man, but very muscular. The former martial arts star had maintained his wiry strength. I wondered if he worked out, I thought, as Bruce gave my arm a quick jerk, popping me to my feet.

"Thanks. Nice outfit, by the way. I've never seen you in a turtleneck and cardigan. It's a good look for you."

There was venom in his stare. I guess he didn't like cardigans. "I'm wearing this because I'm cold, and you're late."

"You're wearing a cardigan because I'm late? Why would that make a difference?" I asked mildly. "Besides, you always say I'm late."

"That's because it's always true."

"Is not."

"Is too."

"Is not."

"Boys," said a voice from the side. "Shut up."

That was Beezy, my boss. The fat old devil, a token number of flies and mosquitoes orbiting his head, was leaning against the wall next to Satan's office door. Beezy usually wore a white suit and black fez, but today he was dressed in an outfit a Mongol warrior might have worn out on the Steppes. He was clad in a knee-length toga; I think the Mongols called them dels.

Anyway, it was a dilly of a del, made of suede, lined with sheepskin and dyed a rich burgundy. The sleeves were very long, long enough to cover his hands, though his claws extended a little beyond the cuffs. Beezy also had on leather boots with upturned toes and a sheepskin-lined felt hat with ear flaps strapped to his chin. As was his fashion with any hat he wore, my boss had it canted back slightly so his horns could clear the fabric.

Odd. Is he cold too? Satan's anteroom did seem a little cooler than its usual sauna-like state. I hadn't noticed earlier because I'd been chilled from freefalling through the sky of Level Nine.

Another funny thing: I don't usually meet with Satan and Beelzebub together. This must be important.

Removing my arm from Bruce's grasp, I walked over to my boss. "What's with the Genghis Khan outfit?"

Beezy flicked a finger in my direction. He didn't touch me, but I felt a jolt, as if someone had put a cattle prod to my cheek. "Don't be a smartass, Minion." Then he opened the door to Satan's office.

A blast of oppressive heat took my breath away. As we stepped into the office, I saw the reason. Striding back and forth in Satan's sanctuary was an enormous red dragon. Each of its seven heads was blasting flames in a different direction. The creature's ten foot tail was swishing back and forth, like that of a cat spoiling for a fight. Each head had a horn, and a crown too, as if someone was playing horseshoes and got seven ringers. There were three extra horns on its back. I didn't know if this was for added scary effect, or if they were spares, in case one of the head-horns broke off.

"Revelation, Chapter 12, right?" I knew my Bible pretty well and liked to show off my knowledge whenever I could.

The dragon batted me across the room with its tail.

I slammed into the far wall, collapsing to the floor like a broken china doll. Despite the pain from what I estimated to be three cracked ribs, I rose to my feet.

I really need to learn to keep my mouth shut. Beezy's right. No one likes a smartass.

As my bones began to mend, seven draconian mouths opened and roared, each slightly out of tune with the other. The sound was pretty unpleasant, and I don't even have perfect pitch.

The dragon shrank into the shape of a tall, thin man in black suit, shirt and tie. He wore dark sunglasses that hid any expression his eyes might reveal. No horns, though. Satan usually reserved those for special occasions, like mixers and costume parties.

"My lord," I said, bowing deeply, remembering the advice I always gave others who were preparing for an interview with Big Red: "Don't screw with Satan. Just be unfailingly respectful and try to get away from him in one piece, as quickly as you can."

I touched my side and winced. If only I'd remembered my own advice before mouthing off to him.

Satan and heights were the only two things I was really afraid of. BOOH used to scare me as well, but no longer. I was even getting a little better with my acrophobia, but I knew my fear of Old Nick would last forever.

Beezy gave Satan a small wave. With a twitch, he changed his clothing back to his Sidney Greenstreet cum 'Casablanca' look. "Thanks for warming the place up."

Satan nodded. "Anything for you, old friend." He didn't really mean it. Satan didn't have friends, but if he did, Beelzebub would be his best one. A massive desk and two chairs, one behind, the other before the desk, appeared in the space between us and the Earl of Hell. A light from an indefinable source struck the furniture, like a spotlight for dramatic effect. The rest of the room was black, and to me the space seemed infinite. I knew it was pretty large no matter what. After all, a monster dragon had just been roaming freely in it.

Executives always have the best offices.

"Have a seat," Satan said, as he settled into his chair. Beezy followed suit.

Of course, there was no chair for me. When there were just the two of us, Satan usually allowed me to sit - though in exceptionally uncomfortable chairs, like that one made entirely out of sharpened pencils, still, a chair is a chair - but with Beezy in the room, the Earl of Hell probably felt that would be inappropriate. Devils are very status-conscious.

Satan and Beelzebub stared at me in expectation. Despite myself, I barked out a terse "What?"

And found myself hanging upside down in the air. There was a couple of popping sounds, and two imps appeared. (Imps are vertically-challenged devils.) They stood on my butt as they stabbed me repeatedly with tiny pitchforks.

"Ow, ow! Shit, that stings!"

"Decorum, Minion," Satan merely said then waved his hand. The imps disappeared, and I fell to the floor. Snap went the wrist of my right arm. I'd already exceeded my quota of broken bones for the day, and it wasn't even noon. Resolving to watch my P's and Q's through the rest of the meeting, I squeaked out a pitiful "Sorry, sir." Hauling myself to my feet once more, I bowed again, and said, "What, Lord Satan, the Great and Powerful?"

Damn! I'm my own worst enemy.

I saw a tiny smile on Beezy's face that he quickly repressed. Satan raised his hand again then dropped it to the desk. "Screw it. I don't have time for this."

The Prince of Lies got out of his chair and began pacing. "Gentlemen, we have a problem."

"What's that?" I asked for the third time, rubbing the pain out of my wrist.

"You mean you haven't noticed?" Beezy chimed in.

"What?" That made four.

"Are you stupid, or just acting like it?" Satan asked. "I know you saw what happened to Old Dependable today."

I nodded. Not knowing what to do with my hands, I let them hang awkwardly at my sides. "I was looking for a work order with instructions to fix it when your note came through the tube. Do I need to light Dependable's pilot or something?"

Satan frowned, drumming his fingers on the back of his chair. Periodically one of his claws would catch on the leather, tearing it, but he didn't seem to notice. "This problem is a lot bigger than that."

"What?"

"Minion!" Satan hissed. "If you say 'what' one more time, I'll make you have sex with Uphir."

Ugh. Uphir was just about my least favorite demon in Hell. He ran the hospital, aka, the Big Toaster, up on Five. Aside from being an exceptionally unpleasant demon, he delighted in upsetting Flo. Things were bad enough between the two of us these days, and having sex with Uphir, beyond being unimaginably unpleasant, wasn't likely to help the situation.

The painful knot in my chest returned. This was happening with fair regularity these days, ever since Flo and I had been estranged, but shaking off my heartache and general self-pity, I turned my attention back to my two bosses. Well, actually,

Beezy was my boss, but Satan was his boss, so I considered both of them as my bosses.

If you think about it, I'm actually pretty high on the organizational chart, to wit:

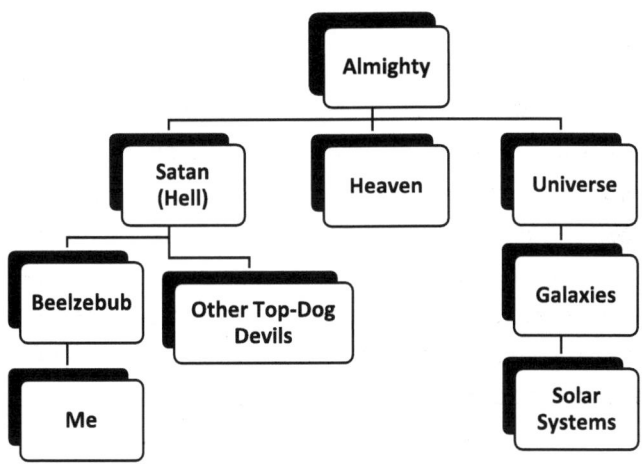

I guess that means I have still one more boss, but I'm not allowed to talk about Him, this being Hell and all. I'm not sure, but this apparently places me on the same level in the organization as a solar system.

Hmmm. Maybe I should gain some weight.

Of course, this line of reasoning would make Bruce, as Satan's personal assistant, nearly the equivalent of a galaxy, and I just didn't buy that. Maybe a black hole.

Once more I bowed to the Prince of Darkness. "Intimacy with Uphir won't be necessary, my Lord. Just tell me wha ... the situation and how you would like me to proceed."

Satan nodded curtly. "Better, Minion."

"Come on, Nick," Beezy said. Beelzebub often called Satan "Nick," at least to his face. I think it was a sign of their familiarity, or maybe it was a subtle bit of disrespect on Beezy's part. Well, if anyone could get away with it, my boss was the guy. "Let's stop playing mine is bigger than yours and get Minion to work."

"I was just getting to that, Flyface," Satan said.

Flyface. Heh. A good one.

Beelzebub is not only "Lord of the Flies;" that's an actual translation of his name from the ancient Semitic.

Satan waved a hand at the air behind him and a large monitor appeared, showing a schematic of Hell. "Minion, you've not had much to do with Hell's HVAC system over the years, have you?"

Heating, Ventilation and Air Conditioning for the uninitiated.

I thought back to the millions of work orders I'd closed or ignored in my time as Hell's Super. I shrugged. "Except for replacing a few burners and lighting the occasional pilot light, I guess not. Seems pretty dependable."

"It is," Beezy said. "I designed it myself. I build 'em good," he said, with a smirk.

"'Well,' Beelzebub," the Earl of Hell said. "Not 'good.'"

"Whatever. In any event, the heating system works flawlessly."

"Until recently," Satan corrected again. "A few hours ago, the system started to act up. I always keep the thermostat at 225 degrees, but the temperature has been dropping."

That's Fahrenheit. No Metric system in Hell. That would make too much sense.

Beelzebub frowned, making his fez slip forward a little, only to be stopped when it caught on his horns. Without thinking, Beezy shoved it backward. "There's no design flaw. Until today, the HVAC system has performed like a Swiss clock. This is the first problem we've had with it in over two thousand years."

"Maybe a pipe is clogged or something," I offered, trying to be helpful.

"Maybe," said the Lord of Hell. "Maybe not. It's your job to find out."

I groaned. This would be worse than fixing the Escalator that bore damned souls from Saint Peter's desk down through the bowels of Hell. That had been my last really big job, along with rebuilding the Stairway to Paradise, though actually Orson had more to do with that than I did. The Escalator was a discrete if enormous piece of machinery, but the HVAC was a complete system, crisscrossing every section of the Underworld.

Beezy snorted. "Buck up, Minion. It's your damnation, remember?"

With an effort, I suppressed the urge to groan again. A hiccup popped out instead. "Any suggestion on how I should start?"

Beezy got out of his chair and walked over to Satan's monitor. "This is a systemic problem, not like a clogged pipe. All of Hell is getting colder. Right now, we're about five degrees off normal, and the temperature is dropping by the minute."

"Five degrees? That doesn't' sound like very much, not enough to put Bruce in a cardigan."

"Bruce has recently been made a demon," Satan said with a shrug, "and demons, like devils, are very sensitive to temperature drops. That's why Beelzebub was dressed for autumn out in my lobby."

Beezy nodded. "Five degrees may not seem like much to you, but we feel it. Besides, the temperature is continuing to drop steadily. If this keeps up, in no time we'll be below 150 degrees, which for Hell is like winter in Vostok."

"Where?"

"Antarctica."

"Oh." I looked over to Satan. "You heated this place up pretty effectively in your dragon form. Couldn't you do the same for the rest of Hell?"

The Lord of the Underworld frowned. "Maybe, but I'm not going to play Big Bad Wolf and huff and puff myself silly. Besides, that would just be a workaround. It's your job to get the system fixed."

"May I continue, please?" Beezy didn't like to be interrupted. If it had just been me, he probably would have sewn my mouth shut, but since Satan was also disrupting his explanation, there wasn't much the Lord of the Flies could do but try to grab back everyone's attention. "The HVAC system is a simple balance of opposing forces. Down here on Level Nine, you have the main jets that heat all of Hell. There are jets on other levels, but those are more for torturing the damned than actually heating the Underworld."

"On each Circle of Hell, the heat is distributed through a series of ductwork, but between levels, it travels through a single pipe that runs up the Throat of Hell."

"Really? I don't recall ever seeing it."

Beezy examined the inside of his right hand; for the first time I noticed a small tuft of hair growing from it. "That's because I put a glamour on the pipe so no one could see or touch it … or fuck with it. Here," he said, and thwacked me in the forehead with his palm.

"Ow!" I said, holding my hand to my smarting brow. "Why'd you do that?"

"What a wuss!" my boss grumbled. "I just adjusted your vision so you'll be able to see the pipes and ductwork."

"Thanks, I guess." My head felt like a boxer had just clobbered me. "What, what about the cooling system?" I knew we didn't use much cold in Hell, but we had some.

"The system works like a sublimation cooler, rather than an air conditioner," Beezy explained.

"Beg pardon?"

Beelzebub frowned and scratched his beard with one of his long, black claws. "You know, Minion, I've seen squirrels with more mechanical aptitude than you. Let me put it in terms you'll understand: think ice box instead of refrigerator."

"Aha! Gotcha."

Sighing, Beezy pointed at a large, stalactite-shaped mass on the upper right of the schematic. "Mount Erebus provides all the cold air and, since cold air falls, it does the same thing as the heater, but in reverse. The heating and cooling pipes between levels are separate, as is most of the ductwork, but they parallel each other. There are also occasional points of cross-over."

"Where?"

"Here, here, here," Beezy continued pointing at the schematic, and at each touch of his claw, a mark showed. He touched a handful of spots, where hot and cold blended to form something I never imagined existed in Hell: temperate.

I noted there weren't very many of them. A temperate zone in Hell was a bit of an oxymoron.

"Sounds complicated," I opined.

Beezy shrugged. "Not really. That's why it doesn't break. The heat rises, the cold falls. Usually we want blast-furnace heat and occasionally bone-freezing cold. The few places we don't, the furnace and cooler work together. The system has never failed."

"So what is wrong now?" Satan asked. I don't think he was really interested. In fact, he was tapping one of his cloven hooves impatiently. Still, as a manager, he had at least to feign interest in what Beezy was saying.

Beezy shrugged. "Dunno. I would have sworn it was impossible to break the HVAC, unless someone did it intentionally."

I thought back to the Escalator incident. The Free Hellions, led by the Three Stooges, had attempted to break the Escalator in order to engineer events that would allow them to escape Hell. I didn't think a human could damage a system he couldn't see, and I couldn't imagine a devil or demon who would want Hell colder than it was. "Do you expect foul play?"

"Always," Beelzebub said. "This is Hell, after all. But if you mean do I think someone intentionally damaged the HVAC, well, I simply don't know. You need to check the mechanics of the system first, though, before you spend any time looking for a saboteur."

Great. He's not giving me any clue as to how I could fix it. "Any suggestions on where I should start, what I should look for?"

Beezy shrugged. "The temperature appears to be dropping uniformly throughout Hell. Like I said earlier, it's not a specific problem; it's a systemic one."

"And what does that mean?" I mean, I knew what it meant. "Systemic" had been in my personal lexicon for a long time. I just didn't know how this demonstration of my impressive vocabulary could help me diagnose the problem.

"It means the problem is likely to have nothing to do with the transportation of heat or cold, but with the sources of each."

"Meaning what exactly?" I was trying my best to absorb the situation, but a paper towel would have done better.

"Erebus is either putting out too much cold air, or the heating elements, mainly on Nine as I told you, though there are repeaters on each of the upper floors, are not putting out enough heat. I don't think it's one of the repeaters, since the temperature is dropping on every level, even down here. Still you need to check them out."

I sighed. "Of course I do."

"Most likely, it's the source burners or Erebus itself."

"Could it be both?"

"Unlikely," Beezy said with a frown, "but possible, I suppose."

I stared at the screen. Beezy had marked it up so much, it looked like a rabid Etch A Sketch. "Could I have a copy of this schematic?"

Satan had had enough. He snapped his fingers, the screen disappeared, and a scroll formed in his hand. "Here," he said, handing it to me.

"Hey!" Beezy protested. "That's mine. My design. You shouldn't be handing it out to just anyone."

"He's not just anyone," Satan pointed out. "He's the one who has to fix the problem. And it's not your design. Remember: work for hire. I own all intellectual property rights down here."

Beezy turned bright red, redder than usual, which was about as red as a maraschino cherry. His mouth popped open then just as abruptly closed.

I was fascinated. I'd seen the two of them together only a few times before. It had always been clear to me that Beelzebub wasn't afraid of Satan, but clearly Satan was the boss, and Beezy knew it.

And so did Satan. A smug little smile formed on his cruel mouth.

What a sweetheart.

Satan gave me a withering look, and I shivered. Right. He can read my mind.

And the Prince of Hell gave a slight nod of his head.

"I ... I assume this is top priority."

Satan grinned, flashing his sharp canines at me. "Of course it is! All of my work assignments are, as you very well know. Though," he frowned, as a sudden thought came to him, "this one is perhaps more important than usual."

"Why's that?" I asked, as I unrolled the schematic and examined it more closely. "Can't everybody just bundle up until the HVAC gets fixed?"

Beezy snorted as he made eye contact with Satan. "He doesn't get it."

"Get what?"

"The metaphysical ramifications," Satan responded, running a hand over the rosewood desktop.

"How can a little cold have metaphysical ramifications?"

Both devils looked at me as if I had a screw loose. "Do you mean," Beezy asked in astonishment, "you've never heard the expression, 'a cold day in Hell?'"

"Well, sure. Back when I was alive, I used it all the time. Like, 'it will be a cold day in Hell before Congress can work together,' or 'it will be a cold day in Hell before I'll be nice to that jerk' or ... " I stopped. My stomach felt a little queasy. "Do you, do you mean ... "

"Yes, Minion," Satan said in impatience. "If things get *really* cold down here, all of those casual statements you humans used to make will start coming true."

"But why?"

Satan lifted a paperweight off his desk and threw it at me. It bounced off my skull, and I crumpled to the floor. "Listen! I don't make the rules. Well, usually I do, but this time I didn't. It's one of ... His." Satan looked upward, a sullen look on his face. "I don't know why, but if you don't get the system back in balance, these unlikely things will start happening just as surely as Beezy will get fatter or BOOH will drool on my carpet."

"Speaking of BOOH," I thought quickly, as I climbed off the floor. "I'll probably need to get around Hell really fast to work on this, so ... "

"No."

"Come on," I whined. "BOOH and I are a great team."

"That alone would be reason enough, but right now you don't need him. Your work starts down here, on Level Nine."

"Really?" I had never been allowed to go anywhere on Nine except the waiting room and Satan's office.

"Yes, really. Beelzebub," the Devil (capital D) said to his lieutenant. "I'm tired of this meeting. I'm going to take a sauna. Finish up." With that, Satan disappeared in a puff of smoke.

Beezy grumbled something in Assyrian. I think it was a curse, but it was one I didn't know. "Give me the diagram." I handed it over.

"On the upper levels of Hell, you'll need to check that the heating and cooling pipes are working properly."

"How do I do that?"

"On a heating pipe, put a finger to it. If your finger burns off, things are working right."

"Swell."

"Don't worry," he chortled. "It will grow back."

It's one of the few benefits of being dead and in Hell. I heal better than Wolverine, as I'd already demonstrated many times since breakfast. "Do I test the cold pipes the same way?"

Beezy's laughter made my skin crawl. "No," he said, still chuckling. "What you do is ... " My boss whispered in my ear.

"No way!"

"It's either that or your dick. Which would you prefer?"

I looked at Beelzebub sullenly. "Fine. I'll do it your way."

"Thought you might. Now, since the main jets that heat the Underworld are here on Nine, you might as well start on this level."

"How do I get to them?"

"There's a door immediately across from Bruce's desk."

"I've seen it. I thought I wasn't allowed to go in there."

"Normally you're not. That's where the Traitors are located."

"Ah," I said with sudden understanding. I'd always wondered where Judas, Cain and the others were kept.

"Go through the door - Bruce will unlock it for you - walk past the Traitors, and at the far end of their, uh, quarters, you'll find a door. Go through, and you'll be in the boiler room. Meanwhile, I'll talk Satan into letting you use BOOH."

"Really?"

"Yeah, really. Normally, I'd let you struggle through this without any help, but a cold day in Hell is just about the most cataclysmic thing imaginable. Satan knows this. He just said no out of reflex. Anyway, I'll see what I can do."

"Well, thanks."

"Don't mention it. I mean, literally, don't mention it. I don't want anyone thinking I'm getting soft or anything." Beezy rolled up the schematic and handed it back to me. "You'd better not lose this. I don't care what Mr. High and Mighty says, this is *mine*, and I don't want it falling into just anybody's hands."

"Yeah, I can see that. You wouldn't want someone like Edison or Ford improving your design and selling it to Satan."

Beezy gave me a half-hearted shove that sent me sprawling. "Minion, I swear, well frequently, but I swear you have a death wish."

The floor and I were constant companions, so I was not particularly fazed by finding myself on it once again. "No, not really. Been there, done that, got the T-shirt."

The Lord of the Flies grabbed me by the scruff of my neck and hauled me to my feet. He snickered. "True. That would be overkill. Bruce!" he yelled, as he opened the door to Satan's office. "Let Minion into the Traitors' quarters."

Bruce looked as if he'd been slapped. "Only the Lord of Hell can authorize ... urp!"

Satan's secretary was suspended in mid-air, grasping at his neck, gasping for breath. Beside me, Beezy was squeezing together his right thumb and index finger. He flicked his wrist, and Bruce flew across the room, going splat against the door he'd just been told to open. "So, Demon, Third Class: open the fucking door."

"kkkkkk ... kkkkaaaa ... kkkkaaaa"

"What are you doing, coughing up a hair ball?"

"kkkkaaaa ... kkkkaaaan ... kkkkaaaan do, Lord Buh, Beelzebub," Bruce finally managed to say.

"Then open it."

"Yessir."

I didn't particularly dislike Bruce, except for the fact that he was an officious twit. Still, I took a perverse pleasure in watching my boss put the little jerk in his place. I also admired the efficiency with which he did it. One thing I always said about Beelzebub was that he didn't mess around.

As Bruce unlocked the door, I turned to Beezy. "Is there anything in particular I should look for?"

"Just ask the fire demon who runs the place. He'll show you around. By the way," he said, as an afterthought, "Surtr's an old one, and an odd one. I think he's going senile, so if he acts a little weird, just put up with it."

"Surtr?" I asked in astonishment. "*The* Surtr? Ragnarok, end-of-the-world Surtr?"

"Yeah. Satan bought him off Odin about a thousand years ago, around the time Christianity had pretty much closed down the whole Norse mythology franchise. Got Surtr at a fire sale," he added in an off-hand manner.

"Bad joke."

"Couldn't resist. Besides, it's pretty much what happened. Odin was desperate to pick up a few bucks. He'd already sold most of his assets, including Valhalla."

"Really? Who bought it?"

"I can't remember, but I think they sold it to Disney about twenty years ago. Mickey Inc. turned it into a theme park."

"Valhalla's a theme park?" I asked in amazement.

"Yeah, in one of those Scandinavian countries. Valhalla's mostly for guys who like to drink a lot of beer and mead and stuff, eat shanks of meat and throw them on the floor, watch the dogs chew up the bones. I popped in there once to check things out. It was pretty boring."

"Well, I bet drinking is a popular activity there. What else can they do in the winter?"

"Ski and shiver, I suspect."

"Yeah." I thought about the fire demon being sold to put a few coins in Odin's pocket. "Too bad about Surtr, though." I shook my head. "How the mighty falleth."

"You said it." Beelzebub mumbled, picking his teeth with a claw. He would know all about falling mightily, since he himself was once a Semitic god … or a fallen angel … or both. "Get to work," he said, disappearing in an explosion. The bodies of dead flies lay on the carpet where he'd just been standing.

Chapter 4

I stepped inside and closed the door. In front of me was a corridor, really just a two-yard span of gray concrete between two sets of cages, each no bigger than eight by eight feet. I couldn't decide if the area looked more like lockdown in Alcatraz or the ape house of a Nineteenth Century zoo.

There were eight cages total, but only those on the left of the corridor were occupied. The first one I came to held a butt-naked, long-haired dude hanging by his neck from a rope tied to a small tree that was growing through the concrete of the cell. A dinner plate was floating in mid-air, right within arm's reach. On the plate were what looked like silver coins. Periodically, the man would take one of the coins and swallow it. This would put his body into spasms, and he would jerk on the rope as if he were choking. I waited a few seconds and heard a plink. Looking down, I spied the coin on the ground. The man took another coin from the plate and swallowed it. Again, ding, like change coming out of a vending machine, the coin fell to the ground. I imagined when he consumed all thirty coins - I was pretty sure there were thirty of them - they would be transported back to the plate, and he'd start eating again.

I left Judas to his meal and looked in the next cage. Here I found an aged man dressed in knickers and a baseball cap. Three of the four sides of his cage were covered with blackboards. The old guy was using a stick of chalk to write, "I will not disrupt class by making unpleasant noises." Each time he touched the chalk to the board, the most irritating screech you can imagine shattered what would otherwise have been an almost eerie silence. The high-pitched grating was augmented by an amplifier as big as a refrigerator in the center of the room.

This was the boy who invented the Screech, and he was one of two recent additions to Level Nine. As a former teacher, well, university professor to be completely accurate, I'd had the Screech happen to me a time or two. By the time students had reached college or graduate student age, they tended not to intentionally make that sound, but it could still be caused accidentally. Of course, I'd been dead so long teachers had probably switched to holograms, which no doubt posed aggravations of their own, but it didn't matter that the Screech was obsolete. In its time, the sound was unbelievably irritating. I just hated it and was glad to see the human who invented the quintessential classroom disruption being punished for it.

Screech Boy finished filling the last blackboard, then he set down his chalk, picked up an eraser, wiped down all the boards, and started again. Wheeeeeeeeee.

I found the second recent addition to the club of traitors in the next cell. Hitler was hanging wallpaper, using his mustache to spread the paste. I noted that he was a really shitty wallpaper hanger, even worse than me, and that's saying something. I don't know why this was a particularly awful version of Hell, after seeing Judas and Screech boy, but things bother some people more than other. Hanging wallpaper would be unpleasant for me, but it was clearly Hell for Adolf.

In the fourth cage was a bestial looking fellow. He had what appeared to be a bright red rash on his face. The inmate was flipping through a family album. I could just spy the figures of Adam, Eve and their first two sons. One of the boys was smiling placidly. He was holding what looked like a 4-H trophy, and his parents looked down on him with obvious pride. The other boy was glaring at his brother, murder in his eyes. In the sky, a beneficent being looked down upon them all. "Mom always liked you best," Cain muttered, sniffling.

Eight cages total. Four empty. Plenty of room for growth, I thought, as I reached the end of the corridor. There I found a closed door. At eye height was a small panel that looked like something the bouncer at a speakeasy would open to make certain there were no cops outside. The door was unlocked, though, so I ignored the panel, decided against knocking, and let myself into the boiler room.

"Gaaaaaaaaaaah!" It was hotter than Hell in there, which made sense, as I thought on it, since it was the source for all of the Underworld's heat.

Beezy had called this the boiler room, but I didn't see evidence of water anywhere. There were plenty of pipes, sure, that went this way and that; they looked like a jumble of linguini. But there wasn't a boiler. Instead, there were rows upon rows of burners, each one superheating air, which then passed into a pipe above it, bound for some destination elsewhere in Hell. Odd, though: I didn't smell any sulfur. *I wonder what they burned: natural gas?*

We humans think natural gas stinks too, but it really doesn't. It's completely odorless. On Earth, an additive to the gas gives it that smell so you'll know if your pilot light goes out, a handy piece of information if you don't particularly relish dying of asphyxiation. Down here, well, we're all dead anyway, so adding smell to gas would be unnecessary, although in keeping with the spirit of the place. I supposed that all the sulfur Management burned in Hell was deemed sufficient to provide the necessary olfactory effect.

The boiler room was a cavernous space. The cement-colored ceiling was high above me, and the floor was as big as a football field. It had to be in order to accommodate the thousands of burners. They looked like blue flowers. Very hot flowers - a field of them.

That's when I saw a row of sputtering jets. They were all but extinguished. Hovering over them was a fiery giant.

"Dear, dear," muttered the creature in an ancient voice, a voice ravaged by millennia of heat exposure. Or maybe he was a smoker, like Dora. Dora, the head of Parts, was a chain smoker, and this guy sounded a bit gravelly, like her. As the flaming head bent lower to examine the jet, I saw a large cancer stick - no filter - sticking out of his mouth.

Surtr, for surely this was he, reached toward one of the flames, as if to nurse it back to health. Instead, the flame went out entirely. The fire demon moved to the other side of the jet, nattering to himself all the while. That's when he saw me. I guess I surprised him, because he took two steps back and rose to his full height.

Yep, he was a big one, twenty, twenty-five feet high at least. But he'd seen better years. Even standing up, he seemed a little hunched around the shoulders, and his flames, while still pretty impressive, guttered out periodically on different parts of his body. He was hot enough to scorch my face though, even from fifteen feet away. I wondered, as I shielded my eyes from the heat, why the little wire-frame glasses he wore didn't melt.

"Sorry, Mr. Surtr, sir," I said, as politely as I could. I didn't care how old this coot was, he could melt me like candle wax, and I didn't want to risk an insult. "Sorry if I startled you."

Surtr cocked his head to one side, then to the other. He was looking at me as if he'd never seen such an odd creature in his life.

"Who are you?" he rasped. Damn he was old!

"I work for Beezy, uh, Beelzebub. He sent me down to check out the burners. Is everything okay?" I asked in genuine concern as another jet winked out.

"'Is everything okay?'" the old demon hissed. "Does it look like everything's okay?"

"Uh, no. I was just being polite."

"Well, stick it up your ass! I've got a crisis here, and I don't have time to bandy words with a little shrimp like you."

That kind of attitude: well, it just pisses me off.

"Look, flamebutt," I said, ignoring any risk of antagonizing the creature, "Lord Satan and Lord Beelzebub ... you *do* remember who they are, right, or are you just too old and senile to remember anything other than where you keep your cigarettes? If you do recall those pretty distinctive names, then you know that Satan *owns* you, and he expects you to cooperate with me."

Surtr roared and threw a fireball at me, which I ducked as if it were a slow-pitched softball. "Hah!" I yelled in triumph. "It's not like that's the first time someone's thrown a fireball at me. I've been around, you know."

Surtr grabbed his head in his hands, as if trying to keep his brain from exploding. Then his body flared. At that moment, he looked every yard the legendary fire demon of Norse mythology. "WHO *ARE* YOU?" he said, in a commanding voice that - despite my earlier bluster - made me quake.

"I'm Steve Minion, Hell's Super."

"Super what? Super jerk?"

"There's no need to get nasty. I'm the Superintendent for Plant Maintenance."

Surtr looked at me suspiciously. "How come I've never seen you before?"

"The boiler room never went on the fritz before. Look, can we stop this pissing contest? Satan ordered me to find out why Hell is getting colder, and that means you and I have to work together, capiche?"

The creature sighed and seemed to visibly shrink before my eyes. "My name is not 'Capiche,' but I understand."

I rolled my eyes. *Finally.* "So all of Hell is getting colder ... "

"Yes," the giant said, as he took of his glasses and cleaned them on a handkerchief.

Funny. Why doesn't that burn up in his hand? Mythological creatures. Go figure.

"And it's about to get much colder. You see this row of jets?" he asked, just as another one sputtered out.

"Yeah?"

"They're not supposed to do that."

"I kinda figured that. What's wrong with them?"

Surtr sat down heavily in a nearby chair. It was the size of an old Land Rover; shit, it could even have been an old Land Rover. That was kind of hard to say, as it was blackened from the heat of his butt. Beside the chair was a table holding an ashtray, a jug of kerosene - probably his drink of choice - and a blue princess telephone. Except for being two feet long and fifteen inches high, the delicate instrument seemed out of place in Surtr's hot and hard-surfaced domain.

"I don't know. They just started turning themselves off a few hours ago. I fear The Spark has gone out of them."

"The Spark?" I said, biting off some loose skin from a cuticle. "What's that?"

"You mean," Surtr said in astonishment, "you don't know what The Spark is?"

"Fraid not. Why don't you fill me in?"

Surtr got to his feet, and as he began pacing the boiler room, all age seemed to fall from him. "The Spark, why it is the animating force of the universe. It is everywhere."

This sounded vaguely familiar. "You mean like the Force?"

He looked at me in puzzlement. "I do not know this Force."

"Never mind. Old movie. You probably never saw it."

"Perhaps it's another name for The Spark."

"I said forget it." I sat down on the floor, thinking this might take a while. "You were saying?"

Surtr adjusted his glasses then began to speak. I recognized the style from my days as a university professor. He was kicking into lecture mode. "There are four forces in the universe which are the most powerful. Well," he said, pausing, "five if you count compound interest. But the other four are … " Turning to the stone wall behind him, Surtr used his flaming index finger to etch them into the rock.

Gravity

Electromagnetism

Strong Nuclear Force

Weak Nuclear Force

As an afterthought, Surtr wrote "Compound Interest" beneath the other four. I appreciated that. I like consistency, and you don't get enough of that in Hell.

"You sound like you're teaching physics. Pretty impressive for an old geezer like you."

"You know, Minion," Surtr commented with a look of disgust on his fiery visage - at least I think it was disgust, though it might have just been gas. "You have a smart mouth."

I shrugged "Yeah, I know. Not one of my better traits. Please continue."

"All right. Some physicists believe there is a single force underlying the five." Surtr drew a circle of flame around the list. "They're right, of course. That power is The Spark."

"Yeah, great. So Hawking was right, after all. There's a single unifying force, and you say it's The Spark." I found it difficult to speak the name in capitals, but I managed, because that seemed important to Surtr. It wasn't just a spark, or even the spark, but The Spark. Got it. "Can you be a little more specific?"

"No, not really." The giant sat back down on his Land Rover. "The Spark is in part defined by its very ineffability."

Ineffability. Pretty good word. "Where did an ancient fire demon learn all this stuff?"

"Don't call me a demon!" he snapped, his flame flaring.

"Sorry." I really didn't mean to offend, at least not on this point. "Why not?"

"Back where I come from, that's considered a racial slur."

One thing you need to know about me. I hate bigotry and intolerance of any kind. "Oh, I'm really sorry. I didn't know. What do you prefer?"

"Fire giant," he said, with simple dignity

"Works for me." After all, he was pretty damn huge. "Besides, I know a lot of demons in Hell, and they are … "

"Uniformly evil, repulsive, and despicable?"

I nodded. "Yeah. That pretty much sums them up. Anyway, where did you learn all this stuff?"

He shrugged. "Correspondence school."

"What?"

"Correspondence school. I'm working on a doctorate in metaphysics."

"This sounds like physics to me."

"I'm not talking about that touchy-feely stuff you humans call metaphysics on Midgard."

"Midgard?"

"Sorry. Before your time. Earth." For a moment, Surtr looked wistful. He was probably thinking about his salad days, when he was the bad ass who was supposed to destroy the universe. With a sigh, he continued. "True metaphysics includes both the physical and the spiritual universes."

"But why correspondence school?"

The fire giant shrugged. "I don't get out much. I have to keep an eye on these," he said, waving at the fire jets. "It's my job. But I've always been interested in these matters, so Satan let me enroll in correspondence school. I'm ABD," he said, proudly.

That's "all but dissertation," for those of you who don't know the arcane vocabulary of academia. "How far along are you on your dissertation?" I asked.

"Well ... "

Hah. I thought so. The dissertation nails so many Ph.D. wannabes. "Do you have your topic approved yet?"

Surtr put his head in one hand. He looked like a fiery version of Rodin's *The Thinker*. "I'm having a little trouble with that," he said, dejectedly.

"Who's your dissertation advisor?"

"Bifrons," he said with disgust. "What's wrong with you, Minion? It looks like your Spark just flared."

I was blushing a bright red.

Bifrons wrote for Hell's newspaper. Not long ago he had published a review of 'Flo Does the Super,' that porn movie I mentioned earlier.

It's a long story.

"He keeps finding excuses for rejecting my proposals."

"That's because he's an asshole," I grumbled.

"You said it."

We sat there quietly for a few minutes, each of us nursing his personal grudge against the demon of arts and sciences. I got off the floor, just as another jet went out. "I understand that you don't know exactly what's going on, but do you have any ideas?" I asked, brushing the dirt off my coveralls.

"N ... no," he said slowly, looking in puzzlement at the rows of jets that were now completely black. "It's as if someone is stealing the fire from beneath our noses."

"Stealing fire, huh? Good clue." Something clicked in my memory, and I headed for the door.

"Where are you going?"

"Just following up on a hunch."

"Keep me informed about what you discover."

"Okay," I said then turned back to him. "You said everything was animated by THE SPARK."

"Just The Spark will do. Overkill is unnecessary."

"Right, sorry. The Spark. What about titans, armadillos, bedbugs ... frost giants?"

Surtr stood very still, looking a little uncertain. At last he said, "Yes, all of them, even frost giants. Their Sparks are just a little colder than ours."

Cold Sparks. Great. "Later," I said.

"Minion, wait a second. Bik!"

I turned to see a small star descend from the rafters. It reminded me of Tinkerbell. The star landed in Surtr's palm. The fire giant whispered something to it, and a small noise, like the squeaking of a mouse, responded. Surtr's whisperings became a little more severe. The star replied with a single squeak. Nodding, as if satisfied, Sutr turned to me.

"Minion, you and I got off on the wrong foot. I am sorry for that. I have a bit of a temper. In fact, I'm famous for it."

"Me too."

"Anyway, I wanted to make things up to you. I want to lend you Bik."

"What's a Bik?"

"This," he said, indicating the star, "is Bik. He's a fire giant like me."

I looked at the glowing orb with skepticism. "Seems a might small for a fire giant."

"He'll grow. He's young still. Bik is my grandson. Here." Surtr extended his hand, as if to give me the star.

"Ah, Surtr, won't Bik burn my hand off?"

"What? Oh, right. Sorry. Bik!" he said to the bright light. "Stifle!"

The light from the star softened then winked out entirely. Standing on Surtr's palm was what looked like a teenager, except he was the size of a Q-tip. "You can take him now. He won't burn you."

With more than a little reluctance I extended my palm. Bik jumped from Surtr's hand to mine. I was surprised that Bik was almost cool to the touch.

The old giant smiled. "He may be young, but he has wonderful control over his flame, and it burns hot as the dickens."

"Thanks, I guess." I examined the little fellow. Bik was dressed in a red danskin, with a similarly colored, tight-fitting shirt. He had bright red hair that stood up straight on his head. Looks like he combed it that way intentionally. Bik was staring up at me with as much curiosity as I had for him. "Why would I want to take Bik with me?"

Surtr shrugged. "Hell's heating system is on the blink, and I don't know what's going on. Bik can be very useful to you. He's small, but The Spark burns brightly in him."

"Yeah, I got that. Listen, I don't think I … "

Surtr rose to his full height. Flames shot from his head, scorching the ceiling. "TAKE HIM!"

"Er, okay, right," I said, and stuffed the little guy in my right coverall pocket, beneath my tool belt.

"mlslfsmdmfmdmf," Bik said, from inside the pocket. I pulled him back out.

"I didn't catch that. What did you say?"

"I said: Could you put me somewhere else? It's crowded and a little smelly down there. And I keep poking myself on your keys." When you were close to Bik, he sounded less like a squeaking mouse, and more like a child with a very high, soft voice. Boy soprano. Or castrati.

Ouch. Always hurts to think about that.

"Sorry." I slipped him into my pocket protector, next to my mechanical pencil. "Any better?"

Bik's head was at about the same level as the pencil. He curled his fingers around the hard plastic of the pocket protector. "Yes, much. And I can see quite well too. This will work fine!"

"Great," I said, without much enthusiasm. *What the hell am I going to do with this guy?*

"Take good care of my grandson," Surtr admonished. "And make certain he calls me often. Otherwise I'll, uh, I'll worry about him."

"I will." *I guess.* "See ya," I said and left the boiler room.

Chapter 5

I retraced my steps past the Traitors until I came to the door on the far side of their holding pens. The door was made of metal and had no handle.

Great, just great. I knocked politely for a moment, but no one came. Slipping my hammer out of my tool belt, I started pounding on the metal.

I heard a rustling on the other side a few moments later. "Mmmmmmmmmm?"

"Open the door!" I shouted.

"Mmmmmmmmmm?" a small panel at eye height slid open, and a pair of dark brown eyes stared in on me. "What did you say?"

"I said open the fucking door, Bruce!"

"Well, you don't need to be vulgar about it. And stop that pounding. You'll dent the metal."

"Bite me. The door?"

"Right." I heard some scratching come from the other side, as Bruce inserted the key into the lock. The door swung open, and I stepped out on the carpet. "Gee, thanks."

"You don't have to be sarcastic as well as vulgar. It's my job to be cautious where that door is concerned. Satan would have my head if one of those four escaped."

I thought about the Traitors. They seemed a pretty depressed lot, not the types to stage a jailbreak. "I think you're probably okay on that score, but never mind. Out is out. I'll be leaving now." I gently pushed past Bruce, figuring it was a good policy not to be too nasty to someone who could sever my spine with a single blow, and now that he was a demon, he was probably even more formidable.

"Minion, wait a second."

I sighed. "What is it, Bruce? More bad news?"

Bruce frowned. "No, not at all. Well, yes, in a way. The temperature of Hell has dropped another five degrees since you entered the boiler room. But," he added, "that means Satan has decided the situation is urgent enough to lend you BOOH."

"Alright!" Beezy had come through.

BOOH was one of my best friends, though the relationship was of recent vintage. He had helped me solve the mystery of Hell's broken Escalator, and while we worked together, we'd bonded. I went up to my pal, who was preening on a large pole stuck in the wall nearby. "Hey, BOOH!" I reached up to give him a high five.

"Skreee!" BOOH, the one and only Bat out of Hell, was about the size of a Piper Cherokee. He reached down with one monstrous foot and gave me a low five.

"Did you hear that, buddy? We're going to be working together again." I turned to Bruce. "Thanks, man."

"Don't thank me," Bruce sniffed. "Thank Satan."

"Thanks, Lord Satan!" I shouted.

"GET TO WORK!" boomed a voice through the door to Satan's office.

"Yes sir! BOOH, could you take me to my office?"

"Skree!" BOOH grabbed me by the shoulders with his toe claws and took off, up the Throat of the Underworld, like a Bat out of Hell. Which he was.

As we ascended through the Throat, I stuck my fist in my mouth to prevent myself from screaming. I'd forgotten how fast BOOH could fly. Closing my eyes, I took a couple of deep breaths to calm down - no mean feat when you're biting through your knuckles - and reminded myself that BOOH was a friend of mine and would never drop me. Feeling a little steadier, I opened my eyes, taking a quick look down at Bik, who seemed to be enjoying the ride, if the big grin on his face was any indication.

We were at the Fifth Circle of Hell before you could count to five, and by six, BOOH was setting me down gently beside the trailer. "Thanks, Big Guy! Hey, I think I have something inside for you."

BOOH settled on the concrete and assumed the position. How a giant, vampire bat could remind me of a dog begging for a Milk-Bone was beyond me, but he did.

"Why's he doing that?"

"What? Listen Bik, if you want me to hear you, you're going to have to speak up."

"Hruhm! Hruhm! Okay, is this any better?"

"Yeah. Thanks."

"Well, I feel like I'm shouting."

"Sorry, but you'll just have to get used to speaking with your big voice."

The little guy frowned up at me. "No need to be sarcastic."

"Hey, it's what I do. Weren't you paying attention down there with Bruce? Never mind. Now what did you ask me?"

"I said: Why is BOOH sitting like that?"

"He expects a treat. Hang on a sec. You'll see."

I went inside the trailer. Orson was busying himself at my desk and paid me no attention, so I walked over to the empty orange crate where we tried always to keep a fresh supply of full blood donor bags. Orson had done his job while I was gone, and the crate was chock-full of bags. I grabbed three and headed back outside.

You might wonder about the orange crate. We consume vast quantities of oranges - oh, and a shitload of sardines - down here. Hell's bad enough; we don't want to be worrying about getting scurvy or rickets.

From the small landing outside the front door of my trailer, I called to BOOH. "Hey, big guy. Think fast!" I threw the three bags in rapid succession, and BOOH deftly caught them all. Then he settled down on the pavement with his treats, poked one with his teeth, stepped on it, and started licking the blood that began to ooze from the holes he'd made.

"Ugh. That's disgusting!"

"You get used to it. And lay off BOOH. He's a friend of mine, and I won't have you hurting his feelings by calling him disgusting."

"Fine," the little pipsqueak said, as we headed back inside.

Orson was still occupied at my desk. He was walking around it now, holding his hands together, thumb to thumb, fingers of each hand pointing toward the ceiling. Orson was framing a scene he had prepared on my desk. I noticed that he wore his director's beret.

On the desk were small figures made from folded up paper, presumably old work orders. Orson had created a scene. At one corner of the desk stood a giant horned devil. In front of him were a dozen miniature versions. Facing them were what I figured to be small, human forms. They were in various poses: some lying on the ground, some standing with little paper hands covering their mouths, others looking like they were prepared to start running.

Orson was working on some dialogue. "ACCURSED HUMANS!" he shouted in a loud voice. "THIS IS YOUR DAMNATION! YOU WILL ALL BURN!"

The fat man then moved to the opposite side of the desk. He picked up one of the small figures, rocking it back and forth, like a child does a toy soldier when he's playing war. "Save me! Aaah!"

Then he hurried back to the big devil, who I assumed was Satan. "NOTHING CAN SAVE YOU!"

"Very nice."

"Huh?" Orson looked up and saw me for the first time. He turned several shades of scarlet and quickly whipped the beret off his head, stuffing it into an inside breast pocket. "Ahem, ah, hi Steve."

"I didn't know you went in for origami, or dioramas for that matter." I walked around the desk. "What are you doing?"

"Well," he hesitated, "I'm working out a scene for the Hell movie I want to make. You remember, I was telling you about it a little while ago."

"I remember," I said, examining the scene with its paper figurines and trying not to smile. I like Orson. Satan would never let him make this movie, but there was no reason for bursting his bubble. "Well, I'm glad those old work orders are good for something."

Orson sighed in relief then took a cardboard box from off the floor and filled it with his paper figures. In seconds, the desktop was clear. "I was just going to throw them out anyway. The office is getting a little crowded."

As the two people responsible for fixing almost everything in Hell, we had to choose our work with care. Over ninety percent of work orders we routinely ignored, with almost no repercussions, well, except for the occasional blast of punitive Hellfire, but we were both used to that and paid it little mind. During our long history together, Orson and I had developed good instincts about what really had to get done and what could be left in backlog permanently. Sure, occasionally we'd get shit from Beezy about the unprocessed work orders, but we weren't all that different from most service departments in Hell. No one could keep up with their workloads; if they could, then it wouldn't be Hell, now would it?

"Orson," I said, unceremoniously pulling Bik out of my pocket protector and placing him on the desktop. "I want you to meet someone."

"Hey! Watch the hair. Do you want me to burn your hand off?" The tiny fellow ran his fingers through his carrot top, making all the hairs stand on end again.

"Sorry. Orson, this is Puck … "

"BIK."

"Oops. Right. Bik. Bik is a fire giant."

"Fire giant?" Orson said in surprise. "He seems a bit sm … "

"He'll grow! He'll grow!" I said hurriedly, as I watched Bik begin to glow. The incident with the hair made me think Bik might have as much of a temper as his grandfather.

"Right." Bik stopped glowing and looked around the room. "Hey, do you have anything to eat around here?"

Orson was staring in fascination at the little guy "Ah, what do fire giants eat?" he asked as politely as he could. My assistant was not known for being particularly polite. He tended to talk down to people, and by virtue of Bik's small stature, it was almost impossible not to do that anyway. Still, Orson was making an effort, which I appreciated.

"Got a match?" Bik asked.

I rummaged around in my desk drawer and found a pack. "Yeah."

"Light one and hand it to me."

I looked over at Orson, who merely shrugged. I lit the match and gave it to Bik. In his hands, it looked like one of those flaming batons you might see at a show in Vegas. Bik inhaled, sucking the flame into his mouth. "Delicious!"

Well, that would make sense, I thought. Fire demons, or, rather, fire giants, eat fire.

"Got another?"

"Sure," I said, lighting up a second one. He consumed the flame this time by placing the tip of the match into his mouth. I'd seen a circus performer do that when I was a kid. It looked pretty neat.

"Uh, want another?"

"No, thanks," Bik said. "I'm on a diet. But you might keep a few packs of matches on you. I need to eat frequently."

Could be worse, I thought, opening my drawer and grabbing all the matches I could find. At least matchbooks were small, and they fit handily into the pocket that held my keys.

Orson looked at me questioningly, so I filled him in on what was happening, while Bik called his grandfather. He did this by summoning up an oval of flame. Though the fiery disc was tiny, I could just make out the age-ravaged face of Surtr.

"Yeah, Grandpa, we got here fine. … Food's good, too. … What? … Yes, I promise to keep you informed."

While Bik talked on his flameophone, or whatever the hell he called it, I finished outlining the situation for Orson. He whistled. "A cold day in Hell. That can't be good."

"Apparently it isn't. And it's not all that great for Earth either."

"How so?"

"Remember all those times you said, 'It will be a cold day in Hell before … '"

"I go on a diet," Orson mumbled then opened his eyes wide in comprehension. "You mean … "

"Apparently, yes. If it gets too cold down here, those things we all said will start coming true. You'll go on a diet; I'll serve on a promotion, rank and tenure committee; and Republicans will increase taxes."

Orson shuddered. "Reality as we know it could be drastically altered throughout Earth, Heaven and Hell."

I looked at him in surprise. "You think this could even affect Heaven?"

Orson waved his arms at the ceiling. "Absolutely. There have got to be people in Heaven who in life used that expression. It could come back to haunt them." Orson was silent for a moment then looked over at me. "And what would happen if all Hell froze over?"

"I don't even want to think about it. Listen, Orson, we've got to figure out why this is happening. It could be a mechanical breakdown, though Beezy thinks that's unlikely, but foul play could be involved. Surtr said something casually, and it got me thinking about someone, a possible suspect."

"Who?"

I told him.

"That makes sense. So you want to go there?"

I nodded. "Right away. And Orson, I'm sorry, but I've enlisted BOOH on this job. We have to travel fast, you see, and ... "

Orson's mouth went flat, and he began making popping noises with his lips, something he always did when he was upset. "And I have to ride BOOH Air with you."

I shrugged. "Afraid so. At least you don't have my fear of heights."

"Yeah, but it doesn't sound like much fun."

"At best, it's an acquired taste. Come on, Puck."

"Bik!"

"Sorry. Bik." I scooped up the fire giant and placed him back in my pocket protector. "Let's go, Orson."

"When you got the blood bags, did you ... did you see Flo?" I asked, as we walked to the door.

"Only briefly."

"Was she okay?"

"She was arguing with some demon who wanted to give an enema to someone in the waiting room. We didn't really get a chance to talk, but she seemed okay. Maybe a little sadder than usual."

"Oh." I didn't know if having Flo sad made me feel better or worse. If she was sad because she missed me, then maybe that was okay. Still, she was such a good person that the thought of her unhappy at all made me sad too. I guess that's what love does to a body, even an ectoplasmic one like mine. I sighed.

"Don't worry, Steve," Orson said, patting me on the shoulder. "She still cares for you. I know it."

"I'm not so sure anymore. It's been months, or what seems like months anyway, since I've heard from her. Maybe ... " Suddenly the floor was very interesting to me. Looking at the floor was better than letting Orson see my emotions get the better of me. "Maybe I've lost her forever."

"Humph," he replied. "I don't believe it, not for a moment."

The linoleum was pulling up in one corner. *Have to do something about that sometime. Maybe put a stack of old work orders on it.* "Well, I do." With that I fell silent.

We stood that way, not two feet from the door, for an awkward moment. Then Orson thwacked me on the shoulder. "Buck up, me bucko! She's not the only fish in the sea, you know. Maybe you'll meet another astonishingly beautiful woman who has the hots for you."

Despite myself, I chuckled. Sometimes Orson knew just what to say to get me out of a funk. "Hah!" I said, making eye contact with him at last. "It will be a cold day in Hell before *that* happens! ... Erp!"

The room seemed to spin as a wave of nausea swept over me. I staggered and would have fallen to the floor if Orson hadn't grabbed me. "Steve! Are you okay?"

The vertigo passed as quickly as it had appeared. "I ... I think so, but maybe I shouldn't have said that."

"Said what?"

"That ... that cold day in Hell thing. I feel like something has just changed in my universe." I looked around the office. Everything looked the same. Like crap. "I guess it was my imagination. Still, I guess we should avoid that particular phrase right now. Careless of me, on today of all days. Let's go."

"Right." Orson held the door for me, which I thought was rather gallant of him. Such niceties were not often encountered down here. "And I still don't think you've lost Flo."

"Hope not." I sighed as we headed down the steps. "But whether or not Satan is going to let me have anything to do with her again is another matter."

He smiled. It was a gentle smile. In a soft voice, he said. "Where there's life, there's hope."

"I'm dead, Orson."

"You know what I mean."

I smiled back, but it was more rueful than hopeful. "Yeah. Thanks. Time to fly."

And we did.

Chapter 6

"Aaaaaaaaaaaaaaaaaaaaaaaaaaaaaaaaaaaaaaaaaaaaaaaaaaaa aaaaaaaaaaaa ... "

"DON'T WORRY!" I shouted to a panicked Orson. "YOU'LL GET USED TO IT. I PROMISE!"

I was hanging from BOOH's left claw, Orson from his right. Since my fat friend outweighed me by more than 200 pounds, BOOH was flying slightly cockeyed. I don't think the extra weight was a particular problem for the Bat out of Hell. He flew with his normal preternatural swiftness, but he did seem to be just a little off-balanced by the unequal load.

"Weeeeeeeeeee!" screamed a tiny voice from my pocket protector. Though Bik was a little hard to hear over Orson's screaming and the loud whooshing of the wind, the diminutive fire giant was still having fun on the BOOH Express.

We barreled up the Throat of Hell, reaching the Second Circle in just a few thumps of my rapidly-beating heart. BOOH hung a sharp left, and headed toward the edge of the Circle, just about as far away as possible from the looming stalactite that was Erebus. Soon we were hovering above deep blue waters, one of Hell's few oceans. As with all seas in the Underworld, the water churned from troubled turbulence.

"Troubled turbulence." I like that, even though it's a bit redundant. There's not nearly enough alliteration in Hell.

We came to a craggy shoreline. BOOH alighted some fifty feet from the water's edge, near a jumble of rocks and boulders that looked as if they had been tossed there by a giant hand and then forgotten.

I was looking for an inhabitant of a particular rock, an enormous slab of granite that lay stretched out atop the pile of stone. To my surprise, when we found the slab, it was empty. All we saw were some massive iron shackles, unlocked and open.

"Hey!" I shouted. "Is anyone home?"

"Do you mind?" came a voice from behind the rubble. "I'm on my lunch break."

With BOOH flapping above us, Orson, Bik and I made our way to a depression in the earth just behind the stones. There, sitting on the ground, was a giant, easily as big as Surtr, but with a body perfectly proportioned, a muscled titan of indescribable beauty clad only in a loincloth. His perfect face, which could have been chiseled from marble by a Renaissance master, was framed by ringlets of dark hair.

In front of him was an open lunchbox - I think it had Buffy the Vampire Slayer on it - from which he was extracting a hoagie as big as a weather balloon. He also pulled out a bag of Fritos that must have been bought at Sam's Club.

"What gives, Prometheus?"

"What do you mean?" he asked, as he took a bite from his sandwich.

I pointed at the slab of granite. "Shackles. Eternal torment, you know?"

Prometheus grabbed his thermos. (I probably don't need to mention it was as big as a garbage can. You know: big stuff.) As he poured some milk into his cup (size of a planter), he shrugged. "It's in my contract. I get a fifteen minute break every two hours, a half hour each for breakfast and lunch, and an hour for dinner."

Orson stroked his beard. "Those are pretty generous terms for one of the damned."

"I'm not 'one of the damned,' Orson, and you know it."

This was true. Like Sisyphus, Charon, Polyphemus and even Surtr, Prometheus was a carryover from a previous religion.

Satan was a born collector. He liked the old stuff, especially characters from defunct mythologies that had iconic storylines attached to them. Like Prometheus. But since he predated Christianity, he wasn't damned. The titan of Greek myth was simply an employee with very long hours.

I nodded. "Prometheus, I need to talk with you."

"Sure," he said between mouthfuls. "What's up?"

"Hell is getting colder."

The giant looked genuinely surprised. "Really?" He looked down at his loincloth. "Well that explains the shrinkage, I guess. I thought I was a little underdressed today ... even though this is what I wear every day."

Orson and I sat down on a couple of boulders, while BOOH settled on a very large tree that was nearby. The limb sagged under his weight but held. BOOH hopped up and down a couple of times, gauging the tensile limits of the wood, then, satisfied, dug his claws into the bark, flipped upside down, and wrapped his wings around his body.

I didn't know bats snored.

There was an excited murmuring from my pocket, and Bik launched into the air, exploding into flame only inches from my face. Reflexively, I pulled back, though the fire giant still managed to singe one of my eyebrows.

Bik flew straight toward Prometheus. The ancient titan smiled and held out his hand. The little guy promptly landed there. He was still burning brightly, but Prometheus didn't even flinch from the fiery star in his palm.

"Gee, Mr. Prometheus!" Bik enthused. "I'm so excited to meet you!"

"And you would be ... "

"Bik, sir. My grandfather is Surtr. He's been telling me stories about you since I was just a little spark!"

"Really? How is the old so-and-so? I haven't seen him in, oh, a thousand years."

"Very well, sir. A little older and creakier, I imagine, since the last time you met, but," Bik ended brightly, "we fire giants are built for the long haul. I believe he could still fry bacon with a glance alone."

The Greek titan chuckled. "No doubt, no doubt. In any event, Mr. Bik, I am pleased to make your acquaintance."

Well. Creatures from Greek and Norse mythologies hung out together. Who knew?

"An honor, sir." Bik bowed to Prometheus then flew over to a nearby rock and settled down.

"Now, Steve," Prometheus said, between bites of his sandwich. "What do you need?"

I shifted on my boulder, trying to get comfortable. That was pretty much impossible. Still, it wasn't much worse than my desk chair back at the office. "Well, Theo … "

"Why do you call me that?"

I shrugged. "Promtheus, that's a bit of a mouthful."

"No it's not," the Greek titan disagreed. "This," he continued, pointing toward his sandwich, "is a mouthful."

"Steve's just in the habit of shortening people's names," Orson explained.

"Really?" I said, genuinely surprised. "I do that?"

"Of course you do that. You even tried to shorten mine, but I pointed out to you that Sonny wasn't any shorter than Orson, and I didn't like being called a bit of pasta."

"Pasta?" I didn't remember any of this, but Orson and I had been together for a long time, and it probably happened when I first met him.

"Orzo."

"Orzo?" I cleared my throat. "I guess that's pretty stupid."

"I'd say so," opined the titan. "Besides, calling me Theo, well, that could apply to a number of people. Theseus, for instance, or Teddy Roosevelt ... "

"Or one of the three chipmunks," Orson added, a twinkle in his eye.

"Yes. Hey! Are you calling me a chipmunk?"

"No, no. Sorry, Theo ... Prometheus. I guess I don't even know when I'm doing it." We were off point. "Anyway, like I said, Hell is getting colder, and you, well ... " I trailed off, trying not to state the obvious.

Prometheus snorted. "And I stole some fire once and, what, you think I did it again?"

"No, no," I said hurriedly. "Nothing like that." Well, it was exactly like that.

Beezy had specifically told me to do a systems check on the HVAC before I indulged myself in conspiracy theories, but this was too obvious a possibility not to check on first. Besides, if I was right, it would save me and Orson a ton of work.

Prometheus was the only person I knew who had ever stolen fire. A quick conversation with him seemed worthwhile, but I now realized that, with his long hours, being chained to a rock and all, he probably wouldn't have had time to do something like filch a little flame. "Still, just to rule you out as a suspect, mind if I take a look at your time card?"

Prometheus shrugged. "Help yourself," he said, popping the last bit of his sandwich into his mouth.

I went over to his time clock and looked at the record. Time clocks in Hell weren't exactly dependable - nothing was - but it appeared that, except for his breaks, Prometheus had a perfect attendance record. He hadn't even taken any sick leave, and you'd think getting your liver ripped out every day by a couple of vultures would leave you feeling poorly every once in a while.

By the way, people don't get sick days in Hell as a general rule, but since Prometheus wasn't Jewish, Christian or Muslim, but instead a titan out of Greek myth, QED he couldn't be damned by our rules. Despite his apparent daily suffering, he probably could get an occasional day off, if he'd wanted to. These ancient Greeks, though. They seemed to have quite the work ethic. In this regard, he was like Ronnie, that is, my friend Charon, the Ferryman of the Dead. Ronnie never missed a day's work either.

I didn't think an hour dinner break would be long enough to steal the fires of Hell. Not even Prometheus could pull that off, I decided. "Thanks," I said, putting his timecard back in its slot. "I didn't think you were involved, but this way I can check you off the list of possible suspects."

Prometheus stood, stretching his massively muscled arms above his head. I felt like I was looking at Michelangelo's *David* after he'd spent a year bulking up at a gym. "Well," he yawned. "That's *certainly* a relief. I sure as heck wouldn't want to be in trouble with the law. Hey, what makes you the law, anyway?"

I grimaced. "Satan views this as a maintenance issue, so he booted it to me."

"Maintenance issue? How does he figure that?"

It was Orson's turn to grimace. "HVAC system."

"Ah." Prometheus nodded then headed toward his shackles. I could hear the loud clang of each lock as he snapped them shut. "Damn," he grumbled. "Hey, Steve, as long as you're here, make yourself useful."

"Hmmm?" I hmmmed in puzzlement, walking over to where the titan had settled on his stone "Sure. What do you need?"

Prometheus pointed to the giant open shackle on which he was resting his right wrist. "The last one is always a bitch to latch on my own, and today the hinge has chosen to freeze up on me."

I bent down to take a closer look. The ancient iron was badly rusted. I tested the hinge. The shackle was heavier than a car tire.

"Rrrr crrr, rrr crrr." Orson said and started chuckling.

"Shut up," I mumbled absently.

Prometheus looked up at my assistant. "Rrrr crrr? What the hell's he talking about?"

"Pay him no mind."

"But what does he mean?"

I pulled a can of WD-40 from my tool belt. "He means oil can. He's referencing an old movie. Not funny, Orson," I said, though my friend was still chucking. "Good idea though." I sprayed some WD-40 on the hinge and let the solvent do its thing for about thirty seconds. Then I worked the shackle's joint back and forth a few times. Satisfied, I snapped it shut with hardly any effort at all.

"Hey, that's pretty good stuff!"

"Yeah." I sprayed some WD-40 on the other three joints, hesitated slightly, then left the can next to Prometheus. "They should all work better now. Just to be safe, though, I'm going to leave the can with you."

Don't get in your head that I'm a good handyman. I suck at it, but anyone can use WD-40. Even me. It was my second most useful tool, after duct tape.

The giant smiled. "Thanks! That's nice of you."

I shrugged. "No problem. Besides, it's the least I can do since …"

"Since you accused me of stealing the fires of Hell?"

"Something like that. See you around, Prometheus."

"Only if you come back here. I don't get out much."

"Guess not," I said, summoning Bik. The fire giant extinguished his flame just before landing on my palm. He was still smoldering a bit when I stuffed him in my pocket protector. "BOOH!" I yelled.

The giant vampire bat cracked open an eyelid and looked at me.

"Time to go."

BOOH released his claws, completing a back flip as he landed heavily on the ground nearby. Still, the move was surprising graceful, like a gymnast. If he'd been competing at the Olympics, I would have given him at least an 8.5.

My winged friend bounded into the air. As he swooped by me and Orson, he dug his claws into our shoulders and lifted us off the ground.

"Ouch!"

"You get used to it. Bye, Prometheus!" I shouted.

BOOH did a quick zig-zag in the air, as he avoided two monstrous vultures that swooped toward Prometheus. My batty friend was curious about what was going on, so he hovered in mid-air to watch for a minute.

As soon as the vultures landed next to the titan, they bent to his side, knocking their skulls together. The hideous creatures hissed at each other.

"Fred, Ethel," Prometheus chided. "Come on. How many times have we talked about this? Where are your manners? There's plenty to go around. Ethel, ladies first."

With a screech, Ethel tore into the giant's right side. Blood squirted everywhere, and the giant howled in pain.

Or at least, it seemed like pain, but I thought I detected a note of boredom in his screams.

Ethel's head came up, and Fred bent to take her place. The female vulture was drenched in the titan's blood, a big chunk of liver hanging from her beak.

I shuddered. I always hated liver.

BOOH," I said, averting my eyes from the grisly scene. "Show's over. Let's scram."

We scrammed.

Chapter 7

We spent the rest of the morning travelling all over Hell, checking the elaborate system of pipes and duct work that enabled the HVAC system to maintain the Netherworld at either insufferably hot or unbearably cold temperatures. In this task, BOOH was a huge help; there was no way we could have covered so much territory in such a short time without him.

"Let's start here on Five." I suggested to Orson, before we began our diagnostics and after we returned to our office from visiting Prometheus.

"Why?" he said, with only mild interest. He was in the middle of cleaning his fingernails with a straightened paperclip.

You may wonder why we spend so much time tending to our nails. Everyone around here does it, even devils. My theory is that this obsessive attention to what seems like a mundane act of personal hygiene is symptomatic of a larger need. On this infernal plane, where everything is wrong and generally chaotic, we want at least one thing under our control, and since fingernails are handy - no pun intended - we tend to focus on them.

I walked to the door. Bik, who had been buzzing around our office like an angry firefly, assuming fireflies got angry, zipped into my pocket protector. "Why start on Five? Well," I said, stepping out on the porch. "Aside from the fact that it's the most convenient place to begin, it effectively bisects the plumbing for the HVAC system."

"You mean ductwork."

"You know what I mean," I grumbled.

"Why the bad mood, boss?"

On the street just in front of our office was a vendor selling roasted chestnuts. When I lived in New York, back when I lived at all, roasted chestnuts were a favorite treat. These were burnt though, and the smell, mixed with that of the sulfur, which was almost always present in the air, was a particularly noxious combination.

"I'm just not looking forward to this particular job. It's a damn sight bigger than the Escalator problem."

"Work's work," Orson said, buying some of the burnt chestnuts off the vendor, an odd-looking fellow wearing a curly reddish blonde wig, top hat and baggy suit.

"Hey," my friend said to the vendor. Orson appeared to know him. "How goes?"

"Honk, honk!"

"Well that's good. Steve, meet Harpo Marx. Want a chestnut?"

"No thanks. It smells burnt to a chrisp. No offense, Mr. Marx."

"Honk!"

"Sorry. I mean Harpo."

We spent a few minutes exchanging pleasantries and honks. Orson thought the Fifth Level Demons had a real chance at winning the pennant this time around, perhaps even the Underworld Series. Harpo agreed, or at least, I think he agreed. It was kind of hard to tell. Since I found baseball more boring than watching paint dry, I didn't express an opinion one way or the other.

Still, a little boredom at that moment was welcome. It put a damper on my concerns over Flo and the "metaphysical ramifications" of a cold day in Hell. Nothing takes away anxiety quite like boredom—unless you start to get anxious about being bored for too long, which can happen if you're an active type.

Me, well, after being Hell's Super for such a long time, I was plenty active, but this was only little boredom. It felt good for a change.

But the job was beckoning. "Come on," I said, finally interrupting the conversation. "Nice to meet you, Harpo, but we gotta go. Later."

"Honk!"

"Why did Harpo get off with only being a chestnut vendor?" I asked as we crossed the street. "Considering other eternal damnations, his seems like pretty light fare."

"Harpo abhors the smell of burnt chestnuts."

"You know, I totally get that."

We were now facing the yawning chasm in the center of Level Five. Thanks to Beezy's magic thwock to my forehead, I could see an array of pipes and tubes crisscrossing the entire circle. "How are the chestnuts?" I asked idly, as we made our way around the Throat of Hell.

"They suck," he grumbled.

"Big surprise. They smell like they've been burning on that grill for two hundred years. So why do you eat them?"

"I like old chestnuts."

"Oh."

After about three hundred yards of walking around the Throat, I stopped. "See anything?"

"No," he said, between swallows of chestnut. "Should I?"

I looked down at the shells he was leaving on the ground behind him. "Hansel, are you making a trail to follow home, or are you just littering?"

"Littering, of course. This is Hell, so who cares?"

"Good point. Anyway, you may not see anything, but just to the left of me are two rather sizable pipes, each about eight feet in diameter. The red one comes from the furnace room down on Nine, and the blue one comes from Erebus up on Two."

Orson looked at me as if I were some kind of lunatic. "I don't see a damned thing. How can you?"

"Beezy used some devil hocus-pocus to hide them," I said with a shrug. "He's temporarily made it possible for me to see them."

Orson whistled. "I wish I could see them."

"Yeah, they're pretty impressive. If we run into Beezy sometime, we'll ask him to give you the second sight." *And I'll be sure to have some aspirin to give you for the ensuing headache.* "For now, you'll just have to take my word for it."

"Will do."

I put my hand on the red pipe. It was quite hot, but not enough to burn me. That wasn't a surprise, since I'd witnessed the failure of those jets on Nine. "Okay, so you don't see anything at all?"

"Other than that big, black hole that looks like a bottomless pit, nope."

I ran my hand up and down the hot pipe.

"You look like a street corner mime. Do the 'locked in a box' bit now."

"Har har. For your information, at this moment, my hand is resting on one of those two big, fat pipes, see? Well, of course you don't, but get my drift? This is the red one. Go ahead and touch it. It's hot, but not so hot that it will burn you."

More on faith than anything else, Orson stretched his hand out and placed it next to mine. When he felt the heat, he pulled back reflexively, but then he tried again. "Amazing!" he enthused, brushing his fingers along the invisible metal of the pipe. "And you're saying these things are all over Hell?"

I glanced around. "Yeah. Level Five practically looks like a spider web to me right now, with pipes and ductwork going all over the place. The one you have your hand on, though, is the main source of heat for all Hell. It leads straight from the boiler room down on Nine."

Orson frowned. "Well, it's hot, that's for damn sure, but I would have thought it would be hotter than this."

"It should be. If the system were working properly, this pipe would burn off your fingers."

Orson jerked his hand off the metal.

"They'd grow back, of course, at least, according to Beezy, so you needn't worry. Besides, you know I'd never let you do something that would hurt you permanently."

"Yeah," he said, slowly, "though I still remember the time you shoved Edison into the Mouth of Hell."

"That's because he was yelling at me for being incompetent. He was asking for it."

Orson pursed his lips. "Maybe."

My assistant was pissing me off. For him to think that I'd intentionally get him hurt, well, it didn't sit well with me. I cleared my throat. "Anyway, we're sure now that the heating system isn't working right. It's even cooler up here than the pipe was down on Nine. We can check some of the upper levels, but I suspect that the pipe will get progressively cooler."

"What about the air conditioning?"

"That pipe is right over here," I said, indicating what must have seemed to Orson like another span of air.

"How do we test to see if it's working properly?"

I told him.

"Come on! You're kidding."

"It's either that or your chestnuts, and I don't mean the ones in your hand." I looked meaningfully at his crotch.

"Well I'm not doing that!"

I frowned. I was still ticked off at him for his lack of faith in me. "You have to. With your tongue, I mean, not your dick. You're my assistant, and you have to do what I say. Besides, I've already done it once. It's your turn."

Orson frowned and started making his flat-mouthed popping noise. "I can't even see the damn thing!"

"Don't worry. I'll guide you."

"Fine," Orson huffed. "You're the boss, and I'm just an underling. And, gee, thanks for rubbing my nose in it."

Now I felt guilty. I was being a jerk, and I knew it, but we had to run the test, and it *was* his turn.

"Let's get it over with." Orson stuck out his tongue, and I moved him slowly toward the blue pipe. "You're in position. Take a lick."

"You know, you're being an asshole, Steve," Orson groused. With great reluctance, he put his tongue to the pipe. "Aye ... uuuh!"

Good thing he just called me an asshole. Now I didn't feel so guilty. "Did you say 'oil can?'" I asked, looking at him with a puzzled expression.

He shot me a dirty look. "Aye eh, aye uuuh!!"

"You suck? Wait a minute. I get it now. You're stuck, right?"

He just rolled his eyes.

I chuckled. "Don't worry. Same thing happened to me. Here, let me help you." I grabbed Orson's waist from behind - I could hardly get my hands around him, and I was impressed by how squishy he was in the middle, sort of like the filling of a Twinkie - and gave him a sharp tug.

Orson's tongue stretched like a rubber band then popped off the pipe. "Aaaghh! Aaaghh! Thyit! Thad hurd!"

The chuckle just wasn't sufficient, so I kicked into a full-throated laugh. "Yeah, I know. Bruce did the same thing for me down on Nine. Same results. Let's see." Orson held his tongue out for me to examine. The top layer of skin - the one with all the taste buds - had ripped off his tongue. I could see it stuck to the pipe. To Orson, though, it probably looked like torn skin and clotting blood suspended in midair. "Don't worry. Your tongue will heal in a second or two, though you might want to wait a bit before finishing your chestnuts. Might not be able to taste much for an hour or so, though down here in Hell, that's usually a good thing."

"Nu … nu … not funny, Steve," he said, as the top of his tongue sealed over.

"Sorry, but it's the only way to test. Well, except that other way, and I did give you your choice."

Orson rubbed his jaw. "You're rationalizing. That was just plain mean."

I shrugged. "Maybe a little, but I was pissed off at you for not trusting me."

Orson put his hands on his hips. He looked pretty indignant. "And so you hurt me to teach me a lesson?"

"No, but … " Blushing a deep scarlet, I shut up. Weren't my actions exactly what I assured him I would never do? "You're right. One of us had to perform the test, but I didn't have to make fun of you in the process."

"No shit."

I sat down on the pavement next to the Throat of Hell. That had been a rotten thing to do to him, probably my best friend in all of the Underworld.

What's wrong with me? Is Satan right? Do I take a perverse pleasure in inflicting pain on others? Am I actually demon material?

I shuddered then looked up at my friend. "Orson, I'm really sorry. I don't know what got into me. Please forgive me."

That was a mistake. Next thing I knew, I was on the ground, slightly toasted and with a mess of coconut cream pie covering my puss.

Satan has a thing about pies. He loves throwing them in the faces of the damned. I don't know if he got the idea from Laurel and Hardy or 'Blazing Saddles,' or if he is the actual inventor of the classic pie in the face gag. Regardless, genuine expressions of positive emotion, saying things such as "I love you" or "I like you" or "You're the best" or sincerely thanking someone or apologizing and really meaning it is frowned upon in Hell and receives a predictable if stupid punishment. The transgressor is flattened by Hellfire then, in a juvenile finale that only a devil, demon or vaudevillian would find funny, hit with a pie in the face.

I'm allergic to coconut. Just a little bit of it on my skin will give me hives. That's why I always get smacked with a coconut cream pie as opposed to, say, Boston Cream or lemon or even butterscotch. On the other hand, Orson's pie of punishment was lemon cream. He hated lemon, because the juice made his eyes sting.

I wiped the pie from my face, using a bit of the cream to extinguish an errant lock of hair that was still burning. The pie and bolt of Hellfire at least proved my sincerity, but I still felt like a creep. I looked up mournfully at my friend.

Orson panted for a second, trying to warm his tongue. Finally he spoke. "Just stop with the puppy dog eyes. Fine. I forgive you."

"You sure we're okay?"

The big man helped me to my feet. "Yeah. So what was the purpose of this little stunt with the pipe, aside from providing you with some amusement?"

"It shows us that the cooling level is staying constant, at least between here and Nine. We'll check farther up, but I bet we'll get the same result."

"What would have happened if the coolant was out of whack?"

"If it weren't cold enough, you wouldn't have stuck. If it were too cold, your tongue would have ripped out of your mouth." Hurriedly I added, "Don't worry. It would have grown back."

"Swell."

"Really, Orson, I was almost positive that wouldn't happen. I'm virtually certain the entire problem stems from the burners failing in the boiler room down on Nine. We have to check out the rest of the system to be thorough, but I'm pretty sure as we move up Hell's Circles, towards Gates Level, we'll find the blue pipe stays a constant temperature and the red one keeps getting cooler."

"Maybe, but next time, you can use your own tongue."

"Fair enough." I determined I'd only do that one more time, though, and that would be on Level Two, where Erebus was. Any more checking was probably a wasted effort, since Nine's pipe was the right temperature, but Beezy liked us to be meticulous. Still, if Two, Five and Nine all passed the tongue test, our boss would probably be satisfied.

It took several hours - even with BOOH's help - to zigzag our way across the Netherworld, checking pipes, ducts, repeaters and so forth. We didn't see anything out of the ordinary, convincing us that the problem was in the boiler room. It simply wasn't producing enough heat to keep the system in balance.

Bik watched our day of diagnostics from his place in my pocket protector. He'd hardly said a thing since we'd left our office.

BOOH whisked us back to the trailer. Orson seemed to have gotten more or less used to flying BOOH Air, but he had some work to do on his landings. Once again, he tripped and sprawled on his face. He was cursing a blue streak as I helped him up.

As soon as I opened the office door, Bik launched from my pocket protector and started a frenzied buzzing around the office.

"Hey, Bik. You doing okay?" I asked

"Yeah," he said, not bothering to stop his aerial calisthenics. "I'm just bored. I don't know why Grandpa was so keen on me going with you. I don't see that there's much for me to do."

"Well, you never know. I'm sure you'll be of some help to us." Though for the life of me, I couldn't figure how. At least he was small and stayed out of the way.

Orson and I spent the next hour drinking coffee and staring at the HVAC schematic. I didn't see any new information to be gleaned from it. "Say, Bik?"

The fire giant was sitting on the edge of my desk, swinging his legs back and forth idly. "Yes?"

"Could you pull your grandfather up on the flameophone again? I want to ask him a question."

"Sure." The little guy stood up on the desktop and swirled his hand before him. A disc of flame formed, and it got bigger and bigger until I could plainly see the boiler room and the giant Surtr sitting in his chair. He was back in his *Thinker* pose.

The fire giant looked up. "Bik, what is it?"

"It's Mr. Minion, Grandpa. He wants to talk to you."

"Well, put him on."

I leaned down and was face to face with a bespectacled Surtr. "I'm still checking on the status of the system. Everything from Level Nine on up is working perfectly, including the cooling system running from Erebus. But the main heating pipe coming from the boiler room gets progressively colder the farther up you get."

"No shit," Surtr grumbled. "What else would you expect, with the burners shutting off down here?"

"Have you had a chance to inspect them ... oh, and what about the fuel lines?"

"Yes, of course. I checked all of that. What do you think I've been doing since this started, sitting on my ass?"

Well, that's kind of what it had looked like just a second ago. "Is there anything broken down there?"

"No, not a single thing. I've checked every burner. Even the ones that have shut off are in perfect working condition."

"And the lines?"

"All clear." Surtr's face was a mask of irritation. "Listen, sonny, you don't need to tell me how to do my job. I've been taking care of the boiler room since your great great etc. grandfather humped up an ancestor for you in some hay loft back in the old country."

"Hey! No need to get offensive."

"Then quit questioning my competence. Everything is working perfectly down here."

"Except for all those burners that continue to fail, you mean."

Surtr frowned at me. I swear if he could have reached through the flameophone and popped me one, he would have. "I don't care what it looks like. The problem isn't down here. Look elsewhere. Surtr out!" The giant waved his hand, and the fiery disc disappeared.

"Is he always so rude?" I asked Bik.

"Yes, usually," he confessed. "Even with me, he's not very nice. I don't think Grandpa's ever been known for his charm."

Orson walked to the coffeepot, to discover it empty. "Considering he was supposed to engulf the world in flames at Ragnarok, I'd say that's putting it mildly."

"So, the system is working perfectly, and yet it's not. Great. Just great." I folded up the drawing and stuffed it in the inside breast pocket of my coveralls.

"We need a fresh perspective," I said, standing up. "I'm going down to Seven to consult with Pinkerton."

Orson dumped the grounds of the Mr. Coffee into the trash, refilling the paper filter with some more from the can of Yuban. It wasn't always Yuban. Sometimes it was Maxwell House or Folgers or even Chock full o' Nuts, but they all tasted the same: like hell. "So you're back to thinking something more than a system failure is involved?"

"Yeah. Beezy implied it was possible when he and Satan first briefed me on this job. Our boss never believed his system was capable of failing on its own."

"Splat! Splat! Splat! Splat!" An all too familiar sound was coming from the pipe above my inbox.

Orson looked with worry at the rapidly growing pile of work orders. "Well, we better get this figured out quickly. As Hell gets colder, even more things seem to be breaking than usual. Our workload's bad enough already, and it's not like we get paid time and a half."

I nodded. "While I'm gone, why don't you and Bik triage the work orders?"

"Right." Orson was used to this kind of work, but Bik looked at the work orders with distaste. "Can I go with you instead?

Grandpa said to help you with the HVAC system. He didn't say anything about an unpaid internship in Plant Maintenance."

"Well," I said with surprise. "That was a pretty snarky retort. And here I thought you were such a polite, accommodating young feller."

The fire giant stood on the desk, his fists on his hips. The envelope of flame that usually surrounded him flared. "I'm at least a hundred years older than you, so watch who you're calling 'young feller.'"

I looked at him mildly. "I guess bad tempers run in your family."

Bik flushed crimson, which was a pretty neat trick for someone already encased in fire. "Yeah, they do. Sorry."

"No problem," I said, holding open my pocket protector. "If you want to go with me, that's fine."

"Thanks," Bik said, flaming off just before dropping into my pocket.

Chapter 8

A great storm raged above the ocean on Level Seven. We arrived just in time to see a monstrous tsunami slam into the pier of the port city where Allan Pinkerton, one of history's great detectives and a close friend of mine, was enduring his eternal punishment. The giant wave shattered the wooden planks of the docks and swamped all the vessels that were moored there. A few terrified sailors and dockworkers managed to get to higher ground, but behind the wave, the enormous tentacles of the Kraken erupted from the water's surface. They snagged the poor damned souls and dragged them down to Davy Jones' Locker.

After the tsunami hit, the rain ceased, and the ocean turned from a roiling chaos back to its normal state, which was still pretty stormy. A fog immediately descended on the city, a blanket of moist air so dense that it hid the buildings.

"Say, BOOH, do you think you can find Pinkerton's shop in this mess?"

BOOH snorted in a way that to me implied, "Of course I can, you dummy." Then he cleared his throat and let out a "Skree!" The pitch of his scream quickly rose, octave by octave, until I could no longer hear it.

"Ouch!" Bik exclaimed from my pocket.

"You can still hear his screech?"

"Yeah. We fire giants have really good ears."

"I'd say."

BOOH panned the city before him, connected with something, and flew toward it. In a second we were hovering before the plastic skyscraper that was next to Pinkerton's small wooden workshop.

Well, that was clever. Sound must bounce back differently from plastic than from other substances, and the skyscraper was the only plastic building I'd ever seen in Hell, or on Earth for that matter. I always knew BOOH was smart, but I sometimes forgot just how smart. Satan had told me once he thought BOOH was more intelligent than I was. Maybe Big Red was right.

BOOH deposited me on the pavement before the workshop and prepared to shoot to the rooftop, where he waited for me the last time I had a tête-à-tête with Pinkerton down on Seven. "Hey, why don't you come inside? I'm sure Allan would be glad to see you." BOOH shrugged and dropped to the concrete beside me. We walked in together, though BOOH had to scrunch down pretty far to get inside the door.

"Bloody Hell!" Pinkerton grumbled. "Ah cannae see a damn theeng!" He was working on a barrel in the dim light of his workshop, a small oil lamp providing him his only illumination. Allan's damnation was to make wooden barrels throughout eternity. He was bad at the work, and he could use all the help he could get.

"Hey, Bik. You said you wanted to be of some use. Do you think you could make like a lightbulb?"

"No problem. It's hard to keep my flame out for too long anyway." Bik flew up into the rafters and made like a small sun.

"Och, mon!" Pinkerton exclaimed, as he shielded his eyes from the glare. "What kinna creetur be tha' totie?"

"Allan, it's me, Steve. Can you drop the blarney?"

"Blarney's Irish, not Scottish," Pinkerton said in perfect King's English. Or Queen's. I really had no idea the gender of the person currently sitting on the British throne. Allan often affected a Scottish accent, since he was a Scot by birth. Yet he had lived in the States for a good portion of his life and been down in Hell even longer, where most of his friends were Yanks. He'd long ago lost his accent, but he used it frequently, thought it was colorful. I thought it was irritating, and he knew it.

"Meet Bik," I said, pointing up at the bright light. "He's a fire giant."

Allan frowned. "Looks a wee small for … "

"He'll grow."

"Ah. The light's good, though. Give me a minute to finish up." Pinkerton tucked his head back in the barrel, cursed a few more times then stood up. "There. Done," he said, taking off his leather apron and hanging it on a nearby nail.

"Better?" I asked.

"No. I was trying to make it better, but I only made it worse, which is what usually happens. At least I'm done making it worse, though. A craftsman I'm not." Pinkerton looked at the shoddy barrel and sighed then stepped forward to shake my hand. "How are you, Steve? I haven't seen you since that day at Gates Level, when we stopped the Free Hellions from using the Stairway to Paradise to escape Hell."

"I'm doing okay, I guess," I said, plopping into a rickety chair at the back of his shop. Allan sat in its twin. Between the two was a small round table.

Allan squinted at the doorway. "BOOH? Is that you? Great to see you! Come over and have a drink with us." BOOH dragged his giant carcass across the shop's floor. Fortunately, the room was large and the ceiling high; BOOH had no problem navigating from the entrance to our table in the back.

"What about you, Bik?" Allan yelled into the rafters. "Care for a draught?"

"No thanks!" came the reply "I don't drink. Can't really."

"Sorry to hear that. Drinking problem?"

"Nothing like that," said our light bulb. "Alcohol vaporizes on contact with me. Sometimes I can get down a little of my grandpa's kerosene, but that's about it."

"Makes sense," Pinkerton said, as he took out a bottle of Scotch and a couple of glasses.

"Uh, none for me, either, thanks. I'm working." Since coming to Hell, I'd never had qualms about drinking on the job, but it was a good excuse. I'd sampled Allan's Scotch before. It was more like motor oil than liquor.

Allan shrugged. "Suit yourself, Steve. But I promised BOOH a drink, and a drink he shall have." Pinkerton got out of his chair and grabbed a bucket and a gasoline can from the corner of his workshop. He poured about a gallon of dark liquid from the can into the bucket then set it before the giant bat.

"So, a fine, fifty-year-old Scotch?"

"Hah. Funny, Steve. It's the best I can do, and you know it. Besides ... "

"Yeah, I know. It's the thocht that counts, aye laddie?"

Allan chuckled as he filled his own glass. "Not bad, Steve. To your health, BOOH."

The bat deftly picked up the bucket in the, relatively speaking, small hands attached to his wings. He took a big swig and burped mightily. Then he slammed back another swallow.

Allan laughed. "Looks like BOOH likes my brew!"

"Nice rhyme, Allan."

"It's good to see you, Steve, but I'm guessing this isn't a social call."

"No. I need your help. Oh, and I changed my mind. I'll have what BOOH's drinking." I thought it might be better than the stuff in the bottle. Allan shrugged and used the gasoline can to pour some whisky in my class.

"To good friends," I said, indicating both Allan and BOOH. Normally, a toast like that would have gotten me in trouble with Hell's Management, but I figured BOOH's special status might provide some cover. Apparently it did: no pies, no Hellfire.

"Here, here!" Allan said.

"Skree!" said BOOH, and we all drank.

I only coughed for about five seconds.

"Are you okay, Steve?"

"Yeah," I sputtered. The liquid wasn't any better than the stuff in the bottle. Still. "Pour me another round." I must have had a death wish. Well, perhaps not. That would have been redundant.

"BURPPP!"

The workshop filled with a noxious odor. BOOH held out his empty bucket.

"Whew! That was one major belch! Still, I'm glad you like the brew." Pinkerton poured out another gallon for our batty friend.

"Skree!"

"You're welcome." Allan turned to me. "So, aside from sopping up all of my Scotch, to what do I owe the pleasure of your visit?"

I looked down at my fresh pour of motor oil, debating about whether or not to take another slug. "What the hell," I murmured, and slammed it back in a single gulp.

When the coughing ended, I squeezed out a few words. "I need your advice."

Allan had dark, piercing eyes, the kind that seemed able to penetrate a dense fog or see the most nuanced expression even in the dark. As he turned those sharp eyes on me, I knew they mirrored the keen mind that lay behind them. I was glad to have

Pinkerton as a friend and advisor. "What is the problem?" he asked.

I explained things to him, pulling out the HVAC schematic for illustration. "Allan," I said, as we both stared down at the complex pattern of lines and circles on the sheet, "I just don't know how it can fail. I now know where the failure point is, which is down in the boiler room, but Surtr, the old geezer running the place, assures me that nothing is broken down there."

"And yet the system has failed anyway. So, why come to me?"

I got out of my chair and walked over to Allan's wall of tools. I picked up one of the adzes.

"Careful with that," Pinkerton warned. "You'll cut ... "

"Ow!"

" ... yourself."

I put the blade back in its place and turned to Allan. "I think," I said, sucking the blood from my finger, "that someone has caused the failure deliberately."

"Why?"

"Because there's really no way I can see for it to fail."

"Now why do you think that? Why would someone want it to fail?"

I shrugged. "Dunno. It's just a gut feeling."

"That's not what I meant," Allan said from his chair. "I mean, what would be the motive for someone wanting the system to fail?"

Pinkerton got up and walked over to a small portable blackboard that was against one of the workshop walls. It was the kind that could be spun around, so someone could write on both sides of it. Allan, during a moment of boredom, had drawn a "Kilroy was here" illustration on the front. For some reason, he wished to preserve it, so he pivoted the board to the other side, which was blank. He drew three vertical lines, spaced evenly apart, creating four columns. At the top of the first column he wrote the word, "Suspects." Above the others, he wrote "Motive," "Means," "Opportunity." Each time he made a stroke on the board, the infamous chalk Screech resonated, putting my teeth on edge. This was, after all, a blackboard in Hell, so it stood to reason that it could do nothing but make that obnoxious grating sound. I tried to tune it out.

"Motive, means and opportunity," he said, as if he were lecturing students in a forensics class. "A good way to dissect a crime or to identify suspects. In my day, we didn't have the process so nicely codified, but we used a similar sort of analysis. Let's start with motive, shall we?"

"Sure," I said, sitting back down.

"You told me that the first person you suspected was Prometheus, since he stole fire from the gods and gave it to man. For now, let's treat this as a theft, all right?"

"Sure. I mean, it might be simple sabotage, but theft is as good a working hypothesis as any."

"I think so, too, so let's use it provisionally. Why would someone want to steal fire?" Allan frowned. "Since we're in Hell, let's start with the Seven Deadly Sins. I've thought about this before, and the Sins make for a pretty good short list of the reasons why someone might want to commit a crime." Under Motive, Allan rapidly listed the Deadly Sins:

PRIDE
GREED
LUST
ENVY
GLUTTONY
WRATH
SLOTH

"Theft could be motivated by several of the sins, though some, like Greed, are more obvious choices than others. For now let's leave them all on the list."

"Works for me. Do you know that some of the top dog devils are specifically associated with some of the sins?"

"Ah, you know your Catholic theology. Good man. I was coming to that in a second. But first, let's hop back to the 'Suspects' columns. Let's assume that whoever did this is a denizen of Hell."

The chair creaked under my weight, and I grimaced. Allan had probably built the seat himself, and since he was a terrible woodworker, the thing was not very sturdy. "That seems a safe assumption. No one from Heaven is likely to be interested in mucking up things down here, the other theological universes stay pretty much separate from ours, and people on Earth can't really get here without, you know, getting themselves damned first, which would put them in Hell as denizens."

"Righto. So let's put down the classes of Hell's inhabitants. There are, of course, devils and demons." He wrote these on the board.

"And humans," I added. "I guess that's about it."

Allan shook his head. "Don't think so."

"What do you mean?"

Allan pointed to my winged companion. "Well, there's BOOH, for instance."

"SKREE!"

"Don't get your dander up, my friend," Pinkerton said mildly. "I'm just giving an example. Bik's another."

"Yes, and also Charon and Prometheus and Sisyphus. And Cerberus, though I don't know how a three-headed dog would have the attention span to pull this off. All he ever wants to do is play fetch with his Frisbee … and eat dog food."

"That too." Allan stepped back to the board. "Let's break these into two categories: mythological beings and magical creatures. Think that would do?"

"Yep." I scratched my head. "I'm about tapped out. You?"

"We could get more precise, how do you say, more granular than this, you know, arch demons for example, but I think this covers the Nether-inhabitants fairly thoroughly."

DEVILS
DEMONS
HUMANS
MYTHOLOGICAL BEINGS
MAGICAL CREATURES

Allan pointed to the word atop the second column. "So, which of these residents of Hell had the means, or more accurately, were capable of mucking up the heating and air conditioning system?"

I rubbed my chin. "I'm trying to decide what it would take to mess up the system."

"Well," Pinkerton said, writing as he talked, "I'm no expert, but I think one would need … "

STEALTH
CUNNING
KNOW
   HVAC
RAW POWER

These he wrote under the "Means" category.

"Well." I walked up to the board and grabbed a piece of chalk. "I think we can eliminate a large number of suspects with a single stroke." I drew a line through "humans," wincing at the loud screech as I did so.

"Hey!" Allan protested. "My chalkboard!"

"Come on. We both can play. Besides, this is how I used to make my living."

That's before I was dead, damned and dumbed down to be Hell's Super. I still liked writing on blackboards, though, screech notwithstanding.

"Fine," Allan said, slightly peeved. "What do you think about the magical creatures and mythological beings?"

I considered them for a sec. "Some are here just for color, like Sisyphus. As strong as he is, he's really just a muscle-bound human. I don't think he could manage it. Some of the others, like Prometheus for instance, are quite powerful, but it seems to me that Satan keeps a pretty close eye on them. Most have 24/7/E jobs in Hell."

"24/7/E?"

"Twenty-four hours a day, seven days a week, for Eternity. It's pretty hard to slip away and create much mayhem with a schedule like that."

"All right," Allan said. "Let's eliminate them provisionally from our list of suspects." I crossed out the two categories. Our list of suspects now included only Devils and Demons.

"I don't think there are very many demons capable of pulling this off."

"Why?" Pinkerton asked.

"Well, they have most of the means you listed - many of them are crafty and powerful, though none as strong as the major devils in Hell - but there are only two demons I know who have even a little knowledge of the HVAC system."

"And they would be ... ?" Allan asked, hand poised before the blackboard.

"Digger, who runs the sulfur mines, and his boss, the arch-Demon Adramalech, the so-called King of Fire." I slipped between Allan and the board, writing their names next to the Demon category.

Allan looked at me dubiously. "You're kidding, right?"

"Well, no. They both have the fire connection, and they both know a bit about the HVAC system, and they both are powerful demons ... "

"And they're both dumb as stumps. Come on, Steve. I've known those two simpletons for a century and a half. If you put either one's brain in a bird, the thing would fly backward. Neither has the cunning to do anything like this."

"Er, you're right about that." I drew a line through their names and, after a moment's reflection, put an x through the entire demon category.

Allan stroked his beard and nodded. "At least for now, that just leaves us with devils."

I frowned. "I think so. They seem the most likely anyway. And not just any devil. Stealth, cunning, technical knowledge of the HVAC system, and raw power. I'm betting we're talking about one of the Princes of Hell."

"You could very well be right." Pinkerton said, nodding. "And that brings us back to the Seven Deadly Sins and their associated devils." Allan used his shirt sleeve to wipe the "Suspects" column clean. Then he wrote down the names of each prince, across from the sin with which he was associated. The chart now looked like this:

SUSPECTS	MOTIVE	MEANS	OPPORTUNITY
LUCIFER	PRIDE	STEALTH	
MAMMON	GREED	CUNNING	
ASMODEUS	LUST	KNOW HVAC	
LEVIATHAN	ENVY	RAW POWER	
BEELZEBUB	GLUTTONY		
SATAN	WRATH		
BELPHEGOR	SLOTH		

"We have Satan down twice."

"Yes," agreed Pinkerton, "in two of his aspects: Lucifer and Satan. But he's not likely to be the culprit anyway. I don't see what he'd get out of it. This is more of a headache for him than anyone."

"Right, right." I drew two quick lines on the board.

Pinkerton studied the chart. "Greed, lust and envy could all be motives for this. Someone who wants power, well, the only way one of the remaining five could get more power is by taking Satan down a notch, or displacing him entirely."

"Do you think any of the other princes would have the stones to take on Satan?"

"Not directly, but perhaps using subterfuge one might try it. I think Mammon and Asmodeus are definite possibilities."

"But not Leviathan?"

Pinkerton shook his head as he drew a line through that name. "I've never heard of him leaving the ocean here on Level

Seven, not even when some of the other princes of Hell get together on poker night. He has too much fun playing Moby Dick or the Kraken. Besides, he's more interested in water than fire."

"What about Belphegor? You didn't mention him."

"That's because he's too lazy to try something like this. He's not only the devil most associated with slothfulness; he is the laziest creature I've ever seen. I also think that of the Seven Deadly Sins, Sloth is the only one that doesn't work as a motive." Pinkerton considered a bit longer then drew lines through Belphegor's name and the word "Sloth."

"That leaves Mammon, Asmodeus and Beelzebub" I said. "Yet I find it hard to believe that Beezy had anything to do with this."

"Why?"

"The HVAC system is his baby. He designed it and seemed really upset about it being broken. Also, Gluttony as a motive for stealing fire seems a bit odd, don't you think? And Beezy's already the second most powerful devil in Hell."

"So who better to topple the first most powerful devil in Hell?"

I frowned. "Maybe, but, well, and I know this isn't a good reason but, I don't want it to be him."

"You're right. It's not a good reason. Why don't you want it to be him?"

"Because ... I like him."

Pinkerton chuckled softly. "Me too. I always have. He's the only devil I've ever known to show any integrity. Don't tell him I said that!" He looked with alarm over his shoulder. "And that includes you too, BOOH!"

BOOH snorted.

"I know what you mean. He's as cruel as any of them, but it's an honest cruelty. Like, he'd never sucker-punch you. He's not a backstabber."

"No, more of a front stabber."

I poked Allan in the chest with my stick of chalk. "Exactly!"

"Still," Pinkerton continued, rubbing the white chalk mark off his vest, "as much as I hate to admit it, he's probably your best suspect. As you said, he knows more about the HVAC system than anyone, he's nearly as powerful as Satan, and he could be a Glutton for more power. I think he needs to stay on the list until you can eliminate him."

Sigh. "Okay, so how do I do that?"

"Ah, that's where opportunity comes in." Allan wiped off the crossed-out names and "Sloth" and replaced the word "Opportunity" with another. The completed chart looked like this:

SUSPECTS	MOTIVE	MEANS	ALIBI
	PRIDE	STEALTH	
MAMMON	GREED	CUNNING	
ASMODEUS	LUST	KNOW HVAC	
	ENVY	RAW POWER	
BEELZEBUB	GLUTTONY		
	WRATH		

"All three could have motive, all three definitely have the means, and all three have lots of independence down here. But not all three of them are likely to have alibis. That's how you will solve the puzzle, Steve. Investigate the three, and see if they have alibis."

Allan sat back down and poured himself another Scotch. He offered me the bottle, but I demurred. BOOH held up his bucket, and Pinkerton topped it off with the gasoline can. We sat quietly while Allan and BOOH finished their drinks.

Another overwhelming task. Hopelessness and helplessness, so familiar to Hell's inhabitants, sat on my chest like heavy weights. They combined with my profound weariness - an exhaustion that had been a constant companion since being damned - to glue me to the chair. Finally, with an effort of will, I stood. "Bik! We're leaving. Come take shotgun." Bik flew down from the ceiling, extinguished his flame and dove into my pocket protector.

"Bye, Allan. Thanks for all your help." Then I sighed. "Let's go, BOOH. We need to see Beelzebub."

Chapter 9

BOOH flew in lazy, ever-widening circles above the endless stretch of sand. Nothing moved on the dunes below, and I was preparing to skip Beelzebub for now and go on to my other suspects.

To think of Beezy as the possible culprit behind the HVAC system's failure troubled me for reasons I couldn't entirely explain. Sure, he was my boss, and I felt a certain amount of loyalty to him, even though he didn't treat me very well. And he *did* seem honest, at least as far as devils went. Maybe my feelings really just went back to what we had discussed in Pinkerton's workshop. I liked Beezy and didn't want to think him guilty of sabotage. Yet, despite my feelings in the matter, in many ways he was the most viable suspect. After all, no one knew more about the HVAC system than Beezy. Shit, he designed and built the thing.

I had decided, at Pinkerton's, to eliminate Beezy as a suspect immediately, if possible, provided he didn't eliminate me first in a more, ah, terminal way. Like all devils, my boss had a temper, but unlike some others in Hell's Management, Beelzebub's reaction would be immediate and most likely quite violent. My boss didn't nurse grudges. He acted or reacted and moved on, usually leaving a bunch of bodies in his wake.

Someone - I don't know who exactly, but I think it was in a Star Trek movie - once said, "Revenge is a dish best served cold." Not with Beezy. If he was pissed off at you, he'd grab and skewer you on the spot, or perhaps reduce you to powder with a blast of flame. Or drop a mountain on you. Or squeeze the ectoplasm out of you. Frankly, I didn't know exactly what he'd do, but he'd do it immediately, no beating around the bush. I only hoped I could survive a really angry Lord of the Flies. Assuming that an existence in Hell really counted as survival in the first place.

Earlier, BOOH, Bik and I had descended on the bazaar that Beezy's office fronted. The screened-in pavilion that was my boss's command center was empty, except for the usual assortment of flies and mosquitoes that he'd managed to evade when he made his escape. Beezy often left his office, usually to spend time away from his tiny worshippers. That the Lord of the Flies really hated bugs was ironic, but I guess anything gets old after a while.

Happening to glance at his desk, I noticed a mass of dead flies - Beezy must have squashed them with his flyswatter - on the surface. Their carcasses had been arranged to spell out a short message: "Taking a walk."

Now, the great Beelzebub can take a walk anywhere he wants, or at least anywhere this side of the Pearly Gates. Although he doesn't instantly transport himself large distances, the way Satan does, he travels pretty fast, faster than BOOH, even.

Well, I say he doesn't instantly travel large distances, but I don't know that for a fact. I know he's capable of teleportation, or whatever technical term the devils use for it down here, at least over short distances. He had once teleported the two of us through an entire pile of rubble, so I suppose it's possible that he could move from his home base on Level Eight to, say, Level Three in an instant. I'd never seen him do it, though. Usually he'd make a showy entrance, like coming on the scene in the shape of a nuclear mushroom cloud.

Anyway, my point is that at that moment Beezy could have been taking his walk anywhere in Hell or on Gates Level or even on Earth. (He'd go there sometimes for a baseball game. He liked the hotdogs and beer, though he agreed with me that the game itself was as boring as watching people queued up to get a haircut.) I was counting on the fact that he preferred to stay on Level Eight. The vast desert that comprised all that I'd ever seen down here must have reminded him of his salad days, when he was a god himself.

Beelzebub is a bit of an enigma as far as the Princes of Hell go. There are two different stories about his origin, one that he was a god who got displaced when monotheism came to the Semites, the other that he was one of the angels that fell with Lucifer after the War in Heaven. If the first were true, Beezy might actually be a mythological creature rather than a true devil. Or perhaps both origin stories are true. While different, they aren't mutually exclusive.

But I digress. BOOH and I were circling the desert, hoping for signs of my boss. Just when we were about to give up, the bat gave a "Skree!" He'd spotted Beelzebub. In a second, I saw him too. A creature that looked a lot like a five hundred foot tall Beezy was strolling along the desert, hands in the pockets of his jacket. Occasionally, he'd kick at a dune, rocketing grains of sand into the sky. The sand would get caught in the wind and begin whirling. There were at least a dozen of these, and they seemed to be following Big Beezy across the desert floor.

"BOOH! Fly near his face and try to get his attention."

That was a mistake. From the perspective of a giant Beelzebub, BOOH, large as he was, must have looked like a big bug, and he reflexively swatted us out of the sky. When my eyes cleared, I found myself lying on the ground, spitting sand from my mouth. Even BOOH looked a bit dazed as he pulled himself to his feet.

I looked down to my pocket. From inside my pocket protector, Bik moaned softly. "What hit us?"

"I DID!' said a monstrous voice from above.

Beezy was standing, legs straddled, hands on hips, looking down at us. He began to shrink, until he was his normal size, which was about a foot taller than me.

"Minion, never, NEVER fly in my face. I can't stand that, remember?"

"Sorry. I forgot." Getting off the ground, I noticed he didn't help me to my feet, but then again, he seldom did. Devils aren't known for their kind natures, you know.

"What do you want?"

"Er, I, uh, that is … " I didn't know how to start this. After just having been swatted by my boss, I didn't relish the prospect of a repeat performance.

"Any progress on the HVAC system?"

"Right, right!" I said, brushing the sand from my coveralls. "I came to give you a report."

The Lord of the Flies grabbed an insect out of the air - even here in the dry air of the desert, one had managed to find him - and stuffed it in his mouth. "Well? I'm waiting."

Good thing he hadn't thought to stuff me and BOOH in his mouth. That would have been unpleasant.

"Orson and I have spent hours checking out the HVAC system. You're right. There's no way it could fail."

Beezy nodded as if he were unsurprised. "Like I said: I build them good."

"Well," I said by reflex.

My boss held a finger to one nostril, then sent a blast of air, and no small quantity of snot, out the other one. I found myself, slightly sticky, back on the ground.

"I'll put up with Nick correcting my grammar, but not you."

"Sorry. Former academic. Old habits die hard."

"Well, watch it."

"Yessir."

"Okay, so my system is unbreakable, and yet it's not working. Have you come to any conclusions?"

"I, uh, well, I suspect foul play was involved."

Beezy frowned at me. "This is Hell, you idiot. Of course there's foul play. Any suspects?"

"A few, yes."

"Who?"

My face felt warm. "I'd rather not say at the moment. I don't want to besmirch anyone's reputation."

"Besmirch? What kind of a stupid word is that?"

"Well," I said, taking the awl from my tool belt to clean my fingernails. I thought the nonchalant look was best at this moment. "Besmirch means … "

"I KNOW what the hell besmirch means! It's just a sissy word, and I don't like it, okay?"

"Yes sir, boss! Anyway, I think whoever did this is trying to go toe-to-toe with Satan. So whoever he or she is will get into a hell of a lot of trouble with the Big Guy. For that reason, I don't want to name the suspects until I've done a little more digging."

"Suit yourself." Beezy grabbed the awl from my hand and threw it at my chest.

"Ow!"

"Quit your whining, Minion. I was doing you a favor. I saw a red slug crawling out of your pocket, and I just skewered it."

A red slug? Oh no!

I pulled the awl from where it was stuck in my pocket protector, and a little bit of my chest, truth be told. As I drew it away from me, I saw a small Bik impaled on the tool.

"Bik! Bik!" I screamed, gently pulling the awl from the body of the fire giant. "Are you okay?"

"Oooh," Bik moaned. Apparently, fire giants were tougher than I thought. Bik had a hole in his chest, but it closed rapidly. He looked up at Beelzebub, shouted "Jævla drittsekk!" - a Norwegian obscenity, I think, though Scandinavian curses are among the few I haven't mastered - and launched himself in the air, igniting as he left my palm. "I'll show you red slug!"

"What the hell?" Beezy said, swatting at the flaming creature. Amazingly, Bik evaded Beezy's swing, something I'd never seen any creature, sitting, standing or flying do before. Beelzebub was deadly accurate with a hand or a flyswatter.

"Lord Beelzebub, that's Bik, Surtr's grandson!"

Beezy swung at Bik again. Once more he missed; he was getting peeved. "I know who he is. I recognize him now. So tell the little cretin to back off, before I demolish him."

"Right. Bik, stop it! That's Beelzebub, the great Lord of the Flies himself! He'll crush you like a coke can!"

"No he won't. Nobody pushes me around. I'll burn that smartass smirk right off his face."

My initial impression of Bik as a generally well-tempered young fire giant might have been a bit off the mark. Certainly, his language was deteriorating the more time he spent around me. I decided in future to watch what was said around him. He was only two hundred years old and obviously still very impressionable.

"Kid," Beelzebub said mildly, "you've got spunk."

"Bik, don't fly at his f ... "

Faster than thought, Beezy's hand flew through the air, swatting Bik back to the desert floor.

"I hate spunk."

"Oooh," Bik repeated. His flame sputtered and died.

"Jeez, boss!" I said with indignation while picking Bik off the ground. He was unconscious, but seemed otherwise okay, so I stuffed him back in my pocket protector. "You didn't have to do that. He's just a kid!"

Beezy drew back his fist threateningly. "You want some too?"

"Ah, no, actually."

"Then shut up and finish your report so I can get back to my walk."

This was it, the moment when I needed to question my own boss about his possible culpability. "I ... I ... "

"Quick stammering, and spit it out. Is this about the work orders?"

"Yes, yes!" I cried desperately, knowing that I had just chickened out. "I've never seen so many come in at once."

"Not a surprise. It *is* a cold day in Hell."

I thought quickly, and an idea came to me. "Yes, but some of these really need to be fixed."

"Like what?"

"Well, another bulb has burned out on the Sign."

Beezy cursed in Ugaritic, an ancient Semitic language. While I might not know Scandinavian obscenities, I *do* know Semitic ones, since my boss's foul temper gave me an almost daily tutorial. Occasionally Beelzebub could whip up something so obscure that even I couldn't understand it, but this one he'd used before. It translated roughly as "son of a bitch."

"And Mussolini's sewing machine has broken."

Beezy spat. "Crap. All of Hell's succubi will soon be without pantyhose. Not that they keep them on any longer than necessary, but they still like the way hose make their legs look. Last thing I need is a bunch of she-demons grouching at me."

"Yes, that's what I thought too. Listen, boss, I don't need Orson right now, so can we let him close off some work orders?"

"Shit, Minion. That again? Just a few months ago, it was, 'Let Orson rebuild the Stairway to Paradise' without me. Now it's, 'Let Orson do my job.' What part of his eternal punishment do you not get?"

"Boss, I understand completely, but some of these orders have to be addressed, and I just can't break away from the mystery of the HVAC system right now. Metaphysical ramifications, right?"

My boss frowned. "Right," he admitted grudgingly.

I was quiet for a moment, trying to think of something that would make this more palatable to Beelzebub. I brightened as it came to me. "Look, we could still accomplish some good, I mean, some bad here. We could make Edison or Ford his assistant temporarily. One of those two pricks would get Orson's eternal punishment. And either one is a mechanical genius. He would have to watch Orson fumble around yet be unable to do anything but assist. It would drive him even crazier than it does Orson."

"Hmm," Beezy said, scratching his forked beard. "That has promise. Okay, do it, but tell Orson that he has to document each completed work order in a memo to you, with a carbon to me. We don't want him to think he's completely in charge."

"Yes sir," I said.

Beelzebub conjured up a piece of paper and handed it to me. "What's this?"

"It's a memo to Digger authorizing you to borrow either Edison or Ford, only one, mind you, not both, to help Orson. Now, go away." Beezy grew back to his gargantuan size and strode off.

In my pocket, Bik was slowly stirring. He was certainly a tough little guy and no doubt soon would be okay. I walked over to BOOH, who had just been sitting quietly, watching with interest as I talked to my boss. He hiked one eyebrow at me. At least, I think it was an eyebrow, though I'm not too sure that bats even have eyebrows. Something was raised, however, and I'm calling it an eyebrow.

"Yeah, I know. I'm a coward. Don't rub it in. Let's check out our other two suspects first. Maybe we can prove one of them is guilty and never have to question Beezy at all. And stop rolling your eyes at me!"

I swear, the giant bat was laughing, but he patted me companionably on the back. BOOH doesn't always know his own strength, though. He knocked me thirty feet.

"Thanks, *pal*," I said, getting up. "Now, if you wouldn't mind, please take me to the office."

BOOH was inhaling and exhaling rapidly on the entire flight back up to Five. I didn't hear any sound, but I was convinced that he was indeed having a chuckle at my expense.

Chapter 10

Orson was sitting at my desk when I returned from the Eighth Circle. His head was resting on his hands as he stared at a six-inch pile of work orders before him. Orson glanced to the door as he heard me open it.

I whistled. "That's a pretty impressive pile of work orders you've got there."

"Yes, and these are only the important ones," he moaned, as the end of the pneumatic tube that hung above my wire inbox spat out five more jobs. "I've set two stacks of low priority work orders on the floor over there." He indicated the new piles in the corner of our trailer. Each stack was over four feet high. The new piles had joined two dozen other ones nearby. Soon we'd have to toss out a few. It was either that or have the trailer tip over from the weight of the columns of paper.

Things broke in Hell constantly, but not at this rate. I'd never seen so many work orders come in in such a short time.

"I've never seen so many work orders arrive in such short order," Orson said, echoing my thoughts, though with better grammar. "Steve, I know how important the HVAC system is, but some of these can't wait."

My assistant started to get out of my chair, but I waved him back down while I perched myself on his stool. "You're right. In fact, I was just talking to Beezy about this very issue."

"And?"

"And I've gotten his permission for you to handle the work orders while I continue to focus on the HVAC."

Orson looked startled. "How'd you pull that off? He never lets me do anything on my own."

"I promised him we'd get you an assistant."

"I get an assistant?" My friend was even more surprised than before. Then his eyes narrowed. "I get it. This person will suck at maintenance jobs, even worse than you and I do."

"On the contrary. Both of the possible candidates are extremely handy, far more so than the two of us put together." I looked up at the ceiling, all innocent. "Of course, whichever one ends up being your assistant, he won't be able to do anything on his own, which should be frustrating for him, even more frustrating than it is for you."

Orson's face lit with understanding. "Now I *do* get it! This is how you got Beezy to agree to this, right?"

"Right."

"But you said two candidates?"

"Indeed I did." I hopped off the stool, got myself some coffee, and rejoined him. "You get to choose who you want."

"Who are my candidates?"

"Hey, gotta light? I'm hungry." a tiny voice said from my chest. Bik zipped out of the pocket protector and landed on the desk.

"Glad you're feeling better." I threw him a nearly empty pack of matches. "Here, knock yourself out, kid."

"No thanks," he replied, lighting a match. "I got enough of that from Beelzebub. My skull is still ringing. Who would have thought that an old fatso like him could be so fast?"

"You should see him with a flyswatter," I said.

"I'll pass on that too, if it's all the same. One run-in with him is enough for me." Bik sucked down the flame of the match then lit another.

"You didn't answer my question," Orson said. "Who are my choices for assistant?"

I grinned all big and toothy. "Do you have to ask? Why, Big Prick and Little Prick, of course."

Orson laughed so hard he began to weep, pounding his fist on the desktop and doing other stereotypical actions that indicated extreme amusement. "I should have known you'd find a way to stick it to those two."

"Yes. Unfortunately, we can only stick it to one of them, though I suppose the unselected will take this as a small blow to his self esteem. So, who is it going to be: BP or LP?"

BP, aka Big Prick, was Thomas Edison. LP, or Little Prick, was Henry Ford. Like I said earlier, they were two of my least favorite people in all Hell. The dislike was mutual. They were envious of my position, because they actually would have *liked* an eternity of being handymen. Besides being inventive, both of them were good at fixing things.

Orson's laughter finally diminished to a soft chuckle. "That's easy. Edison, of course."

"Well," I said, slurping down some coffee, "he would have been my choice, but why did you decide on him?"

Orson leaned back in my chair, clasping his hands over his capacious belly. "Back in 1980, about five years before I died, I made a documentary called 'The Secret of Nikola Tesla.'"

"Really? I didn't know that."

My friend shrugged. "No reason you should. It was pretty obscure, made in Yugoslavia. This was not the best time in my life, you know. I was peddling Paul Masson wines as a way to make a buck. Same reason I made this movie."

"Hey, you're being too hard on yourself. Didn't you do 'The Muppet Movie' at the same time? You had a great cameo in that!"

Orson grinned. "That was a year or two earlier, but yeah, that was fun. Anyway, I played J.P. Morgan in the Tesla movie. A good part of the story was about the AC/DC wars, and Edison didn't come off very well in the telling."

"Ah ha! So you've been holding out on me. All along, you've disliked BP too!"

"Yes, but you've done such a good job pulling his chain whenever you've had the opportunity that I haven't seen the need to do anything."

"Well," I said in mock exasperation. "I hope that you'll take up the slack and do your part now."

Orson grinned mischievously. "Most assuredly."

I finished my coffee and put down my cup. "Then let's go collect him."

"Why don't we just have BOOH do it?"

"Because I'd like to take a quick look at Digger's operation." I didn't tell my assistant that I wanted to decide for myself if the demon running Hell's main sulfur mine was really incapable of mucking with the HVAC system.

"You're the boss, though you know BOOH will have to make two trips."

"He's a fine, strapping bat. He'll manage."

"I think I'll stay here," Bik said, finishing his last light. "I want to touch bases with Grandpa. Besides," he said, looking hopefully at me, "I'm still hungry. That encounter with Beelzebub really took it out of me."

I tossed him another matchbox. "Bon appetit!"

As BOOH was carrying me and Orson through the Throat of Hell from Level Five to Six, I managed to yell, "Oh! One thing: Beezy says he wants every completed work order accompanied by a memo, explaining what you did. Original to me, carbon to him."

Orson shrugged, an impressive accomplishment, since he was in the pincer grasp of BOOH's claws. "That will slow me down," he yelled back, "but I write fast, and if it's the price I have to pay to be allowed to accomplish something, so be it!"

That was all the time we had to discuss these details, as BOOH had already reached the mines on Level Six.

On Earth, you get sulfur as a byproduct of removing sulfur-containing impurities from natural gas and oil. You can also get it from a salt dome by pumping a shitload of really hot water into the dome. In Hell, though, sulfur is as valuable as gold, so Satan has decreed that it be mined in similar fashion.

Hell's primary sulfur mine was an impressive operation. The entrance was huge, a black shadow of football field proportions on the side of a mountain. A train track - a rather poorly maintained one I knew, since it was my responsibility to do the maintaining - ran through the center of the hole. Periodically, a hand cart fully laden with sulfur would be laboriously pushed from the inside of the mine to the outside by five or six of the workers. The track was big enough that a locomotive could have pushed and pulled the weighty cart. Hell, the track was big enough to handle a Super Chief, but that would have made things way too easy for the mineworkers. Scratching the smelly, yellow crap out of the innards of the mine, bringing the sulfur to the surface, and loading it into trucks whose bays were a little bit too high to just dump the cargo in - it had to be shoveled in by hand - was the eternal punishment for the workers here.

Eternal punishment isn't supposed to be easy.

On either side of the track, hundreds of damned souls in white coveralls flowed in and out of the mine like so many ants entering and leaving their anthill. Digging in a mine was dirty work, and by the end of the seemingly indeterminable work day, the coveralls would be filthy, with streaks of yellow and black all over them; yet Digger, the demon responsible for the mine, required that the workers report every morning in spotless white coveralls. Since each of these poor bastards had but a single set of coveralls, they spent the evening scrubbing the sulfur, dirt and general grime from the fabric. It could take all night to get the coveralls clean, and many of the mineworkers would show up in wet, but white work outfits.

Putting on wet clothes is its own form of Hell, as everyone knows.

At the entrance to the mine was one of the Underworld's time clocks, an impressive array of timesheets in hundreds of timecard holders, and a shift whistle. Periodically, the whistle would blow, and an officious-looking demon in a hard hat, holding a clipboard, would grab a microphone and yell into it: "Break time! Smoke 'em if ya got 'em." Three seconds later though, he'd pick up the microphone again and scream, "Break's over! Back to it, you lollygagging fuckers!" No rest for the weary in Hell's sulfur mine.

"Minion!" rasped the demon. "What do you want?"

"Hey, Karnaj. We're looking for Digger, oh, and Tommy Edison."

Karnaj took a fat cigar out of his mouth and motioned inside. "You're in luck. Both of them are together, as it happens, just a few hundred feet inside." He examined us critically. "Good. You brought your own hard hats. Can't let you in without a hard hat. Union rules, ya know."

"Yeah," I said. "I know the rules. We belong to the same union, after all."

That would be the SEIU: Satan's Employees Infernal Union. Every damned one of us is a member. It's mandatory, of course, though we don't get any benefits from belonging. Still, rules are rules.

We walked through the entrance, shouldering our way through the workers, who, depending on the severity of their personal damnation, were digging sulfur out of the walls, ceiling and floor of the cavern with picks, screwdrivers, pocketknives or their own fingers. Second shift had started only an hour ago, but already the hands, faces and necks of these workers, that is, the only portion of skin not covered by the coveralls, and of course the coveralls themselves, were coated with sulfur, making the workers look like golden robots. Nervous golden robots.

In front of us, a clutch of men and women was working at an even more frenetic pace than usual. Seeing the large, humpbacked monster in the middle, I knew why. "Dig!" it shouted. "Dig more! Dig faster! Dig, dig, dig!"

I recognized the voice. Digger.

Digger was a rather large and unusually shaped demon. He measured about fifteen feet, from horns to tail, and he was almost half as wide. Digger's chest, arms and legs were powerfully muscled, and his hands and feet were shaped like big shovels. The demon was using them now, digging at the earth beneath him with speed, ferocity and enthusiasm. Ironic that Digger got as much joy from digging up sulfur as the humans around him got misery.

Different strokes for different folks, I suppose.

The human workers could not possibly keep up with Digger, but they worked as rapidly as desperation drove them. All but two, who were hanging on the fringe of the crowd, pretending to work hard, but not really digging up much of the yellow stuff, as evidenced by the relative whiteness of their coveralls as compared to those of their colleagues.

"Edison! Ford!" I said in a voice much louder than it needed to be. "Why aren't you digging?"

"NOT DIGGING?" Digger howled, looking over to where a very guilty looking Thomas Alva Edison and Henry Ford stood. The other humans, coated in sweat-soaked sulfur, turned and stared. Their eyes narrowed in anger.

"NOT DIGGING?" Digger repeated then brought out a huge whip and thrashed Edison and Ford with it. I was impressed that the demon could even hold the whip with his shovel-hands.

After Digger finished beating them, Edison and Ford pulled themselves painfully off the ground. The bright red whelps on their backs were already closing up, as was the fabric of their uniforms. "Thanks a bunch, Minion," Ford groaned.

"Don't mention it," I said, and began to whistle.

"What Minion and assistant want here?" Digger asked, coiling his whip and attaching it to a belt at his waist.

"Lord Beelzebub has given me permission to borrow Mr. Edison for a while."

The demon stared at me, slowly rocking his head from side to side, as if the motion would somehow shake the words he was hearing into synapses in his brain appropriate for comprehension. "Edison have quota. No can go."

Orson piped in. "Perhaps Ford can take up the slack."

"What?" Ford snapped. "I can barely meet my own quota."

"At the rate you were working just now," I opined, "I'd be surprised if you could ever get it done."

Ford's insult was too vulgar to transcribe here, but it involved some sulfur, a tamp, a lit match and my lowest bodily orifice. Pretty creative, all in all, but I wasn't passing out gold stars. I merely said "Sticks and stones," before turning back to Digger.

"Sorry, Mr. Digger, sir, but I'm working on a special project for Satan, and I need Edison to provide some backfill."

Digger scratched his head. "Backfill?" he said, not comprehending. Then his eyes lit up. "Take sulfur. Use as backfill."

What a moron.

What I *said* was, "Sorry, Digger. Different kind of backfill. I need a human who can work with Orson here to fix things around Hell while I'm working on Lord Satan's project."

Edison's eyes lit up. "So, I'm going to be replacing you as Hell's Super for a while?"

Orson and I had a jolly laugh together. "Not bloody likely," Orson said. "You're going to be replacing me. You'll be my assistant."

"You!" Edison sputtered. "Why, you're even less competent than Minion here."

"Bite me, BP."

"And *don't* call me that! I hate it when Minion does it, and I won't have it from you as well."

Digger interrupted. "Edison can't go. Must dig. Dig, dig, dig!"

"Sorry, Digger, but these are Beezy's, ah, Lord Beelzebub's orders." I handed him the memo Beezy had given me authorizing the temporary transfer. Digger could barely hold the tiny piece of paper. He turned it this way and that, eventually settling on staring at it upside down, with the print facing me instead of him. "Duh, okay. If boss's boss say so." The paper slipped from his grasp, and he turned away and began digging again.

"Dig! Dig! Dig! Dig!"

Boy, I see what Pinkerton meant. Digger really is dumb as a post, and some people say his boss, Ukobach, is even denser. There's no way either one could have pulled this off.

"Why didn't you choose me?" Ford asked.

"I didn't choose. Orson did. Besides, I wouldn't feel too slighted. I doubt your friend will have much fun working as Orson's assistant. Now, Mr. Ford," I said in a loud voice, "don't you think you should start digging? Your fingernails look unusually clean to me!"

Digger's head shot up from the impressive hole he'd made in the ground beneath him. Ford dove for the floor and started digging just as Digger's whip caught him on the butt.

"Bastard!" Ford gasped, shooting me a look filled with venom.

While I was playing with Ford, Orson had been eying Edison. "Hmm. This won't do. It won't do at all."

"What's wrong?" I asked.

"It's the color of his coveralls. They're still white, the slacker. Ours are yellow, and we don't have any spares."

I nodded. "Good point. Do you have any ideas?"

"Well, I have one." Orson tripped Edison. As the Wizard of Menlo Park lay sprawled on the ground, my assistant quickly stooped and started rolling him in the powdered sulfur that covered the soil near the dig site. When he was finished, Edison's coveralls were a bright yellow.

"A little stinky," Orson said, as he brushed the sulfurous residue from his hands, "but at least your uniform is the right color now. Now turn around." He examined the HOTI acronym on the back of the coveralls. (The mining operation was part of Hell's Office of the Interior, just as the Maintenance Department was.) With his sleeve, my assistant wiped the powder from the lettering. "It's not perfect, but pretty close. What do you think?"

"That should do just fine," I said, chuckling. "Let's go." The three of us headed outside, a grumbling Thomas Edison bringing up the rear.

BOOH was playing kick the can with an empty hand cart when we found him. "Sorry, pal," I said, "but there are three of us, so I guess you'll have to make two trips."

The giant bat shrugged, then grabbed me and threw me on top of his shoulders. I managed to right myself, putting my knees on either side of BOOH's ears. Then my batty friend grabbed Orson and Edison with his claws and took off.

I liked being on top.

Oh, I liked riding on BOOH's shoulders too. It made me feel less like a piece of carrion. The only problem was I needed something to help with my balance. I grabbed for the most obvious.

"SKREE!"

"Okay, okay! I get it. Sorry. Not the ears." I locked my fingers through some fur on either side of his ears.

"Urm." *I guess that's okay.*

We were back at the office in two shakes, and I determined that, BOOH willing, in future I'd travel on his shoulders when it was just the two of us. No more BatPassenger for me. Now I really was BatRider.

Chapter 11

When we got back to the office, I noticed the windows were blocked on the inside by piles of paper. Dismounting from BOOH's shaggy shoulders, I snagged Orson by the arm and pointed.

"Just great," he mumbled.

"Well, it *is* a cold day in Hell, ya know. Triage first, I'd advise."

"Always a good strategy," agreed my assistant, or rather, my temporary replacement. "Say, Edison!"

Edison was climbing painfully off the asphalt. BOOH had placed Orson delicately on the pavement, but Edison had not yet earned the giant bat's consideration. I had a feeling he never would. The Wizard of Menlo Park seemed in a daze. Five minutes ago, he'd been dodging work down in the mines of the Sixth Level. Now he was an unwilling gopher in Hell's Plant Maintenance Department.

"Edison!" Orson repeated, a little more insistently.

"Wha … what?"

"Head on into the office and see if any new work orders have come in."

"Where would I find them?"

"Don't worry," Orson said, nonchalantly, as he scraped some sulfur off his sleeve. "They should be easy to spot."

We'd never let BP inside our office before, so he had no idea how the work order system operated. Evidently, Orson was going to show no mercy to his new assistant. Edison took a deep breath and headed for the door. As if Orson had forgotten something, he called to the new guy. "Big Prick?"

The inventor's eyes flashed. "Stop calling me that!"

"I'll call you whatever I want. What year did you die?"

"Let's see." For some reason, all of us down here have a harder time recalling the year of our death than we do that of our birth. I guess it's because birthdays and birth years are causes for celebration. Death days … not so much. "I think it was 1931. Why?"

Orson scratched his beard as he did a quick calculation. He smiled. "Four or five years too early. That means you never heard of Fibber McGee and Molly's hall closet on the radio. That's good."

"What the hell does that have to do with anything?" Edison grumbled, turning the knob on our office door. It flew open as if springs had been on the door jamb, and an avalanche of papers tumbled on top of him.

Now, it's mildly interesting that the door flew outward. It usually opened inward, as do most outside doors, but the Devil will never miss an opportunity to mete out a little punishment that also provides him with a little comic entertainment. He has no problem changing the rules on a moment's notice if he can get a jolly out of it. Orson and I both know that, and my friend had clearly been banking on it. Smart guy.

As the door flew open, Bik shot out of the trailer and into my pocket protector. "Boy!" he gasped. "That was close. A few more seconds and I would have been forced to torch your office!"

I shrugged. "That might not have been so bad."

Edison flailed helplessly against the work orders that had overwhelmed him. "Help! I'm drowning!"

"Only in paperwork," Orson said, laughing. After he and I had a good yuck at Edison's expense, Orson wiped the tears from his eyes. "This is going to be fun. I think I'll call him my best boy."

That's the movie term for assistant, in case you didn't know.

"I thought you hated that expression."

Orson shook his head. "*I don't want to be called best boy.* I prefer assistant, but I don't mind using it with others. Besides, it's nice and degrading, don't you think?"

I whistled in admiration. "I think you may dislike Edison even more than I do."

"Probably. I think you got a lot out of your system when you pushed him through the Mouth of Hell."

I winced again at the memory. "Could we not talk about that anymore? I'm not exactly proud of my actions that day."

Orson looked appraisingly at me. "O … okay."

"And don't be too hard on him. He's your assistant now, and like I said before, he's handier than both of us put together."

"I know that. Should be interesting when he finds out he won't be able to fix anything."

"No doubt. Still, things might actually go fairly quickly with him. He should be able to figure out the fastest way to fix most anything."

Orson nodded as he walked toward Edison, who was still struggling to get out from under the pile of papers that had overwhelmed him. "Yeah, but first I need to teach him our triage system."

"Have fun," I said, heading back over to BOOH, "but not too much fun."

My friend looked in my direction, to find me pointing meaningfully toward the ground. "Right. Beelzebub wouldn't like that very much, would he?"

"Neither would Satan."

"Got it."

"And don't forget to write me and Beezy a memo about each completed work order."

"Will do. Come on, best boy," Orson said, grabbing Edison's arm and pulling him out from under the avalanche of papers.

"Let me show you how we prioritize our work here in the Plant Department."

"Mmph!" Edison replied, then spat out the paper that had gotten lodged in his mouth. I grimaced. Those multipart forms were killer on the throat.

BOOH looked a little disappointed when I returned to where he was sitting on the pavement.

"Sorry, pal," I said, patting his shoulder in sympathy. I had a pretty good idea what he was thinking about. "I can't get at the blood bags right now. Orson and BP have to clear out a little paper first. I'll get you one later, or maybe you'll have time to hunt down some fresh blood while I take care of a little business."

My batty friend raised an eyebrow.

"BOOH, I need to go see Asmodeus over in Lustland. Can you take me there?"

BOOH launched in the air and prepared to grab me with his hind claws.

"Do you think I could ride on your shoulders, instead? I liked it up there."

BOOH shrugged - yes it was a shrug, that much of his body language I could tell, since it was a gesture he used so often - and settled back on the pavement. He flattened down a little and made mounting my trusty steed pretty easy. I grabbed the fur tufts, resisted an impulse to dig my heels into my friend, and said I was ready when he was.

BOOH is always ready.

As we flew up to Level Two, I thought some more about the metaphysical ramifications of a cold day in Hell. Millions and millions - maybe billions and billions - of people had used that expression for hundreds upon hundreds of years, and the possibility of a massive karmic backlash seemed very possible. I recalled my discussion with Orson from earlier in the day. It had been stupid of me to "cold day in hell" (used as a verb here) Orson's comment about me finding another beautiful woman in Hell. While that seemed extremely unlikely, the vertigo I'd experienced right after opening my fat mouth made me wonder.

Don't misunderstand. Vertigo is a common condition down here. Being damned for all eternity, well, it's not conducive to a sense of calm and complacency. Usually, though, I experience dizziness and/or nausea as a result of some torment being meted out by a devil or demon or just something shitty happening because Hell is my home. A casual remark in a conversation on its own won't generally make me lose my lunch.

Well, I didn't exactly throw up, but I was damn close to it, and that had never happened before. I shivered, not from the cold, but out of a sense of foreboding.

All of these thoughts fit into the space of about thirteen seconds, the time it took BOOH to reach our destination. We were hovering over Lustland. The City of Covetous Sin, located on the southwestern edge of the Second Circle, reminded me of a seedy Las Vegas more than anything. The town had a cheesy strip, lined with neon signs advertising gentlemen clubs, aka titty bars, brothels, and comparable establishments that might appeal to heterosexual women, lesbians or gays.

I find it ironic that, while straight guys have plenty of names for the places they frequent to satisfy their baser needs, women and gay men have not developed an entire lexicon around this topic. Or maybe I just don't know it. Still, it makes me wonder why the men in power on Earth maintain such a holier-than-thou attitude about sex outside of marriage, when they are the ones who practice it so frequently and have such a rich vocabulary with which to describe it. The houses of ill-repute for females and non-heterosexual males don't generally have names down here but instead state their meaning with garish neon signs, showing in tubular brilliance the services they offer. There are exceptions, of course, like the Dancing Dildos and the Gay Caballeros.

Brothels in Lustland aren't like those on Earth. There is a definite "look but don't touch" rule regarding anyone a damned soul could possibly find attractive as well as a requirement to "have sex with this repulsive, bepimpled sow" or suffer the lash of a demon. Sometimes you had to have sex with the repulsive one and still undergo the lash. That's called a twofer down here.

Lustland doesn't have the magnificent hotel palaces of Vegas, though there are plenty of roadside motels, the kind you see back on Earth, low-slung, ramshackle buildings with parking lots that consume all the space between building and street, so you can pull your jalopy right up to the front door of your rental room. Most of these places have seedy old farts sitting on the steps before the rooms. These perpetually leering characters are either grotesquely fat or cadaverous, but always ugly, with long, stringy hair, dirty and stinking clothes, and rotting teeth that hold the stubs of long-burning cigarettes. Those are the male versions. The female ones, also ugly, tend to show vast expanses of blotchy, sagging skin, breasts stuffed into ill-fitting bras and hanging six inches below the knees, puffy legs etched with cellulite. None of these abominations is actually human, but demons posing as derelicts. They sit there only to freak out both ladies and gentlemen. Periodically they'll holler out to one of the damned something like, "Looking for a good time?" or "Do me, do me!"

All part of the ambience of Lustland.

At the end of the street was a twenty story office building, the only piece of high-end real estate on the Strip. It was basically a tall cylinder with a rotating observation deck, shaped like a hemisphere, atop it. Huddled at the base of the tower were two geodesic domes. In case that description doesn't conjure up a precise image for you, the building looked essentially like an erect phallus.

Leaving BOOH outside to hunt up a quick meal, I stepped inside the tower. Next to the elevator, located in the center of the lobby, was a brass plaque that said "Lust Unlimited: Corporate Headquarters. Asmodeus: Chairman and Chief Executive Officer." Beneath the plaque was a call button for the elevator. I pressed it and settled in for a long wait.

There was a scurrying from the shadows at the edge of the lobby. An octogenarian dressed in a bellman's outfit ran up to me. He had a big, scoop nose and hair combed back tightly over his skull, revealing a receding hairline that rivaled my own. This guy reminded me of an ugly Bob Hope, but I knew for a fact that this wasn't Hope, because the comic had gone through the Pearly Gates after dying at the age of one hundred. Besides, you can't have Hope in Hell.

"I'm not a crook!" yelled the bellman.

Oh. Him. "I never implied that you were."

"Well, I'm just sayin'." The bellman looked at me apologetically then slapped an out-of-order sign on the elevator door.

"Where are the stairs?" I asked with a sigh.

"Behind the elevator." The old guy walked me around to a door. I pulled on the handle. The metal door was stuck, and I had to pry it open with my crowbar, since there was no glass to throw my hammer through, my preferred method for opening stuck doors, and my screwdriver was only good on softer materials, like wood.

This took ten minutes, and by the time the door finally popped open, I was drenched in sweat. I looked at the bellman who was flashing me the V for victory sign with both hands. I used one of my hands to flash a hand sign of my own - much more expressive, and using fewer digits as well - then stepped inside the stairwell.

I only thought I was sweaty. By the time I'd climbed all twenty flights of stairs, I felt as if I'd gone swimming in my coveralls. The door at the top of the stairs was also stuck, so I repeated my performance from the base of the tower, using my crowbar to push, pull and generally strain against my portal opponent until it finally succumbed.

Soggy me stepped into a beautifully-appointed office suite, with a three hundred degree view through massive, thick plate glass windows of the Strip below. The neon lights were everywhere, forming the garish constellation of promiscuity that was Lustland. I took a moment to gawk, suitably impressed.

"May I help you?"

When I turned and saw the office receptionist, the nausea that I felt earlier returned with a vengeance, along with a migraine that felt like the Acme anvil had landed on my skull. My throat tightened as she stood to receive me. A lower part of me tightened as well, and suddenly my coveralls didn't seem nearly as loose as they had before. I was facing the sexiest woman I'd encountered on either side of the mortal divide, including, I hated to admit to myself, Florence Nightingale.

If this had really been a Looney Tunes cartoon, my jaw would have hit the floor, and my tongue would have rolled out like the red carpet they use on Oscar night. Instead, I just stood there like a grinning idiot - with a migraine.

The receptionist appeared to be four or five inches shorter than me, though, since she was standing behind a desk, that was a bit hard to judge. Her long, curly auburn hair framed a beautiful face; her full, pouty red lips just cried out to be kissed. The woman had a mind-boggling body, with large breasts that were nearly spilling out of a tight, white, low-cut blouse; narrow waist; and generous hips. All of these assets were nicely packaged in a short, form-hugging women's business suit. As she stepped around her desk, I realized she was shorter than I thought, perhaps five-two. Now I could see that her legs were beautifully proportioned as well, shown off to great effect by four inch spike heels and fishnet black pantyhose.

What is it about fishnet pantyhose that we guys find so sexy? Go figure.

"What a babe!" shouted a voice from my pocket protector.

I'd forgotten about Bik. He seldom said anything, but just kept his eyes open, absorbing all our experiences, a sheltered kid who was in the big city for the first time. For some reason, his outburst irritated me, drawing my attention away from the incarnation of sexuality before me. "Bik," I said, a little annoyance creeping into my voice, "go pay your grandfather a visit."

"But I just talked to him!" he protested.

"Do it anyway," I grumbled. "I can handle this. I'll see you later at the office."

Grumbling, Bik shot out of my pocket protector and disappeared down the stairwell.

"What was that?" the woman asked.

I turned back to her. She really was very sexy. And her face was so beautiful ... right down to the two cute little horns that sat on her forehead just below the hairline.

Right. Succubi have those.

I took a deep breath and tried to calm myself. "That was Bik."

"What's a Bik?"

"A fire giant."

"I see," the succubus said with amusement as she came closer. Her breasts were almost brushing my coveralls before she stopped. She glanced down. "Is that another fire giant in your pocket, or are you just glad to see me?"

"Ahem," I ahemed, taking a step backwards. "Don't know what you're talking about."

She smiled, sweetly I thought, which made her look even more sexy. "Of course not," was all she said.

"I … I'm here to see Asmodeus."

"And who might you be?"

"The name's Minion. Steve Minion."

The young succubus lit up. "I *thought* I recognized you!"

"Pardon?"

"'Flo Does The Super.' It's my favorite movie."

Crap. That damn porn movie. Will it haunt me forever?

"I'm your biggest fan!" she enthused. "I thought you had a great part."

I blushed. "The demon who reviewed the movie thought my part was too small."

"Hmph. What does Bifrons know about such things? They're my specialty, and I'm telling you, your part is, er, was far from small." The succubus came closer to me. Now her breasts were really touching my chest, though the rest of her seemed eighteen inches away.

"Are those real?" I asked in disbelief.

The succubus unbuttoned her suit coat and draped it over a nearby chair. Then she took my right hand and placed it on one of her breasts. It felt full, firm, yet soft. I probed her magnificent mammary a bit more, just to be sure, you know. The breast had the right heft, or so it seemed to me. The nipple was soft but erect beneath my fingers. "Well, it feels real enough," I said, as my face heated up again in embarrassment. My discomfiture, however, didn't leave me wanting to remove my hand. She shifted it to her other breast. "Yep," I concluded, finally, after another complete examination. "That one seems *bona fide* too."

"They're as real as you are, honey," she purred.

"I'm ectoplasm."

She giggled, giving my fingers a squeeze before she released my hand. Reluctantly, I dropped it to my side. "Well, there you go," she said, touching my nose with a soft finger. She grinned impishly, and her blue eyes flashed in amusement.

Blue eyes. I'd never seen a succubus with baby blues. They were beautiful. Blue had always been my favorite eye color, until I'd met Flo that is. Her eyes were a rich, chocolate brown that complemented her chestnut hair.

As I thought about Flo, the receptionist's eyes and hair began to darken.

"A penny for your thoughts," she murmured.

I shook my head.

No. Flo is Flo and this succubus is, well, a succubus. Besides, on her blue and auburn are a better fit.

The female's eyes and hair snapped back to their original colors.

I don't think she was reading my mind. I just think that a succubus, like a chameleon, changes colors to match her surroundings, or in this case, a man's pheromonal preferences.

"I loved you in that movie!" she said in a voice that made Marilyn Monroe by comparison sound like Daffy Duck. "You've got great moves!"

"Thank you, I guess," I replied, not knowing if she was just flattering me but feeling absurdly pleased at the same time.

She took me by the hand and led me to a nearby couch. The succubus sat down with extreme grace, I thought, considering how short her dress was. I didn't even see something I wasn't supposed to see, regrettably, though it was a damn close thing, I tell you. She pulled me down next to her, leaning one leg against mine.

"I'm Lilith, by the way."

"Of course you are."

"No, really!" she said, looking as if she were concerned I thought she was lying. "Mom named all of us Lilith."

"And what's her name?"

"Lilith."

I looked up at the ceiling. "Right." Then I thought about what little I knew of succubi. "I remember now. Your mother is *the* Lilith."

"Yes," she said proudly. "Adam's first. His ex-wife, I guess you could say. Also the universe's first feminist."

"Beg pardon?"

"Well, the way Mom tells it, she refused to submit to Adam, saying she was made out of clay just like him and demanded equal rights." Lilith Jr. bit her lower lip, looking impossibly cute as she did it. "Mom got the boot for that, and Eve got the gig."

"But why did she name all succubi Lilith?"

"It was her own little bit of immortality, I guess."

"But she's already immortal."

"You know what I mean. Anyway, our dad didn't mind, so we're all named after Mom. Makes it easy to remember all your sister's names. Of course, my aunts Mahalath, Agrat Bat Mahlat and Naamah also slept with dad, and my cousins - well, they're my half-sisters as well, but I think of them as my cousins - are succubi too. They're also all named Lilith, for reasons that escape me."

"And how many succubi are there?"

"At last count? I think 666."

"That would fit."

"Yeah," Lilith agreed. "A nice, round number."

I looked at her quizzically. She seemed awfully nice for a succubus. "Your father: he's the archangel Samael, right?"

"The very same. The bad boy of the good guys. You know, for an archangel, he sure slept around a lot."

I cleared my throat. "So it would seem."

"Love him to death, though." She looked a little sad for a moment. "I wish I got to see him more, but the bosses upstairs frown on archangels making social calls in Hell."

"Do tell."

Lilith's wistfulness vanished as abruptly as it had appeared. "But you didn't come to the office to hear about my family tree. How can I help you?"

"Well," I said, reluctantly coming to the purpose of my visit. "I'm on special assignment for Satan, and like I said earlier before we got, uh, distracted, I need to see Asmodeus."

She frowned a little, as if the answer disappointed her. Did she really think I'd come to see her? Not that that seemed like a particularly bad idea to me at the moment. "I don't think he's in, and he's usually scheduled up the wazoo, but let me check his calendar."

She got up from the couch as gracefully as she had sat down then swayed her way toward her desk computer. I was mesmerized by the undulating movement of her hips and the shape of her spectacular ass, which was pretty easy to ogle, since the skirt of her suit was so tight and short it left little to the imagination. As she leaned over her computer, I noticed that resting on her, ah, cheeks was what looked to be a small, pink arrowhead, hanging from a short white tassel.

Then I recognized it for what it was.

Lilith turned to look at me, arching an eyebrow. "Looking for a little tail, Steve?"

Lilith had sensed my eyes on her. Of course, any heterosexual male with or without a pulse would have had his eyes nowhere else at the moment. "Yes, I mean no, I mean, oh hell, can I just see Asmodeus now?"

She leaned up from her computer, giving me a full-on view of her incredible cleavage. "I'm sorry, Steve, but he's out of the office."

"Damn!"

She looked hopefully at me. "Maybe I can help?"

"Well, I don't know. I'm here to discuss some problems we've been having with the HVAC system."

Lilith nodded. "I noticed. I've been cold all day."

"I noticed," I said, remembering the feeling of her erect nipples beneath my fingers.

The succubus seemed to read my thoughts and blushed. She actually blushed! It was charming.

"Well," I said, reluctantly getting off the couch, "tell him I need to see him."

"I schedule all his appointments. I have to tell you, it doesn't look good. It's tight," she said with a mischievous smile, looking down at her skirt and then back up at me, "I mean really, really tight, but I'll fit you in somehow."

She did have a way with words. I gulped. "Thanks. I'd appreciate that."

"I know you would." She walked over to me. "Tell you what, handsome ... "

Handsome? She must be nearsighted.

"Meanwhile, maybe I can give you some background information. I'm Asmodeus's personal assistant. I know more about his comings and goings than he does himself." Lilith embraced me, an odd gesture for someone who had just met me, but what the hell. She was a succubus, after all. "But not here," she whispered in my ear. "I get off soon. Buy me a drink, and I'll let you give me the third degree."

She was still holding me, and I found that without volition my arms had folded around her. My right hand was a little lower than it should be, but she didn't seem to mind. "Uh, okay."

"I'd like to get you out of those coveralls."

"What?"

"I mean," she said, smiling innocently, "they're hardly proper for taking a girl on a date."

"This, ah, this isn't a date."

She pouted, looking cuter than hell, then put a hand on top of mine, the one that had now slipped completely down to her ass. I felt like a stallion in rut. She rubbed her body against mine then stepped away from me. "It better be," she purred, "if you want any useful information."

I shook my head, trying to get it above the testosterone flood in which it was drowning. "Ah, o … okay."

"Good," she said, taking me by the arm and escorting me to the elevator. She pressed the button, and it opened immediately. I stepped inside.

"Meet me at the Kit Kat Club in an hour," she said, as the doors started to close around me, "and don't be late."

Chapter 12

I was hot and bothered on my ride back to the Fifth Circle. Straddling BOOH's neck was like riding a broad-bellied mare, and the constant motion did nothing to alleviate the insistent tightness that I felt below my waist. By the time my friend set me down at my apartment, I was just as horny as when I'd left the hot little redhead.

Climbing the six flights of stairs to my studio apartment, I wondered about Lilith. Was meeting her just a normal encounter, a result of working on the job, or did it have something to do with my careless comment from earlier in the day? Another wave of vertigo passed over me, convincing me that a cold day in Hell was not to be taken lightly.

Hiking up all those stairs hadn't calmed down the old gonads. It was time for a cold shower. I twisted the knob on my front door. "Crap." It didn't open, as usual. I fished for my screwdriver, grumbling. "My own doorknob should work today, of all days." I paused, as something occurred to me. "After all, it is a cold day in Hell."

My nausea returned - somewhat diminished, as I seemed to be getting used to it - but something else happened too. As if by magic, the previously-stuck knob turned. Frowning, I stepped through the door jamb. Inside, roaches were skittering to and fro. They appeared to be staging some form of athletic event. An oval track had been laid out on my floor, and six runners, each wearing a number on its diminutive back, were speeding around it. On my table, where I'd left some sour milk in a bowl, three of the vermin were in a dead heat, swimming the breaststroke from one end of the bowl to the other.

My bed was down and unmade. This was unusual. Mine was a Murphy bed, and normally each morning I'd at the very least fold it up, unmade, into the wall just to get it out of my way. My apartment was not much bigger than a jail cell, and I needed all the floor space I could get when not actually lying down on the Murphy. Most mornings, I even made the bed. Flipping it up into the wall tended to throw the sheets all askew, but I performed this ritual bit of housekeeping anyway. It was a matter of discipline for me, one small act of rebellion, creating order in a chaotic Hell. Not today though. For some reason, on getting up this morning, I must have sensed that today was going to be unusual. Or maybe I had had a particularly bad night; I can't really remember. In any event, I'd left the bed down. This worked just fine for the roaches. A number of them were queued up on my sheet, and one after another, they did impressive dives down to the floor where I'd left my pillow.

Great. Roach Olympics. It would be nice to for just one day live in a roach-free apartment.

Hmmm.

I thought back to meeting Lilith and to my experience with the door. Maybe they had been flukes, but this seemed doubtful. Clearing my throat, I said in a very loud voice, "It will be a cold day in Hell before I come home to an insect-free apartment."

This time, I felt no nausea at all. (I'd always had a pretty strong stomach.) Poppity-pop-pop! Every roach in the place disappeared.

Well, this is an interesting side effect of my current troubles. Perhaps I can use it to my advantage.

Off came my boots, as well as my still-damp coveralls, underwear and socks. The clothes were disgusting - pretty damn smelly - so I threw them into the bathtub and turned on the water.

The water had its typical yellow hue; I never knew if it was the result of rust or uric acid. The smell was terrible, but that was also standard fare for my toilette. At least the water was cold, and judging from my still rigid member, that's exactly what I needed. I stepped in the foul, frigid spray. Between the stench and the forty degree water, my parts finally calmed down.

Wow. So that's the power of a succubus.

I mean, I knew that was *exactly* the power of a succubus. I'd just never been on the receiving end of one's attention. Succubi are usually used for tempting and entrapping men on Earth or enticing but not delivering down here in Hell. The latter was probably the situation I was in now, though Lilith didn't seem the type. And of course, I was in love with Florence and would never even look at another woman.

But did Lilith count as a woman at all? Or even a female? Demons were generally not of any particular sex, though some, such as Uphir and Digger, I tended to think of as male. Then I remembered that succubi, and their male counterparts, incubi, were the exceptions to the rule. Their stock-in-trade was sex, so almost by definition they had to have one. A sex, I mean. A gender. I'd even heard of succubi bearing the children of men or incubi impregnating women. The offspring resulting from these unions were usually pretty hideous creatures, though sometimes they were merely watered-down demons and looked more or less human.

So Lilith was definitely female and, if capable of conceiving a man's child, a woman. Sort of. In any event, she looked like all woman to me, except for the tail and horns of course. Any time I spent with her was very dangerous, a threat to my already-strained relationship with Flo.

Flo. I loved Flo, of that I was sure.

I needed to hold onto that thought. It wasn't going to be easy, though, because, well, I was dealing with a succubus, a real pro. Surely if Lilith put her mind to it, no male, in love with someone else or not, would be capable of resisting her.

Yet she was a puzzle. Lilith was an odd combination of the searingly sexy and the kinda sweet. Her blue eyes gave her an innocent quality that made her sultriness even more alluring, at least to me. That would make sense, of course. In the same way Lilith's eyes started to turn brown when I began thinking of Florence, this sexual chameleon's personality might also adjust automatically to whatever her prey found attractive in a woman. And yet, her innocence and kindness didn't seem like an act. I had always considered myself a good judge of character, at least on Earth. I'd been fooled many times in Hell, though mostly by Satan or Beelzebub. Seldom had a demon put one over on me, and after all, a succubus was nothing more than a demon, one that specialized in seduction and fornication.

Hey. There are worse demonic specialties to have.

Were Lilith's friendliness and apparent desire to help just an elaborate put-on? I wondered. Her dad was an archangel, and even though he had a checkered past, Samael was accounted one of the good guys, which meant that, genetically at least, Lilith and her 665 sisters and cousins had some good in them. Yet my Lilith - well, not mine, but the only one I knew - had probably spent most of her life in Hell, so nurture could trump nature here, assuming nurture was a factor at all in the Netherworld.

In the final analysis, though, was anyone, other than the prime movers in this eternal morality play, completely good or completely evil? I had often pondered this. Even those that made it to Heaven couldn't have had souls of unalloyed good.

They just must have had more points in the nice column than the naughty one. By the same token, I knew from personal experience that there were a lot of pretty good people in Hell, folks like Pinkerton, Braille, Orson and Tesla.

I snapped out of my reverie as my body started to shake from the frigid waters. My gag reflex was starting to react to the smell. Time for another magic incantation. "It will be a cold day in Hell before I get another decent shower, with plenty of hot, clean water … and fresh soap!" I added as an afterthought, noticing that again there was no nausea. I was definitely getting my sea legs.

Bibbidi-Bobbidi-Boo.

The water was as clean as that from the Adirondacks. I adjusted the hot water knob and got the temperature just to my liking then reached for the fresh bar of soap, humming as I lathered up. I'd forgotten the shampoo but didn't want to press my luck. I used the soap to clean my hair. Fortunately, or unfortunately I suppose, I didn't have much hair to wash. As I rinsed out my thin mane, a truly seditious thought came to me. Did I dare try it? Satan and Beezy might put up with me getting a break on the shower, but what I had in mind could get me in real trouble.

Screw it. I'm going for it.

"Ahem," I said, clearing my throat. I wanted to get this just right. "It will be a cold day in Hell before I have hair like I had in my twenties … FOREVER!" I shouted triumphantly.

I both felt and heard the hair spring out of my scalp. *Man! This is just too good to be true.*

MINION! Satan's voice yelled in my head.

"Shit, shit, shit!" *Busted.*

A blast of fire seared off the new hair on my scalp. I cowered under the faucet as I put out the flames, hoping the Earl of Hell wouldn't do anything else to me. After a few minutes of my cowering, without anything else happening, I grabbed the soap and scrubbed out the clothes that were wadded in the back of the tub, rung them out, and hung them over the rod of the shower curtain to dry.

As I was toweling off, I glanced at myself in the mirror. My hair had grown back.

Inside my brain, Satan was grumbling.

I headed into my closet to look for some clothes to wear for my date - that is meeting - with Lilith. *Then it's true. This cold day in Hell thing is a real problem for the big guy. He's not overreacting, he's not faking it, and he's not involved.*

I never really had Satan on my list of suspects. While he'd lied to me more times than I could count, this time I was pretty sure the problem with the HVAC system was not of his making. Motive, means, opportunity. He had the means and opportunity, he had a barrel of each in fact, but he had no motive. The prospect of a cold day in Hell was no picnic for him. Then again, it wouldn't be for anyone here, on Earth or in Heaven.

I had no idea how long I'd be able to keep my hair. Adding "forever" to my phrasing gave me some hope that my beautiful new brown locks would stay full, but I'm sure Satan would think of some way to take them from me eventually. For now, I was going to enjoy it. First, though, I had to find something to wear.

The last time I was in this situation, when I needed some appropriate attire to go on a couple of dates with Flo, Satan had obliged me first with a tuxedo and then with a white dinner jacket. No such luck tonight, though. All I had were my clown suit, mauve hot pants and white puffy shirt. I thought briefly about "cold daying" my way to a nice outfit, but Satan was already pissed off at me, and I didn't want to make things worse. With a sigh, I slipped on the shorts, shirt, some reasonably clean yellow socks and my work boots.

At least my hair looked good, I thought, as I ran a comb through it. My locks were still damp, but I'd had wonderful hair in my youth. As it dried, my tresses would fall into a fairly good-looking do on their own.

On my way out the door, I saw my full ensemble in the cracked, yellowed full-length mirror mounted on the back of my front door. The image reminded me vaguely of a brightly-colored duck.

I had a few minutes before I needed to meet Lilith, so I swung by the office to see how Orson was getting along with Edison and the deluge of work orders. I opened the door. Remarkably it didn't fight me, as it did most of the time, but swung right open.

No one was inside. Orson and his new assistant must have been off trying to fix something. Bik had not yet returned from his visit to Surtr, which was fine by me. My puffy shirt didn't have a pocket, and I didn't want him coming with me anyway. The fewer people who knew about this little rendezvous, the better.

The mountain of work orders had been beaten into submission, which surprised me, since I didn't think I'd been gone that long. Still, time being a bit screwy in Hell, I knew my foray up to the realm of Asmodeus didn't necessarily have to sync with Orson's activities. Ten new piles of work orders were neatly stacked in a corner of the trailer. I rifled through a small stack on my desk. Yep, all were top priority items. Beside the pile was a memo from Orson, with a work order paper clipped to it.

HELL'S OFFICE OF THE INTERIOR

"HOTI: We die to serve ... "

Plant Department

MEMORANDUM

TO: Steve Minion, Hell's Super
FROM: Orson Welles, Assistant to Hell's Super
DATE: Whenever
RE: HOTI Form ∞3971\PDYFF 666-327\?///WOE # ∞8911873987

This is a report on the successful resolution of **WOE # ∞8911873987**, to wit, "Replace burnt-out bulb on sign above Hell's Escalator."

After your departure to Lustland, I instructed my new assistant, Mr. Thomas Alva Edison, in the subtleties of Plant Department Work Order triage. Owing to the large number of recently-received service requests, sorting them into essential vs. non-essential was a not insignificant undertaking. In the interest of time, I directed Edison to gather those work orders closest to your wire inbox and give them to me for my perusal, while he stacked as many of the remaining ones that would fit in the corner of our office. A plethora of paperwork still remained ...

Plethora? A pretty high-fallutin' word to put in a memo. I read on.

... These we placed on the curb outside. (They were gone when we later exited the trailer, though they may very well be recycled and appear once again through the pneumatic tube system.)

Top priority, naturellement, was the burnt-out fixture atop the Gates of Hell. I resolved to take the long ladder, but when BP found out that - as assistant - he had to carry it, he insisted we could manage with the painter's ladder. I'm sure you recall how inadequate to the task that particular handyman tool-of-the-trade is. Nonetheless, I acquiesced, knowing what the outcome would be.

After procuring a replacement bulb from Parts, where Edison was introduced to Dora (she wasn't impressed), we caught the elevator up to Gates Level.

The remainder of the job was a veritable rerun of the time you and I replaced a bulb in the sign using only the painter's ladder. When BP found out that, in order to reach the burnt-out bulb, I would have to stand on his shoulders while he stood on the top step of the ladder, his outpouring of profanity was so loud St. Peter came over and pummeled him on the head with a ruler. My appropriately chastened assistant climbed the ladder. Then I stepped up behind him and got on his shoulders. I was pretty sure my four hundred pounds of ectoplasm would be much harder for him to bear than your weight was on my own shoulders, but putting forth an Herculean effort, BP managed to support me. I frankly did not think him capable of the deed. I give him points for that.

The bulb was replaced posthaste, then I made a point to destabilize the ladder, so that it, BP and I fell. As planned, I landed squarely on top of him. I believe, judging from the multiple pops I heard, that all of BP's limbs dislocated from the impact of my bulk on his more modestly-proportioned frame. This was great fun for me, though not for my best boy. Still, a proper orientation is important for a new employee, and there's nothing like a modicum of pain to drive home a point. I think that in future Edison won't argue with me when I give an instruction.

In short, the entire service call was a rousing success, BP was appropriately chastened and I was greatly amused.

I look forward to our next order, which will be **WOE # ∞8911874123**, Mussolini's sewing machine.

xc: Beelzebub, Lord of the Flies

Jeez. What a blowhard.
I knew requiring Orson to file written reports would be a mistake. He enjoyed the written word way too much. It took me almost as long to read his report as it would have to replace the bulb myself.
I left the office, whistled for BOOH, and made my way to the Kit Kat Club.

Chapter 13

The Kit Kat Club was in much better repair than most establishments in Hell, probably because its primary customers were devils and demons. The sidewalk in front of the club was, surprisingly, neither cracked nor chipped. The windows of the Kit Kat were jet black to give its diabolical customers some privacy from the damned that might walk by. Those windows gave the place a dark anonymity as well as a cool vibe that Hell's nightspots generally lacked. The entrance did not have an awning. Instead, the doors were framed by neon figures of voluptuous women dressed in sexy kitten outfits. That entrance clearly wasn't anonymous, but it *was* eponymous, so that was okay.

I hopped off BOOH's shoulders. From the darkness erupted a series of catcalls - my ridiculous outfit was drawing some attention - but I walked with as much dignity as possible to the club's entrance and opened the door. Stepping over the threshold, I heard piano music in the background; surprisingly, it was in tune. I wasn't sure, as a human, that I would be allowed to stay, but the bouncer just gave me the once-over and motioned me to the bar. Lilith must have gotten permission for my presence in the club; there was no other good explanation. The bar was easily thirty feet long and made of a rich mahogany that had been polished to a fine sheen. Yep. Devils and demons certainly had classier places to hang out than did the damned.

Lilith was waiting for me, perched gracefully on a barstool that showed off her legs to good effect. She had had time to change and was now in a short red strapless dress, held up only by her enormous breasts. I had always been a breast man, though, so a substantial rack, well on display, was fine by me. I found it titillating.

Sorry. Couldn't resist.

Lilith's dress seemed to be made mostly of tinsel, reminding me of an X-rated flapper outfit. The look worked for her; she was positively sizzling with sex appeal, and my body responded predictably. My hot pants probably looked like I had more than a diminutive fire giant in there. Felt kind of like the great white whale.

"Hello, Steve," Lilith said in a sultry voice, though her blue eyes flashed in surprise. "That's some outfit. A puffy shirt?"

"Sorry. Satan doesn't allow me much of a wardrobe."

The sexy little succubus stroked my arm. "Well, it's the thought that counts. Besides, the hot pants show off your legs … and that great ass of yours. And, I see," noticing Moby, "something else that looks pretty succulent."

"Why is it," I said with a gulp, "that I always find myself blushing when I'm around you?"

Lilith pulled me into the chair next to her and gave a big hug to my arm. I almost lost it somewhere in her cleavage. "I can make anyone blush. It's one of the things we succubi are good at. You know," she said, running her hands through my thick mane of hair, "I didn't notice before how gorgeous your hair is."

"It needed a good shampooing," I said in embarrassment. "I just washed it."

"Well, I *love* it," she said, stroking it again.

"Ah." The normally facile-tongued Steve Minion was stumbling all over himself. "Would you like something to drink while we talk?"

"Yes, please."

"Okay, what do you want?" I gestured for the bartender, a young demon wearing a polo shirt with the Kit Kat logo on it.

"A black Russian." She looked around the bar then turned to me. "But I don't see one, so you'll do fine."

"Good one," I chuckled, despite myself. "To drink?"

Lilith laughed. She was having a very good time at my expense. "I'd like a crackhead slammer."

"A what?"

"Cinnamon schnapps, peppermint schnapps and Dr. Pepper."

"Yuck," I said, grimacing. "That sounds nasty."

The voluptuous redhead shrugged, setting her breasts to jiggling. I was mesmerized. "An acquired taste, I suppose, but it has cinnamon in it, and that's my favorite flavor. What do you want, Steve?"

"Oh, just some club soda, I guess."

"Sure about that?" she asked, eyebrow raised.

I could have had anything to drink. Drinking on the job wasn't strictly prohibited. Besides, no one except Florence Nightingale could get drunk in Hell, though there might have been others. Maybe some of the magical creatures or mythical beings, like BOOH or Charon, could too. I didn't know for sure, though it seemed to me that BOOH had a little buzz going after he had his two gallons of Scotch at Pinkerton's workshop. On reflection, I decided that Charon probably could not. Since he's a skeleton, any booze he drunk would likely flow right out of him. "Hey, barkeep. Bring me a drink and a mop."

I looked to the bartender. "A crackhead slammer for the lady and a club soda for me."

"Sure thing, Daddy Warbucks."

"Daddy Warbucks?" I said to Lilith.

"He thinks you're a cheapskate."

"Oh."

"You're going to regret your drink order," Lilith said.

"Why?"

"Take a look."

The demon rapidly put together Lilith's slammer, then took a second highball glass and filled it with tap water. In the tray that held maraschino cherries, limes, lemon twists and olives, there was a tiny demon tied to a swizzle stick. The bartender picked up the demon and placed him in the water. After a few seconds of the little guy doing something unspeakable in the glass, the bartender removed him, added some ice then brought both drinks over to us.

Mine certainly had lots of bubbles now. "I see what you mean."

Lilith laughed. "Warned you."

"That's okay," I said, pushing the glass some distance away from me. "I wasn't really thirsty anyway."

"You should have gotten a crackhead slammer," she said, sipping at her drink through a straw. "They're delicious."

"If you say so, though schnapps and Dr. Pepper have never been at the top of my list."

As we sat together, Lilith seemed incapable of keeping her hands off me. She was constantly running her fingers along my arm, or up my leg, occasionally quite far up, as if she wanted to do some major exploration of my privates. Gently, I took her adventurous hand and held it in mine.

"Aw, that's sweet," she said. "No one's held my hand in ages. Other parts of me, sure, but not my hand." She kissed me on the cheek.

And that tightening between my legs got worse.

We sat quietly for a few minutes, Lilith looking thoughtful as she sipped on her drink, me just enjoying the company of a beautiful woman, even if she was a demonic one. "They're cute," I said aloud.

Lilith's impossibly blue eyes opened wide. "What?"

"Your little horns. I've never seen a devil or demon that had cute horns."

A slight frown briefly marred her otherwise perfect features. "Who," she said.

"Beg pardon."

"A devil or demon 'who' had cute horns, not 'that' had cute horns. I'm a person, you know, not a piece of furniture."

"Sorry," I said, genuinely contrite. "I didn't mean to objectify you."

Lilith inhaled, and her swelling breasts almost made the top of her dress explode. "I don't mind that, at least sexually. You know, 'what a piece of ass!' 'great tits!' 'what a tight … '"

"I get it!" I said hurriedly.

"Okay. Just remember though, I'm a person, like you, with feelings and everything."

"I'm sorry, Lilith. I didn't mean to imply otherwise."

The frown faded, and she gave me a smooch on the lips. "That's okay. All is forgiven. Now, what was that about my horns?"

My face burned with embarrassment from my faux pas, but I managed to look her in the eyes. "I...I said they're cute."

"Thanks. Would you like to touch them?"

"May I?"

She smiled, and I noticed her dimples for the first time. "Why sure. Here." Lilith took my hands and placed them on her horns, where they poked from her fair skin just below her hairline.

They were very soft. I was expecting something hard, but they were as soft as the nipples of her breasts. "Nice," I exhaled softly then found myself stroking her auburn hair.

Lilith was practically purring at my touch. "No," she protested, as I forced myself to remove my hand. "Don't stop."

"Have to," I said with a gulp. "While I still can. Uh, Lilith, could I ask you something?"

"Sure, Steve," she said huskily. "Anything."

"Would you ... would you," I paused, not sure this was what I wanted to ask. "Would you check something for me on Asmodeus's calendar?" I said with a rush.

"Oh," she said, a little crestfallen. I doubt that was what she had been expecting. "I don't know. I'm not supposed to. I'm his assistant, and I try to respect his privacy." She chewed on her lower lip for a second then looked at me. "But you're doing a job for Lord Satan himself, aren't you?"

"Yes, I am."

"Then I suppose I have to. Besides, I said I'd help, and I'm a succubus of my word. What do you want to know?"

"I need to find out what Asmodeus has been up to the past couple of days." Motive, means, opportunity. Perhaps with his calendar, I could see if he had an alibi.

Lilith took out an iPhone. "I haven't seen much of my boss recently, but let me check his Outlook calendar."

"You actually can get a signal down here?" I'd never been able to get a cell signal I could depend on, which was why Orson and I had to do so much via the pneumatic tubes or the landline phone system.

"Sure. I have four bars. Don't you?"

I ground my teeth. "No, but I'm one of the damned, remember."

"Does that affect cell service? Well, never mind. Now let me see." Lilith frowned at her phone. Yep, she was adorable and sexy at the same time. "Well, there's not much here. A couple of days ago, he had a few appointments in the office, but all of yesterday and some of today, there was a big block of time set aside. It was marked private."

"What does that mean?" I asked.

"It means he made his own appointment and set it to private. He probably didn't want anyone to know what he was doing then."

Hmm. If the HVAC system was indeed sabotaged, and I was pretty sure at this point that was exactly what happened, Asmodeus could have done it during that private appointment. This prince of Hell had no alibi, or at least, his calendar didn't give him one.

"And you have no idea what he was doing during that period?"

"No, but I can take a guess."

"What?"

Lilith shrugged, and I was again lost for a moment in the wonder of her jiggling breasts. When I came out of the spell, I heard her say, "He *is* the Lord of Lust, you know. Being in the sack with someone is what he does with most of his private appointments."

"Makes sense."

"He's a real rake. Just *loves* the ladies, and he's made a conquest out of almost every female down here."

I looked at Lilith. "In ... including you?" I said, hoping the question didn't offend her.

"Well, sure. I'm a succubus. Besides, how do you think I got my job?" She grinned, but she also blushed a little.

"He's the Lord of Lust," I said, trying to change the focus of the conversation. "I know he specializes in lust, but is it just sexual lust?"

Lilith took another sip of her crackhead slammer. "What do you mean?"

"Well, is lust for power a part of his job portfolio?"

"Yeah, he likes that too. But many of the Princes have a piece of that, Mammon for instance. Sexual lust, though, is the main focus of my boss, so he was probably with a skirt yesterday."

I scratched my chin in thought. Just because Lilith didn't know where Asmodeus had been yesterday didn't necessarily mean he had no alibi. "I really have to talk with your boss in person."

"That will be hard to do. It sometimes takes me a week or two to get someone in to see him. Wait!" she said, brightening. "I know! In a little while, Asmodeus is going to hold a cocktail party in his penthouse above the office. You can be my date!"

"Really?" I asked, surprised. "You'd do that for me?"

"Yes, but only on one condition. Wait, make that two."

"Ah." I had a bad feeling, like I was being trapped into something, but I really needed to talk to him. "What are they?"

"Well, one, find a nicer outfit, like a tuxedo or something. This is a black tie affair, and I can't take you in there looking like that, no matter how much I like your legs."

"That won't be easy, but I'll find a way. Okay. What's the second condition?"

She dimpled again. "I want a kiss."

"What?"

"You *do* know what a kiss is, don't you?"

"Well, of course I do." I thought about Flo, and felt a pang of guilt. Still, a job was a job. "Okay, but not here."

Lilith tossed back the rest of her drink, left some bills on the bar and slipped off her barstool.

The succubus took me by the hand. "Outside, then."

"But ... "

"No buts. That's the deal," she said and, still holding my hand, led me outside.

The streets were dark and deserted. We walked a few yards down the sidewalk then Lilith turned to me. "Well?"

I gulped, leaned over, and kissed her on the cheek.

She frowned. "Not like that. I meant a kiss. A real kiss. Like this."

Lilith pulled my head down to her level and planted a big one on me. At first, I struggled, but I found my lips yielding to hers. As her tongue entered my mouth, followed with scant hesitation by mine into hers, I noticed that her breath was very sweet, with a faint taste of cinnamon.

It was a great kiss. Lilith took my hand and placed it on one of her breasts, and my fingers were once again off exploring her mountains and the valley between. I felt her own hand seek and find the great white whale.

Help! I think I'm drowning! But another part of my brain, the primal part was screaming, *Do it!*

One thought saved me. Unbidden, an image of Flo entered my mind. Beautiful, kind Flo, who currently wouldn't give me the time of day. Yet I loved her. I knew that.

It took all my will to pull away from Lilith's embrace. I even kissed her once more, but it was tender instead of passionate. "That was ... that was wonderful, but I have to go now."

Lilith gasped. "Steve! I haven't been kissed like that in a long time. Please stay," she said, putting my hand on her breast again. I gave it a tender squeeze and let go.

"I really have to leave, but, but I'll see you soon."

She looked at me in astonishment. "No one has ever said no to me before."

"Well," I said with a gentle smile. "You're not easy to say no to."

"I ... I'm impressed," she said. "Maybe even a little stunned."

"I'm a bit surprised myself," though I knew it had been the right thing to do. "Listen, Lilith, I had a wonderful time, but I have some work I must do before the reception."

Lilith nodded and started to walk back to the bar. Then she turned. "You know you don't have to act with me Steve. You don't have to say anything and you don't have to do anything."

"Lilith ... "

"Oh, maybe just whistle," Lilith said. "You know how to whistle, don't you, Steve?"

"Don't."

"You just put your lips together and ... blow."

"Jeez! Does everyone in Hell know 'To Have and Have Not?'" I frowned.

Lilith reacted as if I'd slapped her. "I ... I thought it was your favorite movie!" A discouraged succubus, all five feet two inches of her, looked at me with a pout. "You're just toying with me. You probably don't even like me." Her lower lip began to quiver.

Oh no! I've made her cry. I stepped closer and embraced her warmly. Lilith clung to me like a little child. She really seemed sweet, and I kissed her on one of her horns. "Don't worry about the movie. It's fine. And ... and I like you a lot."

"You do?" she sniffed, turning blue Bambi eyes on me.

"Yeah," I said with a smile. "I don't just pretend to like people. I either do or I don't, and I never learned how to flirt or be coy or anything like that. I'm just not a love 'em and leave 'em sort."

"You don't? You aren't?"

"No, and I promise to whistle for you, at you, and use any other conjunction concerning you, as appropriate, if I need you."

"Really?"

"Yeah, kid," I said giving her a final hug. "Run on inside. Now, when and where shall I meet you for the reception?"

"How about the lobby of Corporate? Three hours?"

"Fine. Here's looking at you, kid," I said, thinking of another Bogart film I loved.

"See you in a while, Steve." She sniffed a final time, smiled demurely and slipped back inside the Kit Kat Club.

As soon as she disappeared, a winged giant dropped to the ground beside me. BOOH stood on the pavement, his shoulders moving up and down convulsively, a rapid exhalation of fetid breath accompanying his silent laughter.

"Don't. Don't say a word," I grumbled, as I climbed on his shoulders. "Just take me down to see Mammon on Four. And stop laughing at me!"

Chapter 14

Usually when BOOH and I flew through one of the orifices separating one level of Hell from another, I was aware of the heat coming from the molten mass of a Circle's interior. The supernatural swiftness of my friend's beating wings, though, kept the air temperature more than tolerable. Besides, we were usually through in the blink of an eye, and intense heat experienced over the course of a single second could be borne by anyone, especially a damned soul. To get to Mammon's domain on Four, we had to pass through two levels, so that would be two blinks, but still not very important.

You would think, also, with the progressive cooling of Hades, due to the failure of the HVAC system, that even the interiors of the circles in Hell would be a little cooler than normal. Yet despite the rapidly dropping temperatures, despite the ceiling fan effect of BOOH's wings, I felt hot, really hot.

I suspected it had nothing to do with the ambient temperature of the Netherworld, but instead with the voluptuous redhead I'd just left. The burning between my legs was predictable, if troubling, but even my skin felt all prickly with heat. I was sweating, unusual for one in my circumstances (Down here, we dead folks are usually not accorded the luxury of the body's natural cooling system, unless it results in uncomfortably wet clothes and objectionable body odor.) I also felt a bit lightheaded.

Never had I experienced such animal attraction for a woman. Not even for Florence Nightingale, I had to admit, who was the most beautiful woman, physically and spiritually, I'd ever known. I knew in my heart that my feelings for Flo were profound, that they were true love, and much more meaningful than the raw lust I felt for Lilith.

Yet that lust was pretty damn powerful too. What's more, I actually liked Lilith. My reflexive cynicism was screaming at me that I was being set up, that Lilith wasn't really attracted to me. This was all caused by my stupid "cold day in Hell" comment, I was sure. She probably wouldn't give me the time of day otherwise. Besides, she was the consummate sexual being; she was a professional. It's what she did for a living, probably many times a day.

And yet ... she seemed genuinely troubled when I pulled away from her. That could simply have been her pride. I doubted a succubus was used to being rejected. On the other hand, there could have been more to it than that.

What's that line from "Macbeth?" Oh, yeah, *"fair is foul, and foul is fair."*

I glanced down at the giant critter who was carrying me. BOOH was certainly foul, foul looking and foul smelling, but he was beautiful on the inside. And Satan, in his Lucifer aspect, was undeniably fair on the outside, while masking the most evil soul in the universe. Hell was the realm of deception, but at least in the case of Flo, the external and the internal matched. She looked like a saint, well, a really sexy one, on the outside, and she was even more beautiful on the inside.

What, then, to make of Lilith, the offspring of a demon and an archangel? Outside: pretty obvious. *But what about under the sheets?* I decided that was a bad though appropriate metaphor in this case. Still, I wondered if she was as nice beneath the surface as she seemed to be.

This was all very confusing. I needed some time to pull myself together, so I asked BOOH to fly around Level Four for a bit. He gave me a quick grand tour, soaring high above the major landmarks of the Circle.

Most of Level Four is a high plain, dry, deserted. It's where people who are afraid of the great outdoors spend Eternity. Four, as I've said before, also has its share of fire pits, but they were burning so low as we flew above them that they barely illuminated the distant Sea of Thorns.

We soared over a smoldering volcano. This one wasn't as dependable as Old Dependable, but it was pretty dependable. In fact, that was its name: Pretty Dependable. Usually you could count on it erupting, but right now, the volcano wasn't living up to its moniker. A bit of dark smoke floated ominously from the summit, but Pretty Dependable looked more like a burnt-out stogie than a dispenser of molten lava. We left the mountain and headed back to the Plains.

The High Plains of Level Four seemed to stretch to infinity, a dusty brown sea of anonymity. While agoraphobics and raging extroverts were down there somewhere, you couldn't see them from my vantage point. Personally, I had never been afraid of the great outdoors. I wasn't much of a people person either. Don't get me wrong. People were fine, but like most academics, I'd always been a bit of an introvert. For these reasons, the Plains struck me as serene, and they tended to have a calming effect on me, even now.

BOOH seemed to instinctively understand this - perhaps he could feel my grip loosening on the tufts of fur beneath his ears - so he just hovered above the Plains, letting me get my fill of the landscape's arid desolation. I took a deep breath and exhaled deeply, felt the tension and heat leave my body. In another minute, I was back to normal.

Good old BOOH. What a friend.

Shoving thoughts of Lilith - and Flo - from my brain, I directed BOOH to the heart of Greed in Hell.

Far from the Great Plains flowed a muddy river. To the north of the river was a shining city, built atop seven hills. Unlike most of the architecture in Hell, which looked like cast-off scenery from the back lot at Universal, the City of Mammon was resplendent in classical architecture.

The home of Greed was, to my mind, what classical Rome must have looked like around 100 AD, or CE to be politically correct. I'd been to Rome once in my lifetime and seen the ruined husks of its Classical period, such as the Coliseum and the Domus Augustana on the Palatine Hill. Full-sized replicas of them were below me now, and these were no ruins, but complete structures made entirely of gold.

In fact, everything in this dead ringer for Classical Rome was created out of gold. That's, presumably, what made it a shining city.

I directed BOOH toward what, on Earth, would have been called the Pantheon. Here, it was Mammon's center of power.

The original Pantheon was first built and dedicated in 27 BC/BCE. A fire took it out in 80 AD/CE, so the Romans had to rebuild it in the year 126. Originally, the building was dedicated to the worship of the Roman Pantheon of gods, which was a knockoff of the Greek one, as I'm sure you know, but as Christianity pushed out the old deities, the structure became a Catholic Church. The Pantheon was something of an engineering marvel. At the time of my death, the huge structure still had the world's largest unreinforced concrete dome, an astonishing 142 feet in diameter.

Like the rest of the city, Hell's version of the Pantheon was made entirely of gold. This defied the physical laws of the universe. No gold dome 142 feet in diameter could possibly exist, but since Hell's management didn't give a crap about the physical laws of the universe, the span was gold. This Pantheon, like the original back on Earth, was in a way also a house of worship. And the god worshipped here was very old: Mammon.

I don't know what's been around the longest, lust or greed or gluttony. Probably gluttony, because the early humans must have chowed down mightily whenever they were lucky enough to take down a mastodon or something. I can easily picture in my mind an overstuffed caveman, with a bellyful of beastie, groaning in the corner of his cave. Lust, like gluttony, is probably older than greed. A man's gotta eat, but after that, he's going to be looking for something to screw. And money didn't come along until tens of thousands of years later; I think they had to invent pockets first. On the other hand, greed isn't just about money. You can be greedy about lots of things. Hoarders, for example, can hang onto old magazines or rocks or any stupid thing you can imagine, so avarice has probably been around for longer than I'm giving it credit. So the jury's still out on which of the three is the oldest, but certainly Mammon has been around for a long time.

I had never met this particular prince of Hell. From what I'd been told, he didn't get out of his palace very often. That's why I was there, to confirm that fact. If Mammon had an alibi, some kind of witness who could vouch for the devil's presence over the past day or two, I could eliminate at least one of my suspects.

A long line of supplicants, carrying weighty bags or chests on their backs or dragging them behind them, stood before the Palace of Mammon. BOOH dropped me at the end of the line, and I queued up and looked at everyone there. Yep, except for me, everyone was schlepping something: a burlap bag, full to bursting, or a strongbox, similar to what a pirate might bury his treasure in or a young maid might use as a hope chest. Most of the people in line were in ripped and tawdry clothing. There was the occasional finely-tailored three piece suit, but it was usually badly frayed.

In the air was the scent of menthol and tobacco. I looked up the line. A fog of cigarette smoke was rising from a lizard with bleached blonde hair, leopard print blouse and skirt. Attached to her ankle were a weighty chain and chest. In addition to this Jacob Marley fashion accessory, the old hag was lugging a Samsonite suitcase. I knew her. It was Dora, head of Parts, and a frequent associate. She of course wasn't really a lizard. Dora just had dry and wrinkled skin, a result of a lifetime of smoking and a retirement under the blistering rays of the Floridian sun.

"Excuse me," I said to the people between me and her, "do you mind if I cut in line? That's a friend of mine."

No one seemed to mind. If anything, they expressed relief to be delayed from whatever punishment awaited them inside. I sidled up to Dora. She was arguing vehemently with a short, round man in black suit and dented top hat, sporting a white, handlebar mustache, carrying a walking stick and dragging a footlocker behind him. He spoke with a pronounced English accent and reminded me of the real estate magnate on the Monopoly cards.

"Come here often?" I said to Dora.

Surprised at hearing a familiar voice, she stopped the verbal chewing out she was giving the man. "Steve? What are you doing here?" She looked at my clothes. "Stupid outfit."

"I could say the same about yours," was my mild reply. "So who's the Brit?"

"He's not British. He's from Jersey, born and raised."

"But that's Briti ... "

"Don't be an idiot," Dora groused. "You're as American as I am. I meant Joisey, as in New Jersey, not Old Jersey. Sheesh."

I knew what she meant; I was just playing dumb. Dora often pulls my chain, but generally I have to be nice to her, since I'm so reliant on her parts, that is, her department, not her privates, which would be gross. Anyway, this seemed like a safe way to irritate her. "Come here often?" I repeated.

Dora sighed. "More often than I care to, but this is the center of Greed in Hell, and periodically I'm required to make the pilgrimage."

"But what about Parts?"

"I have my 'back in a minute' sign hanging on my door."

I just hoped Orson didn't need anything from her. Her 'minute' was likely to take a couple of hours.

"You still haven't answered my other question. Who is that guy?"

"That's George, my fourth husband. You've heard me mention him. GEORGE!" she yelled, and the fellow turned around. "I'd like you to meet Steve Minion, Hell's Super."

I held out my hand to shake, but the old fellow looked as if I was offering him a dead mackerel. Dora elbowed him in the gut and reluctantly he shook with me. "Charmed," he said then turned his back on the both of us. Obviously he wasn't.

Dora grumbled. "I can't stand that superior old bastard. He grew up in Atlantic City, but eventually became an investment banker for Lloyd's of London. He developed that affected English accent. Even in death he won't abandon it."

"See him often?"

She shrugged. "Not if I can help it. It's funny though. Almost every time I have to come up to see Mammon, I'm in line next to George."

"Yeah," I murmured. "Funny. Hell's like that."

"No shit."

"What were you two arguing about?"

"Anything and everything, just like back on Earth during our sucky marriage. If I never saw him again, it would be too soon. Fat chance, though," she said, chewing on her lower lip. How she could do that and inhale cigarette smoke at the same time seemed like a magic trick to me.

"So what's in your suitcase?"

"Cigarettes," she grumbled, glowering at me. "The non-menthol kind."

"I thought you couldn't get regular cigarettes."

"I can get them alright," she said, popping open the latches to reveal a suitcase full of Camels and Lucky Strikes. "I just can't smoke them."

"But how do you get them?"

"I trade parts for them."

"From the department inventory?" I gasped, scandalized. That helped explain why she was "fresh out" of so many things when I needed them. That and her hoarder sensibilities. Not to mention her dishonesty and general orneriness.

Dora looked longingly at her stash. "God, I'd walk a mile for a Camel. Remember that?"

"Yeah, I do." I was old enough to remember the cigarette ads.

"And an LSMFT to you, too," she added with a sigh.

"Pardon?"

"'Lucky Strike Means Fine Tobacco.'"

"I'd forgotten that one."

"Well, Luckies were my brand."

"So, what are you doing with a suitcase full of cigarettes you aren't allowed to smoke?"

Dora used a dying butt to light a new Kool. "You'll see." And then she said no more.

As the line shortened, I could read the inscription above the entrance to the Palace of Mammon. The letters, in the sharp strokes of the Latin you'd find on many an old building back on Earth, said, "Agrippa argentum vestrum." It looked like Latin, and I was fluent in Latin, but I couldn't quite make sense of the words.

"What does that mean?" I asked Dora.

She shrugged. "Nothing really. It's a play on words. Agrippa built the original Pantheon."

"That's right," I said, slapping myself on the forehead. "I used to know that."

"Most of us translate it as 'I grippa your money.' That is what Mammon does, you know."

"That's an awful pun."

"Yeah, I know. Devils seem to have no sense of humor."

"Agreed. And that sounds more Sicilian than Latin."

"You're right about that."

The line moved slowly. Dora, purposely ignoring George, whose very presence seemed to cause her pain, and I talked about little things. Close to the entrance, a devil, dressed like a Roman centurion, stood guard. He eyed the supplicants carefully, making each one stand next to a sign that said, "You have to be this tall to enter the ride."

Being pretty good at estimating length - after all, I'm Hell's Super, so it's part of the job - I figured the height requirement to be a little less than five feet. Every once in a while, the centurion devil would cull a height-impaired individual from the herd and send him to another line off to one side, where a centuri-demon operated a rack. As he strapped the shorties into the torture device and proceeded to stretch them, he would mumble at them incessantly, doing a truly terrible Peter Lorre impression the whole time. It took very little time to do the stretching - ectoplasm is more malleable than the real thing - though the process looked pretty painful. Soon, much taller, though admittedly thinner, damned souls were unstrapped from the rack, where they staggered, dragging their burdens behind them, to the back of the line. I imagined that the stretch was only good this one time, and that whenever they returned, they'd have to endure the same ordeal.

As I stepped between the columns supporting the portico, I got stopped by the centurion devil at the entrance. "Where's your stash?"

"Sin of Pride," I said, pointing at my chest.

He nodded. "Okay, that explains it, but what are you doing here, then?"

"Need to see Mammon."

The devil frowned, and pulled his sword from its scabbard. It morphed into a pitchfork and he pointed it toward me. "I don't know about that. He usually only sees the Greedy."

"I understand of course," I said, trying my best to be polite, always a good policy with devils, especially armed ones, though not that easy to do - they offend easily. "But I'm on a special assignment from Lord Satan, so I think he'll make an exception."

The devil looked at me from side to side, trying to size me up. "I don't recognize you. Who are you?"

"Minion's the name, Steve Minion."

"Minion, huh?" said the devil, nodding again. "I know about you. Hell's Super, right?"

"Right."

"How come I've never seen you before?"

I gestured at the building behind him. "Well, Mammon's palace is modeled after the original Pantheon back on Earth, right?"

"Right, so?"

"So the Pantheon's been around for two thousand years. It's pretty low maintenance."

"Yeah, that makes sense."

"Besides, I *do* get up here occasionally. Only last month I had to unclog one of your Roman baths."

The centuri-devil nodded. "I remember that. The baths are a favorite of mine. That was a real mess."

I thought back to my three broken plungers and the case of Drano I had to use to get the pipes clear. "You're telling me."

"What was wrong with it?"

"The drainpipe was clogged … with devil hair."

"Well, I guess you're legit then. Go on in."

"Thanks." The line shortened, and I stepped inside the building. "See ya."

The inside of Mammon's palace was even more opulent than the exterior. The gold walls and ceilings were inlaid with platinum and precious jewels. The high walls of the palace supported the massive dome. The only light entering the building came from the front door and a small hole at the top of the dome, yet the palace's interior glowed so brightly, I had to shield my eyes. The gold and other precious metals were all buffed to a fine luster. You could see your own reflection in them, and the enormous diamonds protruding from many of the surfaces gleamed like spotlights.

In the center of the palace, atop a massive throne, sat Mammon, all twenty feet of him. At least, that's what he looked like to me. I'm sure he could have been bigger, since as a prince of Hell he probably had powers similar to Beezy, whom I'd just recently seen in a five hundred foot high incarnation. Yet, I suspected Mammon picked his size deliberately to be impressive, almost overwhelmingly so, yet still small enough to interact with the supplicants who were lined up to see him.

Mammon was dressed in a Roman toga. He had white hair cut in a pageboy, and a laurel wreath on his head. He looked much like statues I'd seen of Caesar Augustus, though his horns marred the effect a bit.

Once inside the palace, the line of greedy damned souls lost a bit of its integrity. It splayed out, so we could fill the floor space before Mammon. I wanted to get closer to him, but the crowd pushed me back to a wall not far from the entrance. Above an alcove there I noticed a plaque saying, "Here Lies Raphael." I remembered that the Italian Renaissance painter was buried in the original Pantheon, so I stepped closer to get a better look. In the alcove was a statue of a teenage mutant Ninja turtle.

As the Greedy had their turns before Mammon, they presented their bags or chests or suitcases to him. Inside each was whatever the individual supplicant deemed most valuable. Sometimes it was gold coins, sometimes greenbacks. When Dora reached Mammon, she popped the latches on the Samsonite and offered up her cigarettes. I'm sure it was agony for her to give them away. Each time one of the Greedy made an offering, the entire throng inside the building chanted, "Render therefore unto Caesar the things which are Caesar's." Their voices echoed in the golden Pantheon to eerie effect.

Occasionally, someone didn't present an acceptable offering to Mammon. When that happened, the devil would merely gesture, and from the side a demon would come forward with a cat o' nine tails. After a severe thrashing that would leave the damned soul a bloodied mess, he or she was chained to the interior wall of the building. The chained bodies went entirely around the structure.

Imprisoned on a portion of the wall near me was an old fat dude. He was dressed in opulent manner, though as with most of the damned, his clothes were threadbare. The man was bald, except for a ring of white hair, a bit like Mammon's wreath I idly thought, and a dark handlebar mustache. I recognized him from a picture in one of my graduate school textbooks. It was John Pierpont Morgan.

I'd never met J.P. before, though I knew some of his contemporaries, like Carnegie and Rockefeller. I'd always been impressed by the man's accomplishments. He was the only individual ever to make a loan to the U.S. federal government, keeping it from default. Morgan had arranged the financing for the Panama Canal too. Pretty big stuff.

I also knew he was one of the most ruthless businessmen of all time. In the AC/DC wars, he threatened George Westinghouse with suing him into bankruptcy if he didn't sign over the rights to AC power. Morgan had lost big, because he'd backed the wrong horse, that is, Edison instead of Tesla. He didn't care. He bullied his way to success and in the process helped form General Electric. He also founded U.S. Steel and, of course, the banking empire that bore his name.

"Hey," I said to him. "Aren't you J.P. Morgan?"

"Render therefore unto Caesar the things which are Caesar's," Morgan chanted along with everyone else. "Yes, I am. What's it to you?"

"I was just wondering how long you've been hanging there."

"I don't really have any idea, but since shortly after I died."

"Really?" I was impressed. That would have been almost a hundred and fifty years. "Why?"

"I tried to swindle Mammon."

"Ooh. Bad move."

I stood there for a minute, watching the people give up their treasures to Mammon. Then I had an idea. "So, can I ask you something?"

"Render therefore unto Caesar the things which are Caesar's … what?" Morgan said with a sigh.

"Does Mammon get out much?"

"Out?" Morgan spit out a less-than sincere laugh. "I've never even seen him leave that chair."

"So," I said, stating the obvious, "he didn't leave for a while anytime in the past few days."

"What are you, an idiot? I just *said* he never leaves."

"Good enough for me," and I turned to go.

"Say," said Morgan behind me.

"What?"

"Why are you wearing that idiotic outfit?"

I shrugged. "My eternal damnation?" I left him hanging there.

Chapter 15

My feet made a soft thump as I landed on the concrete in front of the trailer. I had a little more than an hour before the cocktail party, just enough time to check in before changing my clothes. I arranged for BOOH to pick me up at my apartment then climbed the steps to my office.

Neither Orson, Edison nor Bik was around. Some piles had been moved around and the stack of high priority work orders had grown slightly, but otherwise, everything looked about the same as before. Orson was doing a good job of keeping things under control. On the corner of my desk was another memo from him. With a soft groan, I picked it up and began to read.

HELL'S OFFICE OF THE INTERIOR
"HOTI: We die to serve ... "

Plant Department

MEMORANDUM
TO: Steve Minion, Hell's Super
FROM: Orson Welles, Hell's Super Pro Tempore
DATE: Whenever
RE: HOTI Form ∞3971\PDYFF 666-327\?///WOE # ∞8911874123

This is a report on the successful resolution of **WOE # ∞8911874123**, i.e., aka, viz.: "Fix Mussolini's sewing machine."

BP and I found Il Duce, the Great One, in the sweat shops down on Seven. You might recall that the shops are located in Tae Bayan, aka "Shit Town," a tawdry city on the western edge of that very same ocean that on the east fronts Pinkerton's Hellish version of Glasgow. I think of the bit of land on which Tae Bayan lies like a stinking cow paddy to be the Underworld's Pacific Rim.

But I digress. I have never been able to figure out how to get to Tae Bayan via the Escalator, so we took the Elevator, which as you know is capable of moving sideways as well as up and down. Still, it took me and my assistant three attempts before landing in the garment district of what surely must be one of Hell's largest and least pleasant metropolises. I cannot recall if you've ever been to the garment district, but here the buildings are assembled in slapdash manner, adding new floors whenever needed, resulting in such architecturally tenuous structures that I'm frequently reluctant to enter. Each factory in the district, though, is yardarm to yardarm with two more, that is, the buildings here are crammed together in such close proximity that if one started to collapse the other two would likely hold it up.

In any event, BP and I identified the factory in which the Great One was employed. The Pyongyang Pantyhose Factory turned out to be Hell's largest producer of women's sheer stockings. Apparently, Mussolini is a star stitcher, and the former dictator sews all of the pantyhose used by Hell's fleet of succubi.

Mussolini's workstation was on the fourth floor, but we found it empty. Since the Great One was unable to operate his equipment, his demon supervisor had decided to keep the former dictator occupied by shooting him in the chest a couple of times and hanging him out a window on a meat hook.

After retrieving Benito, I queried him about the nature of his problem. His description, "Non funziona," was patently obvious. I could see that for myself. Mussolini was not being particularly cooperative, so the demon shot him again and chucked him back on the meat hook. I then began my diagnosis. After five minutes, I determined the sewing machine was plugged into the power outlet on the floor and the power switch was in the "on" position. I tried unplugging and plugging back in the device, switching the button on and off a few times, but to no effect. To be thorough, I unplugged the sewing machine (you never can tell down here) and tried the switch in both positions. Yet still I was unsuccessful.

At this point, Edison was turning beet-red with frustration, which of course had been the main point of my useless examination. When I allowed him to speak, he pointed out that the plug had been stepped on and probably just needed to be replaced. Edison reached into the pocket of his coveralls and pulled out a replacement plug. How, when and where he got it, I'll never know, but he seemed rather fond of this reminder of his past, when he was "King of Electricity." BP stroked the plug like a lucky rabbit's foot and called it by name, "My Precious" I think, but to his credit he offered it up to the cause, provided he could install it himself.

I knew that was ill-advised, but I also knew that Hell would provide and I needed to do nothing. I stepped away from the sewing machine. With a feral gleam in his eye, Edison pulled some wire cutters from his tool belt and snipped off the damaged plug from the wire's end.

He was rewarded with

* A blast of Hellfire
* A pie in the face, and
* A full 120 volt jolt of electricity from the wire (Yes, I know the machine wasn't plugged in, but when do natural laws come into play down here, unless of course they make things more difficult?)

As amusing as it all was, I still had a job to do, so after helping Edison put out the flames that had engulfed him - Remember how I coated his coveralls in sulfur earlier today? - I allowed the now slightly-charred Wizard of Menlo Park to talk me through the process of installing the plug. This turned out to be easier than I thought, except that attaching the individual wires to the contacts in the plug was an exercise in fine motor coordination that was almost beyond me. Nonetheless, I managed the task, though undoubtedly I took four times as long as Edison would, if he had been allowed to do the work.

As my assistant though, alas, he was not.

I plugged the machine back into the socket and turned it on (the former, not the latter). This blew a fuse and put the entire room in darkness. The demon cursed me in Akkadian. (I find I am developing an excellent ear for extinct Semitic languages, no doubt due to the time I spend with ~~Beez~~ ... Lord Beelzebub.) After he finished his string of invective, the supervisor showed me to the fuse box. I had no replacement, but Edison suggested a copper penny. That was something I did have, so I inserted it in lieu of a fuse (note to file: this may result in a new work order at some point), and the lights came back on, as did the Great One's sewing machine.

We retrieved Benito from his meat hook and set him back at his workstation. Mussolini was a little woozy from the blood that had been running to his head, but he signed off on the work order and got busy on some nice-looking taupe pantyhose. I believe they had a reinforced toe.

At the time of writing this report, I have yet to select the next work order, but I shall do so forthwith.

xc: Beelzebub, Lord of the Flies

I took my stapler and shot a staple into my left hand. As hoped, the pain of the two metal teeth as they dug into my ectoplasm distracted me from the headache that had begun to grow behind my eyes as I'd worked through Orson's detailed memo. I looked around the office. As good a job as Orson was doing keeping the wheels turning on our little operation, I didn't know how many more of his reports I could stand. It was just one more incentive to get to the heart of the HVAC mystery as quickly as possible. There was another danger, I noted. In Orson's first memo, he had listed his title as my assistant. This one said Hell's Super Pro Tem, Acting Hell's Super. Whether consciously or not, Orson was taking a big chance here. With his ego being stroked by success in this temporary capacity, he'd promote himself to Head of Plant Maintenance in no time, and that wouldn't sit well with Beezy.

I filed the memo, along with the work order paper clipped to it, in File Thirteen, that is, I threw it in the trash can. No one in Hell really cares about the official record, and if we kept all the work orders we completed, they would just contribute to the almost overwhelming clutter in our office. The circular file was a fine final resting place.

Leaning back in my chair, I thought about my special assignment. I wasn't much closer to identifying who was behind the failure of the HVAC system, but I had made a little progress. Mammon, at least, was eliminated as a suspect. There were two left, if Pinkerton's and my logic held true, and in a short while, I would have the opportunity of assessing the guilt or innocence ("innocence" being a relative term here - we *were* in Hell, after all, and I was talking about devil nobility) of at least another. And that meant I needed to hie on home and find something respectable to wear before heading up for my date with Lilith. That is, my meeting with Asmodeus.

The wind had picked up while I was inside, and for the first time since being made aware of the failure of the HVAC system, I felt a little chill in the air. True, I'd been used to two hundred plus degree days for a long time, so the temperature might have just dipped down into the double-digits, but there could be no doubt: Hell was suffering from climate change, and by the standards of anyone who existed on this plane, this was a cold day in Hell. Now, even I could detect it. Probably had something to do with the hot pants I was wearing.

As I hurried along the sidewalk, thinking about getting ready for meeting Lilith, I thought again about the powerful attraction I had for her. I hadn't felt anything like it in a while, not since my time with ...

Flo.

A familiar brunette beauty was standing at the bus stop, twenty feet ahead of me. She was dressed in a simple white nurse's uniform, though her sublime figure filled it out in all the right places. All of a sudden I didn't feel so cold. In fact, my face was burning. Months had passed, or what felt like months down here, since I had last seen Florence Nightingale, since our one night of blissful passion.

Being caught in sexual congress by two devils with a video camera had pretty much killed the mood. The last I saw of Florence was her head disappearing under a sheet. She had just peeked out to see me on the floor of her bedroom. I had told her I loved her and been punished with Hellfire and an oversized coconut cream pie.

As far as I knew, Flo still wanted me to keep my distance. Also, since my thoughts had just been on a very sexy succubus, I had another reason for avoiding Miss Nightingale, but it was too late. She had already seen me.

"Hello, Steve," she said, giving me a sad little smile.

"Hi, Flo," I said, coming to a stop a few feet away. "Uh, sorry I didn't spot you earlier. I know you don't want to see me right now."

"That's all right," she said, stepping up and laying her hand on my arm briefly. "In fact, I was just thinking about you."

"You were?" All thoughts of Lilith disappeared from my brain as I stood before the perfection that was Florence Nightingale.

Boy, I had it bad.

"Yes," she continued. "I was … I was just wondering how you were. If you were doing well, and … and why are you wearing those short mauve knickers and that blousy shirt?"

"I, uh, washed my coveralls a while ago," true enough, "and they're still wet." That was probably true also. "This is the only other outfit I own … except my clown suit."

"What about that nice white dinner jacket and slacks?"

She was remembering the outfit I had worn the last night we'd been together. "One of Satan's minions filched them the next day."

Flo nodded. "Just so. My dress disappeared as well."

I closed my eyes briefly and sighed, remembering her ensemble from that evening, a tight black cocktail dress that looked great on her. She wasn't as large topside as a certain succubus I knew, but Florence was very well-endowed and perhaps better proportioned, a classically beautiful woman.

"There's something else different about you, but I'm having trouble placing it." Florence stared critically at me for a moment then brightened. "Your hair! I don't remember your hair being so full. What did you do?"

"Hair Club for Men!" I blurted out then immediately felt guilty for lying to her.

"Is that where men share a toupee amongst themselves?"

"No, not quite. The hair is real. Feel it." This was a pretty feeble ploy, but anything to get Florence to touch me again was worth it.

Hesitantly, Flo touched my hair, running her fingers through my thick brown locks. "What a wonder! It *is* real, and very nice, but ... "

"But what?" I asked, anxiety in my voice.

"Well," she demurred, removing her hand. "I guess I liked the old Steve, thinning hair and all."

Great. The person in Hell I most wanted to look good for, and she preferred me as a balding, middle-aged man. Just great.

"But you didn't answer my other question."

"What?" I said, coming back to the conversation. "You mean, how am I? Okay, I guess, though I have another big project that's taking a lot of my time right now."

"Really? What?"

I told her about the HVAC system.

"Hmm, it seems to me that the poor souls trapped down here could use a little break from the heat."

Which led to me explaining the metaphysical ramifications.

"That's dreadful!" she said, appropriately horrified. "True, many of these unlikely events could be positive, but ... " Florence looked at my hair and frowned.

"But it would be chaos, on Earth, in Hell, and even in Heaven!" I said quickly, trying to draw her attention from my flowing locks.

"Just so," she said primly.

"Flo," I said, taking her hand quickly. "I've missed you so much."

"I ... I've missed you too," she sighed.

"Have you forgiven me yet? You know I was just as humiliated by the affair as you were."

"Affair?" she asked.

"Situation!" I substituted quickly. "The situation!"

"Yes," she said at last. "I know it wasn't your fault."

"Flo, do you believe I love you? I do, you know."

The pie thing was getting pretty old, but at least Flo helped me to my feet, a gentle smile on her face. "Yes, Steve, I know. My feelings haven't changed toward you either, and I am beginning to have faith that they are my own, and not the mere machinations of the Prince of Lies."

"Nice alliteration."

"Thank you." Flo knew I liked alliteration and had probably done it on purpose just to please me.

"Do you," I said slowly, "do you think we could spend some time together?"

Florence smiled her sad smile. "I'm not quite ready for that, but maybe soon."

"That would be wonderful! I'll wait for you Flo, you know I will. Take as much time as you need, darling."

For some reason, I got away with "darling." Either it wasn't a word on the punishment list, or someone was on break. Anyway ...

The founder of modern nursing blushed when I called her "darling," but she smiled as well. At that moment, a bus pulled up to the stop. "I have to go now, Steve. I'll let you know when I'm ready to see you again." On sudden impulse, she kissed my cheek then stepped aboard.

Meanwhile, I stood on the curb with my mouth agape.

Then I thought about my upcoming date with Lilith. True, it was all part of the job, and the fact that I met her at all wasn't my fault. Well, it *was* my fault, because I was being a smartass when I made my "cold day in Hell" comment, but I didn't expect meeting another beautiful woman to actually happen. Guilt pressed down on me like the thumb of a 500-foot Beezy, but there wasn't much I could do right now to change things. I needed Lilith to get to Asmodeus, and if it meant being her escort to a cocktail party, then that's what I had to do, regardless of my feelings about Flo. I hurried the remaining blocks to my apartment building. Six floors later, I was huffing before the door to my studio.

I closed my eyes before grabbing the knob. Satan frequently monitored my thoughts, and I hoped he was doing so now, because I really needed a tuxedo or something similar in order for Lilith to get me into the reception. "I have to have it if you want me to get the job done," I mumbled, and opened the door.

There was nothing draped over any of my furniture. Other than the clown outfit, my still-damp work uniform was the only clothing hanging in my apartment. I plopped down on the couch.

Great. He's leaving me no choice. Might as well get it over with. "It will be a cold day in Hell before I have another tuxedo and accessories that are as nice as what I had on my first date with Flo."

Abracadabra! The outfit was draped across the far end of the couch, the shoes on the floor nearby. After I put out the flames on my head with a pillow, I retrieved them.

This time there was no grumbling in my head. So ... Satan knew I could take care of the problem myself and just used my need for an outfit as an opportunity to punish me. Nice.

By the time I was dressed, my hair had grown back. Looking at myself in the mirror, I realized that I cut a more dashing figure than I had on my dates with Flo. *It's all about the hair*, I thought, running my fingers through the tresses and giving them a rakish, if tousled appearance. *Of course*, I thought, walking down the stairs to meet up with BOOH at street level, I didn't need to make my coif look tousled. Flying up to Level Two would take care of that.

Chapter 16

BOOH was already waiting for me, leaning against a lamppost, trying to look cool, though the metal pole was beginning to buckle. One advantage to riding on BOOH's shoulders was my outfits tended not to get damaged. As precise and gentle as the giant bat was when handling me, his pickaxe-sized claws usually snagged whatever fabric I was wearing. When in coveralls, it didn't make much difference, but a tuxedo, well, you know.

In seconds, BOOH alighted before the corporate headquarters of Lust Unlimited. I hopped off his shoulders. "Shouldn't be more than a couple of hours," I told him as he took off for parts unknown. My friend was very efficient, and if he knew I was going to be occupied for any amount of time, he'd use the opportunity to run some errand for Satan. Didn't matter, though. When I was ready to go, all I had to do was whistle, and BOOH would hear me, no matter where he was in the Underworld. I guess that was one of the benefits of being a creature of magic.

I brushed a little bat dandruff from my trousers, straightened my bowtie, and ran my fingers quickly through my mane.

"So that's how the BatRider rolls," said a luscious voice from behind me. "Pretty cool."

Lilith was wearing a skimpy black cocktail dress that looked to have been applied with a spray gun. The spaghetti straps were straining to keep the black satin fabric of the garment from being catapulted off her enormous tetrahedra; the cleavage she was showing, well, she could have hidden a blowgun in there.

My mouth was suddenly very dry, so I closed it and swallowed a few times. When a little moisture came back to my tongue, I managed to say, "W ... Wow, Lilith! You look great!"

The succubus shimmied her way to my side. Even in her four-inch spikes, I had five inches on her. Nonetheless she managed to get her lips on mine. Levitation, no doubt.

"Mmmm ... mmmm ... ! No, Lilith. People could be watching!"

"Let 'em watch," she said, and ran her fingers down my backside before releasing me. "But if you don't want to smooch in public, shall we head up to the reception?" Lilith held her arm up to me, elbowing me in the ribs. I took the hint, and her arm, then we headed inside the building.

As we approached the elevator, the bellman spotted me and ran for the door with his out-of-order sign. Then he saw Lilith and skidded to a halt, leaving scuff marks on the marble floor behind him.

"That's okay, Milhous," she said, patting the bellman on his ski-nose. "He's with me."

The man gave us a pained grimace and backed away.

"Isn't that ... ?" I began.

"Yes."

"How the mighty falleth," I said, repeating one of my favorite phrases. It always seemed appropriate down here.

Lilith shrugged. "There's a lot of that going around in Hell. That's one of our specialties, you know."

"Do tell."

We stepped inside the elevator. Once the door closed, Lilith pulled out the emergency stop button. "Hey, big boy, ever done the Nasty in an elevator?" She applied a few judicious strokes to just the right spot on my anatomy, and I rose to the occasion.

"B ... better not," I gasped and pulled the zipper back up. "I need to keep my wits about me."

The succubus looked at me speculatively as she twisted one of her auburn locks around a finger. "Okay. I'll just settle for a little face sucking ... for now." She pushed the button back in as she grabbed my head and pulled it down to her level. The taste of cinnamon filled my mouth as our tongues intertwined. Her hand went back to pressing on my privates in a soft but insistent fashion, and my resolve started to crumble.

Bing!

I managed to pull away from her just as the door began to open on the penthouse level. Quickly, I buttoned my tuxedo jacket, thankful to have camouflage with a little style to it.

Lilith took my arm and led me into the crowded room. There were many people I recognized. Well, generally not people, though there were a few humans too, like Giacomo Casanova and Lucrezia Borgia, who were serving drinks and canapés to the guests. The people I was referring to were not people at all; for the most part, they were devils and demons. I saw, for example, Hecate, Astaroth and Baal. Even Bifrons, the film critic who wrote that humiliating review of 'Flo Does the Super,' and little Uphir from the hospital were there. That put a frown on my face, since they were two of my least favorite demons, but a frown beat the look of a horny hellion, so I suppose I should have been grateful they were there.

There was also an occasional mythological creature at the reception, and one of them walked up to me now. "... - . ...- . -- ..-- / .-- .... .- - / .... . .-.. .-.. / .- .-. . / -.-- --- ..- / -.. --- .. -. --. / .... . .-. . ..--.. ?"

Before me, in a charcoal cloak and incongruous black bowtie, was a skeleton holding a champagne flute. It was my friend, Charon. Since Ronnie had no tongue, he communicated through a series of clicks and clacks - or dots and dashes. It was Morse Code which, because of my years in the Boy Scouts, I understood. What he said was, "Steve, what the hell are you doing here?"

I'll continue to translate, since I'm pretty sure most people are a little rusty with their Morse Code.

"I could ask you the same question. Since when do you leave the Styx to attend a cocktail party?"

When my brother talks me into it, my friend grumbled.

Across the room was Mortimer, Death himself. He looked like a twin of his little brother, though if we were honest with ourselves, we'd say the same thing about any two skeletons of roughly the same height, bones bereft of flesh being the great equalizer in human appearance. Morty's black cloak, however, was a better match for his bowtie. Death had a cocktail in one hand, his scythe in the other. He waved at me with his drinking hand, which was nice of him, because if he had waved with the other one, it would have creeped me out. I got along pretty well with Morty, since the old death thing was pretty far behind me at this point, so I waved back.

Mortimer loves these events and, well, he thinks I should get out more.

There were a few extra clacks in there. "Ronnie, are you chewing gum?"

Yes. Grape. My favorite, as you know. What of it?

"Well, you have a glass of champagne in your hand. Are you going to drink that while you're chewing gum?"

I don't see why not. I have no taste buds, as you so frequently point out to me, so it doesn't make much difference. With that, Ronnie slammed back his drink.

Which drained through his bones straight onto the carpet.

Casanova rushed up with a napkin and blotted up the champagne. I looked down at the former philanderer. "Good thing it wasn't red wine," I opined.

I never drink ... wine, not red wine anyway. When I'm forced into going to one of these damnable social functions, which is rare, I always stick with something that won't leave a stain.

"That's pretty thoughtful of you. What?" I said, as Lilith pulled on my arm to get my attention. "Sorry. I'm being rude. Charon, I'd like you to meet a new friend of mine."

Charmed, Ronnie said, taking my escort by the hand and planting a gentlemanly kiss on her knuckles. *Unless I am mistaken, you are Lilith, are you not?*

I rolled my eyes. "Good guess."

Lilith smiled warmly at Ronnie. "Yes. I've always wanted to meet you, Mr. Charon."

Ronnie. Please call me Ronnie. All of my friends do.

Well, well. Ronnie had a bit of the old *savoir-faire* going. I had never thought of him as a ladies' man, but he was pretty smooth.

Lilith, who seemed to have no problem understanding Ronnie, was looking unashamedly at his lower extremities. "Do, ah, do skeletons have bones for all parts of their ... "

I'm afraid not, my dear. Boner is just a figure of speech. However, if you should ever be up on Level 0.5, I could show you how I compensate. I've never had any complaints.

"Ronnie!"

"I'd love to," Lilith replied huskily.

"Lilith! See you later Ronnie!" I said, pulling the succubus toward the refreshment table.

"Steve," my date laughed, "you're blushing! Are you jealous?"

"Yes, no! I don't know." I grabbed a glass of champagne and slammed it back. Since alcohol had no effect on the dead, the drink didn't help calm my nerves, but the action was spirited and seemed appropriate for the occasion.

"You *are* jealous! That's so cute," she giggled, and took a glass offered her by Ms. Borgia.

There was a commotion in the room, and a bright light flashed. Lilith looked up. "I think Asmodeus is making his grand entrance now. I wonder who his date is tonight."

The crowd separated for Asmodeus, an extremely handsome devil, with a black goatee that nicely complemented his white tie and tails, not devil tails, though he had one of them crammed somewhere in his trousers, for sure - or perhaps duct taped up his spine - but the kind of tails on the back of a formal black evening dress coat. On his arm was a spectacularly beautiful woman dressed in a strapless, Empire waist gown. Her long, chestnut hair was in an elegant updo. She wore only a hint of makeup, but she didn't really need any. She had a face that could make an angel - or devil - weep.

It was Florence.

I stood there in shock, and we almost collided before Flo saw me. When she did, she gasped.

"What are *you* doing here?" I asked in astonishment and no small amount of indignation.

Florence disentangled her arm from Asmodeus, who was watching our encounter with great amusement. "I could ask you the same thing!" she said, blushing in embarrassment and outrage.

Then it was that I noticed Lilith's arm wrapped like a serpent around my own. I had a little more difficulty extracting myself from her than Flo had from Asmodeus. Now it was Lilith's turn to be jealous, and she was being appropriately possessive.

"I'm here on business," I said.

"Hmmph. Monkey business, it seems to me," she said, eyeing Lilith with cool disdain, "for I see you have on your monkey suit, which you just told me a little while ago you no longer owned."

"No," I said heatedly. "You asked about the white dinner jacket. Besides, this is a new outfit. I just got it."

"Well, well," Asmodeus said, chuckling. "I see you two know each other, but I'm afraid sir, that I do not know you, or how you got in without an invitation."

"This is Steve Minion," Lilith said with a pout. She didn't need me to spell out my history with Florence. After all, Lilith had seen the movie. She took my arm again. "He's my date."

That's right. And, after all, why should I be defensive? Florence and I aren't seeing each other right now. She has no hold on me, not really.

Except my heart felt like it was being pulped in a juicer. I hated her seeing me with Lilith, and I was pretty sure she hated me seeing her with Asmodeus. Yet I could not imagine why she would be at a reception on the arm of a devil. I took a deep breath. "Lilith is right. I'm her escort this evening, but like I said, I'm here on business. What's your excuse?"

Flo looked a little taken aback. She must have known her presence with the Prince of Lust was every bit as questionable as mine with a succubus. "I ... I'm here on business too," she said at last.

Asmodeus put his hand to his chest, where his heart would have been, if he'd had one. "My lovely, you cut me to the quick. And after all I have done to help you these past two days."

Past two days? "What's he talking about?"

Florence was staring down at the carpet, pursing her lips. "Asmodeus just completed a thirty hour telethon to raise support for renovating the hospital waiting room."

"What?"

"That's right, Mr. Minion, is it? The waiting room was in a terrible state of repair. It seems to me that someone hasn't been doing his job."

"Are you talking to me?" I said, my voice thick with anger.

"Calm yourself, human," Asmodeus said, and flashed his very sharp canines. For the first time, I remembered who I was talking to.

"Sorry, Lord Asmodeus."

"Better, Minion." The Prince of Lust looked speculatively at Florence, then me. "Not that I have to explain myself to you, but I conducted the telethon on the sole condition that Miss Nightingale attend tonight's soiree as my date."

And that explained everything to me. I looked over at Flo, who was sighing softly. She, at least was off the hook. Now, if I could just get myself off too. The hook, I meant. Not that other thing, though if Lilith had her way, that would happen too.

Trying to regain my composure, I nodded briskly. "And that takes care of my reason for being here tonight."

"Beg pardon?" Asmodeus said.

I shrugged. "Lords Satan and Beelzebub have me investigating the breakdown of the Underworld's HVAC system. I suspect foul play, yet there are only a few of Hell's inhabitants powerful enough to pull something like this off."

"And I, as one of the princes of Hell, am one of them, of course. Sorry to disappoint you, but you see I have a ... a, what do you call it?" he asked, all smiles.

"An alibi," I grumbled.

Asmodeus smiled again, delighted. "Yes, that's the word. And Miss Nightingale is it. Would you say she qualifies as a reputable person?"

I hung my head. Where was something to kick when you really needed it? "Yes sir."

"Good. Then if you will excuse us, I would like to show Miss Nightingale the view from the balcony." With that, Asmodeus grabbed two glasses of champagne in one hand and, putting his free arm around Flo's milky white shoulders, led her away. She glanced back at me, wide-eyed.

I had a feeling that at that moment Florence was regretting making a deal with a devil.

"So she's the big challenge Asmodeus has been talking about," sniffed Lilith. "She doesn't seem like such a conquest. Why, he'll have her in the sack before the night is out."

Despite the awkwardness of the situation, I chuckled. "I wouldn't bet the farm on that."

"What farm?"

"It's just an expression."

"Oh."

"Well," I said, looking around the room. "I guess I've learned what I needed to. Might as well be going."

"What? Don't go, Steve. I hate being at one of these events by myself. Please stay a while longer." Lilith grabbed another glass of champagne. "Besides, Asmodeus hasn't told you everything. Let's find someplace quiet. There's more."

"Ah," I said, watching Asmodeus and Flo disappear through the glass doors leading to the balcony. "Okay."

Lilith wove her way through the crowd, leading me by the hand to a room at the far end of the suite. She opened the door and stepped inside, beckoning me to follow.

We were in what looked to be Asmodeus's private study. A modern glass and stainless steel desk dominated the room, along with an executive chair that was about as big as a throne; there was also a large couch in one corner of the room. On the walls was an assortment of erotic art and, incongruously, some framed pie charts.

Lilith sat on the couch and pulled me down next to her. "What's the couch for?" I asked.

"Conquests," she replied. "He's the Prince of Lust, after all. And you think he's gonna just do it on his desk?"

"Good point. So, you said that Asmodeus isn't telling me everything."

The redheaded succubus was twisting one of her curly locks around a finger, a habit of hers that I somehow found very sexy. She looked up at the ceiling then back at me. "I lied."

"What?" I started to stand but was jerked back down on the couch.

"Steve," Lilith said, running her fingers through my hair and nestling her cheek against my own. She smelled both sweet and spicy, and I felt the great white whale preparing to breech. "I really like you."

"And, I ... I like you too. I mean, how could I not? You're a succubus."

"Is that all I am to you, just a demon who seduces men?"

I opened my mouth to say yes but closed it abruptly. I thought about the question with some care. "No," I said at last. "I mean, I know that's exactly what a succubus is, but there's more to you than that. I, well, I confess I like you ... a lot."

Lilith made a cooing sound and started to crawl in my lap. I held her back. "But, but why do you like me so much? I'm just another one of the damned."

My date gave me the same consideration I had given her and pondered the question carefully. "Well, I *am* a succubus. I can't deny that. If you move, I have the hots for you. I'm wired that way. But ... but there's more to it than that."

Exhaling softly, Lilith sat back on the couch. "Maybe it's your puppy dog eyes. And there's something about you, a certain quality I can't put my finger on. I've, well I've never come across it before, and it really turns me on."

"What quality?" I said, mystified. "My big nose?"

She chuckled, touching my schnoz lightly with a forefinger. "I *like* your nose! You do know that all the best lovers have big noses, don't you? But no, that's not it … Well," she said at last, hesitantly, "I'm not sure I'm right, because I only know in theory that this quality exists, but I think it's called integrity."

She looked wistful now. "I saw how you looked at Nightingale back there. I … I'd give anything to have you look at me like that."

"Lilith," I said with a gentle smile, "you could have any man you want."

"Good!" she said, and then she did crawl in my lap. She put her arms around my neck and whispered in my ear. "Because I want you."

"And in here … well, I'd like to show you my pie charts," said a masculine voice from the hallway. The door opened, and Asmodeus and Florence entered the room.

"Aagh!" I screamed. Lilith was dumped on the floor as I stood up in haste, but it was too late. Florence had seen her in my lap.

"Steve!" Flo shouted, fury and embarrassment both vying for facial supremacy. "How could you?"

"How could I what?" I asked, helping Lilith to her feet. "Sorry about that," I whispered to her.

"Occupational hazard," she whispered back.

"And what are *you* doing in here?" I asked. "Alone with the Prince of Lust?"

"You know how I like pie charts."

This was true. Florence Nightingale had always liked pie charts. She used them as a mortal and continued to use them in Hell, frequently to explain some arcane point to a management that couldn't care less.

"Well," I said, finally fed up. "I'm tired of being accused or suspected of doing things I haven't done." I turned to Lilith and gave her a gentle kiss on the lips. "Thank you for a wonderful time, but I must be going now."

The succubus beamed. She had probably expected a brush-off, and my act of gallantry had been unexpected. "You're welcome! I hope to see you again soon." She put a thumb to her ear and her pinkie to her mouth, the universal symbol for "call me."

"That would be nice," I said, smiling, then left the room.

From behind me, I heard Asmodeus say, " … but Miss Nightingale!" Then a door slammed.

Before reaching the elevator, I noticed that Flo was right behind me. "What are you doing?"

"I'm leaving too, not that it's any of your business."

"Why?"

"I only told Asmodeus I'd come to his reception. I never said I would stay long."

"What about him and Lilith?"

"Last I saw, they were sitting, arms crossed, on that couch, glaring at each other."

"Hmmph."

"Hmmph."

We rode down the elevator in silence. As we walked across the marble floor of the foyer, I asked if she needed a ride home.

"No thank you," she said frostily. "I think we would do best to say good day and make our own ways home."

"Fine. Good day," I said and turned my back on her, more than a little angry.

"Good ... "

The door closed behind me before I heard her utter another syllable.

Chapter 17

BOOH took me to my apartment so I could change back into my coveralls. To save me the walk up six flights, my friend flew right to my window. I couldn't open it from the outside - hell, it was hard enough to open from the inside - so BOOH did me the favor of shoving one of his claws through the glass. Then he hovered in place as I got off his back and climbed through the opening.

While donning my still-damp coveralls, I tried to puzzle out what had just happened and why Flo and I were so furious with each other. It was natural that she would be jealous, having seen me in that compromising position on the couch, and I *did* find Lilith attractive. Yet, I had done nothing wrong. Lilith had come onto me, not the other way around, and I'd been doing everything in my power to not succumb to a succubus, especially one I thought was a pretty nice person. All in all, I thought I'd managed myself pretty well.

As I climbed out the window, I realized my anger had something to do with that integrity thing Lilith had been talking about. Flo had been questioning it, and I expected better of her. Back on BOOH's shoulders, I realized this was not the first time Flo had doubted my sincerity. She thought I had been a coconspirator in her seduction all those months ago. Her suspicions were wrong, unjust, and I realized that I had been harboring some resentment ever since.

And yet, as BOOH set me down before the trailer, I understood why she would have doubts. Both situations had put me in a bad light. I probably hadn't helped things by kissing Lilith in front of Flo, but I was mad at Miss Nightingale, and I knew that would push her buttons. Besides, I liked Lilith.

BOOH settled down for a catnap on a nearby trash heap, and I headed for the office door. Climbing the stairs, I suddenly felt less sure of myself, and my anger crumbled.

Fact one: Lilith *was* sitting in my lap on the couch. Fact two: Flo had a right to be upset, because I really was attracted to the little redhead while she, that is, Flo, hadn't shown any evidence of attraction for Asmodeus. *Crap. So much for righteous indignation.* And now my relationship with Florence was even more screwed up than before, just when things between us were beginning to improve.

This wasn't going to be a long stop at the office. I just wanted to check in. Then I had a very unpleasant task to attend to. As I opened the door to my office, Edison came running out. He looked pretty shaken up.

"What happened?"

"Beelzebub happened," Edison replied. He unbuckled his tool belt and handed it to me. "Here. I guess I won't be needing it anymore."

"Why not?"

"Orders. I'm supposed to return to the mines ASAP."

"Orders, huh? Okay then. If you want to get there faster, I can have BOOH ... "

"NO!" Edison almost screamed. "I mean, no thank you. The Escalator will get me there fast enough. See you. I wish I could say it's been fun, but it hasn't. I've enjoyed root canals more." Then he hurried down the street, as if he wanted to put as much distance between himself and the office as quickly as possible.

On stepping inside the office, I found Orson lying unconscious on the peeling linoleum tile. Atop my desk, there was a smoldering scrap of paper. Since the damned weren't unconscious very often in Hell - a second of unconsciousness is just that much less time available for torment - I figured he'd wake up in a second, so I went to the paper. I slapped out the flames with Edison's tool belt then picked up the sheet. It was an unfinished memo from Orson to me.

HELL'S OFFICE OF THE INTERIOR
"HOTI: We die to serve ... "

Plant Department

MEMORANDUM
TO: Steve Minion
FROM: Orson Welles, Hell's Super

I shook my head. Poor Orson. Pride goeth before a fall. A groan emerged from the large smoldering lump on the floor. I put the paper back on the desk and went to help my friend.

"Wha ... what happened?" he said, as I got him off the floor and onto his stool. I would have given him my chair, in view of his condition, but I suspected Beelzebub was watching, and I needed to get our little work universe back in its proper order.

"Beezy probably didn't like you promoting yourself to Hell's Super," I said, pointing at the scrap of a memo he had begun.

"I was doing the work, so I thought I could use the title." Orson rubbed his forehead and winced. He probably had a killer headache going on. "I suppose that wasn't one of my better ideas." My friend looked around the trailer. "Where's Edison?"

"Our boss sent him back to the mines. I guess we're back to a department of two."

"Suppose so," Orson said glumly.

"I never stopped being Hell's Super, you know."

"I know, I know," he replied sourly. "It was a stupid thing to do, I admit it, so can we just drop the whole thing?"

Going to the sink, I grabbed a dishtowel and wetted it then handed the sopping cloth to my assistant. He grimaced, cleaned his face then held the wet fabric over his right eye, which was blackened by the blow he'd taken.

I plopped into my office chair and leaned back, propping my legs upon the battered All-Steel desk that was the command center for the Maintenance Department. No points for posture for me this day.

Our time clock, an old analog model that could have been used in one of Henry Ford's auto plants back in the day, was ticking away with a dull thud thud thud that I could hear even from across the room. The leaden ticking was what I imagined my own heart sounded like at the moment.

Orson sighed. I sighed back. Both of us had our reasons for being glum.

Even through the haze of his pain, Orson could see my discomfiture. "Why the sour expression, Steve?" he asked from his perch atop the stool. He looked to me like Humpty Dumpty in a HAZMAT suit.

With another sigh, I pulled my legs off the desk and leaned forward, pressing my hands flat against the desktop surface. "Female trouble, for one."

My friend looked at me dubiously. "Even if you were a woman, that kind of stuff stops after death."

"Shit, Orson, don't be so intentionally obtuse. It doesn't suit you." I then proceeded to explain what was going on with Flo and Lilith.

He whistled. "A succubus! Man, they're as rare as hen's teeth."

"Not really. According to Lilith, there are 666 of them."

"Yeah, well not down here. Most of them are topside, driving mortal men to distraction ... and damnation."

"That's true," I said slowly. "I wonder why Lilith is kept down in Hell. Perhaps she's too nice to play the seductress."

"Don't know about that," Orson said, switching the cloth to his forehead, where a big knot was beginning to form. Beezy must have been really mad to hit Orson twice. Once was usually more than enough for our boss to get the job done. "She seems to have done a pretty good job on you."

I smiled ruefully. "She's got the talent alright, but Lilith seems a bit too kind-hearted for the job."

"So *you* say. For all you know, she was putting on an act, setting you up for that little scene with Flo in Asmodeus's study."

I frowned. "Maybe, but for the moment I'm giving her the benefit of the doubt." I stood up from my desk and began pacing the office. "Right now, though, Flo and Lilith are the least of my worries."

"What's the most?" Orson asked, grabbing a can of sardines and opening it.

I slammed my fist against the office wall. A framed photograph of Beelzebub fell to the floor, cracking the glass. Hurriedly, I picked up the frame and hung it back on its nail. "Crap, Orson. I haven't a clue how to go about fixing an HVAC system that's unbreakable, especially if there's someone out there intentionally breaking it."

"I thought you had some suspects."

"Yes, three, but I've eliminated two of them." I gave him a short account of my recent activities.

"So who's the third?"

I glanced at the photo I'd just re-hung and then at the speaker of the PA system, through which Beezy sometimes shouted his orders.

Orson's eyes grew wide, or one of them did; the blackened one had swollen completely shut. "Ah."

Without warning, Orson's stool pitched him to the floor. That happened sometimes. Orson's stool, wobbly as it appeared, was perfectly capable of holding all four hundred non-corporeal pounds of him, yet periodically it would just destabilize on its own, dumping Orson on the linoleum. This time, though, I suspected it was just a little extra payback from Beelzebub. I got out of my chair and helped Orson to his feet again.

"I wish it wouldn't do that," he grumbled.

"I know." Leaning over, I picked up the diabolical stool and set it back on its feet. "It's Hell, but whatcha gonna do?"

"Nothing. I'm used to it by now. Mostly." Orson settled his ass back on top of the stool. Rolls of fat spilled around the sides, completely obscuring the seat. How the thing managed to support all of my friend's weight, even when Beezy wasn't pissed off at him, was beyond me.

Orson's black eye faded and the swelling receded. His face would be back to normal soon. "What are you going to do now?"

I reached a decision. *Best get this over with.* "Go have a talk with our boss, I guess."

"Good luck with that." There was a sound like a Gatling gun firing. A mass of work orders had just dropped into my wire in-basket. Orson groaned. "And I guess you know what I'll be doing while you're gone."

"Triage?"

"Triage. See you later."

"Uh huh. If I'm very, very lucky."

Leaving the trailer, I whistled for BOOH. He opened one eye, then the other, then stood and shook out his titanic wings. I guess that was his version of a stretch. Then he bent down and, with great reluctance, I climbed aboard and asked him to take me to see Beezy.

My boss wasn't in his office again. He had always had a restless quality, but he seemed to be wandering more than usual these days. I hoped it didn't have anything to do with the HVAC system.

Beelzebub, the great Lord of the Flies. Number two in Hell. My boss. Could he possibly be the one who had sabotaged the HVAC system? Was he really willing to take on Satan himself for supremacy in Hell? If there was anyone who could pull it off, Beezy would be the one. Of all the devils and all the demons I'd encountered since my death, no one but Satan seemed more powerful, and on any given day, I wasn't even sure about that.

Sure, Beezy had never demonstrated the voodoo mind-reading ability that was Satan's stock and trade, and the Lord of the Flies tended to travel by way of thermonuclear explosion, rather than teleportation, but that didn't mean my boss lacked those skills. He had his own style. He was no infernal impersonator.

BOOH and I searched for a long time on Level Eight but could not find Beezy. Finally we came to a portion of the Circle I'd never been to before. It was desert still, but a high desert, like the Chihuahuan in the United States. There was little sand, but it was dusty. Here and there were tall, broad mesas, rocky outcroppings from the desert floor.

On top of one of these, we found Beezy. My boss was sitting in the lotus position at the highest point, looking out over the land beneath. The air up there was cold, and Beezy was dressed once again in his Mongol del. He glanced at me as BOOH landed then turned his attention back to the land below. I walked over to him.

For a few minutes I said nothing, and he, atypically, did not prod me into speaking. "Kind of pretty," I said at last.

"You mean for Hell," he commented.

"Yes sir." That went without saying. Nothing in Hell was pretty.

"You know," Beelzebub said, turning to me, "you humans just think all of Hell is hideous, but if you could see it through my eyes … " Then he was silent again.

"Chilly up here."

"Yes, I know. Just in case you can't get this HVAC system fixed, I'm trying to get used to a colder climate. Of course, if you don't fix it, I will flail you alive."

"I'm dead, sir."

"You know what I mean."

"Yes sir." I settled next to him, and for a wonder, he didn't object. "Lord Beelzebub, I've come to give you my report."

"Well?"

"I have eliminated two of my three suspects."

He looked at me appraisingly. "Well, that's something I suppose. Who were they?"

"Well, since I've proved their innocence, or at least their innocence in this matter, I guess I can tell you. Mammon and Asmodeus."

Beezy nodded thoughtfully. "Did Pinkerton help you come up with them?"

"Yes sir. He gave me a lecture on motive, means and opportunity. We figured only the most powerful of devils could pull this off, but Satan, Leviathan and Belphegor didn't seem likely."

"And that leaves me. I'm your third suspect, aren't I?" Beezy's black eyes glinted.

"Yes." I gulped. "Yes sir, you are."

Surprisingly, Beelzebub didn't fricassee me on the spot. "Well?" he said at last.

My heart was pounding. Should I ask his whereabouts for the past couple of days? Should I ask if he had an alibi? I closed my eyes and thought hard on how to begin.

"Well?" he repeated.

"Lord Beelzebub," I said finally, opening my eyes and turning to him, "did you sabotage the HVAC system?"

"No."

I nodded, got off the ground, brushed off my coveralls, and headed toward BOOH.

"Wait!" Beelzebub called. "That's it? I say no and you leave?"

"Yes sir. Your word's good enough for me."

Beezy stood and turned toward me. I expected to see anger, but instead all I saw was incredulity. "I *am* a devil, you know. I could be lying."

"Yessir," I said hurriedly. "I know as a devil that you're perfectly capable of lying, it's just that … "I looked at the ground, not knowing how to put this. My boss closed the few feet that separated us. I could feel his eyes on me, and it took all of my courage to return his gaze.

"It's just that what?" he said.

I sighed. *Better to just spit it out.* "Oh, shit, boss, of all the devils I've ever known, you're the only one who's ever been straight with me. I'm not saying you can't lie, but I've never known you to lie to me. Please don't take this the wrong way, because you *are* evil, and really good at your job, but you're not a liar."

Beezy plopped back on the ground. "Hmmph. You're right, of course. I don't lie. Lies are a lot of trouble. They're much more complicated than just telling the truth."

I nodded. "Sir, you have more integrity than ... "

"Don't push it, Minion."

"Yessir," I repeated. No point insulting him.

"And Steve," Beezy said, as I crawled onto BOOH's shoulders. "Thanks. I've not had anyone trust me in a very long time. It's refreshing. But don't tell anyone about this, okay?"

I smiled. "Scout's honor. I'd better get back to Orson now. You did a nice job on him, by the way."

"Well, he was asking for it."

I couldn't disagree. "Later, sir."

"Later," said the Lord of the Flies. Then he shut me from his consciousness and resumed his contemplation of the desert floor.

Chapter 18

I was back at my desk, bad posture reassumed, feet again on the desktop.

Bik had rejoined us after his lengthy visit with Surtr. The young fire giant had enjoyed a growth spurt since we'd last seen him. No doubt Surtr could feed him better than we could with our matches. Bik was now the size of a ballpoint pen, and I thought idly that the pocket protector would be a better fit for him. He was flying around the room in frenzied fashion, like he was on speed, looking at everything in our office with a lot more interest than any of the items warranted. He seemed unusually agitated, and he was glowing more than normal. Apparently, he and his grandfather had had a falling out, but Bik refused to talk about it.

I shook my head.

"What are you thinking about?" my assistant asked.

"What else?" I said, turning from the whizzing point of light. "The HVAC system. No clue how to fix it, and now no suspects." Not to mention that I was so tired I could drop.

Orson had a thoughtful look, which was good, since at the moment I was completely tapped out. "You told me," he said slowly, "that Beezy considers the system to be very dependable, and we spent a good chunk of the day confirming that, right?"

"Right." I pulled the folded HVAC schematic from my pocket. I'd forgotten it was there, and when I'd washed my coveralls, it got washed too. The colors had bled a little, and the paper was a bit limp from being soggy, but it was still perfectly legible. We spent a little time reexamining the design.

After a few minutes, Orson looked up from the drawing. "I just don't see how much could go wrong with the cold side of things. Erebus is an immutable mountain of ice. It's not likely to change."

I nodded.

"But," he continued, "the burners down on Nine: they're another story. Despite Surtr's assurances that everything's working okay down there, you saw several jets blink out, right?"

"Right," I said, barely suppressing a yawn. "They were like Venturi tubes on a barbeque grill get when they are clogged or something."

"Not likely," Bik said, as he extinguished his flame and dropped to the diagram. "Nothing gaseous, liquid or solid flows through the pipes."

"Then what does?" I asked.

"The Spark."

"Huh?" Orson scratched his beard. "What the fuck's that?"

I tried to think of a shorthand way of explaining. "Hey Orson, what gives a Jedi his powers?"

"Are we playing *Trivial Pursuit* now? Okay, I'll bite. The Force."

I nodded. "The Spark is something like that."

"Sounds pretty hokey."

"I thought so too, but go with it, okay?"

"Okay. So where does the spark that fuels the burners come from?"

"The Spark," I corrected him. "But it's a good question." I leaned down to where Bik was studying the tube drawings on Level Nine. "Bik, do you know?"

The tiny redhead stared at my face, hovering like a moon above him. "Grandpa told me that after Beelzebub constructed the system, Satan infused it with his will, and the burners caught fire."

I frowned. "Satan has no shortage of will, but he DOES have a shortage of attention span. I can't imagine that he's funneling his will all the time through those burners."

"I mean he lit the pilot," Bik explained, "not that he was funneling his own Spark through the system on an ongoing basis. I suppose The Spark might come from Satan, but it might come from somewhere else. I don't really know. Grandpa might."

"Maybe," I said, scratching my chin, "but ... "

Splat! A Work Order fell from the pneumatic tube into my inbox. I took a quick look at it and flushed red. Orson, seeing my reaction, checked out the signature.

"Flo? Flo is sending us a work order? That's odd. Almost nothing ever goes wrong for her."

Except me. I had gone wrong for her, but I doubted the work order had anything to do with that. I picked it up and started to read.

"Besides," Orson continued, "considering the chilly relations between you two right now, I would think she'd just put up with it."

"She can't," I said, shaking my head as I put down the work order. "Her lamp needs replacing."

The Lady with the Lamp. That lamp was her trademark. In life, Florence Nightingale had been known to walk battlefields in the dark, lamp in hand, looking for wounded soldiers. The Lamp was as important a symbol of hope as the torch in the hand of Lady Liberty. It needed to be fixed.

"I could take care of it," Orson offered.

This was a chance for me to see Flo, something I would normally jump at, but since we'd parted on a sour note less than an hour ago, the timing was terrible. Yet her work order was important; I could feel it in my bones. Suddenly I made a connection. "Bik? This lamp Orson and I are talking about has a wick and lamp oil. The oil soaks up the wick, you light it, and the fire illuminates things. What causes the flame, do you think?"

Bik's tiny face contorted into a look of disbelief, as if he couldn't fathom why I was so stupid. "Why, The Spark of course."

"That doesn't make sense," Orson said. "All fire can't be the result of this mumbo jumbo 'Spark' thingie."

"What do you know about fire?" Bik said with irritation, his head igniting. "I'm made of fire, so I probably know a little bit more about it than you do, don't you think?"

Orson made a placating gesture. "Don't get offended. I just can't imagine anything magical about a campfire back on Earth."

Bik extinguished his flame. "Now I understand the confusion. You're right, at least in part. The Spark is still involved, because it is the unifying force of both the physical and metaphysical realms, but on Midgard, a fire isn't a direct expression of The Spark the way it is down here. At least, that's what Grandpa says."

I rubbed my chin in thought and felt the rough stubble of my beard. We had a really long day going, with no end in sight. "So you think the failure of Miss Nightingale's lamp could be related to the problem your grandfather is having down on Nine?"

"Well, naturally. The Spark is an energy field created by all things. It ... "

" ... surrounds us and penetrates us," I said, completing his sentence for him. "It binds all things together. Blah, blah. Yeah, I know. I saw the movie."

Bik kicked at my desktop. "You're being snarky again."

"Sorry," I said absently, no longer paying attention to him. I was thinking about Flo's lamp. It was definitely worth checking out.

"Orson, I need to investigate this myself. Especially so after your recent, ah, disagreement with Beezy. You could get the replacement lamp from Dora, I suppose, but I would still have to take it to Flo, light it for her, and get her signature."

Orson nodded, bowing to the logic of his damnation. "I'm just your assistant again. I can't resolve anything on my own."

"'fraid not, but you can come with me. Perhaps Flo will feel more comfortable if I don't show up alone."

"Can I come too?"

"What? Bik, you're mumbling again."

"Sorry. Can I come?" Bik repeated, raising his voice.

"I guess so," I said, holding open my pocket protector. Bik lit up for a second, just long enough to get airborne, then flamed off as he did a perfect jackknife into my pocket.

The air outside our trailer was smelly and damp, like a bandaid you'd forgotten to remove from a badly ingrown toenail before soaking in a bath. A cold bath. The air was noticeably cooler; I could feel it through my coveralls.

We swung by the Parts Department and got a replacement lamp and some fuel from Dora then headed to the hospital. It wasn't far; after we'd walked a couple of blocks, I could see it peeking out from behind the abandoned steel mill. As usual, the hospital's looming all-metal structure made me squirm, but today my reaction was worse than usual.

As we stepped onto the sidewalk leading to the hospital entrance, a sudden attack of the heebie jeebies overwhelmed me. Like most people, I hated hospitals, but my sudden attack of nerves had more to do with my impending meeting with Flo than anything else. I wanted to see her of course. I loved her, and no matter how chilly or even non-existent our relationship was at present, I was sure she loved me too. Yet, after catching me with Lilith plastered to my face and sitting on my lap, Flo probably wasn't real keen on seeing me right now.

"Steve, you okay?"

We were standing just before the entrance to the Toaster. I couldn't move. My feet seemed mortared to the sidewalk. "Just, just a case of nerves, I guess."

Orson put his hand on my shoulder in sympathy. "I could take the lamp in for you."

My smile probably looked pretty lumpy. Certainly the tears in my eyes couldn't be hidden. This whole situation with Flo was turning me into a weepy, pathetic mess. "You know you can't. Beezy wouldn't let you. Probably drop a building on you or something."

My assistant frowned. "I guess you're probably right, but I'd be willing to try for you."

"Careful, Orson," I said, feeling my smile smooth out a bit. "You're getting dangerously close to lemon cream pie territory."

"You're right there," he said, looking cautiously upward. "Come on. We'll go in together. There's safety in numbers, right?"

"Right." We locked arms, and stepped into the Toaster.

Inside the steel building, the temperature was even cooler than outside. In the enormous reception area, amidst the hundreds of patients waiting interminably for admittance, several demons in jackets wandered through the crowds. One in particular I hoped to avoid.

"Ah, Steve Minion, Hell's Super himself," said a nasty-sounding little voice behind me.

I groaned. "Hello, Uphir."

Hell's demon physician, top dog in the hospital as far as I could tell, wore a thick terrycloth robe over his scrubs. "What are you doing here? Aren't you afraid Flo might see you?"

Here it goes, I thought with a sigh. "I'm responding to a work request she made."

"Don't you have something more important to do? It's fucking freezing in here!"

Damn it. Uphir was probably right. The failure of the lamp and the HVAC system were probably unrelated, no matter what my instincts - or Bik - told me. If so, I was wasting time on an insignificant job. "I ... I ... "

The demon snorted. "What are you, a sailor? Then shove off, matey, and get to work on something really important!"

I'd never liked Uphir. Well, I didn't really like any demon, except maybe Lilith now, but Uphir I particularly despised. Aside from being a snotty-nosed jerk, he was always finding ways to make Flo's existence miserable. I gave Uphir my most formidable frown, which was only slightly more intimidating than one from Mr. Rogers. "As soon as I take care of this work order. You always know where she is, so you can speed things up by telling me now. And then I can get back to fixing your heater."

Uphir looked up at a water stain on the ceiling. He stroked his chin while putting his other hand in the pocket of his robe. He looked like a particularly ugly David Niven in a smoking jacket. Then he brightened. "Fifth floor. She's just passed the Nurses' station, Proctology Unit. Looks like she's headed to the Immobility Ward."

"The Immobility Ward," Orson mumbled, rolling his eyes. "Great."

"Thanks," I said, without an ounce of sincerity, and turned to go.

"And tell her that, since she isn't interested in you anymore, if she wants to practice her Floratio techniques, I'm available." Uphir popped open his robe and displayed his equipment for me.

"Fuck off, Uphir!" Orson snapped, beating me to it. My assistant was being particularly protective of me. He must have known how nervous I was about our meeting with Flo.

It's nice to know someone has your back. Even in Hell.

"Yeah," I added, trying to think of some suitable insult. I wrinkled my nose, as if I'd just detected something beyond malodorous. "How long has it been since you bathed that thing?"

"What's a bath?"

"Whatever." We turned to go.

"Wait!" Uphir called.

I wanted to keep walking, but it never paid to ignore a demon. Reluctantly, I turned back to him. "What is it now, Uphir?

The demon physician looked at the ceiling, then back at me, as if something had just occurred to him. "Nothing much. Just say hello to your lady love for me, Steve-o."

"What did you call her?"

"Your lady love. She is, you know. I was kidding earlier. Why," and at this point, Uphir cleared his throat and grinned evilly at me, "all Hell will freeze over before she stops loving you."

"You son of a bitch!" I screamed and punched him in the face.

Bad move. Demons, even twerpy little ones like Uphir, are amazingly strong. And fast. Before I blinked, I was flat on my back, with Hell's demon physician standing on my chest. "Don't ever do that again," he hissed.

"Okay ... okay," I said, slightly dazed. "But why did you say that?"

"Just giving you a little added incentive to get your main job done." Uphir hopped off my chest and, with more dignity than I thought he was capable, left the waiting area.

Orson and I headed for the elevators.

Great. Just great.

"Steve, do you think Uphir just upped the ante?"

I shivered, and not from the cold. The situation was getting worse and worse. "Yeah, I do. It's already a cold day in Hell, and if we don't figure out what's wrong with the HVAC, there's a real risk all Hell could freeze over ... And I will lose Flo forever."

And maybe all the souls in Hell would be destroyed, including my own. I knew I was being selfish, but somehow, losing Flo seemed the worst of it.

We walked by Billing, where there was a glass window, open halfway, behind which sat a demon wearing a green plastic visor, vest and shirt with the sleeves rolled up. The line before the department snaked back and forth upon itself. Every damned soul had at least a ream's worth of paperwork on them. Just coming around the corner was an old lady driving a forklift on which was a pallet's worth of documentation. The guy at the window arguing with the demon had a five-foot stack on a dolly. By the way he kept shifting his weight from one foot to another, I judged he'd just had podiatric surgery. He was wincing in pain with each movement. In his hand was the first page of his bill, a multipart form that was attached, accordion-fashion, to the remaining sheets on his dolly. "But ... but, ten thousand dollars for one aspirin?"

"Ooh, you're right. Mistake that. Should have been twenty. Here, let me print you out a revised bill. Shouldn't take a minute." With that, the demon disappeared to some place far in the back, where the printer must have been located.

I shook my head.

The elevators were broken, so the two of us trudged up the stairs. Orson and I were pretty winded when we reached the fifth floor, and we spent a minute leaning against the wall, wheezing and catching our breath, while we watched the goings-on in the Immobility Ward.

This was one of the larger units in the hospital. Most of the patients housed, or should I say, incarcerated here, were in life control freaks, claustrophobics or both. They, of course, were completely mobile, or would have been if allowed. In Hell's Hospital, they were strapped to beds or wheelchairs or gurneys. Anything that could move on a person's body was bound down in some fashion or other. Their mouths were taped shut and their eyelids sewn open. I noticed idly that instead of medical supplies, their bindings were barbed wire, fishing line and duct tape.

In the center of the Ward was a large open space, currently occupied by half a dozen demons pushing gurneys. On each one was an immobilized patient, eyes wide with fear. The demons were playing bumper cars and having a whale of a time slamming into each other's charges. They had just pulled away from each other, though, and formed a wide circle with the gurneys. The patients' heads were pointed toward the center of the ring, and the demonic orderlies were poised for a grand slam finish.

"One, two…" counted one of the demons.

"Hold!" came a stern voice from down the hall.

A vision of feminine perfection stepped in the middle of the circle, and my heart stopped.

Florence Nightingale was in high dander. She said not a word, but stared each demon down with an expression that could have frozen water. Hell, Flo, in her immaculate, white nurse's uniform and frosty demeanor could have frozen a geyser. None of them could withstand her fury. Grumbling, they one by one wheeled their charges away.

My love took a deep breath before turning away from the ward. That's when she saw me. The frown that had just disappeared from her face returned. "Steve! What are you doing here?"

A cold day in Hell indeed.

"I've asked you not to come to the hospital," she said, dropping the thermometer to zero, Kelvin, "so why would you pick today of all days to show?"

Damn. I cleared my throat. "Your work order," I said by way of explanation.

She nodded but looked to my assistant. "I thought that, knowing my feelings, he'd send you, Orson."

My friend put his arm around Flo, kissing her cheek. I guess he was trying to show my affection by proxy, but it didn't make things any better. Vague feelings of jealousy rumbled through me. "He would have if he could have, Flo, but Beezy doesn't allow me to do any work orders on my own." He shrugged. "I can only assist."

"Yes, of course," she said in a small voice. "I'd forgotten about that."

"Tell me, tell us," I amended, "what happened to your lamp."

There was a faraway look in Flo's eyes, but my voice brought her back from wherever she was wandering in her imagination. I hoped I was wandering there with her.

"I ... I don't know." Flo opened her purse and pulled out the lamp. The thing was iconic, having shown up in several works of art depicting the first lady of the nursing profession: The Lady of the Lamp. "It just abruptly wicked out a little while ago, and no matter how hard I try, I can't relight it."

"Does it have oil in it?" Orson asked, trying to be helpful.

She smiled ruefully at him. "I've been using it for two hundred years. Do you think I would make a mistake like that?"

"Suppose not."

"Well, don't worry," I said brightly, or as brightly as a lovesick handyman could sound. "I've brought you a replacement."

Flo sat down in a plastic chair in the hallway. "I hate to give up my old lamp," she said, staring down with affection at the scratched and dented thing. It had seen better days. "I've had it for a long time."

Her predicament reminded me of Sisyphus and his boulder, so I tried to put a positive spin on the situation. "You can still keep it. You'll have two!"

Flo sighed. "I suppose."

"Here, let me set up this new lamp for you." Quickly, I took the lamp out of its box, filled it with lamp oil, and stuck the wick in the spout. As an afterthought, I pulled out the wick, soaked it completely with oil and reinserted it. I wanted to make sure we got an impressive flame out of the replacement lamp, if only to cheer up Flo.

I rummaged around in my pocket, gouging myself on my keys, and grabbed a box of matches. It took me two or three strikes to get a match lit, but it finally did ignite, and I placed the flame beneath the oil-saturated wick. An impressive amount of smoke rose, but I couldn't light it.

"Ow! Damn!" I said, dropping the match when it scorched my index finger. I sucked on the burn for a sec then struck another match. If anything, it was harder to light than the first one, but light it did, and I went after the wick once more. Still no luck, and I was getting frustrated.

"Bik!" I yelled.

All the while, Bik had been standing quietly in my pocket protector, taking in the scene. He was so tiny that Florence hadn't even noticed him, but her mouth opened in surprise when the tiny fire giant flew from my pocket and hovered before my face. "What's up, Steve? Do you want me to light the wick for you?"

"Would you? I'd sure appreciate it."

"No problem." Bik turned to the wick and shot a blast of fire at it. About a quarter inch was incinerated, but the lamp did not light.

"Odin's Beard!" he said in dismay. "That's never happened before."

"Perhaps," suggested Orson, "a little finesse."

Bik scratched his chin, nodding. "Right."

"Who is this?" Flo asked.

"A new friend of mine. He's helping me on the HVAC project. Flo, this is Bik. Bik, Flo."

Florence smiled at the tiny creature. "Hello."

"Nice to meet you, ma'am," Bik said, as polite as I'd ever heard him. "Let me try again." Bik flew up to the wick, placed both hands on it, and began stroking it gently. The wick began to smoke, and slowly, after considerable coaxing, the lamp lit up. But only for a few seconds. Then it winked out.

"Arrrgh!" Bik screamed and shot up through the ceiling. He was back by the count of five, having apparently burned off some of his frustration. "THAT," he said in his loudest voice, "has never happened before."

Orson, scratching his beard, was deep in thought. "Something odd is going on here. Hey, Flo, let's see if Bik can light your old lamp."

Florence handed the lamp to Orson, who turned to Bik. "Why don't you try again?"

"Okay." Bik repeated his gentle coaxing of the wick on Flo's original lamp. Again, after some effort, he was able to get the thing to light, but it only burned a few seconds before going out.

Bik dropped to the floor, extinguishing his flame, and sat down with his back to the wall. "I must be losing my touch."

"I don't think so," I said slowly. "Something else is going on here."

I looked at Orson, who nodded. He probably had the same thought I did. I had been right. This was related to the problem with the HVAC system.

"Keep the new lamp, Steve. If neither one will light, I'd just as soon hold onto my old one." Flo frowned, and her beautiful face assumed a tragic demeanor that made my heart ache. "I don't know what I'm going to do without it. My lamp has been a symbol of hope to others for a long time."

Unable to restrain myself, I knelt down and took her hand. Flo looked surprised, but she didn't pull away.

"No, dear. You, Florence Nightingale, you have been the symbol of hope. You are the flame that has inspired us."

Yeah, I know. Way over the top, but it's the way I felt at the moment.

Bik looked up and grinned. "She's like The Spark!"

An icy claw clutched at my lungs, and for a moment, I couldn't breathe. Looking closely at Florence, I noticed that she was pale, as if the blood, or what passed for blood in the afterlife, had been drained out of her. Perhaps she was just a little chilled, but maybe Bik was right. Flo was like The Spark, and her fire seemed to be burning pretty low right now. I gave her hand a gentle squeeze - it was ominously cold to the touch - and stood. "Hold onto your lamp. I hope we'll be able to get it working for you soon. I ... I have to go now. There's something important I need to do."

Or rather, someone important I need to see.

Flo nodded and smiled sadly. It was the first smile I'd gotten from her since the bus stop, but it made the fearful claw retreat, and I could breathe again. I picked up Bik and put him in my pocket protector. We bade Florence goodbye then hurried down the stairs.

Orson and I made eye contact as we descended flight after flight. "This looks bad," he rumbled.

"You said it. Big time."

Chapter 19

As soon as we stepped outside the hospital, I handed Bik and the box with the lamp to Orson then whistled for BOOH. I waited for what seemed like forever, but was probably no more than thirty seconds, before he showed.

"BOOH!" I yelled, as my gargantuan friend hovered over me. "I need you to get me down to Satan, pronto!"

"Skree!" And we were off.

Like I said earlier, generally when traveling with BOOH, I was pretty comfortable - well, as comfortable as a soul can be when speeding through the air at warp speed. The air would be temperate: not too hot, not too cold. Not now, though. Frigid air - as opposed to Amana or Whirlpool or some other brand - cut through my coveralls as if they were made of cheesecloth.

I'd told BOOH to step on it, but he didn't seem to be moving as quickly as usual. Was it my imagination, or was he panting a little, as if he were actually exerting himself?

First the temperature of Hell began to drop, then Flo's lamp went out. Now even BOOH was struggling. A lot more than the Underworld's HVAC system was failing. It was as if the fabric of Hell itself was unraveling.

And my hands ache, like I have arthritis or something, and arthritis doesn't even run in my family. Shit.

We needed to get down to Satan as soon as we could, but BOOH didn't seem able to go any faster. With an effort, I tamped down my impatience.

An exhausted BOOH dropped me on the carpet in Satan's foyer - he actually dropped me, as if he couldn't carry me any farther - then the giant bat flew wearily over to his perch near the elevator and plopped down. Even from across the room, I could hear his labored breathing.

Bruce was behind his desk. I greeted him politely.

"Shut up, Minion," Satan's secretary snapped irritably. I guess the cold was getting to him too. "What are you doing here anyway? You don't have an appointment."

"I know, Bruce, but I really need to see Satan."

"Impossible! You know that no one can see the Lord of Hell without an appointment."

I frowned. Time to suck up a bit. Bruce had traded out his cardigan for a ski jacket. Ever the fashion pate, he looked very stylish, so I whipped out a compliment. "Bruce, that's a beautiful ski jacket you have there."

The junior demon brightened. "You like it?"

"Yeah," I nodded, "but if I don't get some answers from Satan, you're going to need to trade it in for a parka soon."

His face turned pale. "But I'd look terrible in a parka!"

"Bruce, this is serious. The temperature is dropping rapidly. It's already a cold day in Hell. Do you know what that means?"

"Of course I know what it means! I wouldn't be wearing a ski jacket otherwise."

"That's not what I meant it means, I mean, it means a lot more than that." I slammed my hand down on his desk, startling him. "Perhaps Satan hasn't explained the metaphysical ramifications of this to you, but let's just say, if you've ever used the expression 'It'll be a cold day in Hell' before, finish that sentence in your head and realize what's at stake here."

Bruce's eyes became as wide as saucers, admittedly saucers with epicanthic folds, but saucers nonetheless. "That means I'd have to make a movie with Ed Wood! Aagh! Have you ever seen 'Plan 9 from Outer Space?' Oh the Horror, the Horror!" Bruce buried his head in his hands.

I looked at Bruce, genuinely concerned. He and I had never exactly bonded over the years, but Lucifer's secretary was clearly distressed. And I *had* seen 'Plan 9 from Outer Space' so knew what was at stake for him. I reached over and patted him on the shoulder. "Buck up, Bruce. It might not be too late. Just get me in to see your boss, and perhaps we can stop all this."

Bruce kept his eyes covered with one hand, but with the other, he reached to a button on his desk and pressed it. The doors to Satan's office opened. I hurried inside as they closed behind me.

The Lord of the Underworld's nexus of power was as hot as ever, and I soon realized why. He was back in dragon mode, wandering back and forth, his seven heads blasting fire in all directions, including my own. I ducked quickly just before he would have fried me extra-crispy.

The head that had done the near-frying stopped breathing fire. "Minion!" it hissed in surprise. "What are you doing here?"

"Lord Satan," I said, groveling my best grovel. "Forgive me for entering uninvited and unannounced, but things are getting very serious out there."

An enormous red La-Z-Boy materialized in the room. There was a hole in it, right where back and seat met, and Satan inserted his tail in the space before sitting down and kicking back to raise the footrest. A seven-headed dragon in a red La-Z-Boy was something I didn't see every day, and even jaded old me found it impressive.

"I already know things are getting bad," said one of the heads, while the other six continued to heat up the room. "And close your mouth, before a fly goes in it."

I snapped my jaw shut. I doubted a fly could survive in the heat of the room, but I didn't want to take any chances. In Hell, you've gotta be prepared for the worst.

The heat of the office actually felt good to me. The chill that I'd caught flying down with BOOH was gone; this gave me an idea. "Lord Satan, BOOH is really suffering from this cold. Do you think he could join us while we talk?"

"My BOOH is suffering?" the dragon head said, showing genuine concern. As far as I knew, BOOH was about the only creature in existence, or non-existence, that Satan really cared about. BOOH was like a pet cat to him. "BOOHSIE!" he called. "Here boy!"

The doors popped open, and BOOH flew into the room. But not far. His wings gave out the last few feet. He was almost crawling by the time he made it to his master.

"BOOH, precious!" the Devil exclaimed, as he scooped up the bat and cuddled it in his dragon arms.

Now, BOOH is the size of a pteranodon, so this gives you an idea how big Satan was in dragon form. In fact, it hurt my neck just to make eye contact while talking to him.

Not that he was paying any attention to me at the moment; instead, he was rocking BOOH back and forth, cooing to the bat. BOOH began to purr. For some reason, the sight of Satan showing my friend, or anyone for that matter, such affection, touched me deeply.

Satan, or at least one of his heads, looked up at me and glared. "If you tell anyone, I'll rip your lungs out."

"Gulp," I gulped. "Of course not."

The dragon continued to blast fire out of five heads, sing a lullaby to the bat he was rocking in his arms, and carry on a conversation with me at the same time. Satan's multitasking skills were impressive.

"Hell is getting colder at a progressively more rapid rate, and I'm not much closer to figuring out the who or the why of it than I was when you first gave me this assignment." I hated admitting that to Satan - he had no tolerance for failure - but he knew that I knew that, and I was counting on the severity of the problem to get me a bye.

"You're right," he grumbled, reading my mind. "Normally I'd fricassee you, but the situation is too grave to waste time on my own personal amusements right now. What else have you observed?"

"Well, there's BOOH, of course. I figured he was nigh on to indestructible, but look at him."

"Yes, yes," the Earl of Hell said impatiently. "Tell me something I don't know."

I thought you knew everything that goes on in Hell.

That was a mistake. "Of course I do!" he snapped. "Or I do if I put my mind to it." The dragon looked a little troubled. "Besides, all this cold, well, I've got too much to deal with right now to follow everything, so talk!"

"Yes, sir." I proceeded to tell him about Flo's lamp.

He nodded thoughtfully. "That makes sense."

"Not to me ... sir. I always thought Flo was basically immune to anything that happens down here."

The dragon cursed under his breath. "Generally she is, but her lamp isn't. Besides, what's going on right now is affecting everyone and everything. Remember the metaphysical ramifications." Then Satan stopped talking. He looked very thoughtful.

"What?" I asked.

"WHAT? Don't you mean, 'What ... ?'"

I slapped my forehead. "Sorry, sorry. What SIR? What, sir, are you thinking about?"

"Harrumph. That's better. It may be a cold day in Hell, but that's not an excuse to show less than the proper respect."

"About that cold day in Hell business: is anything, you know, starting to happen topside?"

Seven dragon heads frowned. "Yes. The U.S. Congress has unanimously approved a sensible balance-the-budget bill, and the President has signed it into law."

I stared dumbfounded at my lord and master. "But that's impossible! It would be a cold day in Hell before ... " and of course I stopped myself.

"Right," Satan said. BOOH had fallen asleep in his arms, and the Lord of Hell gently dropped the footstool of his La-Z-Boy and stood. He placed the bat in the chair, summoned an afghan out of thin air, and covered my friend. Then he morphed into his man-in-black persona. With a gesture, he motioned me away from the chair so that our talking wouldn't wake his pet.

"Other things are happening too," he whispered. "North Korea has renounced communism, and unification talks are underway with South Korea. The United States has given Cuba favored nation status, Parliament has made coffee the official drink of Great Britain, Russia has joined NATO, and Ralph Feenie has asked Bridget Johnson out on a date. She said no, of course, but he did it."

The Devil removed his sunglasses. His eyes were a dull gray; he looked tired. I wondered how long it had been since he'd slept.

"Not quite fourteen billion years," he said, answering my unasked question. "I don't need much sleep."

"I guess not." I opined. "All of those things on Earth. They really happened?"

"Yes. And the scientists are saying that they'll have fusion power perfected in ten years."

"Incredible!" I said, marveling. "They've been saying twenty for as long as I can remember."

"Indeed," he said, slipping his sunglasses back on his nose. "Normally, I don't give a crap about what's happening on Earth, but I like discord, I like things to go wrong. All this good stuff happening, well, it's unsavory."

I nodded. "Even Bruce is worried. He's afraid he's going to have to do a kung fu remake of 'Plan 9 from Outer Space' with Ed Wood."

Satan snorted. "Well, that one at least won't happen. Wood ended up in Heaven."

"Really?" I said, mildly astonished. "After all those terrible movies he made?"

"Rotten artistic sensibilities don't usually land you in Hell."

"Well, they ought to," I said.

"In that we agree."

"Boss," I said quietly, realizing as I said it that he might take that as a sign of disrespect. I called Beezy boss all the time, but not the Earl of Hell. Yet he seemed not to notice. "What happens if ALL HELL FREEZES OVER?"

Satan grimaced. "Well, my poker night would be cancelled, at the very least."

That sounded like a joke, but it wasn't. The Lord of Hell and his lieutenants took their weekly poker party very seriously and had often said Hell would freeze over before they cancelled it.

"And even more dramatic things would begin to happen back on Earth. Bridget Johnson would say 'yes' to Ralph, and eventually they'd get married and have really ugly babies. Cuba would become the fifty-first state, which would piss off Puerto Rico to no end." Satan rubbed his chin in thought. "That part sounds pretty good, but the point is that impossible, chaotic things would happen, and it would be chaos that I didn't devise myself. I'm the epitome of chaos. I AM Chaos, damn it, and I will NOT tolerate chaos to which I haven't consented!"

Satan began to pace his office. A chair appeared in front of him so he could kick it, then a table, which he crushed beneath his fist. Then he shot a blast of Hellfire at the ceiling.

Boy, was he pissed off.

After the Earl of Hell had given an impressive display of his pique, he turned on me. "And you've got nothing?"

I looked around desperately. I didn't want to be the next target of Satan's anger. "Well, yes! I have figured out a few things!"

"Then out with them! I'm in a shitty mood, Minion, so give me something."

Two office chairs appeared nearby, and we sat down. "Okay," I said, gulping. "I've studied the HVAC schematics, and Orson and I have checked out every choke point in the system that I can find. Beezy is right. It's a simple system, and he built it well. It's functioning properly."

"But then why is the cold getting worse? Why are fires winking out all over the underworld?"

Yes, why? I thought, and then a tumbler clicked in my head. I stood up and almost shouted "Eureka," but Satan's head jerked up, and I realized I was standing above my lord and master. You weren't supposed to do that, so I sat back down. "I think," I said slowly, "I think it's a fuel problem."

"Impossible! The supply is inexhaustible!"

"What is it? What fuels the fires of Hell?"

Satan looked speculatively at me. "I'm not sure I should tell you. It's a company secret. Or, rather, it's my secret. Beelzebub doesn't even know."

"Huh?" I scratched my head like a hayseed staring at the Empire State Building. "How is that possible? He designed the system didn't he?"

"Yes, all except for one important part. I built the fuel line myself, and no one else in Hell, not even my chief engineer, knows what's inside it." Satan was silent for a moment. Then he nodded, as if he'd made some kind of decision. "Let's see the schematic of the system."

I pulled the drawing from the inside pocket of my coveralls. Satan caused a drafting table to materialize between us and spread the diagram out on top of it. "I hate to do this, but if you're right ... " Satan waved his hand over the paper, and a faint green line appeared. It ran from Gates Level all the way down to Level Nine, snaking this way and that in a nonsensical fashion. The distance it needed to travel was only nine miles, but there must have been at least fifty miles of pipe laid.

"Why does the line go in all these screwy directions?"

The Lord of Hell slapped me, making sure in the process to dig the claws that passed for his fingernails into my cheek. I yelped. "Don't be a moron, Minion. To keep the pipeline out of the view of others, I had to run it through every backwater corner of Hell, hiding it behind mountains, fire pits, you name it. Tell me, stupid, you've been all over Hell in your pitiful attempts to fix things. Have you ever noticed this particular pipeline before?"

Satan's sour mood seemed to have left him. I guess there's nothing like inflicting "ouch" to cheer a body up. Insults helped too, I supposed. I rubbed my cheek, noting without surprise that there was blood on my hand from where he'd gouged me. "Well, there're a lot of pipes in Hell going every which a ways, so it's a little hard to tell, but I don't think so."

"You don't think so. Geez. These are the tools you let me have." Satan looked upward and sighed before returning his attention to me. "Of course you haven't. I'm the Master of

Deception, as well as being the Prince of Lies. Beelzebub himself has never spotted them."

I wonder why he didn't put a glamour on them, like Beezy did on his own pipes.

"I'll answer that," Satan responded, reading my mind, "though usually such a thought would put you in the iron maiden. The simple reason is it's more fun to hide things in plain sight than to use magic. Besides, the other princes of Hell - especially Beelzebub - wouldn't have been fooled."

"If you wanted the pipe to remain hidden, why give me a schematic now?"

"Because I don't think you can handle this on your own." Satan frowned. "As much as I dislike interfering in a soul's eternal punishment, you need a little help."

He stood, and the chairs disappeared. I landed on my ass then scrambled to my feet. "Thanks. I could use all the ... "

At that moment, I got hit by the usual combination of Hellfire and pie and found myself back on the floor, cursing this time. "Man, I did not see that coming," I mumbled, wiping the coconut cream from my face. "I didn't even see you throw it."

"Oh, I never throw my own pies."

"No?"

"I have a service."

"Ah."

"You have something on your mind." He put his hand to his brow momentarily and I wondered if the cold were affecting him as well. "Not really," he said. "I'm just a little busier than usual. Go ahead and ask your question."

"Well," I said slowly. "It's about Flo's lamp. It's not connected to Hell's HVAC system at all, yet I couldn't light it. And I was having difficulty even lighting a match a while ago."

Satan folded up the HVAC blueprints and handed them to me. The table summarily disappeared. "But that's not your real question, is it?"

"No. No sir, I mean." I was struggling to put in words my ill-formed hypothesis. "When I was talking to Flo, she said her lamp was a symbol of hope for all who saw it. I told her that she herself was the symbol of hope that inspired us. Then Bik said something really interesting."

"Which was … ?" Satan yawned. He was getting bored with our conversation. It was clear he wanted me out of there.

"That Flo was like The Spark. When he said that, I felt a chill. I think in some way Bik was right."

"The Spark, huh?" Satan chortled. "Spare me the fire giant mumbo jumbo. But he's basically correct."

"Lord Satan," I hesitated, "is The Spark hope itself?"

"Close, but no cigar. It's far bigger than that. But I'm tired of explaining things to you. Go up to Gates Level and ask Pete to show you the Well of Souls. Maybe you can figure out the rest for yourself."

"The Well of Souls?"

"Yes." He leaned over to me and hissed. "Meeting adjourned!"

Chapter 20

Satan walked over to his La-Z-Boy and gently shook BOOH. The bat opened one eye then began purring when he saw his master. The Earl of Hell smiled and whispered something in BOOH's ear. He nodded eagerly then hopped off the chair.

The nap, and time spent in Satan's presence, had done BOOH a world of good. He seemed his old self.

The Devil nodded, satisfied. "Minion," he said, not taking his eyes of his pet. "Take BOOH with you up to Gates Level. But I don't want you wearing him out. Use the Elevator. It's waiting for you two now."

"Uh, okay. Come on BOOH. We're going to talk with St. Peter." I looked to Satan. "You know he doesn't like me, right?"

"So what do I care? He'll answer your questions. He's such a pompous know-it-all, he won't be able to help himself. Now, get out of here before I toss you out."

As promised, Hell's Elevator was outside Satan's office, door open, waiting for us. The demon who animated the Elevator must have really hated being so accommodating.

Hell's Elevator is really big, but it's not hangar size big, and getting a bat the size of a small Cessna inside was a bit of a trick. BOOH squeezed himself into the metal box, bending his head until it almost touched his stomach. By the time he pulled his last foot inside, the Elevator was almost completely filled with a solid furry ball of scrunched BOOH. I couldn't even see his mouth, just his beady red eyes.

I wasn't sure how I was going to get in myself. "Yikes!" I squawked as BOOH reached out a claw and pulled me inside. He draped me across his belly. The situation reminded me of something I had done back in college with ten of my dorm mates, and I started laughing. "BOOH," I said, still chuckling, "do you think you can punch the button for Gates Level?"

The furry monster stretched out one toe and snagged the GL button with a claw. The doors closed, and the ELEVATOR blasted upward.

The demon running the thing was almost as fast as BOOH, and before we knew it the GL light started glowing. The Elevator dinged once then stopped.

Now, on Satan's level of Hell, the Elevator door will open automatically. It's a rare courtesy that he extends to the occasional guest who comes from Gates Level. On GL, however, there is no automatic door opener, so BOOH and I needed to open the thing ourselves. Normally, that's only a mild inconvenience, but being stuffed as we were in the elevator, like two sardines - or rather, a sardine and a blue whale - this was going to be a challenge.

I couldn't do a thing, being smooshed face-down against BOOH's chest the way I was, but he managed to slip a claw under the lip of the door (which was on the scale of one fronting a garage) and pop it open. In a couple of seconds, we tumbled out of the Elevator, like the Marx Brothers did in the stateroom scene from 'A Night at the Opera.'

Gates Level, the neutral zone between Hell and that other place, seems made of clouds, though the walking surface is solid enough. Today was more overcast than usual. The Pearly Gates were only visible as a bright glow behind a veil of precipitate gauze. The Gate to Hell was all-too-visible, though. I noted that the "Abandon all Hope" sign above the Escalator was dark again. Normally, the sign was top priority, but the HVAC system was taking precedence over everything else at the moment, especially now that Orson couldn't work independently anymore. The sign would stay a black rectangle until I had time to put in a new bulb.

Things were pretty quiet up on Gates Level. Only a few souls were standing in line before Peter, and he dispatched them quickly. The saint frowned at me as I approached. Since he didn't like me, this wasn't much of a surprise. "Why is BOOH hitching a ride on the Elevator? Ah, never mind. Are you here to fix the sign? Welles and Edison obviously didn't do a very good job. And what about that pile of rubble over there? I've been waiting for you to clean that up since the incident with the Hellions."

I glanced over at the debris that was blocking the entrance to the Stairway to Hell. Or the Stairway to Paradise. It all depended on which end of the stairwell you were at.

Everything's relative, I suppose.

The Hellions, or Free Hellions as they more properly were called, was a gang of damned souls that had tried to escape Hell by means of the Stairway. I'd stopped them, with a little help from Pinkerton, by collapsing the exit from the stairwell to Gates Level. I frowned. There really needed to be a proper, dramatic entryway there, but my masonry skills were about as good as Lucy Ricardo's. At the very least, though, I needed to tidy things up.

I painted a smile on my face and did my best to be polite to the prickly saint. "I know, St. Peter. Unfortunately, we've got sort of a crisis on our hands right now."

"And when do you not?"

"Well," I said, shuffling my feet a bit. "It's true there's always some sort of mess down in Hell. Sort of by definition, if you know what I mean."

Peter snorted. He had a way of doing it that I found particularly irritating. Heaven's Concierge could communicate more disdain and patrician superiority in a single snort than others could manage with a paragraph of disparagement. "What's wrong now?"

"Heating system's on the fritz. Air conditioning too, though we don't use much of that."

Peter looked amused. "No heat in Hell? I can see that would be a problem for you."

Okay. I knew it wasn't his issue to solve, and he clearly didn't give a shit about my troubles, but I had questions to ask and wanted good answers, so I decided it was time to get him invested in the situation. "It could be a problem for you too."

"Really?" he said, picking up his letter opener - it was shaped like a sword and had been given to him by the archangel Michael - and slitting open some envelopes that were piled on his desk. "And exactly why would it be a problem for me?"

"Why, Pete," I said casually, the informal tone making his head pop up like a Whac-A-Mole mole. "Have you never heard the expression, 'a cold day in Hell?'"

This was the best part of my day so far. I got to watch Peter's expression change from puzzled to thoughtful to horrified. The saint paled, as the ramifications sunk in. "How," he stammered, "how can I help?"

Better. I shrugged. "Don't know, but Satan sent me up here to see something. And he thought you could answer some questions for me."

Peter placed the letter opener on the Book of Life then took a small sign with a little gold chain attached and hung it on a nail that had been hammered into the front of his desk. I took a look at what the sign said: "On break. Back soon. St. Peter."

"What do you want to see?"

"The Well of Souls."

The saint shook his head. "You can't see that. It's behind the Pearly Gates. Wait," he said with sudden understanding. "I think I know what Satan means. Follow me."

Peter led me and BOOH, who hopped along behind us, past the Gates of Hell and toward the pathway that led to Charon's ferry, one of the other ways to get down to the Netherworld. Peter walked past the trail, though, and I soon found myself in an area of Gates Level I'd never visited before.

In the distance, obscured by some of the low-flying clouds that littered the landscape of the GL, something was glowing. As we got closer to the source, I gave a whistle. Before me, was a gigantic lake, filled with golden light. "Wow!" was about all I could muster.

"Yes, impressive, isn't it?"

"I thought you said the Well of Souls was behind the Pearly Gates."

"It is, but this is another Well of Souls. The one in Heaven holds those waiting to be born on Earth. This is the Well of [Damned] Souls."

"What's that noise you just made?"

"Hmm?" Peter was staring thoughtfully at the well. "That's the sound of brackets. It's a little hard to do. Sort of a constriction of the glottis, a little like the "ch" sound in the German 'Ich.'"

I tried it a couple of times. "Close enough," the saint said.

"Okay, so this is the Well of [Damned], *cough*, Souls. But that doesn't tell me much. I really don't get it."

"No reason why you should. It's not talked about much. But think back, if you can, to the moment I told you that you were damned."

I closed my eyes and tried to remember. It was harder than I thought, as if a veil had been drawn over my memory. Perhaps that was part of the procedure, or perhaps I had repressed the memory. The saint must have realized this, for I suddenly felt the gentle stroke of his hand on my forehead. Suddenly I recalled standing before St. Peter's desk for the first time. Peter, looking exactly as he did now, flipped rapidly through the Book of Life, looking for my name.

I didn't know much about the administrative procedures of salvation, but I always thought things were pretty binary. If your name was in the Book, you entered the Pearly Gates. If it wasn't, you won the Booby Prize. In my case, I was a booby.

I thought harder and remembered that a frown crossed Peter's face. Then he reached in his pocket and pulled out a quarter, which he flipped in the air.

"Hey!" I yelled, my eyes popping open. "Was my damnation determined by a coin toss?"

"Whoops!" St. Peter quickly removed his hand from my brow and looked away. He started paying close attention to a small cumulus puppy that seemed to have wandered away from others of its kind. "I don't," he said finally, "I don't know what you're talking about."

"You do too! You tossed a coin. I remember now." Funny that I couldn't before, but it explained why my memory was so cloudy. "How many souls had been damned by a coin toss?"

"Well," Peter said finally, "you were a borderline case - funny how many of those we get - and that's how I usually decide in those instances."

I plopped down on the cloud surface. "Shit," I grumbled, "I'm in Hell because I lost a coin toss."

"Never mind about that!" the saint finally snapped. "I don't answer to you. Besides, that's all ancient history, and you're not remembering what's really important. Keep trying to recall what happened at the precise moment of your damnation."

Still grumbling, I closed my eyes again. *What* did *happen?* And then I remembered. "There was a bright flash of light."

"Right," Peter said. "That was the moment when your soul left your body."

"What??" I said, scrambling to my feet. "First I learn I went to Hell because of a lost coin toss, and now you're saying I don't have a soul." I found that my fists were clenched. I was about to slug a famous saint.

Peter sensed my anger. "Calm yourself. Of course you have a soul, it's just that once you're damned not all of it resides in you."

My anger turned to hurt and despair. I felt like a little boy who had just lost a puppy.

"That bright flash of light you remember was the pure portion of your soul. It separated from you at the moment of your damnation and came here." Peter indicated the lake. "Once you're damned, the unsullied part of your soul stays up here. It can't descend into Hell. It's still yours, though," he said hurriedly. "A connection remains."

"You said only the pure portion of my soul leaves me. So what's left is ... "

"The dregs," St. Peter said, patting my shoulder sympathetically. "Sorry about that."

"Dregs. Great, so I really am all evil."

"No, no, there's still plenty of good stuff there. Some great beer comes from the bottom of the barrel."

"Your metaphors leave something to be desired."

"Good grief, Minion. Quit feeling sorry for yourself. Some good in a damned person's soul is pure," he said, pointing at the lake. "It remains here. The rest is either entirely bad or good, sometimes even substantial good, that is so tightly alloyed with evil that the two cannot be separated. If it makes you feel any better, in your case, there's more good than bad floating around inside you."

"If there's more good in me than bad, even now, after you filched the pure stuff, then why am I in Hell?"

"You lost the coin toss."

"I know, I know," I grumbled. "but if I'm more good than bad, why was the coin toss even necessary?"

Peter shrugged. "Being good alone is insufficient. You were deficient in good works. You didn't do enough of them in your life."

I felt like I was being sucked into a theological argument that had been going on since at least the Reformation. "Yeah, well what about faith?"

St. Peter looked at me appraisingly. "My guess is you were a little deficient in that as well."

He was right, I knew. "So ... so just being good ... "

"... isn't good enough," St. Peter said, finishing my sentence. "Look. They're all important: being a good person, doing good works, having faith. When someone doesn't make it into the Book of Life, it's because they are deficient in one or more of the categories."

Swell. That explained a lot, though, such as why a number of obviously good people were rotting in Hell. Especially if there were so many borderline cases that a coin toss was necessary.

"Minion, we're drifting from our main topic."

"Hmm?" I said, distracted.

"The Well of Souls."

I shook my head to clear it. "Right. You were saying?"

"The pure portion of your soul is in the Well."

"I heard that already, but why?"

"Don't know exactly," Peter said, sitting on the bank next to the lake of golden light. I sat down beside him. "What I've been told is that a few people upstairs," he said, looking up to some place I couldn't see, "had once considered experimenting with recycling ... I mean reincarnation. You've got to remember that this Well of Souls is just as unsullied as the Well of Unborn Souls in Heaven. In fact, they're connected."

"What? Why?"

"Well, the thinking was, if the level of Heaven's well dropped too low and demand for souls exceeded supply, the valve between the two would open and we'd use some of these old souls. They're really good as new, you know."

"Has that ever happened?"

"Not to my knowledge."

I had a sudden awful thought. "What would happen if the Well of [Damned] Souls got too low?"

Peter laughed. "Not likely that. Far more people go to Hell than to Heaven. We've had to widen the lake several times just to handle the influx of new old souls."

"But if it did?"

"Not sure," Peter admitted with a shrug. "I wasn't involved in designing this system. It was here when I arrived. Why do you ask?"

"Nothing." The fact that the two wells were connected made me very uncomfortable. "I was just wondering if the valve between the two is one-way or two-way."

"Meaning what, exactly?"

"Meaning if this Well of [Damned] Souls got too low, would it start to drain the other well?"

St Peter looked at me. I looked at St. Peter. We both shuddered.

For a few moments, neither of us talked. Then I ventured another question. "Did you ever wonder what the Well of

[Damned] Souls is for, other than being a holding tank for stuff that can't go down to Hell?"

"As far as I know, that's its only purpose."

A flash of insight hit me, and my nausea returned with a vengeance. I was pretty sure that Pete was wrong about the well. I shuddered again.

"What's wrong, Minion? Catching a chill?"

"Hope not," I mumbled. Then a final question popped into my head. "St. Peter, this may seem a little off-topic, but I was wondering, is a soul a form of hope?" I know Satan had said no, but I was interested in getting another perspective, especially one from the other side.

Peter scratched his beard. "I've never thought of it like that, but in a way, yes. Every soul is hope, hope for good, hope for salvation. Potential."

I got to my feet. "Thanks, St. Peter. I think I've learned what I came to find out."

Peter rose. Literally. He floated up, then when his head had reached about the level of mine, he unfolded his legs and touched his feet to the ground. It was a pretty neat trick. "Well, I'm glad I was helpful. I hope you can stop that cold day in Hell before things get too chilly down there. If you don't, next time you come up here, you might be dealing with another saint."

"Pardon?"

"An, ah, infelicitous statement I made once to Paul, involving that 'all Hell freezes over' expression."

It seemed even saints weren't above using the phrase. "Come on, BOOH. I'm sure St. Peter wants to get back to work, and it's time for you and me to go."

But BOOH wasn't paying any attention to me. He was standing on the edge of the Well of [Damned] Souls, staring into its depths. Then he dove in.

"What's he doing?" Peter shouted.

I looked down at my friend, who had just surfaced and begun to swim for shore. "The backstroke, I think."

"He can't do that!"

"No, look. He's really pretty good at it. He could put Johnny Weissmuller to shame."

Peter punched my arm. "That's not what I meant. I meant, it's not allowed."

I rubbed the spot where the saint had hit me. That was gonna make a bruise. "Will it hurt the souls?"

He frowned. "Well, no. They're pure, like I told you, and not really vulnerable to anything but the bad choices of a human's free will during mortal life. As far as I can tell, BOOH hasn't a gram of evil in him. He's morally neutral."

"Then there's no problem," I said, as BOOH bounded to the shore. The giant bat, completely rejuvenated, was glowing with a golden light. He stretched his wings high overhead. He was like Superbat.

I nodded. BOOH's sudden recovery convinced me that I was right.

"Looking good, BOOH! Thanks again, Peter, for the information." Though I still wasn't very happy about the coin toss, or my sore arm, he had been helpful. "Come on BOOH, let's get back to the Elevator."

"Skree!" BOOH shot into the sky. He was stronger and faster than ever. Like a falcon on speed, SuperBOOH plummeted to the ground, snatched me up, and shot toward the Mouth of Hell.

I could no longer see Peter or the Lake. We had left him behind in the wink of an eye. As we entered the Mouth, I realized we wouldn't be needing the Elevator for a while.

Chapter 21

Lying on top of my desk was the HVAC schematic, with a little addition of my own. On a piece of butcher paper (that's all we really have to write on down here - that and work orders) I had sketched the Gates Level, along with my best sense of where the Well of [Damned] Souls was in relationship to the Pearlies, the Escalator, the Elevator, the Stairs and the pathway to Charon's boathouse.

I had done my best to draw this to the same scale as the HVAC schematic, and I tried now to place my sketch above the blueprints, aligning things the way I thought they fit. "Hmm."

"Hmm, what?" Orson asked, as he came into the office, his hands full of supplies. Above him, Bik flew in a lazy sort of loop-the-loop.

"Just looking at the HVAC drawing some more," I said, as I walked over to the Mr. Coffee and poured some coffee into my "I'M NOT WITH STUPID. I AM STUPID" mug. I took a sip and did my involuntary wince. As usual, my cup o' joe tasted like hell. "What's all that stuff in your hands? It looks like you raided Dora's warehouse."

"I did," Orson said, dumping the supplies in a corner of the trailer. "While you were off visiting who knows who, I did some more triage on our work orders. Things are backing up pretty badly, so I picked up the supplies we'll need for the top priority items. Might save us some time when this HVAC crap is over with."

The HVAC. I hadn't discussed with Orson my growing concerns about the true severity of the situation, though I knew he had some notion that this was more serious than a heater being on the blink. A shiver went down my spine, as much from fear as the drop in temperature.

"Cold?"

"Maybe. That was good thinking, by the way, picking up those supplies." A good supervisor should always praise the initiative of a subordinate.

But Orson frowned. "Don't patronize me."

"Sorry."

I stared at the two drawings, placed end to end. "Say, Orson, pour yourself some coffee and come take a look at this with me."

Orson grabbed his mug. It was bright yellow and said Blimpie's on it. There was a big blimp on the mug too. I always thought whoever had given Orson the mug had been making a joke about his weight, but I never mentioned that to him. My assistant topped off his cup with some coffee then, as an afterthought, grabbed a can of sardines.

"Rickets?" I asked mildly.

"Not so far, thank goodness. No. I'm just hungry." Orson opened the tin, cutting his finger on the jagged edge of the can. "Shit!"

Orson stared at the drawing for a minute, dripping, oil from his sardine can on the paper. "Sorry," he said, blotting it up with his sleeve.

"No problem."

"Did you add the little drawing on top?"

"Yeah."

"Why?" Orson took a sardine out of the tin, stared speculatively at it then dropped it in the coffee. He took a sip and grimaced.

"Any better?"

"No, a little worse in fact, but I'd never tried it before."

"Nothing ventured, nothing gained," I offered.

"You didn't answer my question. Why did you graft the Gates Level on top of the schematic? And where did these green lines come from on the blueprint? I don't remember them from before."

I grabbed an orange from the crate we always kept in the office. Well, the one with oranges in it. We had the other crate, but it was full of blood bags. Orson must have gone back to the hospital to pick up some treats for BOOH. Copying Orson, I put a slice of orange in my coffee and took a sip.

"Any better?"

I spat on the floor.

"Didn't think so. That's why I tried the sardines instead. Now, about the lines?"

"Satan added them."

"What are they?"

"Company secret. Need-to-know basis. You'll probably need to know later, but for now, I'll keep it to myself, so I don't end up in the shithouse with Satan."

"Fine by me. I don't want to know anything Satan would rather keep secret. That's a death w ... never mind. It's a bad idea."

"Can't argue with you there."

Orson studied the green lines. "They're a bit of a mess. Like green spaghetti smeared all over the page. Or the line you've drawn when you've solved a maze puzzle."

"Maze puzzle?"

"You know, you have a maze drawn on a piece of paper, you take your pencil, start at one end, and you have to get to the other end. There's only one solution."

"Yeah. I remember those. Satan did that on purpose. Tell me, though, can you find the two ends?"

"Probably. I used to be pretty good at these things. Look here," he said, pointing to the terminus down on Level Nine. "Here's one."

Orson was pointing at the end that fed into Surtr's boiler room. "And here's the other at the top."

"Yeah. That's what I thought too, but I wanted a second opinion. See any other loose ends?"

My assistant did a quick double-check. "Nope."

I tapped the end at the top of the schematics. "Where do you think this one finishes?"

My fat friend ran his fingers through his beard. "Hard to say, since it goes all the way to the top of the page, but if you've placed your drawing in the correct spot, I'd say it ends ... here!" Orson pointed to a round circle I'd drawn.

"Yes," I agreed. "That's the Well of [Damned] Souls."

"What's that funny sound you're making before and after the word 'damned?'"

"Brackets."

"What's the Well of [Damned] Souls?" Orson made a perfect brackets sound without any practice. He had always been good at making noises, though: cat calls, farts, squeaks, even vocal impressions. He probably picked up the skill during his years in radio. Anyway, it was impressive.

"Believe me, you don't want to know." But then I reconsidered. Satan had been reluctant to share the information about the fuel line with me, but he hadn't actually told me anything about the Well.

Making a decision, I closed my eyes and tried something I'd never done before: I attempted to project my thoughts. In my head, I said, "Lord Satan, I need to tell Orson all about this. I need his help."

I hadn't really expected a response, but to my surprise, the Devil's voice hissed in my head. *Go ahead, Minion. But tell Orson to keep his trap shut, or I'll feed his fat butt to the Kraken. And never do this again! I'm not an answering service, you know. Make an appointment like everyone else.*

My eyes popped open, and I saw my assistant peering intently at me. "What just happened?"

"I … I had a conversation with Satan."

"What? How?"

My heart was hammering in my chest. That may have been the single most terrifying thing I'd ever experienced in Hell. I always felt that a man's thoughts should be his own, and even though the conversation was at my own initiation, I still felt violated. "We're … we're working on something that's really important, and I guess Satan was monitoring my thoughts. Mind reader, remember?"

Perspiration began to form on Orson's forehead. "Scary."

"You said it. I've never done that before. Wasn't even sure it would work, but I needed an answer right away. I guess Satan thinks the situation is serious enough to indulge me."

"Indulge you how?"

I sat in my desk chair, feeling a little faint. That was creepy-scary, and it made me wonder if the Earl of Hell really was omniscient. I hoped not. The prospect of never having a private thought unnerved me. "I … I need to be able to tell you what's going on, or what I suspect is going on, and I wanted Satan's permission."

"And he gave it to you?"

"Yeah." I wiped my forehead with my sleeve. The fabric came back soaked, as if I'd just had a panic attack, which was probably exactly what had happened. I took a few deep breaths and began to explain. "Orson, as you've figured out, the green lines are actually just one. It's the fuel line for the heating system. We've always known that what little cold we need down here is provided by Erebus. It's like a slowly melting, gigantic stalactite. It should last us forever. But the heat, well, we need to burn something. It's not sulfur. All the mines in all of Hell couldn't produce enough fuel to keep Hell hot."

Orson nodded. "I know. The sulfur is just for effect. And the smell of course."

"Of course. Now, the line at the bottom is going into the boiler room where I met Surtr. I'm pretty sure it feeds the main burners down there."

"If that's the destination for the fuel, then you're saying the source is this Well."

"It's only a theory, but ... " I nodded.

"Then, then you think our heating fuel is ... "

"Say it. Say it, Orson. I don't want to."

"Souls? My Go ... damn it, that's diabolical!"

Satan's laughter echoed in my brain, sending me to quaking in my work boots. "Sort of by definition. Satan designed this part of the system. Even Beezy doesn't know what fuels the system. Satan didn't want him to, which is why the line is all in curlicues, taking the pipe wherever it needs to go to stay out of sight."

I left my desk and walked over to the window. Outside, Hell was bustling. The traffic on the Road to Hell was snarled, and some demons were out in the middle of the cracked asphalt trying to make it worse. They were all wearing hoodies. Yep, things were definitely getting colder. No self-respecting demon would wear a hoody unless he was really cold. I turned back to my friend. "It gets worse."

Orson looked at me aghast. "How could it possibly get worse?"

Aside from the fact that a chunk of your soul, and mine, is in that vast well? I didn't tell him that part, though if he thought long enough, Orson might figure it out. He was smart. Until he did, though, the owners of the Well's souls was a ghastly secret I would keep to myself. What I said instead was, "There is another Well of Souls inside the Pearly Gates. It's the source for all the newborn Christian, Jewish and Muslim babies on Earth."

"And why is that relevant to our problem?"

"The wells are connected. If one gets too low, a valve will open and ... "

"You mean Hell could potentially start burning baby souls?" Orson started to gag.

"Man up, old chum. I don't think Satan wants that any more than we do. I suspect that would get him in deep shit with his boss."

"Satan doesn't have a boss," Orson mumbled, then his eyes widened. "Oh. HIM."

"Exactly. Burning damned souls is bad, but Satan's responsible for the damned anyway. Besides, at worst, it's no more than a bit of petty larceny, and I think the guy upstairs pretty much expects that of the Devil. Burning souls of the unborn, though, I think that would qualify as grand theft."

While we had been talking, Bik had settled on the counter where we kept the coffee pot. In the air he had formed one of his flaming discs and was speaking intently into it.

"Hey, Bik," I hollered. "Do you have your grandfather on flameophone there?"

The fire giant glanced at me over his shoulder. "Yes. I was just filling him in on our adventures."

"Do you think I could talk with him for a sec?"

"Sure! I'll try to make the disc bigger. Ugh. This is hard," he said, as he swirled his hand, increasing the diameter of the disc. "I'm having more and more trouble manipulating The Spark."

"That's because we're all in deep doo-doo," said a smoked-ravaged voice from the disc. I leaned in closely and saw the ancient fire giant.

"And why are we in deep doo-doo?" I asked, fully expecting a certain answer.

"Because the last jet on the heating system just went out."

I stared at the tiny image of Surtr. It was hard to tell, since I was staring through a monitor made of flame, but it seemed to me that Surtr was burning like a house afire.

"Well, you look pretty good, considering your job's on the line, not to mention probably freezing your fanny off."

The old giant bit down on his cigar, turning it to ash. "What do you mean?"

"Well, you're burning so hot you're practically blue."

"I'm mad, damn it! And frustrated! I take pride in my work, and whatever's going on is making me look like a nincompoop." Surtr screamed in rage, the monitor filled with a blinding light then went out.

"He's right, you know," Bik said. "Grandpa takes his work very seriously, and he's got a wicked temper. The madder he gets, the hotter he gets."

"Interesting," I said, but I was thinking about the information Surtr had given me. "Thanks, Bik."

I wandered back over to where Orson was still studying the schematic. "It's as I thought," I said to him quietly. "The fires of Hell just went out."

"And what exactly do you think that means?"

"It means we're out of fuel."

"How can that be? You said yourself the Well of [Damned] Souls is plenty full."

"I think we've sprung a leak somewhere."

Orson frowned. "Then, somewhere in Hell, souls are spewing all over the place."

"Possibly. There's a problem, somewhere, that's for sure, but how do you find 'somewhere' in all of the Nine Circles?" Then an idea popped into my head. Pulling open my bottom drawer, I rummaged through its contents. "Rubber duckie, no. Wet Wipes, uh uh. Ah, here it is," I said, pulling out a stethoscope.

"What's that for?"

"We're going to try to find the leak."

"With a stethoscope?"

"I think so," I said a little sheepishly. "The souls aren't on fire as they travel through the pipeline, so the only thing I can think to do is listen for the flow of their passage through the pipe."

"That's stupid."

"Hey, it's what I do. Besides, you got any better ideas?"

Orson walked to our parts closet. "No," he said, lifting another stethoscope off a shelf.

"What's that for?"

"You may need a second opinion." Orson put the ear pieces of the stethoscope around his neck, doctor style. "Man, this is going to take forever."

"Maybe," I agreed, "but it's all we've got right now. Look here," I said, indicating the green line that crossed at Level Five. "That's not far from here. Let's go take a listen."

My assistant closed the door to the closet. "Yes, let's. Bik you coming?"

"Huh?" The fire giant was recreating his flameophone. "In a minute. There's something I forgot to tell Grandpa."

I taped together the HVAC diagram and my own drawing and folded them under my arm. "Well, shake a leg. We're going to be just across the street."

"'kay. I won't be long."

As we stepped onto the road, I wished we'd had on white lab coats. The stethoscopes looked stupid against our yellow coveralls, but we could only work with what we had.

Though there was plenty of activity in the oil refinery, the tall iron gates were closed. Orson and I shouldered one open and went inside. We were looking for a pipe, but there were plenty of those here. The place was littered with them. I only hoped the sketch was accurate enough to help us spot the one we wanted.

"Crap! Crap, crap, crap!"

Looking to our right, we spotted a man in overalls who was struggling with a valve on a pipe that was stretched across the ground. He looked ancient, close to a hundred, and frail enough to snap between two fingers. The skin on his cadaverous face was like parchment; his thin, white locks looked like wisps of smoke on an otherwise bald pate. "Hey, J.D.," I said. "What's the problem?"

J.D. Rockefeller was drenched in sweat. He must have been working on the valve for some time. "I can't get this damn thing open. It's stuck."

"Of course it is," Orson replied mildly. "This is Hell after all. What do you expect?"

Rockefeller grunted as he gave the valve another go. "A little less lip from another one of the damned, Welles, would be something."

"How about a hand instead?" I offered.

"That," he gasped, trying again, "that would be appreciated."

I gave him a standing ovation. With a smirk, Orson joined in.

"Very funny," he grumbled.

"Got the idea from Bruce the Bedeviled, so you can thank him. Besides, we couldn't resist," I said, grabbing the valve with him. Orson, chuckling, did the same.

Man, was it ever stuck. It took all three of us five minutes of grunting and straining to get the valve to move. We finally got it open.

As I stepped away from the pipe, I studied the workman. J.D. Rockefeller was the world's first billionaire, having reached that milestone in 1916. At that time, his personal wealth was nearly two percent of the gross domestic product of the entire US. I did a little mental math and figured that, accounting for inflation, he probably would be a trillionaire in the present era, which, although I didn't know for sure, was probably around the year 2050 back on Earth. Some people say old J.D. was the richest man to ever live.

I didn't like Rockefeller very much. He wasn't a nice guy at all, although very religious in life, not that it did him much good in the end. The only one of those captains of industry from the Guilded Age that I gave a flip about was Andrew Carnegie, and that was mainly because he liked libraries, like me. Not to mention he built Carnegie Hall, were I once heard Isaac Stern play. Rockefeller didn't bug me as much as Edison and Ford, but he still wasn't any favorite of mine.

However, meeting him this way could prove fortuitous. "A favor for a favor?" I asked.

Rockefeller was as ruthless as the rest of his kind, so I'd never thought of him being the most giving person. That's probably unfair, since he set up a substantial foundation that was still doing good in the world in the mid 1990s, when I was killed. His foundation helped the human race, I guess, but would he himself help a single person? I wondered, noticing that he hadn't even bothered to thank us for our assistance.

"Why should I?" he answered predictably. "I've already got what I want."

I shrugged. "Okay. Orson, help me close this valve again."

J.D. tried to stop us, but Orson used his prodigious girth to block him. "Okay, okay! Just leave the valve alone. What do you want?"

Orson and I smiled at each other, and I picked up the blueprints from where I'd laid them on the ground. "I'm trying to find a pipe ... "

"Well, look around. We've got plenty to choose from."

"Yeah, I know that," I said, rolling my eyes. "That's the problem. Take a look at this."

Rockefeller took the blueprints from me, and I indicated the green mark that represented the pipe. "Do you know where this is?"

J.D. laughed. The sound was like a carburetor dying. "Yeah, that one I know. I bet even you two assholes could have found it given enough time." He pointed to a spot fifty feet before us. There it was. A straight green pipe.

I hadn't really expected it to be green.

"Well, that might make things a little easier," Orson opined.

"Yeah," I said. "Thanks Rocky. Oops! Sorry. That was your grandson, Nelson. Well, if I had a name like Nelson, I'd go by Rocky too."

"Fuck you, Minion!"

"You too!" I replied gaily. "Have a nice day."

As we left Rockefeller, I heard a terrible squeak. Turning back to where the man stood, I saw the valve turning itself off. "Aaggh!" he screamed. J.D. grabbed the valve, trying desperately to keep it open, but the valve just continued to close, dragging Rockefeller along the pavement until he flipped over the pipe. He landed on his back, and I heard the crack of fragile bones breaking. "Ow! Damn."

We left the founder of Standard Oil sprawled on the pavement. As we approached the green pipe, I began to whistle.

"You know, Steve," Orson said, with a twisted grin, "you're not always a very nice person."

"I know, I know. What can I do though? The guy's a prick, not like Edison or Ford, but still a prick. He wouldn't have given us the time of day if I hadn't blackmailed him."

"True enough. And now, doctor," Orson said, putting the stethoscope to his ears. "Shall we examine the patient?"

I nodded and stuffed my own rubber ear tips in place. We must have looked pretty odd, two yellow-garbed maintenance types listening for the heartbeat of a fat green pipe. I moved the chest piece up and down the metal cylinder, listening for anything that sounded vaguely like a whooshing sound. Orson did the same. I couldn't hear a damn thing.

At last, I took the rubber tips from my ears. "Well?" I asked my assistant.

Orson shook his head. "He's dead, Jim."

I snorted. "Thank you Mr. Spock. Or should I call you Dr. Spock?"

"I don't think so. Wasn't he a pediatrician?"

"Right." I stuffed the stethoscope in a pocket. "You're more of a pipe doctor. Besides, wasn't it Bones who was always saying that, not Spock? Anyway, assuming we can hear the swooshing of souls as they pass through this pipe, then I think the leak must be somewhere above us."

"That's a logical conclusion, assuming, as you say, that swooshing souls make a sound at all. We should go someplace where we're more likely to hear it. Any ideas?"

At that moment, Bik flew across the street. He flamed off and dropped into my pocket protector. Absently, I patted my pocket.

"Hey, watch it!"

"Sorry. You okay in there?"

"Yeah," grumbled the little guy. He seemed to be in a bad mood. Probably talking to his grandfather did that. I know it would do it to me, if Surtr had been my granddad.

I showed Orson the diagram. "What do you think?"

He nodded. "Looks right. Besides, maybe we can play a few holes. I haven't been on a golf course in a long time, except for Beezy's on Eight, and it's just one big sand trap. Hey, as long as we're up there, we can do a work order too."

As we walked back toward our office, I noticed that Rockefeller was back on his feet, struggling with his stubborn valve. He looked up imploringly, but we just grinned and walked by him.

Once inside our trailer, Orson went to the back wall. He rifled through a tall stack of work orders until he found what he was looking for. "Eureka! It came in this morning. Didn't seem very important, so I put it in the Dead Letter department, but as long as we're going to be there anyway ... "

"Sure," I said, as we headed outside again.

Orson looked at me speculatively. "I don't suppose we can take the Elevator."

I shook my head. "No. Besides, you won't get used to it unless you keep trying. This is a job for SuperBOOH!"

"SuperBOOH?"

"You'll see." I whistled loudly. "BOOH!"

BOOH was still glowing with vitality when he scooped us off the pavement. "Skree?" he asked.

"First Level, please. The Pro Shop." And we were off.

Chapter 22

The sky, or what passed for sky above Level One, was a bright cerulean. The day was beautiful, and I looked for the sun, which was stupid, since there is no sun in Hell. On all the other levels of Hell, the sky was gray and polluted, but in Limbo, every day was grand and the temperature always perfect, owing no doubt to One's proximity to Gates Level. After all, the people on this level were good. They were just the victims of bad timing.

As I've noted, most of the inhabitants of Limbo are babies who had never been baptized. I'm not sure what the age cutoff is, but I think it's around two. After that, a youngster starts to develop a personality, and in the terrible twos, a kid could quite possibly knowingly do something terrible.

Hey, I already told you I feel bad about this. I don't like the idea of babies being in Hell any more than you do, not even in the cushy section of the Underworld, but I'm just a humble civil servant. The powers-that-be don't really give a crap about my opinion.

The more interesting residents of One were the virtuous pagans, people like Socrates, Homer, Cicero and other folks like that. I always enjoyed striking up a conversation with a virtuous pagan. You'd often leave with something to think about.

Except for Socrates. Well, he left you with plenty to think about, but he was so irritating I could hardly stand him. What with his constant asking of questions, you'd think he was a failed psychologist. The dialectical method: bah. You can have it.

BOOH set us down at the clubhouse, near the first tee, then skedaddled back down the hole. He wasn't really supposed to spend time up there, since his very presence tended to scare the shit out of people, and One was not a place for punishment.

Limbo was more of a holding tank to put good people who didn't fit into the scheme of the Catholic universe.

Like I said earlier, Roman Catholicism got to Christianity first, so their beliefs shaped much of the topography of the metaphysical cosmos. There are some elements from Orthodox Christianity and even from the Christianity practiced in Ethiopia, which are also quite old, that got worked into the scheme of things, but Lutherans and Anglicans, Presbyterians and Methodists, not to mention the fundamentalists, are usually a bit peeved when they see how much of Heaven and Hell resembles the Catholic view of things. Doubt the Jews and the Muslims like it much either.

It never really bothered me. True, I was raised Catholic, but even if I hadn't been, well, you've got to admit that the Catholics have the best churches and religious art. And Dante: well, his *Divina Comedia* makes for a lot better read than Luther's *Ninety-Five Theses*.

But I digress. We were standing before a fairly modern clubhouse near an emerald green fairway. The scent of freshly-mown grass made me smile. I didn't get to smell that very often.

A while back, Level One had been converted to a gated golf community. That added to the security of the place. People didn't try to sneak in very often, but every once in a while, one of the damned attempted to use the Stairway to Heaven or Hell's Elevator to get to One. They were seldom successful, and even when they were, they were quickly tossed down the Throat of Hell, only to land at the Level from which they had escaped. Yet these occasional stowaways disturbed the locals, so Satan upped the security. He keyed the Elevator to only allow a handful of people - like me and Orson - access to the level. He had the two of us install a pretty impregnable door off the Stairway, so people couldn't get into One that way either. For a while, Beezy even had us dismantling the Stairway itself - but that's another story. Around the perimeter of the First Circle, Satan had brick walls and gates installed. I'm not sure what the purpose of that was. I don't know how anyone could slip in from the outer edge of Circle One without falling back to a lower level or, shudder, spinning out into Chaos, which is what I assume to be the only other possibility. Still, Satan was taking no chances.

Orson and I didn't work on the renovation. Beezy oversaw that himself, and he even had some help from Heaven. The result was a rather beautiful spot, with lovely little bungalows for the residents that backed up to the many fairways down here. Some of the homes even had swimming pools. Nice.

And the golf courses: I have no idea how many of them there were. I tried to count them once but gave up at around a thousand. Yet they needed that many. Level One was the largest Circle in Hell. It had to be to accommodate all the babies. You'd be surprised how many people die in infancy. Kind of sad really, especially since that leaves them on the short side to really enjoy a good eighteen holes. Hell, the walk alone is killer, but most of them buzzed around in dinky little golf carts and used custom-made clubs. Some of them were even pretty good players.

The First Circle has courses that ranged widely in difficulty. The easiest is the Par One, dead center in the Circle. That one only has nine holes. Well, to be more accurate, it has nine fairways, and a single hole, which is the Throat of Hell. The Throat is so huge, it's pretty much impossible not to knock the ball in. Even if you duff it, the fairways are only a few feet long; there's also a slight downhill pitch to the land near the Throat, so the ball will eventually roll in. See? You made par. Must be great for building self-esteem.

I don't know what happens to the golf balls. Probably most of them burn up on descent, but I wouldn't be surprised if occasionally some poor damned idiot on a lower level of Hell gets clobbered on the noggin with a golf ball, without the advance warning of someone yelling "Fore!"

The other courses are at varying levels of difficulty. Many people actually like a challenge, to play a golf course that's really hard, and even though Limbo is only the first level of Hell, it *is* in Hell, and man, do we know how to make golf courses. Naturally, up here, the courses are merely difficult. On the lower levels of Hell, where golf is used for eternal punishment, you could spend a decade in the rough or a sand trap, or knock ball after ball into a water hazard the size of Lake Michigan. On the golf courses of Two through Eight, foursomes queued up to tee off can have a century-long wait. That may not sound like much as far as eternal punishments go, but my friends who play the game say the wait is agony. There are lots of reasons for the slowdowns. For example, a great golfer might be paired with three beginners. The length of the holes could be another factor; some of them are as much as a thousand miles, and that might be for a par three. The biggest problem, though, is that everyone has either a wicked slice or hook, assuming they can get the ball in the air at all, and not just dribble it down the grass a dozen feet, or miss the ball entirely. Those damned golfers who can get some heft on their balls, though, drive them so far to the left or right that they could end up in the rough of a fairway on another course entirely. There are no golf carts on the lower levels, either. Everyone must walk and carry their own clubs, usually in their hands, instead of in a bag, and if they do have a bag, it's often covered with barbed wire. Satan seems to really like barbed wire.

But here on One, the hard courses are merely hard, often designed by famous golfers of days gone by, like Ben Hogan or Bobby Jones or people with nicknames out of 'The Wizard of Oz': lions and tigers and bears. Oh my. These individuals of course don't reside on One. They are just allowed to consult on a project before being sent back to whatever eternal damnation Satan has devised for them. The courses they have created, however, are marvelous, and quite beautiful. Aside from lush grasses, towering trees, pure white sand traps and shimmering blue water hazards, many courses had views that would put Pebble Beach to shame. Green fees on One are really cheap, too.

We entered the pro shop. Many of the ancient Greeks had become particularly good at golf, and they took turns staffing the office. It really wasn't much of a hardship, because they got to play with the equipment, chat with people or have a beer with their buds at the 19th Hole (that's the bar, for all you non-golfers). Behind the counter was Socrates.

Lucky me. My favorite Hellene.

"Γιατί δεν έρχεσαι;"

It was Greek to me, but fortunately Orson and I could both understand it. English is sort of the *Lingua Franca* for most of Hell (sorry about that, France), but on Level One, we mostly heard Greek and Latin, so we had to be reasonably proficient in them. Even the virtuous pagans whose native tongues were not one of these two had picked them both up over the centuries.

What he said was, "Why do you come?"

To which I responded, "Ηρθα για αυτή τη σειρά εργασίας," which means, "I came about this work order." I'll translate from now on.

The old Greek looked at me questioningly. *Do you not come seeking truth?*

Great. It was going to be one of *those* kinds of conversations. Like I said, you usually got a philosophical third degree from Socrates. He did love his dialectical method.

No, I mean yes, I mean, oh here, take a look at the work order, I said, shoving it in his hand.

Is this work order real, or is it only seeming real? Is it merely a shadow on the wall of a cave, and are we poor brutes, chained to ...

Shit, Socrates! Can we not play this game today? I've got a lot on my plate.

Is the plate half empty or half full?

I slammed my hand on the corner. *Would you stop it and just look at the fucking work order?*

The old philosopher - he was indeed pretty old for an ancient, having slammed back a shot of hemlock (not his idea) at about the age of seventy - looked a little sheepish. *Sorry. Old habits die hard.*

No kidding.

Let me just take a look at this. Socrates studied the paperwork. *Ah, yes. The ball washer at the sixth tee of the clubhouse course. You know, this is the most popular course in Limbo, since it's so close to the bar. And this ball washer being down, well it's been very inconvenient. Players have had to go an entire two holes with a dirty ball. At this rate, the extra use of the washer for the seventh hole will shorten its lifespan, though who can predict what the lifespan of a ball washer can be?*

Enough with the questions, please, Orson chimed in. He sounded about as irritated with the old Greek as I was. *Thanks for telling us where it is. We'll go take care of it now.*

Orson and I hurried to the exit. The door was just closing behind us, when we heard Socrates begin, *What is the care that a ball washer needs when ...*

267

Brother. That guy drove me crazy.

To speed things up, we commandeered a golf cart from Homer. Orson and I argued about who got to drive, but a round of rock, paper, scissors ended that discussion pretty quickly.

"Quit grumbling," Orson said from behind the wheel. He was whistling. "Just relax and enjoy the ride."

It was a nice day, and riding beat walking, so things could have been much worse. It's just that driving a golf cart is so damn much fun.

In no time, we were closing on the sixth tee. Four virtuous pagans had just pulled up to the tee box. Two were dressed in tunics, one in a kilt, and the fourth in a polo shirt and khakis. All were wearing golf cleats.

My guess was that the two in tunics were Greek and the others Roman. I've always found the Greek pagans more traditional. The Romans would borrow from anybody - especially the Greeks - and that included fashions.

The four were gathered around the broken ball washer. They'd look to the golf balls in their hands, then to the washer, then back to their balls again. They were completely nonplussed, but they visibly relaxed when they saw us draw up behind their golf cart.

Steve, and Orson too! cried one of the men in tunics.

Now that we had pulled up to the tee, I recognized the foursome. *Hi, Sophocles. How goes?*

Great, now that you're here. We weren't sure what to do.

Aye, said the fellow in the kilt. That was Aeneas. Aeneas had told me once that he learned to play golf from St. Andrew himself. Andy had nothing to do with the invention of golf, but since the town in Scotland that was named after him was widely considered to be the birthplace of the sport, he was an early adopter, even considering himself the patron saint of golf, which of course was not true. Andrew was a very good player by all accounts, however, I don't think he was as good as his brother Peter.

What do you mean, you didn't know what to do? Orson asked. *You mean the ball washer?*

Aye, Aeneas repeated, in an affected Scottish brogue, which is much harder to pull off in Latin than you would expect. *Saints be praised!*

Now that's not something you typically say in Hell and get away with, yet Aeneas was not struck by Hellfire or anything. There was, however, a sound like thunder in the air. I recognized Satan's grumble at once.

Orson scratched his head. *Why didn't you just play through and clean your ball at the next tee?*

Ovid, the guy in the polo, shrugged. *We did that last time, but, well, playing with a dirty ball is* so *unsatisfying.*

So you could have used another ball, Orson persisted.

We don't have any other balls.

What if you lose the one you have? I asked as I stepped up to the ball washer.

Och, mon, we ne'er lose golf balls, so why carry more than one?

Orson and I looked at each other then shrugged. "Figures," Orson mumbled in English. "They probably all play scratch golf too."

"Nah," I said lightly, elbowing him in the side. "Satan, now *he* plays Scratch golf." Orson started laughing, and I joined in, but a warning rumble in the sky shut us up. The virtuous pagans might have been spared the pains of Hellfire, but we knew we had not.

The foursome, not speaking English, had not followed our conversation, but they recognized the word "Scratch," and they nodded happily. *Yes,* Sophocles said. *We always break par.*

Orson's look was worth bottling.

I stepped up to the cleaner. There was no knob on top, but the stick thingee was still in the washer. I pulled it up and down a couple of times. It moved freely enough. *Aeneas, Ovid, let me hold your balls for a second.*

I beg your pardon? Ovid said.

Your golf *balls, I meant.*

Oh. The two Romans handed their balls to me. I pulled up on the stick, revealing the place to insert a golf ball. The receptacle was wet and soapy. I plopped in a ball, plunged the stick back into the cleaning reservoir, and pulled it up and down a few times. I could feel the brushes inside the washer scrubbing the ball. I pulled up on the stick, stuck the other ball in the washer, and repeated, with the same results. After drying the two balls on the green towel attached to the washer, I gave the now-white and shiny orbs back to their owners.

This isn't broken. It works just fine, I said.

The four pagans looked at me in disbelief, then Ovid stretched out his hand, palm down, fingers curled. *There's no knob.*

As Orson was in mid eye roll, he spotted a ceramic orb lying on the ground and picked it up. *Here it is. Why didn't one of you just screw it back on the plunger?*

Not our job, Sophocles said solemnly.

Well, said Orson. *I think this one even I can do.*

"Orson," I began in English, as he started to screw on the knob, "I don't think that's a very goo ... "

The smell of brimstone was unfamiliar to the pagans, and they stepped back quickly, as if they'd just stepped on some skunks. Orson, his beard still burning from the blast of Hellfire, got off the grass. He was cursing.

"You know ... " I began.

"Yeah, I know, I know. Assistant. Mustn't fix things. My eternal damnation, etc., etc." He looked in disgust at the knob then tossed it to me.

"Sorry about that," I said, as I proceeded to screw the knob back on.

Hmph. He probably can't even fix it.

Always the Cynic, eh, Diogenes? I said over my shoulder.

It's my job.

Whatever.

Truth be told, I had a bit of difficulty getting the threads to catch. Must have taken me five minutes to get the knob on straight.

As I was working, and cursing, I eavesdropped on the pagans. Ovid was telling them a story, and my ears perked up when he mentioned St. Peter. *Yes, it's true, according to Socrates, who is pretty tight with him. Peter used to be the pro at the golf course just on the other side of the Pearly Gates. Guess he was moonlighting. Anyway, he could never get together a foursome for Jesus. Seems no one wants to play golf with someone who gets a hole in one every time. But the rules of that course are that only foursomes can play. After this happened three times, Jesus fired him.*

Diogenes rubbed his beard. *Why? What did Jesus say to him?*

Well, first, I have to tell you that a crazy rooster started crowing in the background. Then Jesus said, "Doest thou not remember what I told thee once, Simon Peter? 'Before the cock crows, thou shalt deny me tee times.'"

Orson groaned.

I don't get it, Aeneas said.

At that moment, I finally managed to line up the threads on the plunger and knob and screw them together. I pulled up and down on it experimentally then nodded in satisfaction. *Diogenes,* I said, bowing to him, *if you will do the honors.*

The Greek philosopher pulled up the knob, inserted his ball, and cleaned it. After drying the white orb, he inspected every dimple, looking for any sign of dirt. *Hmph. I suppose it's fixed.*

Sign here, please, which he did, while Sophocles cleaned his ball. Then the great playwright stepped to the tee and set up his drive.

By the way, Orson said, right at the moment when Sophocles was bearing down on the ball with his driver. He shot Orson a dirty look. Sophocles only managed to drive his ball 375 yards, straight down the fairway.

Sorry, Orson apologized, without much conviction. *I was just going to ask if any of you has seen a big green pipe anywhere on the course. It should be pretty near here.*

The four pagans looked at each other dubiously, but then Ovid brightened. *Well, maybe you're talking about Satan's Column. It's pretty big.*

Maybe, I said doubtfully, but since we had no other lead, there was no harm in checking it out. *Okay, where is it?*

If you step off the path between the twelfth hole green and the thirteenth tee box, you'll see it, Ovid said.

Thanks. I folded the completed work order and stuck it in my pocket. "Let's go, Orson."

"αντίο," I said to Sophocles and Diogenes.

"vale," Orson said to Ovid and Aeneas.

"Bye!" the four replied in unison. In their respective languages, of course.

It took maybe ten minutes to get to the green of the twelfth hole. To our right, towering above us, was a massive Corinthian column, the largest I'd ever seen. Or at least so it seemed. A hundred feet up, an elaborate capital topped the column. Above the column, there appeared to be nothing but blue sky. We parked the golf cart and walked over to the structure.

Orson laid his hand on it. "Ah, as I thought. Trompe l'oeil. The Greeks invented the technique, you know."

"No, I didn't know that," I said. "But I bet I know why they call it Satan's Column. I didn't know he was so good with a paintbrush." This had to be the green pipe, carefully painted to resemble a column, but I marveled at the seeming three dimensionality of it, including what looked like a base carved out of marble. I used my fingernail to scrape an inconspicuous spot near the base. Yep, underneath all that paint was something green. I looked up and whistled. "Satan must have painted the pipe blue above the fake capital to blend in with the sky. This is much classier than a green pipe."

"Indeed," said my rotund friend. "About what you'd expect up here. You know, Steve, if Limbo is this nice, can you imagine what Hea ... what that other place must look like?"

"Nope, not in my wildest imaginings. Don't want to either."

"Why not?"

"Too depressing. I'm stuck with what I've got, so why should I torture myself with what I can't have?"

"Point taken," he said, pulling his stethoscope out of his tool belt. I did the same, and in moments we were repeating the same examination we had performed on Level Five.

This time, though, we heard a definite swishing.

"He's alive! He's alive!" Orson screamed to the sky. "Bwa ha ha!"

"Very funny. So, now we know the leak is somewhere between One and Five."

Orson pursed his lips and nodded. "Shall we split the difference and go to Three?"

"Why not? That will limit our maximum number of additional examinations to two levels, Three and Four or Three and Two. Once we've figured out what Circle the problem is on, we'll still have to isolate things further."

"I just hope the leak isn't somewhere high above ground," Orson said as he climbed back in the driver's seat of the golf cart.

"Me too. Orson?"

"What?"

"I know you won at rock, paper, scissors and all, but could I...?"

Orson smiled and got out of the cart. "Sure. Knock yourself out."

Humming, I drove us back to the pro shop.

Chapter 23

We dropped off the golf cart with Homer, then I whistled for BOOH. He was a little slow getting to us. At first I worried that he was feeling peaked again, but I needn't have. In under a minute, we saw him, flying very low to the ground, trying to be as quiet as possible. He still had his golden glow.

BOOH scooped up me and Orson and made his stealthy retreat to the Throat of Hell. Homer, being blind, didn't even know the creature was there, though the poet complained about an awful smell.

It's true, of course. I love BOOH like a brother, but he *is* a scary, giant and most of all stinky vampire bat - complete with dried blood on his face - who regularly flies through sulfur pits, excrement and other foul substances in the execution of his duties. Not his fault, and Orson and I have gotten used to the smell.

But otherwise, my hematophagic (look it up) colleague was in stealth mode; he slipped beneath everyone else's radar and dropped into the Throat. Once he was out of view of the Circle he gave me a questioning, "Skree?"

"Third Level, please," I answered. "And if I'm remembering the schematic correctly, I think somewhere near Glutton's Gap."

Glutton's Gap looks like a ghost town from the Old West, a single, unpaved street lined with weathered buildings. On many of these, the doors and window shutters are nearly off their hinges. Hitching posts are in front of each establishment, but they are just for show. If there were ever any horses in Glutton's Gap, they long ago had been eaten.

The faded lettering above each door advertised all sorts of businesses. On my left was the First National Bank of Hell, but since no one in Glutton's Gap kept checking accounts or took out mortgages for that nice little ranch house north of town, and since saving for a rainy day seemed too little and too late, the bank was closed. Likewise the whorehouse on my right: Lustland on Level Two had all that business. In fact, most of the establishments in Glutton's Gap were closed. The Gap incongruously did have an über modern store devoted to cheap and shi-shi clothing, and it was still open, but I think that was the result of some clerical error by one of Hell's underlings. The merchandise didn't move very well ... except the jeans of course. You wore a lot of jeans in the Old West, by law, I think.

The exceptions to all the closures were the restaurants. I saw a sign in a cracked window advertising "all you can eat beef jerky," another one pushing a blue plate special. There was a particularly prominent sign over one big establishment. It said, "Donner Party Planners. Have your friends for dinner, and we'll do the cooking!"

Ugh.

A loud "SKREE!" came from behind me, and I turned to see what was up with BOOH. He had just sprung off the ground like he'd been bounced from a trampoline. When I finally got him to come back to my level, he was making unspeakably nasty sounds that I'd never heard before. I think he was swearing.

BOOH had picked the wrong spot to take a nap and lain on a cactus. I had a devil of a time, so to speak, getting the thorns out of his hide, even with my pliers. BOOH was tough, but after all, these were cacti from Hell, so I guess even the big guy could get an owie from one of the succulents down here.

"There," I said, slipping my pliers back into my tool belt. "That's the last of them. See if you can find a less treacherous place to sleep." BOOH, still grumbling, flew up to the top of the bank and made like a gargoyle. A very grouchy and sleepy one.

"Where is everyone?" Orson asked. "The streets are deserted."

"Well," I deadpanned. "That's the problem, don't you see? Now, if they were desserted, you might find someone out here."

"Har, har," said my friend. "Very funny. Your puns suck, you know."

"That's not the first time you've told me that."

"Probably won't be the last either."

"Anyway, in answer to your question, it beats me. They're probably inside somewhere. Hey, Bik!" I shouted at my pocket.

"What?" he groused. Bik sounded as if I'd woken him. The fire giant had been keeping a low profile ever since we'd left the office. He seemed very low on energy; the thought was worrisome.

"Would you please find us some people?"

Bik shimmied out of my pocket protector. His movements were lethargic, but with an effort, the fire giant flamed on and took off, buzzing in and out of about a dozen places before he returned. He powered down and practically dropped into my pocket. "There," he panted, "there are several places with people inside, but I saw the most in a Luby's Cafeteria, about a block up on the left."

In the United States, large commercial cafeterias such as Luby's and Furr's are primarily a southwestern phenomenon. In the north, there are diners aplenty, but since the demise of the automat, cafeterias where you can buy, a la carte, as many salads, entrees and desserts as you can balance on a tray, are confined to states like Texas and Oklahoma. These eateries are perfect for Hell though, because they specialize in excess; not to overindulge is nigh on to impossible.

"Let's go, Orson," I said, kicking us into action.

The entrance to Luby's was a saloon door, and it opened onto the largest waiting area I'd ever seen in a restaurant. Thousands of people were standing in line.

A minute passed while we figured out the different forms of glutton punishment, which in the case of Luby's was only two. Many people looked like they'd been queued for food for centuries. Their eyes were hollowed madness, and their bellies probably were too. Other gluttons sat at tables in the restaurant, and food was brought to them before they even asked for it. In fact, most of the diners were being held down by demons, while their associates used small shovels to force feed their charges.

"No more, please, no more!" begged an immensely fat man in the corner. He was dressed in a suit, vest, and cravat; the garments must have been quite fine in their day. The outfit looked to be from the early Twentieth Century, though the buttons and seams had long since popped off or split, so the fabric hung loosely on his corpulent frame.

The demons ignored his pleadings and kept shoveling in the grub. I recognized the man from old photos in history books: William Howard Taft. The former president had been famous for his appetite. I remembered reading somewhere that he was so fat he'd once gotten stuck in the White House bathtub. They'd had to use butter to get him out.

Thinking about butter reminded me of butterball turkeys, and that's what Taft reminded me of too. Then he let out a tremendous fart, filling the cafeteria with the odor of rotten eggs just as effectively as burning brimstone would have. His humiliation was painful to watch, and I turned away.

Orson and I looked around the room for someone in charge. The most likely candidate was a rather bored-looking cashier, a devil in a blue dress and equally blue wig. Since none of the gluttonous damned probably ever left this place, we doubted she ever had to use her register. We walked over to her station, noticed the dust on the cash register's keys and were sure of it.

"Got a second?" I asked.

"I'm busy," she said. "Get lost."

Now, as I've said, devils are neither male nor female. If, however, one is wearing a dress, I usually call him/her/it a she. "Listen, Miss ... ," I looked down at her blouse. There was an employee pin that identified her as "Laverne."

"Listen, Laverne," I amended. "My name is Steve Minion ... "

"Big, fucking whoop. I told you I was busy."

"And I'm doing a job for Satan."

"Sure you are. And I'm Hecate. Now, like I said, get lost."

Orson walked over. "What's the problem, boss?"

I indicated the cashier. "She doesn't believe I'm on assignment for Satan."

"Maybe she needs some convincing," Orson said, cracking his knuckles.

"From you, fat guy?" Laverne sneered. "Why you ought to be in line for some meatloaf and mashed potatoes."

"Not from *me, dear* lady," Orson said, with all the contempt he could muster, which believe me, even being a damned soul Orson could summon in large quantities. In fact, he could have taught many of the devils and demons around here lessons in contempt.

Orson whispered in my ear. "Good idea," I said and gave a loud whistle.

The front doors, as well as the door jamb, were knocked ten feet into the room as BOOH made his way inside. The roof was a little low for him, so he had to sort of shimmy his way over to the register.

Laverne stood with her mouth agape.

"Have you ever met BOOH?" I asked.

The demon cashier nodded up and down rapidly, her chin going like a jackhammer.

"BOOH, Laverne here doesn't believe I work for Satan."

"SKREE!" BOOH screamed in her face. He gave me a smug look and waddled back outside.

I ran my fingers through my hair, removed from my sleeve some dust it had picked up while resting on the counter. "NOW do you have time to answer a question for me?"

The jackhammer started up again.

"That's great. I'm looking for a big green pipe. It should run from the bottom of Level Two all the way to the surface of Three. Can you tell me where it is?"

"Uh, no. I haven't seen anything like that."

"Are you sure?" I pulled the schematic out of my pocket and showed it to her, careful only to reveal the portion that corresponded to the Glutton's Gap area of Level Three. I didn't want to show too many people the drawing. Satan or Beezy might not like it.

Laverne, who despite her nasty nature, seemed to have a pretty good sense of spatial relationships, looked curiously at the drawing. "Well," she said slowly, "I don't recall a green pipe there, but there's an old grain silo on that spot."

More camouflage? "Where?" I asked.

"Just take the road maybe half a mile past town, and you'll see it."

"Fine, and thanks for your cooperation. I'll make sure both Satan and Beelzebub know how much you helped us." Since Beezy is the patron devil for gluttony, this operation was his.

"No, no," she said hurriedly. "It was an … " she almost choked on the expression, "an honor just to be of service."

"I bet," Orson grumbled, and we left.

We stepped through the demolished entrance of the cafeteria and out on the gravel road. Not far away, BOOH had settled back down on top of the bank. His eyes were closed and he was snoring loudly.

"Let's let BOOH get his beauty rest," I said to Orson. "It's just a short walk."

"Fine by me. Got your stethoscope?"

I pulled it from my trouser's pocket and slipped it around my neck. "Ready when you are, Dr. Welles."

Just outside of town was a chuck wagon. Donner Party Planners, which must have been operated by a cartel of devils and demons, was throwing a barbeque for some residents of Glutton's Gap. Many of them were soon-to-be diners; others were soon-to-be-dinners, the latter skewered on large rotisserie spits and turning over bonfires. Slow-cooked, my mama always told me, was the best way to do barbeque. Makes the meat nice and tender. I took a whiff and almost gagged. *Ugh. They're using a sweet sauce.*

In life, I was quite fond of barbeque and often sought out the different varieties that could be found in many regions of the States. The North seemed to favor sweet sauces, my least favorite. Some places in the South, like South Carolina, had mustard-based sauces. My favorite, Texas barbeque, was smokier and more vinegary. If I had been running the show, I'd have opted for that from the Lone Star state. It would cover up the quinine tang of human flesh.

Not that I've ever tasted any, of course. I'm just sayin'.

The devils had really put on the dog. Well, actually, they'd put on the people, but they had all the fixin's: potato salad, beans (pinto not fava), loaves of sliced white bread, pickles and onion slices, banana pudding for desert - a lot of it - and of course iced tea.

There was one devil, probably the boss, who was standing near the wagon, overseeing the preparations. He had on an apron that said, "Kiss the cook." Except for the fact that humans would be eating humans, and that everyone would no doubt have to eat until they were near to bursting, it looked like a nice affair.

Anyway, the food-to-be was in agony, and the expectant diners looked green at the gills. I imagined that once they'd finished eating and then passing their neighbors, the groups would switch roles.

"Creepy," Orson whispered.

"Yeah. I'll never eat barbeque again."

"Just as well," my friend said. "It's really terrible for you. That charred meat - all those carcinogens - could give you cancer."

"Well, since I'm already dead, that's not much of a disincentive."

"How about cannibalism?"

"Yeah. That works."

Beyond the festivities I spied cornfields. There looked to be miles and miles of stalks in long and, for Hell, surprising straight rows growing out of rich, black soil like what you might find in Illinois. The corn was "as high as an elephant's eye," ripe for the picking, and I pulled an ear off a stalk. I tore the rich green husk away from the ear, but the yellow kernels turned to black dust when they were exposed to the air and blew away. With a sigh, I tossed the naked cob over my shoulder.

A couple of more minutes walking, and we spotted the silo, about a hundred feet off the road. The storage structure did indeed look abandoned; there were no signs of activity. As we got close, I noticed flecks of green beneath the peeling yellow paint. "I think we found our pipe."

"Yeah. You know, Satan is good at this camouflage stuff."

I shrugged. "Would you expect anything less from the Prince of Lies?"

"Not really. Hey! Look at that." Orson pointed to a nearby hitching post. Hanging from its underside was a small icicle.

Chapter 24

"We're running out of time, Orson. At this rate, all Hell will soon freeze over, the devils will miss their poker night, and chaos will ensue."

Worst of all, said that selfish portion of my brain, I'd lose Flo forever. A familiar anxiety grasped my chest, but with an effort of will, I shook it off. This was not the time to panic. Well, it was exactly the time to panic, but that wouldn't have done any good. If Flo and I were to have any chance together, if the entire universe were to be saved from bedlam, Orson and I had to stay focused on the job.

"Then we'd better get at it," he said, putting his stethoscope to his ears. I followed suit.

The pipe was as silent as the dead, or at least the dead before they made it to the afterlife, where we all tended to be on the mouthy side. We pulled off our stethoscopes. "That clinches it, Orson. The problem is somewhere on Level Two."

"Or in the ground beneath either One or Two."

"Hadn't thought of that," I said with a frown. "If it's buried in the ground, I'm not sure we'll be able to handle this on our own."

Orson scratched his beard. "Well, let's isolate this as best we can. Pull out the HVAC schematic."

I placed the drawing on the curved walls of the faux silo. Together, we studied the drawing for a few minutes.

"Looks to me like the pipe is right next to the Elevator on Two," Orson concluded.

"Yeah. That should make this pretty easy." I whistled for BOOH, and he came roaring out of Glutton's Gap. "BOOH, it looks like our next stop is the Elevator doors on Two." My winged compadre grabbed the two of us by his claws and shot upward.

The easiest way to hide something is in plain sight. Satan had made the column appear to be part of the Elevator shaft on the Second Circle. The shaft looked especially large on this level, but I knew from experience that the car inside was the same car that served all levels of Hell, so at least a portion of the shaft, the back portion I was pretty certain, since the front was taken up by the Elevator doors, was fake, like a secret compartment in a desk or suitcase. Sure enough, there was a very slight roundness to the back of the shaft. I was positive I'd never seen that on any other level. "I bet money that's the pipe."

Orson nodded and pulled out his ears' augmenter.

Again there was dead silence. I unplugged my ears and hung the stethoscope around my neck. "Somewhere between here and the tee box on One."

"I concur," replied my supercilious friend. "What do you propose now?"

"At this point, I think the best thing to do is for you to wait here while BOOH and I trace the pipe all the way to the top of this level. I'll take a listen periodically to make certain the failure isn't somewhere in midair, though I doubt that's the case."

"Wha … what's going on?" Bik asked, pulling himself out of my pocket. I placed him on my palm.

He looked terrible, as if the life was being sucked out of him. "How long has it been since you've eaten?" I asked him worriedly.

"Don't know. I feel kind of woozy."

I dug into a pocket of my coveralls and pulled out a couple of matchboxes. "Orson, feed our diminutive friend while I'm gone, would you?"

"Sure, Steve." He looked as concerned for the little guy as me, as he took Bik and the matches from my hands. He set the fire giant carefully on the ground, then struck a match. After a few attempts, Orson got it to light. "Here, little one," he said gently. "Have a bite."

While Bik sucked down fire, BOOH and I flew up to the shaft and began paralleling its ascent. A few hundred feet in the air, the tube separated from the elevator shaft. Because of the constant haze found on every level of Hell except Limbo, no one on the ground would have been able to see the pipe from this distance. Since there was no need for additional camouflage, the pipe reverted to a bright green. I took a listen about twenty feet from where it had made its right angle divergence from the shaft, but there was no sound to be heard.

The course of the pipe was now a beeline. I saw where we were heading and shivered. It was hard not to. We were shooting straight for Erebus.

As we approached the summit, or nadir, depending on your point of view, BOOH slowed down. He seemed to be having difficulty getting close to the mountain; as he struggled against some invisible force, his golden glow began to fade. Finally, about twenty feet from the tip of the giant stalactite, BOOH was reduced to a hover. He let out a Skree! in frustration.

"Hold on, big guy!" I said. "Just let me take a listen to the pipe then we'll back off."

The pipe was deader than a doornail, this close to the summit. I tapped BOOH on the shoulder, and he retreated about fifty feet from his position, still close enough to see the pipe - which traveled along the side of the mount, a giant, slithering green snake frozen to a great big icicle - but not close enough to take a listen.

We weren't able to get near the pipe again until we reached the underbelly of Level One. Less than thirty feet from the base of Erebus, the supply line emerged from the bottom of the First Circle of Hell. Attached to the pipe, running along the underside of the circle, was a horizontal service ladder. I put the stethoscope to the green metal of the fuel line.

I heard the loud swish, swish, swish of souls flowing through the pipe. BOOH tried to fly closer to the base of Erebus but hit the same invisible force that had stalled him at the summit. From our vantage point, I examined the green tubing as it started its climb up the mountain. The pipeline was undamaged as far as the eye could see.

Back on the ground of Level Two, I told Orson. "The location of the sabotage must be somewhere on Erebus, but for some reason, BOOH can't fly me to the mountain. We're going to have to find the failure point ourselves."

"Are you kidding?" Orson spluttered. He had just picked up Bik and put him in his own pocket protector. Bik's color was better, but he was still very lethargic. "Are you telling me that, in order to find the leak or blockage or whatever the hell it is we're contending with, we have to climb Mount Erebus ... upside down?"

"That's exactly what I'm saying, but before we do, I need to talk with Satan again to find out what we're getting ourselves into."

"Not Beezy?"

"No, I don't think so. Beezy doesn't even know the source of the fuel that fires his own HVAC system, and I think Satan wants to keep it that way. I need to talk to the big guy himself, and since he said no more 'mind phone calls,' this will have to be in person. On the way, we'll have BOOH drop you at Parts. Get Dora to give you every bit of mountain climbing gear she has, and tell her no holding back, unless she wants her butt chewed on by a dragon."

We took off and flew down to Five. The temperature on all levels was dropping rapidly now, and we were shivering by the time we got to Parts. I took Bik from Orson, thinking the fire giant might benefit from visiting his grandfather while I talked to Satan. BOOH whisked us down to Nine. After placing me on the carpet before Satan's office, the bat hopped on his perch near the Elevator. Even though he had lost his golden glow, BOOH's dip in the Well of [Damned] Souls was still standing him in good stead. He was as fast as ever, but like Bik, he now seemed to tire after each of our jaunts, requiring frequent naps. The giant bat closed his eyes and was soon snoring.

Bruce was at his desk, clad in a powder blue parka and thick ski gloves. In all my years of dealing with him, he had never looked more miserable. "Bruce. Give me the key to the Corridor of Traitors. Bik needs to see his grandfather."

Normally, Bruce would have argued with me, but I guess he didn't have the energy. Instead, he just fished in his pocket and pulled out the key, handing it to me. Then he laid his head on the appointment book and fell asleep.

Shaking my head, I walked over to the door. After unlocking it, I pulled Bik from my pocket protector. "Do you think you're strong enough to fly in and see your grandpa?"

"I ... I think so."

"Can you get through the boiler room door?"

"Special opening ... on door. Just my size ... be fine."

Bik's voice was so soft that he was almost inaudible, but I could make out enough to know he was talking about the peephole. "Good. Stay with Surtr for a while. Maybe he can help you get your strength back."

"Okay." Bik flew off at a slow, looping pace, like a yellow butterfly that could barely stay aloft.

I left the door cracked open and placed the key on Bruce's desk. He was snoring slightly. I tried to wake him, but he wouldn't budge, so even though I knew it was a bad idea, I walked over to Satan's office, pushed open the doors, and stepped inside.

Satan was standing in front of his desk, arms crossed over his black Armani suit, eyes hidden by dark sunglasses. There was no expression on his face as I approached the Earl of Hell. Then, without warning, he slapped me. Hard.

"You are getting insolent, Minion. This is the second time you've barged into my office without invitation. It is the height of hubris."

Satan frequently knocked me around when I met with him, but those punishments were the reflexive act of a consummately cruel being. This slap, though, came from a deep sense of personal outrage, that I had violated the rules of engagement, made a huge breech of protocol. And perhaps I had. After all, a man's office is a man's office, even if he happens to be the Devil. Not only did I not have an appointment; I didn't even knock before entering. The slap was deserved.

I bowed my head. "Sorry, my Lord, really I am, and I wouldn't have done it if I didn't think we we're running out of time. Things are getting colder on every level. I saw an icicle on Three, Bruce is out there wearing a parka, and I fear that very soon all Hell will freeze over. That's much worse than just a cold day in Hell, isn't it?"

"You have no idea," Satan said under his breath as he walked around his desk to his chair. He sat down, pointing at one of the visitor chairs that regularly appeared and disappeared in his office. Grateful for an opportunity to get off my feet, I sank into the cushion. I was no longer merely bone-tired; I was exhausted to the point of collapse. This was turning out to be a very long day.

"I visited the Well of [Damned] Souls, sir. Peter told me about it in some detail. Burning human souls to heat the Underworld ... that's pretty diabolical, even for you."

A comment like that would normally have gotten me flame-broiled, but Satan only frowned. "Yes. That's not a secret I want too many people to know about - it would cause me a major PR problem - so you and Orson keep your mouths shut, get it?"

"Yes sir. And I think I know where the problem lies. It's ... "

"Erebus. Yes, your mind has been ringing with that one word since you stepped into my office. Why don't you tell me what you've discovered?" The Lord of Hell emitted a long sigh. Until today, I'd never seen him exhibit any weariness; it was very unsettling. More, in the past, whenever he wanted to know something, he'd just pluck the information from my brain. I had a feeling he was just too tired to do that now. The seriousness of our situation was becoming more and more apparent.

Quickly, I outlined our efforts to identify the break point in the supply line and the conclusion we had drawn. "It has to be somewhere on Erebus, sir. The pipe is working fine at the base of the mountain, but shortly after leaving the summit, the pipe is silent."

The rest is silence. I wondered who said that.

"Shakespeare," Satan replied, answering my unspoken question. "It's the last thing Hamlet says before he dies." The Earl of Hell took off his sunglasses and laid them on the desktop. One eyebrow formed an impossibly high arch. "I'm tired, Minion, not dead like you. If Hell were to be destroyed, I'd be the last to go."

"I always figured that, sir. But to get back to Erebus, I have to somehow climb the mountain and trace the line to the failure point, unless," I added hopefully, "someone else more appropriate for this task could handle it."

Satan frowned at me. "Trying to get out of your eternal damnation, Minion?"

"No, no sir, but things are getting pretty serious in Hell, and I wasn't sure you wanted to waste any more time with my stumbling around."

He shrugged. "You're doing okay, all things considered. Besides, most devils and all demons are incapable of dealing with the cold on Erebus. Only one of the princes of Hell or a human could make the climb, and I'm not ready to call on one of the princes yet."

I nodded. "Especially since you're trying to keep the existence of the fuel line a secret."

"Yes. Once again, Minion, you show your gift for clear thinking. Being Hell's Super may be your eternal damnation, and you stink at fixing things, but you've shown your mettle on more than one occasion. Without letting the cat out of the bag about the Well of [Damned] Souls, the only other being who could effectively deal with the Erebus situation is me, and I'm not ready to climb a mountain to fix it. Well," he said, considering the possibility, "I'll do it if I have to, but straits are not yet so dire as to make that necessary. You have a go at it first."

The Lord of Hell had just paid me a compliment. He didn't deal those out very often, and he surprised me.

"Sir, there's something funny about Erebus. Well, there are a lot of things funny about Erebus, starting with it hanging upside down. BOOH, for example, can't fly me there. He can only get so close."

"Only about twenty or thirty feet, I imagine. Erebus was here when I bought this bit of real estate from Hades and rebranded it as Hell. The mountain exists in its own pocket universe, and gravity is flipped on its head within that universe. As BOOH gets closer to the mass of the mountain, he reaches a point where the gravity of Erebus and the gravity of the Underworld cancel each other out."

I nodded. "That's why he could only hover when he was near the mountain."

"Correct. But there is actually no physical barrier between Hell and Erebus. Get to the base of the mountain, and you should have no problem climbing it. I know you already noticed the service ladder on the ceiling of level two. BOOH can fly you to it, then you and Orson can use it like a jungle gym to climb to the base of the mountain."

Satan waved at the black void behind him, and a screen appeared. He and I shared an interest in old movies. He projected a scene from 'Royal Wedding,' where Fred Astaire was dancing on the floor, then walls, then ceiling of his stateroom. "It'll work like that, Minion. Once you get close enough to Erebus, up will be down and down will be up. Shouldn't be more than a few seconds of disorientation, then you will be looking up at the mountain instead of down."

And facing one bitch of a climb.

"And facing one bitch of a climb," Satan agreed, voicing my inner thoughts. "I suspect you will find the problem with the fuel line near the summit."

"Why sir?"

Satan didn't answer immediately. When he spoke again, it was as if he'd changed topics. "Beelzebub told me about you and Pinkerton trying to narrow down the field of suspects. What you didn't know was that there isn't a human, demon or even devil who can keep something from me if I want to know it. Well, except for Nightingale," he added sourly, "and she doesn't have the horsepower to screw with the HVAC system."

I frowned. "Sure wish I'd known this before. It would have saved a lot of time."

"But what fun would that have been?" Satan said, grinning wolfishly. "Anyway, there is one class of Hell's inhabitants whose minds I cannot read."

"Really? Who."

"All those mythological beings I've let into the Underworld. They're all a bit of a cipher to me." He shrugged. "I should boot them out of Hell, I suppose, but what can I do? I'm a collector of creatures from dead religions. They fascinate me. Usually, I don't have a problem with them. Sisyhpus, Prometheus and Charon, for example, are model employees."

"But what does this have to do with Erebus?" I asked.

"Ymir," was his simple response.

"Ymir." I ran my fingers through my hair in thought. Satan frowned at my full mane but said nothing. "He ... he's from Norse mythology, right?"

"Yes, part of its creation story, a frost giant. He maintains the cooling plant at the summit of Erebus, though there's really not much for him to do, since the mountain itself does most of what's needed. Still, he's the only creature on the mountain at all, and since I can't read his mind, he's probably the one who's at the bottom of this whole mess." Satan frowned again. "Though I wouldn't have thought him capable of it."

"Not enough horsepower?" I asked, using Satan's own metaphor.

"Ymir's plenty strong. He's just a mental midget. Digger is Albert Einstein by comparison."

"But ... but he's still the likely candidate here?" My mind filled with an image of a monstrous and vicious sentinel made entirely of ice "A frost giant? And Orson and I are going to go up against him on our own? With what?"

Grinning, Satan held out empty hands to me. I don't know whose hands they were, but they were empty. "Got me. Duct tape?"

"Great," I said, scooting back in my chair. It was time to go.

"Good luck, Minion," the Devil said mildly. "You're going to need it. And watch your back, because I won't."

"Gee, thanks."

"Now get out of my office."

"Getting," I said, and hurried out of Satan's lair.

Chapter 25

Opening the door to the trailer, I heard the mellifluous voice of my assistant.

"Rope."

"Check," the voice of Bik said in a high-pitched squeek.

"Pitons."

The fire giant, who looked much improved since the last time I saw him, was buzzing over a mini-mountain of gear piled in the center of the floor. Orson was sprawled on the floor beside the hillock. "Uh, what's a piton?" Bik asked.

Orson had wasted no time getting us provisioned, probably asking Dora to give him everything she had that could remotely be used for mountaineering, including the book I saw in his hand, *The Idiot's Guide to Mountain Climbing*.

I wish I'd thought up that little franchise. I could have made a bazillion dollars.

Just stick *"The Idiot's Guide"* in front of anything - *The Idiot's Guide to the Marimba, The Idiot's Guide to Bestiality, The Idiot's Guide to Insider Trading* - and you had a best seller. Orson was perusing a page near the back of the book, where he must have found a mountaineer's checklist, and he was confirming that we had what we needed.

Orson checked the index, turned to the appropriate page and read, "Let's see. Says here a piton is a stake that a climber drives into a rock or crack in the side of a mountain. I guess you can grab it with your hand or use it to support a rope."

Boy, if we need to do that, we're in trouble.

"I like my steaks medium rare," I said in as light-hearted a tone as possible.

"Hi, Steve. I got the gear."

"So I see. Bik, what are you doing here? I thought I told you to stay with your grandpa."

Bik flew to within a few inches of my face and hovered like a hummingbird. A big hummingbird. He'd grown again, and was now larger than a Sharpie. He had a frown on his face, but all he said was, "I'm fine. Grandpa fed me and told me to get my butt back up here, in case you needed my help."

"Well, you didn't waste any time. You must have flown like a bat out of Hell to get here ahead of me."

"Yeah," he said, turning from me quickly to get back to helping Orson with the inventory.

I looked at my assistant. "Do you have any idea how to use this stuff?"

"Not much," he admitted. "I'm a speed reader, though, so as soon as I finish checking the inventory, I'll read the book."

"I took a speed reading course in college. Evelyn something or other. After the training, I used my new skill to get through my biology textbook in one night."

"Let me guess. That would have been the night before the final."

"Right you are," I said, plopping down on the floor and sifting through the gear.

"And ... ?"

"And somehow I passed my final."

"And ... ?" he asked again. "What do you remember about biology?"

"Let's see." I thought for a minute. "Nucleotide ... mitochondria ... scatology."

"That's it?"

"Yeah, and just the words. I don't know what they mean - except scatology of course."

Orson grinned. "I bet you know a bit about eschatology too."

"Yep, they both figure pretty prominently in my day-to-day afterlife."

"Mine too, but in view of your rather pathetic speed reading skills," he said, ripping the inventory out of the back of the guide. "I'll use the book to take a crash course on mountain climbing while you and Bik finish the inventory."

"Check," I said.

"No," Bik said, buzzing past me. "You call out the item, and *I* say check."

"Well, I didn't hear you say check about the pitons."

Bik hovered in space, his hands on his hips. "That's because I didn't know what they were. I do now."

"And?"

"Oh, right. Check."

Orson sat down in my desk chair and cracked open the front of the book. "I still don't know how we're going to climb upside down."

"It won't be upside down after the first few yards." I explained to Orson about the reverse gravity of Erebus. "So, after we do our hand to hand thing for about twenty feet, gravity should flip, the ceiling will become the floor, and we'll be fine."

"Sounds swell. I haven't done a jungle gym since I was twelve," he said, "and I've only gained, what, three hundred pounds since then."

"Sorry. Can't be helped."

Grumbling, Orson started to read.

Meanwhile, I continued with the inventory. "Hammer."

"Check, check - two of them - though they don't look very much like that one in your tool belt."

"The ones you got from Dora are specialized, I assume. Uh, carabiners."

"What?"

"Clippy things that you can snap over ropes or tie ropes to."

"Man, you guys are going to get yourselves killed," the fire giant said.

"Thanks for the vote of confidence. Besides, we've already gotten ourselves killed. Everything else has been pretty anticlimactic since then. I imagine we'll do okay," I concluded, not feeling particularly confident about it, but trying to put on a brave face.

Bik dropped to the linoleum and extinguished his flame. He charred a little bit of the tile, since he performed these tasks in the wrong order. He looked troubled. "Well, maybe you'll be all right, but I think I should go along, just in case you need me."

"Bik," I said, touched by his concern, "I really appreciate it, but would that be wise? We're going to climb a mountain of ice and fight a frost giant. Ice should be anathema to you."

"What's a 'nathema?'"

I sighed. "Not nathema. Anathema. It means, well, oil and water, they just don't mix. Neither do fire and ice. And you've been feeling puny for a while now, ever since The Spark started to fail in Hell."

The pout on Bik's face made him look like a thwarted toddler. "I wanna go. I might be useful to you. Besides, look at me. Do I look puny right now?"

I admitted that he did not. Surtr must have given the boy a tonic or something. In addition to his growth spurt, he was positively glowing with energy, but then he did that most of the time anyway.

"Fine," I said, sighing again. "You can stay inside my parka. Uh, we *do* have parkas somewhere in that pile, don't we?"

"Check, I mean yes, two of them, bright red, one large, for you, and the other XXL for ... "

"We all know who the XXL is for," Orson griped. He was running his index finger down page after page. He was already a quarter of the way through the book.

Hmm. So maybe I just didn't do the speed reading thing right.

"So what have you learned so far?"

"Crevasse … altitude sickness … oh, and that we're a couple of chumps for even attempting this."

"That's positive thinking. Go, Orson, go."

He shoved his lower lip beyond his upper one, blew at his mustache and made the hairs rise until they were perpendicular to his mouth. That was a pretty neat trick. "We'll manage," he said, quietly. "We have to."

We needed a little more confidence than that. I got off the floor and spoke in a loud voice. "It will be a cold day in Hell before we successfully climb Mount Erebus."

Orson looked at me in amazement. "Does that really work?"

I gave him a smug look. "How do you think I got my hair to grow?"

"I've been wondering. Been a little too busy to ask about it, though."

"Well, now you know."

I felt a rumble beneath my feet, but I didn't know if that was the irritation of an angry Satan, if a dump truck had just driven by or if the fabric of reality had just shifted in our favor.

"Maybe I could lose some weight." Orson stood and cleared his throat. "It will be a cold day in … "

"Stifle, will ya?" I said and put my hand over his mouth. "Satan was furious with me over the hair. He's burned it off twice now. I thought he'd let me buy a little insurance for our climb without getting too peeved, but if you wish yourself thin, there'll be Hell to pay."

"Okay," Orson said, somewhat deflated, and sat back down to finish the book.

"Bik, I think we can dispense with the inventory. We probably have everything we need to make the climb. I'll just stuff the gear in our packs and … "

"No check," the fire giant said. He was still on the linoleum tile, flame extinguished. "Dora told us that was the one thing she didn't have in stock. Orson said you had a couple of burlap bags in the trailer you could use."

"Great. It will be tons of fun using burlap bags to haul all this crap up the side of a mountain." I grabbed two bags from the orange crate where we kept BOOH's treats and started stuffing the gear into the bags, with the exception of the parkas and hammers. I replaced the one in my tool belt (the hammer, not the parka) with the one for climbing the mountain then put the second one on the desk for Orson. "We'll look like a couple of St. Nicks, especially with those red parkas."

"Especially me," Orson groused as he turned another page. He was nearly finished with the manual.

I had both bags packed in a matter of minutes. There wasn't much point taking care with the job; things tend to get jumbled up when you throw them into formless burlap bags. I did try to put the soft items on the outside, so we wouldn't have things like, oh, pitons digging into our backs. "Ready," I said, pulling the tie strings closed on the second bag.

"Ready," Orson said. He had just finished the book, but he opened his bag and slipped the volume inside. "Just in case I need to check my memory on something."

"But … but you know how to do this now, right?" I said hopefully.

"Crevasse … altitude sickness … oh, and falling, I picked that up too."

"Cute."

"Just a second." Orson went to the back of the office and grabbed something else, adding whatever it was to the contents of his sack before pulling the strings tight again. "Now I'm *really* ready, or as ready as I'll ever be. Can't say what I'm looking forward to more: climbing the mountain or battling a frost giant." He'd been listening to my conversation with Bik, apparently.

"Well, one step at a time." I didn't want to think about it any more than Orson did.

We slipped on our parkas and threw the bags over our shoulders.

"Ho, ho, ho," said the not-so-jolly fat man.

"Very nice. Bik, I have a warm inside pocket for you to travel in. Bik?"

The diminutive giant was still on the floor, a thoughtful look on his face. "Steve, I've been wanting to talk to you about something that's been bothering me."

"Ah, sure, but later. This isn't really a good time."

"But ... "

"Listen Bik, we really need to get going. Maybe on a rest stop we can talk, okay?"

"Well, okay," he said reluctantly.

"Good." I reached over, grabbed up the little guy, and stuffed him in my pocket.

BOOH was waiting for us outside.

"I think we should tie our bags to our belts for right now. They'd be in BOOH's way during flight. And afterwards, we're going to need both of our hands for the first twenty feet or so."

The weight of the bags, tied to our waists, was so great that we stood hunched over, as if we had spinal conditions. I wasn't looking forward to climbing that infernal jungle gym with an extra fifty pounds hanging from me.

"Now, BOOH," I explained, feeling a little winded already, "I know you can't fly us to Erebus, but remember the ladder mounted near the base of the mountain, hanging from the ceiling of Level Two?"

"Or the underside of Level One," Orson added, trying to be helpful.

"Yeah. It's all a matter of perspective, I suppose. Anyway, if you can just get us as close to the base of the mountain as possible, and within reach of that ladder, we'll climb the rest of the way ourselves. Any questions?"

"Skree?"

"No, I think once we get on the mountain, you should fly somewhere where you can rest up. Listen for my call, though. I may need you quickly. Got it?"

"Skree."

"Okay, then … "

"Wait a minute," Orson interjected. "You understand BOOH's skrees?"

"Well, we spend a lot of time together. Now, let's go."

BOOH had finally lost all the extra pep he'd gotten from the Well of [Damned] Souls. In fact, he looked a little ashen. I hoped he was up to making the climb. Like the trooper he was, though, he scooped up the two of us - three, counting the little guy in my pocket - and shot skyward.

Unsurprisingly, BOOH flew a bit slower than usual on the climb to the base of Erebus. He seemed to be breathing harder than usual too. The temperature of Hell had dropped so much now that only in the times when we were within the actual Circles of Hell, surrounded by the molten rock on which each level sat, was the air warm. Orson and I had on our parkas, and we were human, so had at least experienced cold in our lifetimes. BOOH, well, he wasn't used to this.

"Steve!" Orson yelled as we flew. "What do you think we're going to encounter when we reach the summit?"

"You know *exactly* what we will encounter. A frost giant."

"Yeah, you said that earlier. How about some details?"

Quickly I filled Orson in on my conversation with Satan. He needed to know that it was Ymir himself who would be waiting for us on top of the mountain.

By the time we reached the ceiling of Level Two, the giant bat could hardly breathe. The reverse gravity of Erebus, so close to us, was a giant hand, pushing against the efforts of my friend. I wondered how much longer BOOH could hold out.

"There!" Orson shouted. "There's the jungle gym!"

"Ladder."

"Whatever. There it is!"

Orson was right. There was the bright green ladder, and as I remembered, it was attached to the green fuel line that was poking out of the underside of Level One, where it made a perpendicular bend on its way to the base of Erebus.

BOOH was struggling to get us up to the level of the ladder. He was practically clawing his way, foot by foot, against the resistance of the mountain's inverse gravity. Then it was all he could do to hover in place, his breath coming and going in great gasps.

"BOOH! It's okay! I ... I've got my hand on the ladder." Then I put my second hand on the next rung. "Orson! Have you got a grip on it?"

"Yeah!"

"Good. Let go of us, BOOH. Let go!"

Reluctantly, it seemed to me, my batty friend opened his claws, and we were hanging by our hands from the ladder. My arms felt as if they were going to pull from their sockets, but with an effort I let go of one rung of the infernal jungle gym and grabbed the next one, then the next, moving foot by foot toward the base of Erebus.

Fifteen feet ... ten feet ... oh, hell, this is murder ... five feet ... four ... three ... two ... one ...

And then I felt as if I were in the middle of doing a cartwheel. Kicking my legs in the air, I sent myself tumbling forward and stood up. "Whew!"

Behind me, Orson was having more trouble, over two hundred pounds more. He had only managed to move about ten of the twenty feet necessary to reach the mountain.

"Steve!" he shouted. "I ... I don't think I can do it! Go on without me!"

"No! Hang on." Quickly I rummaged in my bag and pulled out a length of rope. I tied it firmly to the ladder, which was now at my feet. "I'm going to throw our rope to you. Grab it, then make like Tarzan, understand?"

Orson's face was turning from a bright red to a deep purple but he managed to nod. "Hurry!" he said with a gasp.

It took a couple of attempts before I got the rope close enough for Orson to catch it, but catch it he did and, hanging by one arm, he put his full trust in the strength of the line, relinquished his hold on the other rung, and swung toward the mountain.

When he crossed over the invisible barrier where Hell's gravity was nullified and that of Erebus took over, he dropped up, that is to say down, making a very nice parabola with his swing.

"Ow, ow, ow! My arms feel like they've been stretched!" Then Orson just lay on the ground, gasping as he stared up at the peak of the mountain.

"BOOH, no!"

My batty friend was trying to follow us. He was hanging upside down, holding on by his claws. He had managed a few rungs, but seemed ready to drop. Perhaps if he weren't already exhausted, he could have made it, but as it was, he was almost out of strength. Even if he could reach the base of Erebus, though, he'd likely be of little use to us in his weakened condition.

"BOOH!" I thought quickly. "I need you to get away from Erebus. You can't help me here, but I may need you later, and you have to be rested. Drop, dive and glide yourself to somewhere safe!"

But BOOH refused to abandon me. He reached out with a claw, trying to move forward another rung. Then his strength failed, he lost his grip, and he dropped like a stone.

"BOOH!" both Orson and I screamed. But he was gone.

A feeling of great loss overwhelmed me. I found that I was crying. No. Bawling.

Then two big arms wrapped around me. "Don't worry, Steve," Orson said, trying to comfort me. "BOOH's one of the toughest creatures I've ever known, and that includes most devils and all demons. If anyone can take a fall like that, he can."

I wiped my eyes and nose on the sleeve of my parka. "Hope so," was all I could say.

"Besides," continued Orson. "We've got problems of our own. Look," he said, indicating the mountain.

Above us loomed Erebus, a mile high mountain of ice. Its summit was draped in dark storm clouds; they looked as if they would drop snow on us at any moment. This was going to be a bitch. "Get the rope, would you?"

"Okay." My assistant took a step and fell flat on his ass. I tried to help him up and found myself lying next to him. The icy surface of Erebus was as slick as a banana peel in a Buster Keaton movie.

"Maybe we put our ice cleats on now?" he suggested.

"Good idea." We rummaged around in our Santa sacks and found them. The ice cleats were less like cleats than snow chains for tires, and they slipped over our boots in a not dissimilar fashion. We now had pretty good traction against the slick surface of the mountain, and while Orson untied and coiled the rope, I walked over to a portion of the fuel line. Pulling the stethoscope from my coveralls, I took a listen.

Swish swish.

"The pipe is still live."

"With our luck," Orson said, dropping the rope into his pack and pulling the drawstrings taut, "we'll have to get to the top of this damned Popsicle before we find the problem."

"That's what Satan thought, though we'll check the pipe every so often, just to make sure. Come on," I said, looking up ruefully at the mountain. "The sooner we start, the sooner we finish."

Bik peeked out of my pocket. "Damn. It's cold out there!"

"No kidding," I said, mildly peeved. "What did you expect, the Sahara?"

"What's that?"

"Skip it. I told you not to come."

The little guy climbed out of my pocket and sat on my shoulder. His flame was still out; I guess he was saving himself for later. "No," he said, a glum expression on his face. "I needed to come. Besides, I have something I want to tell you."

"Not now, little guy," I said, handing him a toboggan (not the variety that you go down snowy slopes with, but the kind you put on your head), which he promptly wrapped himself in.

"But Steve ... "

"Later, Bik. Rest break, remember? Come on, Orson."

And so we were off, two Santa lookalikes and a pint-sized fire giant, wrapped in a toboggan (the other kind).

We decided to stay close to the fuel line. We could see it, a green zigzag climbing up a snowy white peak until it disappeared in the storm clouds above. The path the pipeline traveled up the mountain side seemed to be the least treacherous way we could go. For one thing, we could use the rope to secure ourselves to the braces that supported the pipeline as it wended its way up the side of the mountain.

This soon became the standard approach to our ascent. We would loop the rope around one of the braces and tie the ends around our waists. When we reached the next brace, usually about fifty feet up the mountain - linear feet, unfortunately, instead of vertical feet, which meant we would travel far more than the mile distance from base to summit - we'd untie one end of the rope, haul it up, make another loop around the pipe support we'd just reached, and tie the rope back to whoever's waist it had come off. In this fashion, we at least had the security of knowing that we couldn't fall more than fifty feet without the brace and our own weight catching us.

This worked great until we got to a rather nasty crevasse that had opened in the ice of the mountainside. It was only ten feet across, but that was farther than either of us could jump. Then Orson surprised me. Turns out he could throw a pretty mean rope. He said he learned the trick from Will Rogers, but I think he was just name-dropping. Anyway, he tied a rock to one end of our line, and after three or four attempts managed to throw it across the ravine, hooking it on the next brace up the slope. We secured the other end to the brace behind us, threw our bags to the uphill side then shimmied our way across. Hanging upside-down, legs wrapped around the rope, hands pulling us along: not fun. Fortunately it was a short distance, we were each fifty pounds lighter without our bags, and we were across in no time.

Of course, now we were without a rope, or without a good portion of it. We salvaged what we could, but our line was now only fifty feet long instead of a hundred.

Not that it mattered. Five minutes later it was gone entirely. We had decided that, since the rope was now too short to be doubled and provide us with a little insurance between pipe braces, we'd try to copy Orson's trick of throwing the rock and rope uphill, hook the next brace, and get our security that way.

But I wanted to try it.

"Steve, it's not as easy as it looks. You'd better let me."

"No, I've got this. You'll see."

He saw, all right. He saw me build up lots of centrifugal force as I spun the rock around in the air, like David using his sling to pop Goliath in the noggin. Then I let go and watched the rock overshoot its target by ten feet. That, in and of itself, wouldn't have been a problem, but I didn't have a firm grip on the rest of the rope. It slipped through my fingers, and Orson and I watched in frustration as the rock-powered rope shot into another crevasse.

"Great. I *told* you to let me throw it."

"Sorry."

"Now what are we going to do?"

I thought hard then opened my parka and removed my toolbelt. Zipping the coat closed, I put the belt on the outside, resting my hands on the two rolls that now hung low, near my hips. "Duct tape?"

"Swell," Orson grumbled.

"Hey! I'm good with duct tape!"

"Yeah, you are, but duct tape is a crummy substitute for rope."

"Well, maybe we won't have to use it," I said. "We've mostly been walking, and the rope has only been important for getting over that crevasse."

"Not to mention the two or three times that one of us slipped. The rope kept us from playing Jack and Jill. I for one don't relish the thought of breaking my crown."

I spun my two rolls of duct tape. "If you fall, I'll catch you. Promise."

"You'd better. This place is weird, and I don't know what would happen if I fell down the mountainside."

"You'd break your crown. You already said so."

"Yes, but would it heal?"

"I ... I don't know." Satan had implied that the rules for Erebus were different than those for the rest of Hell. So far, that had only applied to gravity, but there might be other ways things were different up here.

Like, for example, what if I can't handle duct tape as well on Erebus? Then we'd really be in trouble.

There was nothing for it, though. We had to keep moving, so with a sigh from me and another one of Orson's patented grumbles, we continued our climb.

Chapter 26

After what seemed like an eternity of scrabbling up the icy side of Erebus, we were near its peak. But we had hit a serious check. The way above us would require a vertical climb. Actually, more than vertical, since the cliff we needed to reach hung behind as well as above us. We looked to see if there was an alternative, but without some serious backtracking, we could not avoid the climb.

Orson set down his bag and started rummaging through its contents.

"What are you doing?"

"Time to break out the pitons."

"And then what?" I asked.

"Then it will be, 'drive one into the mountain, grab, pull yourself up; drive another one higher up, grab again, pull again; repeat.'"

"Sounds like a lot of work."

Orson shot me a withering look as he handed me a mess of pitons. "What did you expect? We're climbing a mountain here."

"Why are you giving these all to me?" I asked, pocketing them in my parka.

"You're lighter than I am, and you're better with a hammer."

"So what?"

"So you'd better get hammering."

Orson was right about that. I *was* better with a hammer than he was. Marginally. I couldn't use the hammer with the gloves I had on though, so I took them off. The cold of the mountain felt like tiny pricks of frost poking my hands in dozens of places. It made me even more awkward than usual, and I hit my thumb more than once as I drove the pitons into whatever cracks in the icy surface I could find. Fortunately, my hands were so cold that I didn't even feel it when I hit myself.

The going was slow, but foot by foot we were climbing the face of the cliff. Orson had also removed his gloves so he could better grasp the pitons. The downside was that our skin would sometimes stick to the steel, but fingers pulled off metal more easily than tongues, so it wasn't any big deal.

"Hurry up, Steve. I can see the top of the cliff and ... Ow!"

"Ow what?" I said looking down. Orson had been following a little too closely and, when I shifted my weight, I had stepped on his hand. In my distraction, I let go of my own handhold.

We were both scratching at the side of the cliff, in a desperate but what would ultimately be futile attempt not to fall. There was only one chance. Quickly (which for me is very quick - I'm preternaturally gifted with duct tape), I looped some tape around the ankle that in my fall had all too quickly become at eye level, pulled out seven or eight yards more, and made a lasso. Then just before gravity claimed me completely, I tossed my noose of tape over the stony outcropping twenty feet above me.

Perhaps I should have attached the duct tape to my waist instead, because I was flipped upside down, suspended in midair. Yet this gave me a chance to help Orson. Just before he fell off the side of the cliff, I grabbed his wrist.

The Santa Claus bags were a bit of a nuisance. We had tied them to our waists for the climb, and they were now hanging somewhere around the backs of our heads, thumping us near where I imagined our medullas must be.

"Don't let go!" he screamed.

"I'm not letting go!" I said, trying to figure out how we were going to get back on terra firma. Or Erebus firma anyway.

"For Go ... for Heav ... oh, shit ... just DON'T let go!"

"I'm NOT letting go!"

My fingers were slick with sweat, and I was beginning to lose my grip on him. At once a thousand fears hit me. Fears of losing my friend, fears of losing myself.

"Ow, ow, ow!" I would say periodically. I kept slamming my nose against the side of the cliff, and each time I did, I could hear cartilage break. Then we'd swing out again, giving my nose a chance to heal, if only briefly. Each time we swung out, though, my grip on Orson grew more tenuous.

"Steve! Do something! You know what will happen if I fall."

I didn't, but I didn't want to find out either. With my left hand, I spooled out some duct tape and somehow managed to secure it around my wrist and that of my friend. We were now in no immediate danger of falling. Duct tape is strong, and the Infernal version, well, I'd bet my life on it, if I had any life left to bet.

Our initial pendulum-like momentum had ceased. We were dangling, upside down, a dozen feet from the cliff face. "Orson! Can you get us swinging again? We've got to get closer to the cliff and see if we can grab it."

"I ... I think so, now that I'm not worried about falling and crushing every bone in my body."

"Okay, but wait a ... Ow!"

"What?"

"Let me turn my head so I don't break my nose again."

"Again?"

"Yeah, that made the fifth time since we began dangling here."

"Sorry. You ready now?"

"Uh huh. Go ahead. Each time we get close to the cliff, see if you can find something to grab onto. I'll do the same."

"Right."

Swinging back and forth, while all the while my nose was bleeding, was making me a little nauseous, but I tried to add my own body weight to the not inconsiderable momentum a four hundred pound assistant was capable of generating. Soon we were swinging like the pendulum on a grandfather clock. On our third close encounter with the slope, I spotted something dark sticking out of the ice and reached for it.

It was Bik's toboggan. It had gotten snagged on one of the pitons. When I reached for it, Bik appeared from the inside of the hat and grabbed my sleeve with a surprisingly strong grip. He pulled me up against the wall.

"Are you okay?"

"Yeah, thanks. Hey, you been working out?"

"Even a small fire giant is pretty strong."

"No shit. Orson!" I yelled. "Do you have a handhold?"

"Yes. Now let's get off this infernal cliff!"

Orson cut our wrists free with a penknife, but I left the lasso in place for security sake, though I moved the loop on my person from ankle to waist. As an afterthought, I tossed down a loop for Orson to put around his own waist, then fastened the new span of duct tape to our shared lifeline. My assistant handed me his hammer, since I'd dropped mine when I lost my grip on the mountain. I drove piton after piton into the cliff, and we inched our way to the top.

"Good grief!" Orson exclaimed, as I helped him over the lip of the precipice. "That was close."

"No kidding," I said, panting, as I slipped Orson's hammer into the vacant loop of my tool belt. "Let's rest here a while."

Looking above us, I felt as if I could almost reach out and touch the storm cloud. The cold was fierce, worse than anything I'd ever encountered on either side of the mortal divide. Orson's beard was covered in ice particles. My nostrils were nearly frozen shut, and at that moment I felt we were very close indeed to all Hell freezing over. We were also very close to the summit, and probably Ymir as well.

Ymir: a primordial creature, one of the oldest in Norse mythology. In a way, he was like Surtr's opposite, Ymir at the beginning of time, Surtr at the end. Bookends almost.

Hmmm. That seems a little too tidy for coincidence.

"Steve," Bik interrupted. "I *really* need to tell you something."

"Not now, Bik. I'm thinking." An idea occurred to me. "Orson," I said slowly.

"What?" He was cutting the duct tape loop off his waist.

"Don't you think it's strange that Ymir and Surtr, two characters from Norse mythology, are responsible for Hell's HVAC system?"

"Hmmph. That does seem a little odd. Do you think Surtr's involved in this?"

My brain made a few more connections. "Yes, in fact, I think he must be running the show."

"Why?"

"Because Satan said Ymir was as dumb as a stump. And I *know* Surtr isn't."

"How do you know that?"

"Well, he's ABD for one thing."

"Ah," Orson replied knowingly.

"Also, I talked with him. He's a pretty smart guy." A final connection closed in my skull, and I pointed at Bik. "Smart enough to plant a spy in our midst."

We both turned to Bik, who was hopping up and down in my hat like he needed to take a pee.

"You!" I spat out, with all the venom I could manage. I grabbed his toboggan and shook it. "You've been spying for your grandfather."

"Yes. No. I mean, not intentionally! That's what I've been trying to tell you!"

"Tell us what?" Orson sneered. "That you're a spy?"

Bik stared down at the snow. "I didn't know I was spying for him. Grandpa just said to give him a call periodically and let him know how we were doing."

"I'd been suspicious for a while now, but it wasn't until you and I went down to Nine together that I figured out what was going on. Surtr is planning a takeover, and he's been keeping The Spark all to himself."

"How? Where? And why should we believe you?"

Bik looked up at us with a pout. "Because I just saved you from falling off the mountain. Why would I do that?"

"He's got a point, Steve."

"Maybe. But you've been looking pretty chipper since you got back from visiting him."

"That's because Grandpa took one look at me, said, 'you haven't been eating enough,' then threw me in his secret stash of Spark."

No wonder Surtr has seemed to burn hotter, while the rest of us have been turning into frozen leftovers. "Where's he keep it?"

"Under his chair."

Orson was still suspicious. "And why did he give you some of the good stuff?"

Bik almost spat. "Because he was trying to buy my loyalty. He wants me to be some kind of page for him after he takes over Hell."

"Take over Hell!" Orson laughed. "That's a good one! Why, all Hell would freeze over before ... "

"DON'T FINISH THAT SENTENCE!" both Bik and I shouted.

"Oops," my assistant said sheepishly. "That ... that would explain a lot."

"If Hell freezes, anything could happen. Even the overthrow of Satan." I turned to the young fire giant. "But why wouldn't you stay loyal to your grandfather, Bik?"

Bik's kicked at a nearby snowdrift. Okay, it was really the size of a rock, but for him it was a snow drift. "Because ... because my grandfather isn't a very nice person. You know, he was supposed to destroy the Earth, and he would have too, if the Scandinavian religion hadn't lost out to Christianity. If Grandpa takes over Hell now, I bet he'll get around to doing it eventually."

"And I haven't even mentioned my personal reasons. Grandpa, well, he's always been pretty mean to me. Little things, like sending me to bed without supper, eating my parents ... "

"Gaaah!" Orson gaahed. "He ate your parents? Why?"

"He was hungry ... and he wanted their flame. He's greedy like that, and generally short-tempered and unpleasant. Nothing like you and Orson ... and BOOH." Bik got quiet for a moment. "Gee, I hope BOOH is alright."

That put a chill on the conversation. It also made me sympathetic to Bik ... but just a little. "Okay, I believe you, provisionally anyway. So can you give us any information that will help when we get to the summit?"

"Only that, as you've suspected, you'll find the problem with the pipeline up there. And that Ymir is waiting for you. Grandpa, see, well, he knows you're smart, Steve. He said you'd end up here eventually."

"How would Ymir know I'm coming?"

"Hotline. There is a direct phone link between the two of them. Grandpa told me Lord Satan put it in place so they could coordinate the running of the HVAC system."

Ah, the blue princess telephone I noticed the first time I met Surtr. This didn't explain why he had chosen the princess line, but the color seemed appropriate.

"Okay," I said, "that all checks out, and if he ate your parents, you certainly have reason enough to hate him."

"You forgot sending me to bed without supper.'

"That too. So, any helpful hints on how we tackle Ymir?"

Bik shrugged. "Not a lot, I'm afraid. I don't know much about him, except that he's a little, well, slow."

"Yeah, Satan said the same thing. Not exactly a mental giant."

"He also *moves* slow."

"Slowly," Orson corrected. He hated adjective/adverb confusion.

"Really?" I said, ignoring our resident pedant.

"Uh huh. Grandpa says that in the beginning, Ymir was pretty much all by himself. There weren't any natural predators for fifty foot high frost giants, so he didn't need to move fast. Also, he apparently has such a tiny brain that it takes all his concentration to do even the smallest thing. Of course," Bik added, "if the smallest thing he decides to do is take a swat at you, and he connects, you're a pancake."

"Great," Orson rumbled.

"Don't worry, Orson. I'd be a pancake. You'd probably be more of a waffle."

"Har, har."

"He could also shoot a blast of freezing air or ice at you."

I was scratching my chin, thinking hard. I looked above us. The top of Erebus was less than fifty feet away. "Okay, he can be deadly, but he's dumb and he's slow. Orson, I think we should approach the summit from opposite directions. That should confuse him."

"Hell, it sounds like most anything could confuse him. If I had three balls, I could go in juggling. That would probably confuse him too. Wait!" he said brightening, digging into his bag and extracting three brightly colored orbs. "I have three oranges! Grabbed them from the crate just before we left the office. What?" he said, noticing my frown. "I thought I might get hungry."

"You didn't bring any to share?"

"Sorry."

"Skip it." My stomach was a little queasy anyway. An orange probably wouldn't have sat on it very well at the moment. "When we find Ymir, I'll start the talking, but chime in whenever you want. Perhaps two people talking at once will overload his brain."

"So, that's our plan?" Orson said, stuffing the oranges in the pockets of his parka. "Approach from opposite sides, juggle some oranges, and talk at him? Then what?"

I had no idea what we'd do next. "Then we improvise."

"Super."

"Hey, it's who I am."

"I might be able to help," Bik piped in. "I've been feeling pretty good since Grandpa submerged me in his Spark tank. Even up here, I'm pretty confident I could burn up the pavement, and I bet Ymir hates fire as much as Grandpa hates ice."

"Well," I said, trying not to sound negative, "you've certainly grown since we first met you, but you're still kind of little."

"You might be surprised by what I can do."

"Okay, but, ah, why don't you get in my parka pocket instead of back in the hat, you know, stay out of sight until we need you?" I didn't want the little guy to get hurt.

"A pocket's fine with me, but let me get back in your pocket protector instead. I can slip in and out of that quickly."

"Fine," I said, opening my jacket and stuffing Bik in the plastic sheath. "Ready?"

"Ready."

"Don't mumble."

"Sorry. Ready."

From my tool belt, I pulled Orson's hammer. It wasn't likely to help me much against a giant, but I felt better with some sort of weapon in my hand. Orson took out an orange and tossed it up and down while he considered things then shoved it back in his pocket. I guess he wanted his hands free for the climb.

We left the Santa bags in the snow. The less encumbered we were, the better.

Turned out the way to the summit was pretty easy. Our ice cleats were all we needed to climb the last few dozen yards. We were briefly plunged in darkness as we ascended through the cloud cover, but on reaching the top, we discovered ourselves above the storm.

Orson and I made a complete circuit of the summit, in opposite directions, in our hunt for Ymir. There was nothing to be seen except a few large boulders and a bunch of ice. And the pipeline, which on reaching the summit, bent, continued its way in horizontal fashion for a while then made a second bend toward the Elevator and the surface of Level Two. As I crawled over the pipeline, I noticed something was attached to it, at the point just before it left the mountain. The anomaly was a large rubbery sac; it looked like a giant tick. On the downstream side of the sac, a large chunk of ice was crushing the pipe, choking it off. The sac seemed to be slowly expanding.

"I think we found out where the fuel is going," I said when we crossed paths while reconnoitering the summit. Orson only nodded.

In a couple of minutes, we were back where we started, with no sign of Ymir. "Where the hell is he?" Orson fussed.

Long moments passed. Then a hillock of ice on the side of the peak twisted, and I found myself looking into eyes as blue as the ice of Antarctica. Slowly, the giant got off the ground where he had been sitting and stood. Ymir was every bit of fifty feet, just like Bik had said. In fact, I had thought he was part of the glacier that covered most of Erebus, though he moved faster than a glacier. Not much faster, but some.

"Ymir!" I shouted. "I am Steve Minion, Hell's Super, and you, sir, are in violation of 49 CIR 193!"

"What's that?" Orson yelled.

"The Code of Infernal Regulations," I said, not taking my eyes off the frost giant. "It's the part that governs construction and maintenance of pipelines. I looked it up."

As we had been talking, Ymir slowly looked from one of us to the other, trying to keep up with the conversation. Then he smiled, having finally processed at least some of what I said. "MIN ... ION!" he said in a ponderous voice. Ymir reached out a fist. It hovered above me, a while boulder of ice - with knuckles - then the giant let it drop.

He may have been slow, but gravity wasn't, and the fist fell with the rapidity of anything dropping forty feet to the ground. I rolled to one side, and the blow fell six feet away from me. Not too close, but close enough to make me nervous. "Now, Orson, now!"

Quickly, Orson reached in his pockets and grabbed the three oranges. "Hey, Ymir!" he shouted, juggling for all he was worth. "Check this out!"

As Ymir turned to face Orson, the giant's arm froze in midair. Well, it was already frozen, but you know what I mean. Apparently, Ymir had difficulty doing more than one thing at a time.

Shit, this guy was so dumb, he really did make Digger look like Einstein. In Ymir's defense, though, he was so fucking huge his little brain probably had to work overtime just sending a neural impulse to something as far away as his fist.

"Steve!" shouted a voice from my pocket. "Now, while Ymir is distracted, throw me at him."

"But, you'll get hurt."

"Don't argue! Now!"

So what else could I do? I reached in my pocket, grabbed the little guy and …

Flicked my Bik

Straight at the frost giant. By the time he reached Ymir, Bik was in flames. He burned a fairly significant hole in the center of the giant's chest.

Ymir, hand still frozen in midair, looked down at the wound. "WHA … ?" he managed to say before slumping back against a large boulder. His fist nearly got me again, but then the entire arm collapsed against his recumbent body.

But where's Bik? Has he been crushed by the falling giant?

I breathed a sigh of relief as a flash of light came toward me at great speed. Bik started zooming around my head. "See? See?" he yelled excitedly. "I told you I could help."

"That was great, kid!" I said. "Now it's my turn." I didn't know if Ymir was dead or just unconscious, but I was taking no chances. As I rushed over to the fallen giant, my hands were already spooling out duct tape from both rolls. Round and round him I ran, taping Ymir to the boulder against which he had fallen, and none too soon, for the hole in his chest was already closing, and he was regaining consciousness.

Or as conscious as he ever got.

Ymir tried to lift his arms, one at a time, but the duct tape held fast. "WHY ... WHY CAN'T MOVE?"

"Because you're under arrest, uh, you're my prisoner, uh, Satan says be still!"

"SATAN? NOT SURTR?"

Orson was still juggling the oranges as he walked up to us. "I still got it," he said, tossing the three in the air then catching them one at a time in his parka pocket.

"OOH! MA ... GIC."

I ignored the antics of my assistant. "Ymir, why'd you do it? Why'd you help Surtr?"

The ice giant slowly cocked his head from side to side, then he looked at me with his baby blues. He really did have beautiful eyes. "SURTR SAID ME HAVE MORE COLD ... IF HELP HIM."

My foot was resting on one of Ymir's toes. He could probably have given it a flick and sent me sprawling, but I wanted to communicate to his primitive brain that I was alpha dog. "Surtr lied to you. He played you for a sucker, Ymir."

The giant's eyes clouded over as he tried to process this. Finally, he bellowed, "THAT NOT NICE!"

"No, it isn't. Now, if you'll excuse me for a second, I've got a pipeline to fix. Bik, you stay here and keep an eye on our frosty friend. Come on, Orson."

We went over to the boulder of ice that had pinched the pipe closed. For ten minutes we put our shoulders to it, but the thing wouldn't budge. "What now, Steve?"

"Steve!" yelled Bik. "Watch out!"

Ymir's foot was moving in our direction. With his big toe, the giant pushed the ice block off the pipeline. The soul stuff, trapped in the sac, was like a system under pressure, and it forced open the line, removing the dent. I didn't even need my stethoscope to hear the swishing of souls passing through the far side of the pipe. In seconds, the sac was deflated.

Puzzled, I walked back over to the prisoner. "Why did you do that?"

"SURTR LIE TO ME … TRY … TRY TO MAKE RIGHT."

I looked into those clear blue eyes for any sign of guile, but there was none. He may have been dumb and easily manipulated, but he wasn't bad. And that was good enough for me. "Orson, cut Ymir loose, would you?"

"What? Are you crazy?"

"Maybe, but not about this. Look at him."

Orson shot me a glance that as much as said I was an idiot, but then he too stared into Ymir's eyes. "You're right," he said, and reached for his knife. "He may be a patsy, and a bit lacking in intellectual wattage, but he's not a monster."

"WHO 'PATSY?'"

"Don't you worry about that, Ymir," I said, patting him on the knee. "Say, can I borrow your phone?"

"SURE. OVER THERE."

In a grotto nearby was a four foot phone. It had no buttons or dial, but the phone was bright red, and I had a pretty good idea who would be on the other end of the line. With both hands I shoved the receiver out of its cradle. It fell to the ground, and I put my head to the earpiece.

"One ringy-dingy," I said to myself, waiting for a connection, "two ringy-dingy."

"Ymir!" rasped an all-too-familiar voice. "You moron! I told you to stay off this line! It could be bugged."

I moved over to the mouthpiece. "Wrong, flamebutt. It's Minion."

"Minion!" I didn't even need to move back to the earpiece to hear him, and the sputtering coming from the end of the line was most gratifying.

I was on my hands and knees above the mouthpiece. I wanted to make very certain Surtr could hear me. "I took care of your pal, Ymir. And I fixed the pipeline. Now I'm coming for you, you son of a bitch!" Then I yanked the phone line out of the back of the phone.

"Time to go," I said, returning to the group.

Orson had just finished pulling the last of the duct tape off of Ymir. The giant just sat there. He was smiling, though. If ignorance was bliss, I was looking at one happy camper.

"Go? Go where? Not back down the mountain." Orson gnashed his teeth.

"No," I said, eyeing the pipeline. I drew my assistant's attention to the ladder that ran along its top. "You and Bik stay here. I'll go first. If this works, you can follow me. If not, well, you two can climb down the old fashioned way."

"I don't like it, Steve. If you fall, you might still get caught in some Erebus mumbo jumbo."

"I have faith."

"In Hell? Are you kidding?"

I looked at my friend and smiled. "I have lots of faith. I have faith in you, Orson. I have faith in Bik, now." The fire giant was sitting on Orson's shoulder, beaming, literally, and I had to squint to look at him. "And I have faith in a few others. I think it will be fine."

With that, I made my way to the ladder. I crawled along it, keeping a firm grip on each rung as I went. I didn't know when
...

Gravity shifted, and my legs dropped. I was hanging from the ladder by my hands.

Here goes the faith part.

I whistled for BOOH and let go.

Chapter 27

I had fallen twenty feet and was just beginning to resign myself to going splat on the surface of Level Two, when I heard a rustling of wings. BOOH, looking a little worse for wear, but otherwise intact, snagged me with a claw.

"Boy, am I glad to see you!" I said, stroking his foot, and trying not to cry. "Are you okay?"

"Skree!"

I looked up. Orson was already out on the ladder, Bik no doubt in one of his pockets. In moments he'd hit the gravity flip-flop point. "Up for catching one more?"

"Skree!"

Orson's legs were now dangling toward us, and he looked at me with a hopeful and mildly desperate expression. I grinned and flashed him the thumbs up. My friend let go of the ladder, fell a bit, then BOOH snagged him too.

"You two okay?"

"Yes, I believe so," Orson said. There was a slight sheen of sweat on his forehead, but he was maintaining a brave face.

"You bet," Bik replied. He had crawled out of Orson's pocket and was sitting in the hood of the parka. The young fire giant had a fierce look in his eye.

"BOOH! We fixed everything and found out that Surtr's been behind this whole mess. You feel up to helping us kick his fiery ass?"

"SKREE!"

"Then let's fly!"

Drawing from some hidden reserve of strength, BOOH took off for the Ninth Circle like the Bat out of Hell that he was.

We landed in front of Bruce's desk. Satan's personal secretary was standing on its surface, looking uncertainly at the crowd of devils and demons trying to force their way through the door leading to the traitors and the Boiler Room.

But not for long. Soon, they were scrambling away from the blasts of flame coming from inside.

Leaning against the wall of Satan's reception area, in pretty much the same spot he was when this adventure began, was Beezy. "That would be Surtr," he said, pointing at the flamethrower-type discharge coming out of the door. "Those poor schmucks," he continued, indicating the retreating members of the Devil & Demon Squad. "They didn't have a chance against that old fart."

"How did you know it was Surtr?"

The Lord of the Flies shrugged. "Satan read your mind as soon as you got clear of Erebus. He ordered the attack of the D&D Squad. I think he was curious to see how they'd do against the bastard."

"Not too well, I'd say."

"No. I think they need to earn some continuing education credits." Beezy cracked his knuckles. "I'd love to go in there and take a swat at that traitorous SOB myself."

"Why don't you?"

"Because I'm reserving that pleasure for myself," said a voice behind me.

I gasped. Exiting Satan's office was a huge and savage creature. He was naked, with legs of a goat, complete with cloven hooves. Sprouting from his forehead were the horns of a ram, but the ends curled forward, terminating in points that could skewer an opponent. The creature's tail was long and barbed, his chest broad, hairy and rippling with muscular power. Satan's eyes were no longer gray; they glowed now with a scarlet fire, and he was wreathed in flames.

He didn't have a pitchfork, though. No sense in overdoing things.

I had never seen Satan like this, and I shivered at the violent potential of Hell's ruler. The devils and demons parted before him like the Red Sea for Moses. Well, perhaps not the best simile, considering the parties involved, but the D&D Squad *was* in red and it did split up the middle to make way for the boss. The Earl of Hell took a swipe at the metal door the devils and demons had slammed shut to block the fire. His black claws shredded it with a single blow.

Yep, Satan looked pretty pissed off, and ready to rumble. I had hoped for something like this. I hadn't really wanted to take on Surtr myself - that seemed like suici ... Scratch that. Let's just say I was hoping Management would want to deal with an insubordinate employee its own way.

And how. The flames were still coming through what little remained of the door, but Satan merely absorbed them.

"Come on, Steve," Beezy said. "You too, Orson. This should be fun. I haven't seen the big guy go one-on-one with someone else in millennia."

"Okay, but after you," I said, indicating the doorway. If the flames got out of control, I wanted a major devil between them and us. "Bik, you might want to stay here."

"No," the little guy said, a look of malevolent anger on his face. It made me shudder. "I want to see Satan stick it to Grandpa."

We walked through the corridor fronting the cells of the traitors, all but one of whom were cowering in the corners of their cells. Cain however, was pressed against the bars, trying to see what was going on. His thirst for violence was showing, and the mark of the murderer on his forehead glowed a lurid red.

Satan confronted Surtr in the latter's seat of power: the boiler room. Orson, Beezy, Bik and I, oh, and also Bruce, which I thought interesting, were the only ones who'd come in to watch the fight.

The boiler room was as hot as any place on Hell I'd ever been. Flames were everywhere, and in the center of the conflagration stood a savage and desperate Surtr. Gone was the pretense of an old giant. Instead, Surtr stood at his full height, sending blasts of flame in all directions.

"You'll never take me alive, copper!"

Ah, he was a Cagney fan.

I looked from the giant being to, by comparison, a rather small guy, admittedly with great pecs, but small nonetheless. Yet Satan merely yawned as Surtr sent a blast of white heat against him.

"I can take you, you little pipsqueak, you," roared the Norse fire giant. "I kicked Freyr's butt. I even engulfed the world in flames, or I would have, if given the chance. You think you have a chance against me?"

The Earl of Hell stared at one of his claws, frowning. He reached in a pocket that was secreted somewhere on one of his hairy legs and pulled out a nail file. He spent a long time filing the offending claw, then satisfied, returned the file to its hidden compartment. "Undoubtedly ... you dirty rat," he added as an afterthought, which I thought was a nice touch.

I leaned over to Beezy. "Do you," I began, "do you think Satan can take him?'

"Are you kidding? Just watch."

The Lord of the Underworld held up one hand and closed it, extinguishing all of Surtr's fire. Then Satan grew to gargantuan size, which was quite a trick, since the boiler room had a thirty-five foot ceiling. But Big Red made the rules in Hell, so the room expanded to accommodate him. The Devil was now so large that Surtr, by comparison, looked like a small kitten. With one hand, Satan picked up the fire giant and shook him. "You! You were behind this all the time. Why?"

Surtr struggled against a grip of steel. He was caught, but the old geezer was rebellious to the end. "I was going to keep the fire all to myself," he said with a growl, "and when Hell froze over, I figured you'd get the boot for incompetence."

"Hmm. Interesting, just as I'm now about to do with you. Surtr, you're fired."

"You can't fire me," Flamebutt snarled. "I quit."

"Fine by me. That means you don't get unemployment." Satan casually threw Surtr over his shoulder. A hole in the boiler room floor opened to reveal a dark, whirling vortex. Surtr, still cursing, fell into it and disappeared in the blackness of Chaos. The hole closed behind him.

Satan shrank down to a more human scale. "And now to turn on the heat." A hiss of sound began to fill the room, the essence of lost souls that had finally made its way from Erebus to the boiler room. Fire blasted from Satan's eyes, igniting the essence leaking from the burners. At once, all the jets burst into flames.

"Neat!" Bik enthused.

Satan arched an eyebrow at us and walked back to his office.

* * *

We were back at the trailer, sitting on the front steps. There was no room for us in our office - it was full of new work orders - but for the moment we didn't care. We were still in the blush of victory. Bik was with us, sitting on the steps' railing, and

BOOH was sprawled on the pavement nearby, chowing down on half a dozen blood bags I'd managed to pull out the back window. Satan had left the scene of Surtr's humiliation without a word, so - after getting Beezy to sign off on the completed work order for the HVAC system - I took advantage of the situation to have BOOH bring us back to Five.

My giant friend looked as good as new. Admittedly, that was pretty grisly, seeing as how he was a giant vampire bat, and his face was covered in blood, but he had his strength back. His color looked good too. For a bat, again.

"Wow!" Orson said, peeling an orange. "That was really something."

"Boy, isn't that the truth? You know, I've never seen Satan show that much of his power. Actually, Beezy is more prone to demonstrations of puissance."

Good word, puissance. It doesn't get out nearly enough.

"Well, maybe Satan is so secure in his strength that he doesn't feel the need to show off. Want an orange?"

"No thanks," I said, shifting my butt on the step. It wasn't very comfortable, but I wasn't yet ready to tackle the paperwork inside. Besides, it had been a really long, cold day in Hell, and it was almost quitting time. I began to think we might just let things wait until tomorrow.

The air around us was already warming up. Devils and demons walking the street were stripping off jackets and parkas and toboggans (still the hat kind), tossing them to the ground. Things were getting back to normal. Of course, normal sucked in Hell, but at least it was more predictable.

I ran my fingers through my full head of hair. I still had it, which was amazing to me, but I *had* thought to throw that little "forever" into my "it will be a cold day in Hell" statement, and that seemed to have done the trick. "I don't think Beezy intentionally shows off. Lots of times when he makes a demonstration of his power, he's by himself. I'm not even sure he's aware he's doing it."

"How are you doing, Bik?" Orson asked. "Any regrets?"

The fire giant shook his head. "Grandpa got what he deserved. Besides, he won't die out there in Chaos. He's been there before. I'm sure he'll get another job."

"Probably," I agreed. "Maybe in Diyu." Diyu was Hell's Chinese doppelgänger.

"Yeah, I hear Diyu uses lots of fire to torture people. Grandpa would do okay there." The little guy was quiet. "I wonder what Satan will do with Ymir."

"Nothing," I said. "Beezy told me that Ymir gets to keep his job. The boss said everyone has always known what a moron Ymir is. In fact, Beezy described the ice giant as sort of an innocent. It's no wonder he was so easily duped by Surtr."

"You broke his phone, you know," Orson pointed out.

"Yeah, and I'll be going back to fix it soon. Think I'll take Ymir some Popsicles when I do."

"He'd like that, I'm sure, but are you going to climb Erebus all over again?"

"No. I have a better idea. In fact, I wish I'd thought of it sooner. It could have saved us a lot of trouble."

Orson stuffed another slice of orange in his mouth. "Whth tht?"

"Pardon?"

"Sorry," he said, swallowing. "I said, 'What's that?'"

"You remember the ladder running parallel to the summit of Erebus?"

"How could I forget? Between it and the one at the base of the mountain, my arms are still aching."

"Well, I'm going to get BOOH to fly me just as close as he can to that ladder, then I'm going to take a page from your book and throw a rope up to it. Shimmying up the line won't be much fun, but I'd rather do that than climb Erebus again."

"And what if you drop the rope?"

I blushed. "I'll practice with you until I'm a little more proficient than when we were on the mountain. … And I won't let go of the rope."

Bik stood up. "Well, say hi to the big fellow for me. Now, I've got to get to work."

"Work?" Orson and I said in unison.

"Yeah. I had a talk with Lord Beelzebub, too. He's offered me Grandpa's position in the boiler room, and I'm going to take it."

"Really? Well congratulations!"

"Thanks. See ya!" And with that, our new friend ignited and shot skyward.

"Isn't he a little small to be running the boiler room?"

I smiled. "He'll grow into the job."

An enormous belch rattled the trailer, accompanied by an overpowering stench of blood. BOOH got off the concrete and stretched his wings.

"You takin' off now, BOOH?" I said, getting off the steps.

He nodded.

"Well, thanks again for all your help. As usual, I couldn't have done it without you."

"Hey!" Orson shouted, half joking. "What about me? If it hadn't been for my oranges, you know … "

"You too," I said with a smile. "Thanks to both of you."

"You're welcome."

"Urm." Then BOOH took off as well.

"You know," Orson said, "BOOH is a really nice guy. Handy to have in a pinch too."

"That's an understatement." I stretched, yawning. "Feels like quitting time, don't you think?"

"Yeah. I don't really want to start sorting work orders. This has already been a hell of a long day."

"Well, see you tomorrow then."

"Steve, wait a second. I... " Orson looked a little awkward. "I just wanted to warn you about something."

"Warn me? About what?"

"Well, I don't know how to say this, but," he leaned over and whispered to me, "you're getting too good at your job."

"Me? Nah. I'm a crummy handyman."

"Maybe, but you're getting better. You generally fix the stuff that really needs fixing. Not like your predecessor."

Orson had predeceased me by ten years and had immediately been made Assistant in the department. He actually had seniority over me. I was his second supervisor in Plant Maintenance. "Hey, who was my predecessor anyway?"

"Charlemagne."

"Karl der Magnus? First Holy Roman Emperor?"

"Yeah. Charlemagne was the head of this department for over a thousand years. Needless to say, he was a slow learner, but by the time I got here, he was beginning to get it figured out. And once he got good at his job ... " Orson shrugged.

"What? Did Satan move him to another job where he could feel incompetent all over again?"

My assistant, looking very serious now, stared me straight in the eyes. "No. Satan made him a demon."

A chill went down my spine. The Lord of Hell had already been making noises about promoting me to demon. Up until now, I'd managed to talk him out of it. I wondered how long I could keep doing that.

"Thought you'd like to know."

"Thanks, Orson," I said, putting my hand on his shoulder. "You're a good friend."

As a good friend, my assistant helped me up from the pavement and gave me a rag from his pocket. I used it to wipe off the coconut cream pie that had just pounded me. "You think I'd know better by now."

He shrugged. "It happens to all of us down here. It's Hell, isn't it?"

"Sure is," I said, wincing as the painful welts from my coconut allergy popped up all over my face. "See you tomorrow."

"Right," he said and headed toward his apartment.

I had a lot to think about as I walked home: the very long day I'd just finished, the duplicity of a certain fire giant, and the friendships I'd made here in the most unlikely of all places: Hell.

As I turned a corner, I saw my favorite friend. Flo was just exiting the hospital. When she saw me, she waved. I waited for her to catch up. By the time she did, the welts on my forehead had disappeared.

"Hi, Steve," she said, breathlessly.

I smiled a tired little smile. "Hey, Flo. What can I do for you?"

"I wanted to let you know that I was able to light my lamp a little while ago."

"Well," I said slowly, "that's good."

Flo blushed slightly. "I ... I also didn't want to leave things the way we had at the hospital. I know you didn't do anything with that horrid succubus."

"She wasn't horrid. Actually, she was pretty nice," I said then caught myself. Quickly I added, "But you're right. Nothing happened between us."

"Good, I mean, I, I do trust you, Steve, and seeing you today, well, I've missed you."

My heart was thumping hard. Taking her hand, I said, "Me too. I mean, I miss you. I don't miss me. I've got me around all the time."

"You sound a little flustered."

"You have a way of doing that to me."

She gave me a big smile. "Good. I want to see more of you, but I need to take this slowly. Perhaps … perhaps we could have coffee together sometime? The coffee in the hospital isn't very good, but … "

"That would be great!"

Flo kissed me then, a sweet, chaste kiss on the lips. "Call me soon?"

I felt a little lightheaded. "How … how about in five minutes?"

She grinned. "How about tomorrow, instead? You look a bit tired."

I rubbed my face with my hands. "I am a bit peaked. It's been a long day. Tomorrow then."

She squeeze my hands in her own, gave me another breathtaking smile, and left.

Despite my fatigue, there was a bounce in my step as I went up the six flights to my studio apartment. On the floor before my door, there was a small box with a note. I picked it up.

The box contained some hard cinnamon candies, shaped like hearts. The note said:

Hey, hot stuff,

So glad I got to spend time with you today.

I know you may find this hard to believe, since we succubi are not known for our sincerity, but I like you sooo much, in fact more than I've liked anyone in eons. If you ever want to get together, give me a ring. I could show you some moves that you wouldn't even find in the Kama Sutra.

Yours if you want me,

Lilith

P.S.: Hope you like the candies. They're my favorites.

I thought of the luscious redhead, and a familiar warmth suffused my nether regions. I shook my head to clear it.

"Great," I said, as I broke into my apartment. In the background, I could hear the chittering of my roachy roommates. "Fifty years without a girlfriend. Now I've got two. What a helluva situation."

From the back of my brain came an all-too-familiar diabolical laugh.

An extract from the sequel to 'A Cold Day In Hell'

Deal With The Devil
(Circles in Hell, Book Three)

Chapter 1

A dull, red glow, like that of a wildfire in the distance, or the burning ocher of a lava flow, suffused the sky, driving back the shadows of night. They weren't gone. They were never gone, but lingered always along the edge of sight, nightmares that would not end but lost some of their potency in the light of day.

Well, they would have anyway, if this weren't Hell, where nightmares are pretty much the steady diet of the eternally damned. Besides, the lurid radiance I'm talking about was emanating from the Throat of Hell, that great yawning chasm that stretches from the Mouth of Hell at Gates Level all the way down to Satan's office suite in the Ninth Circle. Still, the scary shadows weren't as obvious, because the Infernal Realm was now cooking on high instead of a slow boil. A new day, or what passes for day around here, had begun.

I took in Hell's version of dawn from the steps leading to my office. To be accurate, it was not really an office, but more of a beat-up trailer that wouldn't have been allowed its rectangle of concrete in any self-respecting trailer park back on Earth. Still, it was command central for the Underworld's Superintendent of Plant Maintenance (me) and my trusty sidekick, Orson, as we endured our never-ending punishment of being lousy handymen.

Hey, it's a lot worse than it sounds. Have you ever been bad at something? I mean really, really bad, stinko, like someone with two left feet and an inner ear infection trying to execute a pirouette during the climax of *Swan Lake*? Not pretty. So doing something you really suck at, not to mention hate, for all eternity is an excruciating, if highly specialized, form of Hell for me and Orson.

Speaking of Orson, he had beaten me into the office that day, something almost unheard of, since he was famous during his lifetime for being late and I was obsessive about being early. I knew he had preceded me because the door was already slightly open, so for once I didn't have to fight the stupid doorknob to get into my own office.

That the great Orson Welles got to work before me was noteworthy. I'm an early riser, as evidenced by my getting to watch Hell's version of sunrise every morning. Orson, on the other hand, didn't give a damn about punctuality, but there he was, early for work, sitting on his work stool, waiting for me, his Blimpie's mug in hand.

"Morning, Steve."

"What are you doing here so early?" I asked, closing the door behind me.

"Couldn't sleep," he said.

For some reason, this struck me as funny, and I chuckled. "Good grief, Orson. This is Hell. Nobody can sleep."

He shrugged. "Yeah, but last night was worse than usual." Probably true, judging from his eyes, which were especially bloodshot this morning, with dark bags under them, as if he'd stayed up the night, drinking and smoking while he pondered the mysteries of the universe. "I keep thinking about my Hell movie."

"That again," I said, rolling my eyes. "You know there's no way, correct that, there's no way in Hell that Satan's going to let you make a promotional video about Hell."

My assistant's face reddened. "He might. It would help get him some more demons. You know he always needs more demons."

Orson had a point there. While a few demons, like incubi and succubi, were native-born, most were converted humans. They actually volunteered to be repulsive devil-wannabes. "Okay, that's probably true. But it's not going to happen."

"And why not?" he snapped.

Okay, we'd started the morning off on the wrong foot. Now it was time to calm things down. "Look, Orson. I know you'd make a great movie, but you'd, well, you'd enjoy making it, right?"

"Well, of *course* I'd enjoy making it, and ... oh ... well. Right. We're in Hell." Orson's face assumed a mournful expression, like I'd just killed his dog or something.

I smiled sympathetically. "Yeah, and we don't get to enjoy anything down here."

The smell of burnt java filled the room, so I stepped away from my disgruntled assistant and his hanged-dog expression. From my desk, a rusted and dented All-Steel model that could have been constructed from a World War II depth charge, I grabbed my "I'm not With Stupid. I AM Stupid," mug and headed to our antediluvian Mr. Coffee. I took my first sip of the day, straining loose grounds with my teeth. "Shit," I mumbled, singeing my tongue.

"Nothing like a good cup a' joe, eh?" Orson said, a little twinkle coming back in his eye. Only one of them, though. The other was hanging onto its depression.

"Yes, but unfortunately, this isn't one," I grumbled, using thumb and forefinger to pick a ground off my still-burning tongue. "I haven't had a decent cup of coffee since the grande Sumatra I got at Starbucks the day I died."

Orson set his cup on the edge of my desk and stretched expansively. Of course, since my friend's ectoplasmic frame was a reasonable facsimile of his mortal one toward the end of his life, said frame was pushing four hundred pounds. Almost by definition, Orson was expansive, and so, gargantuan as he was, he had a hard time doing anything in less than expansive fashion. "Starbucks was around when I died in 1985, but I never got around to trying it."

"Just as well," I said, wincing as I took another sip. "I still remember, which makes our morning coffee ritual just a little enhancement to my eternal torment."

"Lucky you," Orson said, grabbing his own mug and taking a swallow of the hot, black liquid. "Still, even Folgers was better than this. Speaking of coffee, are you and Flo still on for this morning? ... I guess so, judging by the way you're blushing."

"She has a way of doing that to me," I replied with a rueful grin.

"Nervous?"

"A bit." Florence Nightingale (yes, that Florence Nightingale - is there another one?) and I had only recently gotten past an early rough patch in our relationship. Rough patch: that's a euphemism for Satan and his underlings humiliating us by filming me and Flo in the sack and then turning the footage into the most popular porn movie the Underworld had ever seen. And by Underworld, I mean all of it. Apparently, everyone in Hell had seen "Flo Does The Super." Many devils and demons even owned it on Blu-ray, complete with 3-D and Smellovision®. Pretty humiliating, though that's par for the course down here.

Anyway, Flo had been particularly upset by the movie. After some months, though, she had adjusted to the situation. Only a few days ago, after the successful conclusion of the HVAC Affair - hmmm, doesn't have the same panache as "The Thomas Crown Affair," but there you go - she had confessed the surety of her love. (That's exactly how she'd said it: "surety." I'd never even used that word in a sentence, but then I hadn't been born in the Nineteenth Century, as she had, back when the language had a lot more elegance to it than what I'd lived and died with in the second half of the Twentieth Century.) We had agreed to take it slow. Well, she had wanted to take it slow, and I'd reluctantly acquiesced. Me, I would have been perfectly happy to get back in the sack with her immediately, but then I'm a guy. We are simple creatures, driven mainly by lust and bacon.

Having coffee at the hospital today was our way of restarting the relationship. I was a bit nervous, but mostly excited. Now if only nothing important came up that the Plant Department had to handle. As Hell's only maintenance team, Orson and I were expected to fix everything that broke down here. That was a boatload. After all, no one really expects Hell to function flawlessly. If it did, it would be Hea … the other place.

Well, we didn't fix everything, as evidenced by the four-foot high piles of unresolved work orders filling one corner of our office. There was no way we could take care of everything that broke. If it were even possible to do so, this wouldn't be a particularly good form of eternal punishment, now would it? Still, we did our best to fix the important stuff.

I looked around our trailer. The office could use a little repair itself. All of the wallpaper, a drab gray pattern that added nothing to the décor except that it was something else to maintain, was sagging like a dowager's chin. One piece, damp from a leak in the roof that we'd never been able to find, had finally pulled away completely from the wall. The top half of it was now touching the floor. Without thought, I lifted the stapler off my desk and, with a rapid series of clicks, tacked the sheet back to the wall. No more than a second after I finished, while admiring my own handiwork, the staples began to pop out of the drywall. One of them hit me in the right eye.

"Shit," I cursed, without much enthusiasm - after all, I'd only had half a cup of coffee and didn't really feel awake yet - and reached to one of the two spools of duct tape hanging from each side of my tool belt. With a quick pull, I dispensed about eighteen inches of the stuff, what I judged the width of the wallpaper to be, made a clean tear, and taped the top of the paper to where it met the ceiling.

"I'm surprised you didn't reach for the duct tape first," Orson commented.

"Me too," I said, once again admiring my handiwork, and once again being struck in the same eye by a tardy but nonetheless rebellious staple. The wallpaper stayed put, though. Duct tape, the one tool of the handyman trade with which I had any competence, had never failed me. It was also gray, so it didn't look particularly bad against the wallpaper, though the paper in the middle of the wall still sagged like that chin I mentioned earlier.

Splat! A long, skinny package, about the size of a salami, emerged from the pneumatic tube above my wire inbox. That's how we got most of our work orders, but this obviously wasn't one of them. Curious, I picked up the package. It was addressed to both of us.

"What the hell?" Orson said, when I showed him the return address. It said Sintas Uniform and Apparel. "You don't think it's two of those HOTI gimme caps they were trying to get us to wear last year, do you?"

HOTI was the acronym for Beelzebub's operation down here: Hell's Office of the Interior. Plant Maintenance was a department within the HOTI division. The hats hadn't worked out very well. They made us look too dignified, so we'd had to return them.

"One way to find out," I said, opening the parcel. Inside were two long, narrow maroon-rimmed ovals, with yellow centers that matched the color of our coveralls. There was also a set of simple instructions: "Peel off the paper and affix fabric to the location indicated by the diagram."

Orson slapped his hand to his forehead. "Great, just great."

I shrugged. "We knew this would happen sooner or later, so let's just get it over with. Turn around. I'll do you, then you can do me."

"Fine." My friend put his back to me, displaying the maroon HOTI insignia on the back of his coveralls. I peeled off the wax paper from the back of the fabric and affixed the oval to the narrow space between the O and the T, doing my best to stick it on straight. Then I turned and let Orson do the same for me.

Our divisional acronym now read, "HOOTI," except that one of the "O"s was extra skinny to fit in the limited space available to it. This was a pretty cheap solution, but actually better than getting a whole new, properly-spaced logo that we would have had to sew on ourselves. After we took the old ones off, of course. Since I'm a terrible seamstress, a skinny peel-and-stick letter was okay by me.

Still, this was a regrettable if completely predictable eventuality. The old acronym had never accounted for the "of" in "Hell's Office of the Interior." This new one did.

Orson was staring over his shoulder, examining the logo in the cracked and yellowed shard of mirror we had in our office. "HOOTI. Just marvelous."

"Actually, it says 'ITOOH.' Mirror, you know."

"Very funny," he grumbled. "Dora will have a field day with this."

I nodded. "It was the first thing I thought of too." Dora, who ran the Parts Department, was fond of calling us Hotties. "Now she'll call us Hooties, I guess."

He frowned. "Knowing Dora, she'll probably call us a big pair of Hooters."

"Ooh!" I said, grimacing. I went over to the Mr. Coffee and topped off my mug then sat back at my desk. "Hadn't thought of that."

Splat!

"Now what?" Orson groused.

"Work order?" I said, not looking up from my coffee.

"No. Wrong color."

I glanced at my inbox. Our work orders were printed on paper stock that was the color of bile, but this packet had blue and white sheets stapled together. With suspicion, I picked it up and got popped in the left eye this time by the staple holding the packet together. All the papers tumbled to the floor.

On my hand and knees, I gathered the pages from off the linoleum and put them in order then took a gander at what I had and scowled. "Crap!"

"What is it?" Orson asked, putting down his coffee cup.

"I HEARD that!" boomed a voice from the office PA system.

Fuck! Beezy was paying attention. I got off the floor and pressed down the talk button of the intercom that sat on a corner of my desk. "Come on! A performance evaluation?"

"Union rules," said Beelzebub, the great Lord of the Flies and, not insignificantly, my boss down here.

I had been on the last bargaining team for the union, so I knew the current contract by heart. There had been no such provision in it. "I don't remember the SEIU agreeing to personnel evaluations."

That's Satan's Employees' Infernal Union. Don't confuse it with the Earth-bound union having the same acronym. Just a coincidence, like the APA standing for both the American Psychological Association and the American Poolplayers Association.

Beezy laughed in that endearing way of his. It sounded like a rock polisher working on a large chunk of concrete. "You don't remember it because Management slipped it into the contract when you weren't looking."

Swell. That means they rewrote the contract without telling us. Nice.

"Besides," Beelzebub continued, "it only applies to humans in positions that report directly to one of the princes of Hell."

"Oh," I said, somewhat mollified. "There can't be too many of us in that situation."

"You're right about that. Demons supervise most of you."

I thought about all the princes of Hell, and realized with some surprise that almost none of them had direct contact with humans. "That," I said hesitantly, "that would narrow it down to just me and Bruce then, right?"

Bruce the Bedeviled was Satan's personal assistant.

"Not Bruce," Beezy said. "At least, not anymore. Remember he was promoted to demon recently."

"Oh right, right." I stared in bemusement at the speaker mounted on the wall. "Then, that means this portion of the contract only applies ... to me?"

That piece of concrete got a little bit shinier. "Right you are! But if you're going to report to me, you must be held accountable for your actions, Minion, even in Hell. Besides, it's best practice. All the management consultants, and believe me, we have a lot of that type down here, agree."

In life, I had been a professor of economics. Faculty members, probably more than anyone, hate having their performance evaluated, but in most cases, they only have to put up with it for their first seven years on the job. After getting tenure, I thought I was done with that forever ... well, except for those stupid evaluations done on Scantron forms I had to let students fill out - number two pencil - for the occasional course. Seems I was wrong. My lips curled down into a fair imitation of a toddler's pout. "It just doesn't seem fair that I'm the only one in all of Hell that has to have a performance evaluation."

Polish, polish. "Tough shit. Besides, Hell isn't about fair play, and you know it. Now quit your whining and come down to my office this morning. Make sure you complete that self-evaluation before you get here."

"Yessir," I mumbled, as an ear-piercing screech came from the speaker. The PA system had lasted just long enough for Beelzebub to ruin my morning before failing.

It failed about twice a week.

Great. Though it could be worse, I suppose. At least he didn't say immediately. This means I have time to have coffee with Flo then fill out the stupid personnel form as I ride down on the Escalator to the Eighth Circle.

"What's the point of an evaluation?" Orson said, sharing my outrage as he stared at the forms crushed in my hand. "We're in Hell. Everything we do sucks, not to mention being completely pointless. And even if you did a great job, Beezy would never admit it."

I stroked my chin. "Don't know about that." My boss and I had been getting along pretty well, especially since I'd had success with some big projects recently. Also, despite his bluster and innate cruelty, Beelzebub was the most fair-minded of all Hell's princes. *Good thing I don't report to Asmodeus. He'd rake my butt over the coals.*

Asmodeus, the Lord of Lust, had a double axe to grind with/on me. Only the other day, Flo had very publicly snubbed him at a reception at which she'd been the honored guest. That had been partly my fault.

Not to mention that his own assistant has the hots for me. As I thought about the redheaded succubus, I began to blush. She was one sexy demon, the only woman in Hell other than Flo who I'd ever been attracted to.

But this was the worst time to think about Lilith, right before my date with Flo. Putting my coffee cup down on the desk, I stuffed the self-assessment form into my pocket, stepped before our mirror and tried to make my hair appear a little less unkempt.

"Orson, while I'm gone, would you take a pen and draw some narrow O's on our letterhead?"

My friend flexed his right hand and frowned. "That sounds like a guaranteed hand cramp. Couldn't we just order fresh stock?"

"Sorry. We're over budget in the Supplies line."

"Oh, okay," he said with a sigh.

"Thanks." Pivoting on my heel, I headed toward the exit.

"Good luck, Steve! With both Flo and Beelzebub!" Orson yelled, as the door closed behind me.

Made in the USA
Columbia, SC
21 May 2022